THOSE WHO RESIST

THE WAYSTATIONS TRILOGY
BOOK 3

N.C. SCRIMGEOUR

CONTENTS

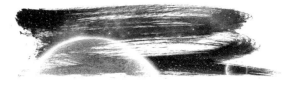

ONE

ALVERA

Chase was gone.

It didn't seem right to fixate on any one particular loss, not when Alvera saw the scale of their combined losses in the form of glowing numbers and jagged lines on the holofeeds all around them. The galaxy was turning dark on the dimly-lit screens, systems flickering and disappearing like little lights snuffing out. Every day, more and more enemy forces poured through the hole ripped in the fabric of space. Every day, more and more planets fell to the curators' unrelenting numbers. Entire worlds burned. Settlements lay slaughtered. Yet all of it was inconsequential compared to the persistent, aching hole in Alvera's chest.

Chase was *gone*. And she wasn't.

She'd come to Alcruix expecting death or imprisonment, but what remained of the Coalition's chain of command seemed to have understood the value in keeping her alive. But a relationship of necessity—of desperation—wasn't the same as having an ally, and for the first time she could remember, Alvera felt helplessly, shamefully lonely.

"If we're all ready, we should get this summit underway. We don't exactly have time to waste."

The dachryn who'd spoken was more familiar to Alvera than she was entirely comfortable with. Rivus Itair, Supreme Commander of the legionnaires—or what was left of them, at any rate. The scarred, black-and-white bone plates of his exoskeleton shifted as he glanced around the room, his green eyes sharp and wary.

When he locked his gaze with hers, an unpleasant shiver ran down her spine. Looking at Rivus was like looking into a memory she had no right to see. The strands of consciousness that had connected them when she'd been trapped in the curators' hive had been severed, but a shared understanding still lingered between them. Maybe because they'd both played a part in starting all this. Maybe because they both knew what it might take to end it.

A low, menacing rumble from somewhere deep underground broke Alvera from her thoughts, and she readied herself for the ensuing shockwave that rattled around the room. Some of the Idran-Var chuckled as the legionnaires stiffened in alarm, but the tremor soon passed without incident. The near-constant quakes and sporadic eruptions of the broken, scarred planet didn't unsettle Alvera like they did some of the others in the room. Alcruix's volatile temperament was a reminder of the atrocities it had suffered. A reminder that she was not the only person in this galaxy capable of terror on a scale few could imagine.

"Captain Renata, did you hear anything I said?"

Heat rushed to Alvera's cheeks as she blinked away the haze. Rivus was watching her intently. The rest of the room turned their attention to her as well, staring at her through helmets and breather masks and everything in between.

She'd never have lost her step like this with Chase. Sharing her head with an artificial intelligence had given her processing capabilities no other living being—human or alien—could match. But Chase was gone. All that was left was the shell of the woman Alvera was without her.

She forced herself to swallow, her mouth unbearably dry. "Sorry. I was...distracted."

Rivus twitched his bony face plates in disapproval. "It's hardly the time for distractions. Every hour we delay, more worlds fall."

"More *Coalition* worlds fall," one of the Idran-Var corrected, a siolean with bright blue-green skin and distrusting eyes. "Your precious capital is the epicentre of this shitstorm. Why would we send our forces to die trying to save the allied systems instead of holding them back to protect our own planets?"

Rivus gave a warning growl. "Because if you don't—"

"You'll die anyway. It will just take longer."

All the heads in the room swivelled back to Alvera as the words left her lips. This time, no warmth flooded her skin. This time, she knew exactly where she was and what she was saying. She shifted her balance, grounding herself in the way her boots scraped across the floor, in the way her next breath steeled inside her chest and straightened her spine. Chase had given her a second shot at life for a reason. It might have been a cruel shadow of the life she'd once known—the life they'd shared—but she'd be damned if she wasted it on petty squabbles.

"Captain." Rivus inclined his head. "You have the floor."

Alvera moved into the centre of the room, ignoring the shimmering lights that danced across her face as she walked through the holographic feeds.

"How long do you think you can protect a planet?" she

asked, turning to the Idran-Var who'd interrupted Rivus. "A few years? A decade? Would that count as a victory to you?"

The Idran-Var glared. "As long as it takes."

"As long as it takes?" She laughed, the sound thin and hollow. "You could hold out against them for centuries, and it still wouldn't be long enough. The curators don't see time the way we do. As far as they're concerned, the passing of millennia might as well be the blink of an eye. You won't win this war by trying to outlast them."

The Idran-Var's headtails flushed a dark, angry blue, but before he could open his mouth to bite back, one of his companions held up an armoured hand. The room fell silent at his gesture, submitting to the small, quiet movement with a deference that made Alvera shiver. This Idran-Var was different. He hadn't removed his helmet since she'd arrived. He wore no expression apart from the glowing red lines of the grille-like visor that ran around the middle of his helm.

"Explain," he said, his voice mechanical through the filters of his helmet.

"The curators are a hive mind," Alvera replied. "A collective consciousness on a scale impossible for anyone with such a fleeting lifespan as ours to comprehend. Put bluntly, they are the galactic memory of every being that ever existed."

An outbreak of soft, hushed murmurs rippled through the room. Alvera sensed everyone's eyes on her. Not believing. Not *wanting* to believe.

The Idran-Var leader sat as still as ever. "How is that possible?"

"Because we made it possible," Alvera said. "Once, the curators were like us. They *were* us. But that wasn't enough for them. They wanted more. Stronger muscles, sharper claws, harder plating. Longer lives—*endless* lives. Our ancestors chased immortality. They craved perfection." Something seized in her chest. "They used cybernetics to upload their consciousness into a collective neural network. It was small, at first. Small enough for them to retain a sense of the individuality they once held. But it doesn't take long for those kinds of distinctions to become blurry."

Alvera knew that better than anyone. Chase had never been anything as simple as a programme in her head. They'd become something so connected, so entwined, that it was impossible to extricate the parts of themselves that had once been their own. It was only now Chase was gone that Alvera realised how much she had been made from her. The empty spaces in her head felt hollower than ever.

She cleared her throat, trying to ignore the prickling at the back of her eyes. "The more minds the curators added to their network, the less regard they gave to the fleeting lives of the species they'd once been part of. With each passing century, each passing millennium, their perspective skewed further and further from what they once were. The flesh and blood and bone they'd been made from became too perishable, too transitory, to afford any kind of significance to." She shook her head. "Consider it from their perspective. How much value can a singular, finite lifeform hold against the memories of millions?"

The room fell into an uneasy silence as those gathered glanced between their neighbours, exchanging worried looks.

"Does that answer your question, Rhendar?" Rivus turned to the faceless leader of the Idran-Var. "Do you see now what we're up against? Why we need to stand together?"

"Stand together?" The other Idran-Var was back on his feet, his turquoise skin darkening. "Like we did on Aurel? We know too well what a legionnaire's word is worth when they talk of cease-fires and peace agreements." He gestured to a hardened white scar curving down his face. "Don't talk to me about standing together."

Rivus stepped back. "That wasn't me. I tried to stop—"

"Enough." Rhendar cut through the argument, his strained

voice like rust on the tip of a blade. It carried a tiredness Alvera recognised all too well, but there was still an edge there capable of damage. "Stand down, Serric. The time for righting past wrongs is over. For all of us." He turned to Rivus. "That goes for you too, Supreme Commander. Serric isn't the only one in this room with a grudge to bear."

It wasn't possible for a dachryn to flush, but Alvera noticed the anger that lit up Rivus's eyes. He twitched his jaw plates and let out a huff of air from his nostrils. "I wouldn't have come here if I wasn't committed to setting that aside. For now, at least."

"Good. Then we can focus on our common enemy." Rhendar turned back to Alvera. "What do these curators want? To add us to their network? Make us part of their hive?"

"No," she said. "At least, not yet. They've been patient, carrying out this experiment for hundreds of thousands of years, whittling down all life in the galaxy to ensure all that's left is the pinnacle of evolution."

"That's why they created the colonies, right? As environments for their tests?" The human woman who interrupted her had messy red-brown hair and a cybernetic graft over her left eye. Her expression was animated, almost giddy, as her words spilled out one after another. "It's fascinating. They simulated evolutionary conditions on a planetwide scale, limiting resources so each colony could only sustain its inhabitants for a finite amount of time. The fact they were able to—"

"Zal," Serric said through gritted teeth. "We're trying to kill them, not study them."

"We don't have a hope of killing them unless we understand them," Alvera replied. "What she's saying is relevant. The colonies were tests. If their inhabitants made it back to civilisation before they died out, that species was given another chance. Those who didn't make it were absorbed along the way —the curators used them as lessons in failure, in weakness."

Rivus let out a low breath. "Those aliens we faced on Ossa..."

"The azuul. The velliria. Dozens more. All remnants of past civilisations. Fallen, forgotten civilisations." Alvera grimaced. "After the curators uploaded their collective memories to the hive, they took the genetic material from their bodies to breed mindless shock troops. That's what their army is made of—all the civilisations that didn't make it this far. That's what we'll be facing."

Rhendar shook his helmeted head. "When you humans arrived a year ago, it meant all of the colonies made it back. According to your theory, shouldn't the curators be sparing us?"

"They are sparing us. At least, that's how they see it." Alvera shrugged. "As far as they're concerned, they're resetting the experiment. Reducing our numbers so they can start from scratch. They'll keep running it until one of us doesn't make it back before our colony dies out. Four becomes three, then two, then one. After that..." She trailed off, the words dying in her throat. "Their goal is perfection. I don't know what happens beyond that. I doubt any of us will be left to find out."

Zal's cybernetic eyegraft blinked green in the dim light. "They're intelligent. They must be able to communicate. Can't they be reasoned with?"

"Would you reason with the microbes under your boot?" Alvera twisted her lips into a bitter smile. "They don't see us as anything more than material to be manipulated. They're nurturing us in their own way. Growing us from primitive seeds and not hesitating to prune off dead leaves when the conditions necessitate it."

Rhendar grunted. "The question isn't whether we can reason with them—it's whether we can stop them. They're breeding an infinite army to throw at us. How can we fight against those kinds of numbers?"

"We can't," Alvera said bluntly. "If we want a chance at

something that resembles a fair fight, we have to cut off their supply of bodies."

Rivus snapped his head up. "You want to take out the Omega Gate."

The Omega Gate. That's what the newsfeeds were calling the monstrosity suspended in orbit above Ossa. The four waystations had converged, twisting apart and re-joining in a terrible, colossal superstructure that had ripped a hole between the galaxy and where the curators were lurking in the reaches of what was beyond.

"It's our only shot," Alvera said. "If we don't shut down the space tunnel it created, the curators will keep coming through."

"They already have an armada protecting that thing," Rivus pointed out. "I don't like the chances of us breaking through their defences."

"That's why we need to join our forces together. All of us."

The tension in the room was already unpleasantly thick. Now, Alvera felt like it might smother her. The quiet was full of grudges and grievances, some centuries in the making, others still fresh and raw. What she was asking for was impossible.

Maxim ras Arbor leaned forward, the silver speckles in his coarse hair glinting under the lights. He wore the same amused expression he always did, but there was a graveness in his eyes Alvera hadn't seen before.

"You have to admit, it's a bit of a tall order," he said, his Rasnian accent coiling around his words. "The galaxy has never been as fractured as it is now. Ras Prime and the secessionists, the jarkaath and the iskaath... And now we're meant to be playing nice with the Idran-Var?" A grin broke out across his face. "How long do we expect that to last?"

"I was thinking the same thing." Serric shot Rhendar a disapproving look. "Nothing in this summit has convinced me the Idran-Var should be anywhere near this war. The allied systems aren't our problem. I say let them burn. We'll take care of whatever is left at the end."

Rivus let out a sharp growl. "There won't *be* anything left at the end. Have you been listening to anything, you arrogant bastard? Or is the siolean bloodlust rushing around in that skull of yours too much for you to see things clearly?"

Serric leapt to his feet. "Call me siolean one more time, *skrita-kelar*, and see what happens." His armour misted with a blue-green vapour that made the room waver. Several of the Idran-Var behind him reached for their weapons.

It wasn't just tension anymore. It was a storm about to break.

Alvera closed her eyes. This was how they'd lose. Numbers didn't matter if all they did was bring together people who'd sooner kill each other than those they were meant to be fighting against. Max was right. The galaxy was in pieces. Maybe there was too much that separated them. Maybe any attempt to bring them together was ill-fated, destined to end in a death of their own doing instead of the curators'.

"You said there were four species left."

Rhendar's voice cut through the tension. He had been quiet, but now he was staring at her through that eerie red visor like they were the only people in the room that existed. All the chest-pounding and simmering violence faded away. It was just the two of them, and between them, the spark of under-standing.

"Four," he repeated. "Then it becomes three, then two, then one. But you've miscounted—or maybe they have. We are five. We are Idran-Var."

Alvera gave a strained smile in reply. "I'm not sure the cura-tors see it like that."

"It doesn't matter how the curators see it. It's how we see it. How we see ourselves." There was a note of urgency in his voice now. "We're a part of their experiment they never accounted for. Something made from all of us, yes, but something *different*. Something more than civilisation."

A disbelieving laugh rumbled from Rivus's throat. "All the Idran-Var have ever accomplished is violence."

"What we've accomplished is *resistance*. And we have done that by standing together as a single people. By transcending distinctions of species or civilisations. If we do it again, if we do it right here, then the curators' experiment is already over. They just can't see it yet."

Something in his words took root inside Alvera, loosening the tightness in her chest. What if Rhendar was right? Maybe the Idran-Var were a variable that tipped the scales of this twisted game they'd been forced into playing. Maybe they were the key to escaping the extinction that had been planned for them.

It was a reach. An idea half made from hope and half from desperation. Those were the odds they were up against.

Rivus bristled. "Standing together is one thing, but don't tell me that makes me Idran-Var. You can't pretend our differences don't exist."

"It's not that our differences don't exist—it's that they don't matter. Not when we come together to face something greater. To *become* something greater, through the action of facing it." Rhendar tilted his head. "Call yourself whatever you like, Supreme Commander. All I need is for you to fight alongside me. That will speak more of you than any name."

Rivus didn't say anything. Alvera watched the slow rise and fall of his chest, the way his thick plates shifted as he frowned. The black, blistered scarring down the side of his face looked like ragged shadows under the dim lights. He was the only other person who'd known what was coming. It was a burden visible in the stoop of his shoulders, in the hairline fractures of his bone spurs. If he couldn't do this, then she was on her own. She wasn't sure she could handle that, not after everything she'd done to get here. Not after everything she'd already lost.

Then Rivus straightened his spine, turning towards her with discerning eyes. "We'll gather our allies. All of us. Not just the legionnaires, not just the Coalition, but everyone we can spare from the entire allied systems and beyond. We'll call on the independent planets in the Rim Belt. We'll call on the pirates and mercenary crews." He turned to Rhendar. "We'll call on the Idran-Var."

"You'll find us ready to answer," Rhendar said. "We've been waiting for this fight longer than any of us realised. We'll be there when the time comes."

Max shifted in his chair, looking between them all with a sceptical expression. "The human fleet is one of the biggest in the galaxy, but the Rasnian systems have gone dark. We haven't managed to get any communications in or out. You want firepower, you need to deal with Cobus and whatever he's up to. He'll be feeling brave with the ambassadors gone. Nobody's left to stop him breaking away from the Coalition like he always wanted."

"There's someone left," Rivus said, an edge to his gravelly voice. "Maybe the human governor needs reminding exactly what this white cloak represents. In the meantime, we need to consolidate our forces. Send out envoys, arrange rendezvous locations. You heard Captain Renata—our window of opportunity is already small, and it's closing fast. If we don't do this now, we'll not get another chance."

"Agreed," Rhendar said quietly. He stood next to Rivus, the dark, glassy metal of his armour reflecting the white of the legionnaire's cloak. The red lines of his visor blinked rapidly as he turned his gaze around the room. "This is where our fight begins. Only we get to say when it ends. *Idra ti gratar, var-fael.* Now I need you to fight better. For yourselves. For all of us."

A hushed murmur of assent broke out around the Idran-

Var, quickly echoed by the other scattered factions gathered in the room. All of them here through necessity or desperation. All of them choosing to stay, choosing to fight. It wasn't enough, but it was a start.

Hey, look—galactic peace. And all it took was the inevitability of extinction.

Alvera smiled. Chase's voice would never echo around her head again. All she could summon were fragments of words never spoken, guesses at what she might have said. But it was still an existence, if only in memory. If nothing else, it made her feel a little less alone.

"Captain."

The rest of the room was filing out. The holograms of the star charts had been lost to the raised lights, and someone had cranked open a window, letting in the icy breath of the planet outside. Only Rhendar remained unmoving, his steely presence watchful and observing as the room emptied, leaving the two of them alone.

Alvera folded her arms. "Something else you needed?"

The clang of his boots on the hard floor filled her ears with an uncomfortable ringing as he closed the gap between them. She saw her reflection in the gleam of his metal shell, pale-faced and dark-eyed, with too many lines to count. He was close enough that she could hear the hiss of recycled air escaping from the filters of his helmet, tinged with the harsh modulator that distorted his voice.

Rhendar lifted his head towards her, trapping her in the unfathomable glare from behind the glowing red lines in his visor.

"Yes," he said. "I think there's something we should discuss."

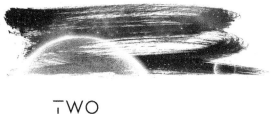

TWO

KOJAN

The sterile smell of the medbay was giving Kojan a headache. Not a cybernetic-induced headache, just a plain old regular headache. The throbbing through his temples was a pain he was profoundly grateful for. A pain that was relatively benign, all things considered. For once, it didn't mean something was wrong with the implants inside his head. It didn't mean that a circuit was threatening to blow and rupture his brain. It was a normal, unremarkable headache.

And he had Alvera to thank for it.

Not for the first time, the thought brought an involuntary scowl to his face. She'd saved his life. There should have been a part of him capable of summoning gratitude for that, no matter how begrudging it was. But all he felt was a simmering mixture of anger and resentment festering in the pit of his stomach, every bit as corrosive as the quickening.

The Idran-Var medic rapped him on the shoulder and

Kojan drew another breath, his lungs burning from the effort. His oxygen saturation was still far below normal levels, and the latest set of lab results had shown a significant loss of function in his right kidney. Alvera might have stopped the quickening before it killed him, but there was no easy fix for the damage it had left behind. The rogue code in his implants had turned his cybernetics against his body, eating through tissue and weakening his central nervous system. The recovery would be long and painful, even with the help of the Idran-Var med centre.

Not that Kojan intended to stay there.

He stifled another hacking cough as he turned to the medic. "I feel a lot better, all things considered. You sure we can't cut down on all these check-ups and tests? If I'm not needed out there yet, I will be soon."

"You've responded well to the oxygen therapy, but it's still early days," the medic replied shortly. "I can't stop you if you choose to leave, but it's in the best interests of your recovery if you adhere to the treatment plan."

"You're Idran-Var, aren't you? Surely you of all people should understand."

She bristled. "Not all Idran-Var are warriors. What I *understand* is the merit of following a treatment plan to its conclusion. I'm sure there are plenty of other space jockeys who can replace you in the meantime."

"Space jockey?" Now it was Kojan's turn to be affronted. "There's not another pilot in the galaxy who can do what I do. If you knew half the things—"

"Harassing the med techs again, I see?" Cyren entered the room, her long jaws split in a sharp-toothed grin. The Idran-Var medic took the opportunity to excuse herself and shuffled off as Cyren made her way over to the bed, her yellow eyes gleaming with amusement.

A painful jolt shot through Kojan's heart. Cyren's scaled neck still showed the incision scars from where the cyber surgeons had inserted her new implant. She was a living test subject. The first iskaath to trial Alvera's modified trauma regulators. She stood before him bare-jawed, no breather mask or toxin supply in sight. It was everything Eleion had ever wanted. For herself, for Cyren, for her people. If she could have seen her now...

Cyren's grin faded as she studied him with keen, discerning eyes. "When are you going to stop looking at me like that?"

"Like what?"

"Like you'd rather be anywhere else than in my company."

Kojan flushed. "I didn't mean—"

"I know." Cyren let out a long, quiet hiss. "You think I don't see her every time I look at you, Kojan? My daughter didn't have many friends. She didn't have a bondmate. You were the only person she ever..." She broke off, her voice constricted. "Part of her lives on because of what she meant to you, and I'm grateful for that. Grateful for you."

The raw emotion behind her words buried itself somewhere deep beneath Kojan's sternum. He was still carrying too much pain, too much guilt, to take comfort from them. Still, there was something bittersweet in the shared sorrow. Eleion was gone, but everything she'd fought for had been made real. Cyren was proof of that.

"How does it feel?" he asked, gesturing to her jaws.

The scales around her nostrils rippled as she let out a tentative huff. "Strange. Like I've forgotten to put something on. I imagine it's how you humans might feel if you found yourselves wandering around without clothes."

Kojan laughed. "And apart from that? Are the implants working as intended?"

"Better. I admit, I was never as eager as Eleion to leave the nest and travel to new planets. The risks were too high. But now, being able to breathe without filtration systems and toxin supplements, being able to go wherever I choose, wherever I'm needed..." Cyren smiled. "It's like a freedom I never knew I missed until I got it. The freedom Eleion always knew our people deserved. Not all iskaath will choose it—nor should they—but the fact we have the choice now...that's what she died for."

Kojan swallowed the hard lump lodged in his throat. "I wish she hadn't needed to."

"So do I. But she'll not be the last to fall in this fight, not with what's coming," Cyren said. "This alliance needs greater numbers. The iskaath can provide that. We're turning all our factories on Kaath towards production of the trauma regulators Alvera designed. In a few weeks we'll be ready to fight alongside the rest of you."

"Is that what you want?"

"It's our duty. We iskaath aren't a violent people, but we fight to protect our nest. With this gift Alvera gave us, our nest got a whole lot bigger." Cyren tightened her jaws. "We won't let this galaxy fall now that we might finally have a place in it."

Her words sent a swell of determination through Kojan's chest. She was right. The galaxy belonged to all of them now. They were responsible for defending it. There was no way he could sit this out, not when so many others were ready to give their lives to stop what was coming.

He swung his legs over the edge of the bed and ripped off the monitoring nodes taped to his skin. He was getting out of here. No matter what it took. No matter who he had to plead with or threaten to do it.

The Idran-Var medic rushed back across the room, her plates quivering with irritation. "Where do you think you're going?"

Kojan pushed himself to his feet, ignoring the trembling in his legs as he set his eyes on the med centre doors. "To find someone with the authority to put me back in the fight."

He found Alvera in a room on one of the building's upper levels, looking out over Alcruix's rugged, volcanic terrain. Her reflection blurred in the glass, melding with the ice-covered peaks and blackened craters outside. There might have been pain in her expression, regret even. Or it might have just been a trick of the light.

"The summit went that well, did it?" Kojan asked.

Alvera turned around, dark-eyed and unsmiling. A shadow of the woman Kojan had once followed—once feared. It was like all the rage and bristling indignation had been sucked out, leaving her withered and empty. Her light olive skin had paled so much it looked translucent, with webs of thin blue veins underneath.

"As well as could be expected," Alvera said, her voice heavy. "Though I'm not sure I like how much our survival depends on everybody *not killing each other*." She allowed herself a thin smile. "It's good to see you up and about. You're looking a lot better."

"After you fixed what you did to me, you mean?"

The words were out before he could stop them, filled with a bitterness clinging to the tip of his tongue. He'd carried the resentment inside him for too long. Seeing her was all it had taken to send him over the edge.

Alvera blanched. "I never knew—I never thought Ojara would have used it on her own son."

"What does it matter who she used it on?" Kojan shook his head. "You handed her a weapon that let her turn innocent people into ticking time bombs. Have you any idea what that's like? To feel your own cybernetics turning against you, destroying you from the inside out?"

Alvera's face was stony. "The quickening was a mistake. Not my first, and certainly not my last."

"Creating that kind of horror isn't a *mistake*. You knew what you were doing. You must have worked hard to come up with something that terrible."

"I suppose I did." Alvera shifted back towards the window. "It still stings to admit it, but there was a time I wasn't all that different from Ojara."

"I don't see how you're all that different now."

She gave a hollow laugh. "Maybe that's true. At least now, I know who I am. There was a time that wasn't the case. A time before Chase. I don't remember much about the person I was then. It was a different life. A darker life."

"Maybe all Chase did was make you a different kind of monster."

"Possibly. I wonder what that means for me now she's gone."

Kojan stilled. "Gone?"

Alvera turned to face him again. This time, there was no trick of the light. He could see the tear-stained streaks on her face, the bloodshot colour to her eyes. It was like looking at something impossible—something that shouldn't have been able to exist. Alvera Renata. The captain, the agitator, the woman who'd changed everything. This was all that was left of her.

It wouldn't be enough.

"Gone," she repeated.

The emptiness in her voice chilled him. There was a time not so long ago when he might have taken satisfaction from seeing her like this. It might have been easier if he hated her the way he hated Ojara. She didn't deserve his pity or forgiveness, not after the things she'd done. But too much was at stake. Whatever she'd become, he needed the old Alvera back. They all did.

"I wanted to kill you," he said quietly. "Ojara told me she'd reverse the quickening if I did."

Alvera gave a sad, strained smile. "You wouldn't have gone through with it, Kojan."

"Eleion said the same thing. I don't know what made either of you so sure."

His throat tightened arounds the words as he spoke. Eleion's name was a wound that would never close, one he'd carry with him long after the last scars from the quickening had healed. Eleion was dead because of Alvera. Dead *for* her, which somehow made it worse. She'd given her life to save Alvera's. Now every time Kojan looked at his old captain, he couldn't help but wish for the trade to be reversed.

Alvera stared at him. "Kojan, I—"

"It doesn't matter," he said. He couldn't handle an apology. Couldn't handle her regret, if that was what she'd been ready to offer him. "I didn't come here to go over things that can't be changed. I need a favour. Get me out of that med centre and back in a ship. It doesn't have to be the *Ranger*, but I need to fly. I need to do something to help."

She looked him over, eyes wary. "What did the medic say?"

"She's not keen on me leaving. But she doesn't understand what your trauma regulators are capable of. Now that the quickening is gone, my implants will be able to fix the mess left behind."

"Eventually. They'd work a lot faster with proper medical care."

Heat rushed to his collar. "Is that a no?"

"No." Alvera sighed. "I don't have any right to stop you, and the truth is we need everyone we can get. Too many systems have gone dark. We can't get communications through. If we're sending envoys, we need pilots who can—"

"Kojan, finally! I've been looking everywhere for you."

He snapped his head around to see Ridley Jones burst into the room, wide-eyed and breathless. The black coils of her hair had grown longer, half-covering the shaved sides of her head.

She carried herself straighter than he remembered, the square-ness of her shoulders making her taller.

Then she caught sight of Alvera, and something inside her seemed to deflate. "Captain Renata. I didn't realise..." The warmth in her voice evaporated, replaced by an unforgiving edge. "I heard about your summit. Let's hope it goes better than last time."

The lines in Alvera's forehead deepened. "What do you mean?"

"It's easy for you to forget the people you leave behind, isn't it?" Ridley laughed, the harsh sound echoing off the walls. "All of us go, or none of us go. That's what you used to say. Of course, it didn't matter when you left us at the mercy of a madman with a loaded gun and a grudge to bear."

"I didn't know—"

"You brought Shaw onto the *Ranger*. Don't tell me you didn't know what he was capable of. You knew. You must have."

Alvera lowered her head. "I'm sorry."

"Sorry?" Ridley echoed. "Half the crew are dead because you couldn't control that monster. I only survived by abandoning them to save my own skin. Do you have any idea what it's like to carry that kind of guilt? Or is coming back here to play the hero enough to make you forget?"

"I'm not trying to play the hero, Ridley."

"Of course you are. That's what you do." Ridley shook her head. "I believed in you. I told myself I could finish what you started. I travelled past the edge of the galaxy searching for answers. But when I came back to warn everyone about what I found, it was too late. You'd already done it." She gave her a pained look. "Guess that really does make me *obsolete*, doesn't it?"

Alvera flinched. "I would never call you—"

"You didn't have to." Ridley let out a slow breath. "Us

surfacers weren't on the *Ranger* because you needed us. We were there as a symbol. A reminder of your promise."

"I thought I was doing the right thing."

"Part of me thought you were too. But you were too busy trying to save the world to see how much danger you were bringing to those of us you wanted to protect. And now…" Ridley's jaw trembled. "Tell me something—what happens to New Pallas if we destroy the Omega Gate?"

Alvera's silence left Kojan's stomach churning. "What do you mean?" he asked, his voice dry. "The tunnel we punched is still there, isn't it?"

"For now," Ridley said. "But I've learned a thing or two about punching tunnels these last few weeks. A ship's drive only causes a tiny tear in the fabric of the galaxy. A miniscule pinprick on either end of a hairline fracture, relatively speaking. But the tunnel from New Pallas wasn't made by the *Ranger*."

"No, it wasn't," Kojan said, cold realisation creeping over him. "It was made by Exodus Station."

"Exactly. The size of the hole it tore, the distance it had to bore through… That kind of energy leaves a trauma. It makes the tunnel unstable. The only things keeping it from collapsing—"

"Are the waystations themselves," Alvera finished.

Ridley snapped her head towards her. "You knew?"

"Not for certain, but it makes sense. They must act as anchors on either end of the tunnel. And if we remove one of those anchors by destroying the Omega Gate…" Alvera stared at them both, her eyes bleak and empty. "These past few weeks have forced me to reckon with the possibility that keeping a door open for New Pallas condemns the rest of this galaxy to death. We might not be able to save both."

Kojan rubbed his forehead. "This doesn't make any sense. The plan was to shut down the space tunnel, not destroy the

Omega Gate. If we get control of it, we can cut off the curators while still keeping the waystations active, at least for as long as it takes to evacuate New Pallas."

"And if we don't manage to get control of it?" Alvera asked, her voice heavy. "If all that we're left with is the choice of destroying it, even if that means destroying New Pallas's hopes of survival?"

Kojan didn't answer. He couldn't. His head flooded with thoughts of the iskaath, memories of his time spent among them on their homeworld. How could he possibly balance their lives against the lives of all the people back on New Pallas? How could anyone make that kind of decision?

He met Alvera's dim, broken eyes. This was why she had come back. It was her. It could only be her.

Ridley's complexion had taken on a sickly undertone and her eyes were stricken, as though she'd inevitably come to the same conclusion Kojan had. It was an impossible choice. One neither of them were capable of making.

Alvera nodded, slow and stiff. Kojan saw the weariness in her eyes as she acknowledged their silent resignation. She'd already accepted this burden from them, this weight nobody else could carry. Her face was wrought with lines and shadows as she made her way towards the door, the wispy grey strands of her hair pale against the darkness.

When she reached the threshold, she turned back. "I was wrong," she said, her voice half a whisper. "I was wrong about a lot of things. Whatever happens next, I'll be wrong about this, too. There can be no right choice with what we're about to do. Remember that, when these decisions come to you instead of me. Try to forgive each other, if you can. Because the void knows you'll never be able to forgive yourselves."

Then she was gone, leaving them with nothing but the disturbing wake of her departing words.

Kojan turned to Ridley. Her chest rose up and down as she stared out at the empty doorway. "Hey."

"Hey." She shook herself out of her trance and stretched her mouth into a strained, weary smile. "What's new?"

"You tell me. You seem...different."

"I'm angry. Took me a little while to learn that that's okay." She let go of a long breath. "It's good to see you, Kojan. You look like you've been through it."

"We all have."

"I suppose that's true." Something pained flitted across Ridley's face. "I can't believe I came all the way here just to tell this stupid summit what they already know. Nothing I did these past few months matters now. I might as well have stayed with —" She broke off, clenching her fists. "It doesn't matter. It's done now. I'm here. Might as well find a way to make myself useful."

"You're staying? You're going to help, even after what Alvera said?"

"We have to. I don't see how there's any other choice."

Kojan didn't reply. A quiet, unspoken understanding filled the gaps between Ridley's words. Heavy with dread, laden with a possibility neither of them wanted to consider. Alvera had taken the decision out of their hands. Just as she always did. Just as they'd always needed her to.

"What are you going to do?" he asked.

Ridley shrugged. "They're sending people out across the galaxy to gather allies. It's a nice plan, but there are places it will never work. The pirates and mercenary gangs in the Rim Belt won't agree to help just because some Coalition envoy asks them nicely. They only respond to power. Or force, if that's what it takes."

Kojan let out a nervous laugh. "When we get some downtime, you have to tell me how you've ended up an expert on Rim Belt politics. I assume you have a plan?"

"I know someone who could bring them all in line. If we get her on board, the rest will follow."

He raised an eyebrow. "Can you? Get this person on board, I mean?"

A cackle cut through the air from the open doorway. "Not a chance."

A long-limbed jarkaath sauntered into the room, his bronze eyes bright and amused. He was shorter than Eleion or Cyren, and his scales were still dusted with the lingering remains of the silvery coating his species shed in their early adulthood. His green-black jaws were long and bare—not because he had implants, like Cyren, but because he'd never needed them in the first place.

Ridley sighed. "Drex, we've been over this. It's worth a shot."

"Do you need reminding of what happened the last time you spoke to Skaile?" the jarkaath replied, his words accompanied by a hiss from the back of his throat. "She tried to kill you, and then your ex-girlfriend shot her in the head. Well, her android head. Her real head is probably very much intact, more's the pity."

Ridley blanched. "If you came here to talk me out of it..."

"I've given up on trying to talk you out of anything. Just wanted to offer your friend an accurate assessment of the situation." He flicked his long, lean head towards Kojan, his eyes sharp and keen. "I came here to talk to him, actually. I hear you're close with the iskaath."

Kojan crossed his arms. "What's it to you?"

"No need to be hostile." The jarkaath held out his clawed hands. "Drexious, by the way. Nice to meet you. We're all friends here, aren't we?"

"Depends what you want with the iskaath. Your people don't exactly have the best track record of treating them with anything other than contempt and intolerance."

"I take your point." Drexious swished his tail from side to

side, his eyes darting between them nervously. "Normally, this would be where I jump in to defend my people, only I stumbled across some information that does nothing but add to our track record of contempt and intolerance."

Kojan tensed. "What are you talking about?"

"I have a contact in jarkaath intelligence." Drexious glanced at Ridley. "Yes, I know it sounds unbelievable, but it's true. We grew up in the same nest, but while she went into government work, I went into—"

"Thieving and smuggling," Ridley cut in. "Go on."

"We've worked together over the years to help each other out. I pass her any rumours that might affect jarkaath security, and she tips me off about black-market investigations and what smuggling lanes are being watched." He shrugged. "It's an arrangement that's worked well for both of us. Only this time, *she's* the one passing on rumours about suspect jarkaath activity."

"What kind of activity?"

"The violent kind. She got a tip that a jarkaath terrorist organisation is planning a strike on Kaath's factories. Some militant group that doesn't want to see the iskaath gain any kind of political standing." He met Kojan's eyes with a steady, unblinking stare. "They're going after the trauma regulators."

Kojan clenched his jaw. He'd seen this too many times—the belief that the only way to set yourself apart was to beat down anyone who tried to get themselves on equal footing. Ojara's hands were bloody with it, Shaw's too. He'd be damned if he let the jarkaath inflict it on Eleion's people, not after she'd given her life for this kind of chance.

"Why did your contact pass this on?" he asked. "I don't think the jarkaath government would lose much sleep over a few bombings on Kaath."

"You're right, they wouldn't. Which is why they're sitting on this information and not doing anything about it. I guess my contact thought someone should know. Someone who might be able to do something about it." Drexious's scales rippled. "Not all jarkaath agree with our government. Why do you think I spend so much time in the Rim Belt? Once you get away from the allied systems, you start to realise we're all just people. Aliens. Whatever." He groaned. "Shit, I've only been on this planet for a day and I'm already talking like an Idran-Var."

Ridley turned to Kojan. "I know what Eleion meant to you, what the iskaath mean to you. I know you have no reason to trust the word of a jarkaath, but I trust Drex."

"A sentiment that's not shared by many others, in my experience," Drexious added. "That's why I brought this to you, human. Word has it you have a direct line to the Supreme Commander himself. Or a direct line to the direct line, as it were."

Ridley frowned. "You're talking about Alvera?"

"Not unless Alvera is a swaggering, purple-headtailed siolean who wanders around the base in a flight suit two sizes too small for her."

"Not the last time I checked." Ridley gave Kojan a pointed look. "Seems like you have your own stories to share when we finally get that downtime."

Kojan flushed. "His name is Kitell Merala—he's the legionnaire that rescued us from Nepthe. He was there when..." The words caught in his throat. "I don't see what he's got to do with any of this. He's just a fighter pilot."

"A fighter pilot who came through the ranks with the Supreme Commander himself. Maybe the only friend he has left, what with the old Supreme Commander getting himself blown to pieces." Drexious huffed at their questioning glances. "What? I listen to people."

"When they don't know you're listening," Ridley said dryly. "If the Idran-Var caught you spying on them..."

"The Idran-Var don't scare me half as much as those things

coming through the Omega Gate," he shot back. "The only reason I'm still here is because I have a personal stake in making sure we don't all die. I'm *helping,* all right? We need all the backup we can get, and the iskaath are no good to anyone if they can't fight offworld. Someone needs to make sure those factories don't get blown to hell."

The memory of Eleion's face swam before Kojan's eyes. Her bright gaze. Her long jaws grinning behind the translucent material of her breather mask. She'd died to give her people this chance. If the jarkaath thought they could take that away...

No. He wouldn't stand by and watch it happen. Drexious wasn't the only one who had a personal stake in this fight.

"I'll do it," Kojan said. "I'll talk to Merala and try to get help from the Supreme Commander. If he agrees to give me a ship, we can stop the terrorists before they get near the factories."

Saying it out loud released something in his chest, like a vice-tight grip had relinquished its hold on him. The time for waiting around was over. He'd lost too much already. All he could do now was fight to save everything that remained.

"I had a feeling you'd say that," Ridley said. "So much for a New Pallas reunion."

"Not this time."

"Maybe not. But we'll get there, Kojan. We have to."

He nodded, accepting the silent promise exchanged between them. They would meet again. Not just him and Ridley, but all the people they'd been separated from, in this galaxy and the world they'd left behind. That was what they were fighting for.

Kojan smiled. It was time to get himself a ship.

THREE

NIOLE

The base was starting to move. Niole felt the energy like one of her flares. The buzz had become tangible—an unspoken call to arms, a feeling of being ready to *do* something.

Reflections from the ceiling lights bounced off the surface of her armour as she climbed the narrow stairs to the roof. Every now and then she caught herself looking down at her arms, still unable to believe that the dark, glassy metal covering them belonged to her. She'd fought for this armour. She'd earned the right to wear it. She was Idran-Var.

A blast of icy wind caught her headtails as she emerged onto the roof. Somewhere in the distance, a volcano spewed ash into the atmosphere. At any moment, another fissure might open in the already-scarred surface of the planet. Yet Niole couldn't help but find a broken sort of beauty in Alcruix. Whatever this rock had been before, it had changed because of what the Idran-Var did to it. Once, she'd been terrified of that kind of power, that kind of violence. Now, the only thing that terrified her was knowing how much they needed it.

Rhendar and Serric were already waiting for her on the exposed, ash-swept rooftop. Like her, Serric was wearing a breathing aid to contend with the planet's thin atmosphere, the snaking tubes connecting his nostril slits to the oxygen supply inside his armour. His blue-green headtails were bright against the monochrome landscape, and the stirrings from his flare already tugged at Niole's insides.

Rhendar looked the same as he always did, his face hidden behind the helmet that had become so symbolic to the Idran-Var. When he caught sight of her, he inclined his head. "Glad you could make it."

"We couldn't have met somewhere warmer?" Niole asked. "Or at least somewhere that wasn't raining ash?"

"Too risky. Alcruix may be our planet, but this base is neutral ground now. You never know who might be listening."

A shiver ran down her spine. "I thought we were all on the same side."

Rhendar tilted his head. "We might all be working towards the same goal, but that doesn't mean we'll agree on how to get there. There are some operations we're better off planning on our own."

"Operations like what?"

"Like breaking into the Bastion," Serric answered bluntly.

Niole couldn't speak. She wasn't entirely sure she'd heard him right. But there was no humour in his expression, no sign that this was anything other than exactly what he said it was.

She let out a weak laugh. "You can't be serious. The Bastion? Of all the places..."

"I'm deadly serious." Serric folded his arms. "Numbers mean nothing if we don't have the firepower to back it up. You were on Ossa. You saw what those aliens were capable of. Any force that tries to take the Omega Gate will get ripped to shreds.

We need hard hitters, and nothing causes devastation like a flare-sick siolean let loose from their leash."

The way he said it made Niole's stomach churn. Like those sorry bastards down in that underwater prison were nothing but weapons, little better than the mindless thralls the curators were using themselves.

The worst part was that Serric was *right*. Niole knew better than anyone how much an *ilsar* could turn the tide of a fight. The same violent energy ran through her too. The legionnaires had hunted her for years, and every time they came for her, she'd left nothing behind but bodies. The fact that she was still free only spoke of the blood she'd shed to keep it that way.

"You're talking about releasing some incredibly dangerous people," she said slowly. "Anyone locked up in the Bastion is there because they can't control their flares or because they don't want to. Honestly, I'm not sure what scares me more."

"We don't need them to control their flares," Serric said. "We need them to fight. I bet they'll only be too happy to trade their cells for a shot at the Omega Gate. Wouldn't you?"

Niole didn't need to meet his eyes to feel the disappointment coming from him—it was evident enough in his voice. She should have been hardened against the sting of Serric's disapproval by now, dulled to the way it hit her, but there was something in the way it burrowed under her skin that made it impossible to ignore.

"It's a risk," Rhendar said heavily. "But we may be asked to do worse before this war is over. The more you prepare yourself for that possibility, the less it will break you when it comes to pass."

Somewhere in the coldest, darkest part of her, Niole knew he was right. This was what being Idran-Var meant. To fight. To resist, no matter what the cost. But there was another part of her, buried under all she'd put herself through to get here, that squirmed and fought against it. Part of her that longed for a better way, that glimmered in her mind like a green cloak in the breeze, and not the dark sheen of armour.

She swallowed. "I'll do it. I don't like it, but—"

"If you don't like it, then don't come," Serric said, cutting her off with a wave of his hand. "I need someone who has my back. If that's not you, I'll find someone else."

Heat rushed to her headtails. "You'd say that to me after everything we've been through? How I feel about the mission has nothing to do with me having your back. Question whatever you like about me, but don't question that."

Serric said nothing, but the turquoise of his cheeks turned a ruddy blue. His displeasure radiated from him like a flare pulsing across her skin. Half of her wanted to push back against it, but Serric would only take that as a challenge. Niole wouldn't let things go back to how they'd been before, not when they'd finally carved out some kind of understanding between them.

"We have enough enemies as it is, Serric," she said quietly. "Don't mistake me for something I'm not."

"Niole is right," Rhendar said, the metallic tinge to his voice taking on a harder tone. "You know what we're up against. You know what's at stake. If we're to win this, we need to take strength from each other, not turn it against ourselves."

Serric let out a long breath. "Fine," he said, not meeting Niole's eyes. "I've got a ship fuelled and ready to leave in three hours. Docking bay C-93. Make sure you're ready."

He was gone before she could reply, stalking off through the grey drifts of ash with stiff shoulders and a long stride. Watching him leave released a tension Niole hadn't realised she was carrying. It left behind an ache too, a pain as unexpected as it was unwelcome.

"This is more dangerous than he thinks," she said softly. "He has no idea what that place will do to him."

"He'd have found a path there eventually," Rhendar said. "I

used to fear it would mean the end for him. That he'd die alone down there, destroyed by his own rage."

"And now?"

He turned the red lights of his helmet towards her. "Now, he won't be alone."

His words were like two edges of a blade—Niole couldn't tell if they offered a sliver of hope, or a warning. If she went into that watery hell with Serric, would either of them come back?

"What will you do while we're gone?" she asked, shaking the thoughts from her head. "I heard some of the *varsath* were returning to Maar."

"Our forces suffered considerable damage during the evacuation of Ossa," Rhendar said. "We need to regroup and resupply, and the *varsath* will oversee that. But I won't be joining them. I have a different task."

Niole furrowed her brow ridge. "Does this have anything to do with what you were talking to the human captain about? I saw you speaking after the summit."

For a moment, Rhendar said nothing. His faceless helmet was as expressionless as ever, giving nothing away. It was times like these the old fear crept back in, the fear that despite all they'd been through together, she didn't really know the man behind the mask—or what he was capable of.

After the silence had stretched out so long it was almost unbearable, Rhendar spoke. "Contingency," he said.

It was all he needed to say. A single word with a thousand possibilities, each of them more terrifying than the next. It filled Niole with dread and left her grateful that he had said no more, grateful that he had spared her—if only for a little while —from the horror on the horizon.

The last time the Idran-Var had elected a war chief, they'd gone on to kill a planet. When Rhendar had the title thrust upon him, Niole told herself it was different—*he* was different.

We may be asked to do worse before this war is over, he had said. *The more you prepare yourself for that possibility, the less it will break you when it comes to pass.*

Contingency. Their last, desperate hope when all else had failed. Survival at the cost of the unthinkable. Preparing for something like that was impossible. It *would* break her. And all she could do was wait for it to happen.

————

The journey to Pxen passed in near-silence. The stuffy, recycled air was thick with tension as Niole moved around the cramped quarters of the ship, and every time she ventured near the cockpit, she felt the simmering of Serric's flare like a barrier warning her against getting too close. She sometimes wondered what might be left behind if that rage was ever taken away, but those thoughts too often turned to guilt, like she was longing for a person that didn't exist, that *couldn't* exist. The galaxy had made Serric what he was. There was no changing it. Maybe she had to learn to accept the gap between them instead of forever trying to bridge it.

The intercom crackled overhead. "Making our final approach."

Serric's voice was gruff and brusque; it was hardly an invitation. Niole made her way towards the cockpit anyway. Her skin prickled with energy as the door slid open, but there was no response from Serric as she slid into the co-pilot's chair. He seemed strangely calm, almost subdued.

Niole cleared her throat. "Any sign of curator ships in the area?"

Serric shook his head. "Not yet. We might be in the heart of siolean space, but this system is pretty isolated. Not much here apart from an asteroid belt and a couple of gas giants. And Pxen, of course."

There was a bite in his voice when he spoke. Maybe

Rhendar was right. Maybe Serric would have always found an excuse to come here. He'd killed so many to escape it, just as Niole had. The fear of it had made them who they were, for better or worse. There was power in a place like that. It made it dangerous.

"Serric, are you sure—"

"I shouldn't have said what I did before," he interrupted, his headtails flushing with colour. "Vesyllion, Aurel, Ossa... You've proven yourself more than once. You don't deserve my doubt, not anymore. But coming here... I can't help but wonder how things might have been if I'd let them take me away that day. If I hadn't fought back. Hadn't resisted." He turned his eyes towards her. "You don't want to let these prisoners out, do you? You think they deserve to be here."

"That isn't what I said."

"It's what it sounded like." He shook his head. "If I thought they deserved to be here, I'd have to believe I deserve it too."

"I'm not saying they deserve to be here. *Nobody* deserves to be here." Niole placed a hand on his shoulder. Something inside her rushed at the contact, like a current fizzling through her skin. There was a time she might have recoiled from it, but now all she wanted to do was dive deeper into it. Deeper into *him*—if only to make him understand. "But that doesn't mean these people aren't dangerous. Some of them enjoy hurting others. They enjoy killing, enjoy losing themselves in their flares. I know what it's like to be *ilsar*, but I'm not like that. You're not either, whether you see it yourself or not."

Something on the navigation console blinked, and Serric tapped in a command through the interface. "Hitting atmo soon. Make sure you're strapped in. I don't expect a particularly warm welcome."

Niole adjusted her flight restraints and looked out the viewport as Pxen loomed closer, a glistening ball of blue in the black depths of space. The ship buffeted gently as they hit the atmosphere and swirling clouds of white and grey rose up to meet them. Below, the ocean heaved with waves so huge she could make out their cascading shapes even from this high. They roared and crashed like monstrous creatures of blue and green, ever-moving across the horizon. Somewhere amongst them was a landing pad only big enough to hold half a dozen ships. And below that, underneath the weight of the writhing waves, was the Bastion.

"Do you know what we're up against?" Niole asked, peering out the viewport.

"Not as much as I'd like. The siolean government likes to keep its records about this place sealed—even the intel we managed to gather from the Coalition was vague. According to their logs, there's no major military force stationed here. The whole prison is built underwater and can only be accessed by submersibles. I guess the guards don't exactly have to worry about people getting out."

"Or getting in. What happens when we reach the landing pad? I doubt they leave their submersibles lying around."

"Looks like we're about to find out. We've got an escort." Serric brought up one of the external feeds. A small, streamlined fighter was following in their wake, its sharp wings cutting easily through the air. "Our siolean identification codes are holding up. They're sending us an approach vector, telling us to follow them down."

"That seems friendly enough. As opposed to blasting us out of the sky, at any rate."

"Maybe." Serric paused. "Still, for a prison, I'd expect them to have a little more firepower than a single—shit, I knew it!"

He tightened his hands on the controls as the fighter blasted past them and banked hard. One wing skimmed the surface of the water as it flew in a large, sweeping circle around the landing pad they were headed for, then pointed its nose downwards and crashed through the tumultuous waves below.

"What happened?" Niole said. "Did they lose control?"

"No." Serric's voice was grim. "They're heading back to base. Those fighters double up as submersibles. The Bastion does have a fleet protecting it after all—it's just below the surface."

Niole couldn't see anything beneath the churning waters. There was no sign of the fighter. It had disappeared below the waves like one of Vesyllion's water-hawks, as sleek and graceful in the depths as it was in the air. How many more of the strange aqua-fighters were lurking under the surface? She imagined the water glowing with hundreds of lights rising up to meet them. If Pxen had a fleet at its disposal, they had already lost.

The floor rattled as Serric guided the ship down to the landing pad. The grey concrete platform towered above the waves on steel stilts, but its impressive height wasn't enough to stop the spray showering the hull as they hit the ground. After a moment, the rumbling of the engines faded and died, leaving Niole with nothing but the crashing of waves echoing in her ears.

"I hate this place already," she muttered, half to herself.

Amusement tugged at the edge of Serric's mouth. "We haven't left the ship yet."

"Exactly."

She pulled her helmet over her headtails and hit the release for the access ramp, giving an involuntary shudder as the door slid open and the roar of the water grew louder. Even through her helmet's filtration system, she tasted salt in the air. It was unlike anywhere she'd ever been. Unlike anywhere she'd ever wanted to go. Like being in a vacuum, if a vacuum could fill her lungs with saltwater and crush her body under the weight of its depths.

This was where people like her were sent to die. Plunged below the waves to be held in an inescapable tomb. Buried under hundreds of metres of water, confined by an invisible pressure bearing down all around.

Serric nudged her, motioning his head towards one of the pillars on the far side of the landing pad. He'd put on his helmet too, staring out across the dull grey platform through the diagonal slits of his visor.

A curved door in the pillar slid to the side, and two sioleans in bulky, riot-grade power armour came out. As soon as they caught sight of them, their hands flew to the weapons on their belts. Niole could hardly blame them. There was a time she'd have had the same reaction to seeing an Idran-Var somewhere they shouldn't have been.

"Let me do the talking," she said quietly to Serric, keeping her eyes trained on them.

"Why?"

"You can be abrasive."

Niole walked towards the middle of the landing pad, holding her hands in the air. The wind howled over the exposed platform, and the blue-grey waves stretched as far as she could see.

"That's far enough," one of the sioleans barked, raising her rifle. "Don't make me test that armour of yours."

"Take it easy," Niole said, keeping her hands high. "We're not here to cause any trouble."

The other siolean, a gnarled older male with too many headtails to count, drew his mouth into a hard line. "Two Idran-Var show up out of nowhere and tell us they're not here to cause any trouble? How stupid do you think we are?"

"These aren't normal circumstances. Surely we all agree that the situation is desperate."

The female guard furrowed her brow ridge. "What are you talking about? Does this have something to do with our long-range communications going out?"

"Don't tell them anything, Lilosa." The older guard shot them a venomous look. "They're Idran-Var."

"Your comms are out?" Serric asked, cocking his head.

Lilosa nodded. "Almost three standard weeks now. We sent a runner to the next system to see if they could get word out, but they never came back. When we saw your ship had a siolean-registered identification signature, we thought..."

"If your comms are down, then you've no idea what's happening," Niole said gently. "The waystations have opened up a gate to curator space. They've been sending through invading forces for weeks. We're working with the Coalition, or what's left of it, at any rate. Things are bad out there—bad enough to make a lot of people desperate. All we're trying to do is find a way to beat these things attacking us."

The two guards shot each other a look, but neither of them loosened their grip on their guns. They were already on edge. It wouldn't take much to spark this impasse into violence. Maybe that was what Serric wanted. Maybe that was why he'd come here.

The old siolean grunted. "We've not seen any kind of invading army out here."

"You will soon enough," Niole said. "I know it's not what you want to hear. It's probably too much to believe. Fyra, I sometimes wish I didn't believe it. But the truth is that—"

"Fyra?" The guard drew the wrinkled skin of his cheeks tight and narrowed his eyes. "You a siolean under there?"

Niole stilled, her heart thumping against her ribs. The word had left her mouth before she realised she'd said it. It was too commonplace on her tongue, too familiar for her to have thought anything of speaking it. She'd been careless, sloppy. Now the guards knew she was siolean. If they figured out the rest, if they suspected she was *ilsar*...

The guard's flare came without warning. One moment Niole was on her feet, the next she was sent sprawling, the air knocked from her lungs as she hit the hard concrete of the landing pad.

Before she could catch her breath, another burst of energy

slammed into her. The old guard wasn't letting up. His flare didn't have the same potency as an *ilsar's*, but that didn't mean he wasn't capable of hurting her. He pushed against her, trying to draw her flare out, trying to make her lose control.

He was testing her.

Niole turned cold. This wasn't an ordinary prison. This was the Bastion. They knew how to deal with people like her. How to break them. Her Idran-Var armour might protect her against blades and bullets, but the Bastion guards had other weapons at their disposal. If she couldn't control herself, if he provoked her into showing what she really was...

It would be so easy to make it stop, to give in to the energy simmering under her skin and unleash her flare. She could reach past the guards' armour. She could force herself into their cells, boiling their blood and setting fire to their nerves. She could tear them apart from the inside out, and in doing so, prove she'd always deserved to be here.

"Enough of this." Serric stepped in front of her. The next blast from the old guard caught him square in the chest, but Serric didn't flinch. He drew the flare past his armour and absorbed it into his body, each movement calm and measured.

The guard hesitated, his brow ridge twitching in confusion. Then Serric threw out a hand and sent a violent, blue-green flare across the platform. It slammed into the guard, sending him flying backwards with a ferocity that took him perilously close to the edge of the landing pad, where the waves roared below.

Lilosa stared at them, her eyes wide. "*Ilsar?* Both of you?"

Serric reached out a hand and Niole took it, hauling herself up from the ground with a groan. His flare pulsed around her, and her own leapt to meet it. She'd never be free of the urge to release it, the call from her body to surrender itself to violence and drown in the power it gave her. That's what being *ilsar* was.

But she was more than that now. She was Idran-Var.

She turned to Lilosa. "Yes. Both of us."

The siolean's green skin paled. "Shit. Of all the days I could have pulled surface rotation." She grimaced. "You know I can't let you leave, right? Besides, they'll blow your ship out the sky now that they know what you are. There's no way off this platform for you now but down to the Bastion."

A chill ran down Niole's spine. This was what they came here for. But walking into this prison willingly, handing themselves over to people who would seal them away under the weight of all that water and slowly kill them with anti-radiation drugs... If they went below the waves, would there be a way out for them?

Above the whistling wind and crashing waves, Serric laughed. "Lead the way."

FOUR

RIVUS

R ivus woke to the sound of an alarm blaring through the ship. The fact that he'd been able to sleep at all was a small comfort, in spite of the ear-splitting wail of the siren. For the first time in months, his dreams had been quiet and free from terror. Maybe it was all the exhaustion catching up with him. Or maybe it was because the nightmares plaguing him had made their way from his dreams into his waking reality.

The noise continued to screech around the walls of his quarters as he retrieved his power armour from the footlocker under his bed and pulled it on piece by piece. The polished white metal had a gleam to it, even in the darkness. The last thing to go on was the cloak. A reminder of everything Rivus had become, and everything he'd lost on the way.

When he caught sight of himself in the mirror, he almost looked like the Supreme Commander everyone expected him to be. He might have believed it himself, if only he could stop seeing Tarvan in the shadows of his reflection. The pain had a habit of catching him off guard, re-emerging when he least expected it, no matter how much he tried to push it from his mind.

He shook off the tired fog around his head and blinked his way to a state of alertness. The alarm was still ringing around his head, painful and persistent. What the hell was happening out there? Were the Rasnian systems already crawling with curator forces, or was this the doing of the humans themselves?

Alvera Renata was waiting for him on the bridge, her eyes grimly focused on the series of lights flashing on the interface. Her silver hair was pulled tight behind her head, and her forehead creased with worry as she tapped the controls. "Figured something like this would happen, though I hoped they'd make an exception considering the situation."

"Exception to what?"

"Rasnians don't like outside ships polluting the air of their homeworld. If you're not on their list, you have to dock at one of the orbital stations and take a solar shuttle down. Normally, you'd figure the Supreme Commander would make the list, but for some reason, they don't seem to like you."

"Don't like the company I'm travelling with, more like." Rivus grunted. "The jarkaath government aren't the only ones getting bold. The whole galaxy is under attack and all everyone wants to do is find ways to take advantage of it."

"I'd call it human nature, but it looks like everyone is getting in on the action." Alvera released a long breath. "I don't like where this is going. If we go down in one of those solar shuttles, we leave ourselves at Cobus's mercy. I only managed to get off this planet the first time because he *wanted* me to escape. We'll have no ship, no reinforcements—"

"Bringing reinforcements would have sent the wrong signal. We're coming here to ask for an alliance, not bully them into submission," Rivus said pointedly. "Cobus may be an opportunistic asshole, but he's not stupid enough to attack the Supreme Commander."

"Maybe not before." Alvera shrugged. "Now though? I'm not so sure. Like you said, people are feeling awfully brave with the Coalition gone. They'll try as much as they can get away with."

After they docked, they made their way to one of the solar shuttles, surrounded by stern-faced Rasnian military police. Ras Prime glittered against the darkness of space, all bright greens and rich, vivid blues. White clouds streaked the atmosphere as they descended, giving way to lush emerald forests and snow-covered peaks as far as the horizon stretched.

It was a beautiful planet. Rivus could see why the humans wanted to protect it so badly. Was that why Cobus wanted to break away from the Coalition? Did he think the curators would leave these glistening lakes and fertile vales unspoiled while the rest of the galaxy burned?

Maybe Alvera was right. Maybe the humans had been waiting for this kind of opportunity. The Coalition had held strong for millennia. Rivus had always believed the rest of the galaxy respected that kind of stability, that the peace he'd sworn to protect *meant* something. Now, it seemed like everyone had been waiting for it to fall.

"We're here," Alvera murmured. Her eyes had a far-away look in them, and she'd set her jaw squarely. Most humans were softer around the edges, but there was something in the rigidity of her face that reminded Rivus of a dachryn. *Unyielding,* he thought. Like Tarvan. He wasn't sure whether the comparison gave him comfort or left him uneasy.

The Rasnian police escorted them towards a towering glass building, stiff-shouldered with their hands firmly on their weapons. There was no pretence of courtesy, no polite greeting as they ushered them through the doors and across the marble-tiled atrium.

"I've been here before," Alvera said. "This is where I stood trial when they arrested me on those bullshit charges of stealing the *Ranger*."

"They're taking us to a courthouse?" Rivus bristled. "That's hardly appropriate protocol for—"

"Do you think Cobus cares about protocol right now? He's looking for a win, and we're about to give it to him freely." She shook her head. "This was a bad idea. We should have brought a fleet. And guns. Lots more guns."

"I never asked you to come. You were the one who insisted."

"Only to stop you getting yourself killed. You're the only one who understands, Rivus. I can't do this by myself. Not anymore. Not after..." Alvera paused, her face hardening. "We started this, you and I. It's up to us to finish it."

"We agree on that much, at least." Rivus surveyed the chamber they'd been escorted into. The ceiling was a glass dome, glinting with sunlight reflecting off the surrounding panels. At the far end was a carved wooden bench sitting above the floor like a podium. He recognised Governor Cobus behind it with his shrewd, thin features and long black hair. The woman next to him was familiar too. She had a hard, pointed face and near-white hair scraped back into a series of intricate spirals at the back of her head. When she saw them, her cheeks pinched and a slow, vicious smile crept across her painted lips.

Rivus glanced at Alvera. She had turned deathly pale apart from two angry spots of colour in her cheeks. Her mouth twisted into a snarl as she glared up at the podium.

"What are you doing here?" she spat, staring at the woman by Cobus's side. "Haven't you done enough damage already, you deranged old bitch?"

The smile on the woman's face stretched a fraction wider. "Insults? I've come to expect little else from one such as you, murderer and traitor that you are."

"Ojara, I swear—" Alvera took a furious step forward but

stopped in her tracks at the sight of a dozen military rifles being drawn and pointed in her direction. Red targeting lasers splayed across her face as she froze in place, her fists clenched.

"I'll kill her," she muttered. "Give me half a chance and I'll drop her dead on the ground like she deserves."

Ojara. Rivus remembered now. The human who had arrived on the *Ranger* with Alvera. The one who'd claimed mutiny and murder and wormed her way into the role of chief diplomat. At the time, the Coalition ambassadors had considered her a useful tool, but ultimately harmless. Now they were dead, and Ojara stood at the side of one of the few leaders left in the galaxy.

Cobus appraised them, steely caution in his eyes. "Strange company you're keeping these days, Supreme Commander Itair. Or does that title no longer apply? I wasn't sure you had anything left to command."

Rivus kept his expression steady. Rising to Cobus's taunts would only play into the human's hands. There was more at stake than his own pain and pride. "These are unprecedented times, Governor. We're not in a position to be turning down allies, regardless of the things they might have been accused of."

"Renata still has a galactic arrest warrant out in her name. She killed one of my finest military police officers."

"I'm also one of the only people in the galaxy who understands what we're up against," Alvera retorted. "Or do you have some grand plan to save your sorry asses from the curators that you'd like to explain?"

"If I did, I'd hardly share such classified information with the likes of you." Cobus's face hardened. "I don't know why you came here, Supreme Commander, but it was a waste of time. The Rasnian systems no longer recognise your authority. You may have missed it, what with the communications blackout, but our government enacted emergency legislation last week to withdraw from the Coalition. Humanity is no longer subject to your rule."

"In case *you* missed it, there's no longer a Coalition to withdraw from," Rivus said, fighting to keep the growl from his voice. "We're all just trying to survive now. You don't have a hope if you do this alone."

"That's where you're mistaken. Humanity's strength has always been in our numbers. Even without New Pallas, we far outnumber the rest of the allied systems." Cobus chuckled. "Why should we hand over human ships—the largest military fleet in the galaxy—when we could use them to protect the Rasnian systems instead? No curator ships have breached our borders yet, but if they do, they'll find us ready to answer them."

"It won't be enough," Rivus said flatly. "It may take years, or decades—stars, it may take centuries—but eventually, the curators will overpower you. They have an infinite army, one you can't stand against on your own."

Ojara drew her lips into a thin line. "So we give our forces over to you instead? You, who couldn't even protect Ossa? Where was the Coalition when its capital burned? Where were the mighty legionnaires?"

Her words rocked Rivus like each one was a blow. She had no *idea*. She didn't see the blackened skies and charred bodies Rivus saw every time he closed his eyes. She didn't have to live with the weight of all the fallen legionnaires left behind. Ossa had been the heart of their civilisation—now it was a graveyard. That kind of loss was something she'd never understand. Not until it was her own world burning.

"Throw my failures in my face all you want," Rivus said, his voice low. "I didn't come here to argue about what I should have done, what the Coalition should have done. I came here to warn you not to make the same mistakes."

"You're wasting your breath," Alvera said. "Ojara doesn't

care about Ras Prime any more than she cared about New Pallas. She'll watch it burn to be there at the end of it all, ruling over whatever rubble is left."

She turned to Cobus. "Take it from someone who knows from experience—Ojara will stick a knife between your ribs the first chance she gets. The fact that you've allied yourself with her makes you either desperate or stupid. If it's the latter, there's nothing we can do to help you. But if you're doing this because you think you have no other choice, listen to what Rivus is saying. Let us work together."

For a moment, something changed in Cobus's eyes. A glimmer of contemplation, perhaps. But it was over all too quickly, replaced by a derisive sneer. "The Rasnian systems don't need the protection of whatever is left of the Coalition and its once-proud legionnaires. Humanity can stand on its own."

"It's useless," Alvera said to Rivus, keeping her voice low. "He can't see past whatever bullshit Ojara has filled his head with. We won't get any help here."

She was right, but that didn't make it any easier. Even if the Coalition was gone, Rivus couldn't help but feel responsible for what it had once stood for. Abandoning the Rasnian systems felt like a betrayal, no matter what Cobus proclaimed.

"If you refuse to listen to reason, I see little else we can do here," Rivus said tightly. "I've done all I can. I hope you will do the same—for the sake of your people, if nothing else." He turned to Alvera. "We should go. Our job just got a lot more difficult."

"We?" Ojara's voice carried across the chamber, ringing through his ears. "I'm sorry, Supreme Commander, but while you're free to go, I'm afraid your companion has a long list of crimes to answer for. It's past time for her to face the punishment she's been running from ever since we arrived in this galaxy. Alvera Renata will not be leaving Ras Prime."

"You don't have the authority to make that kind of demand."

"But I do." Cobus clasped his hands together and leaned over the wooden bench. "I have no quarrel with you, Supreme Commander, but my advisor is correct. The agitator faces charges of murder, theft of government property, treason..." He shook his head. "Even your own Coalition had a galactic arrest warrant out in her name. You of all people should understand we can't simply let her go, not with the danger she poses to the galaxy."

Alvera gave a short laugh. "You have no idea what kind of danger I pose." She glanced at Rivus, her face hard and steady. "Get out of here while you still can. There are people out there who need you to lead them. This was always my fight, not yours."

Rivus could hear the sense in her words, even if he didn't want to admit it. Cobus was right too—there was much Alvera had to answer for, and not all of it was forgivable. But the same could have been said about Tarvan, about him. They'd all done things that could never be taken back, never be made right. Maybe it wasn't about forgiveness. Maybe it was about the chance to do some good in the galaxy before they got the end they deserved.

"This started with us," he said. "That's what you told me before. You said it was up to us to see it through. There's not another person in this galaxy who understands how much is at stake. I can't do this alone either."

The sad ghost of a smile spread across Alvera's lips. "I don't know if I was hoping you'd say that, or afraid of it. Guess we've both got a stubborn streak to us."

"Together, then?"

"Together."

The military police advanced upon them, their guns still painting Alvera's face with the red pinpricks of their targeting lasers. But each time one of them stepped forward, one of the dots disappeared. One by one they flickered out, until all that was left were the frown lines on Alvera's pale face.

"What are you *doing?*" Cobus hissed, his face flooding with colour. "Did we learn nothing after last time?"

"Go easy on them, Governor. The upgrades to your targeting systems are actually quite impressive. It's just, well..." A smirk broke out over Alvera's lips. "I've never come across a system I didn't want to hack."

An explosive crack echoed around the room, followed by a dozen more. Rivus didn't understand what had happened at first, only that Alvera had somehow caused the chaos. The military police yelled in confusion as the rifles in their hands erupted into a shower of sparks. Some let their guns clatter to the ground. Others stepped back as they frantically scrambled to fix their malfunctioning weapons.

"Bring all the safeties and firewalls you want," Alvera said. "You can't keep me out."

Her cybernetics. Rivus should have known. It wasn't long ago she'd helped him tap into the capabilities of his own mechanical arm. She'd visited his head when she was trapped in the hive, lending him her knowledge across the strange connection they'd inadvertently bridged between themselves. He'd always known what she was capable of, but seeing it in person was another thing entirely.

"Watch out!"

One of the officers drew a blade and thrust it towards Alvera. Rivus barrelled forward with as much ferocity as he could muster, charging into the human and knocking him to the floor with a loud crunch. If the blade had nicked his plating, he hadn't noticed. Sharpened steel was little match against an exoskeleton of hardened bone, as the unfortunate officer on the floor had realised.

He looked up at Rivus, gasping for breath as blood pooled around his mouth. Rivus had probably broken half the poor bastard's ribs. He hadn't even hit him that hard. Humans were just so soft, so easily damaged. He didn't want to kill these people, not unless they left him no other choice. They weren't enemies, just fools following bad orders.

Another officer appeared beside him and slid a knife between his plates, driving the blade into the soft tissue underneath. Rivus let out a grunt of pain and swung around, cracking his plated skull against the human's forehead with an ear-splitting crunch. This time, he felt decidedly less sympathy.

He cast a glance at the useless guns on the floor, some of them still sputtering sparks. "You could have left one functioning for me to use," he muttered to Alvera.

"I'm not sure I'm capable of that kind of finesse at the moment," she replied, wiping a stream of blood from her nose. "It's been years since I used my cybernetics without an AI in my head to handle the processing. Turns out it's a little more strenuous than I remembered."

"Will you be all right?"

Alvera gave a grim nod, her skin pale and clammy. "I'll have to be."

One of the officers leapt towards her and she skipped aside, pushing him hard in the back as he stumbled past. He went down clutching one of his ears, blood seeping from between his fingers.

"Blew his auditory implant," Alvera said, by way of explanation. "Could have done worse. Might still have to if they send reinforcements."

"We need to get out of here before that happens."

"Yeah. About that…"

Rivus followed Alvera's gaze towards the domed roof of the chamber. The panels trembled with the roar of something above. The sunlight disappeared, obscured by the shadow from a rumbling hull descending closer and closer. Soon after, the entirety of the pale blue sky above was blocked out by the belly of the ship as it hovered metres above the chamber roof. Its shape was sleek and streamlined, like something out of a vid.

Or a newsfeed.

Recognition jolted through him. "I know that ship."

The glass exploded, sending a shower of shards crashing to the floor. Rivus pulled Alvera out of the way as the roof panels shattered into pieces around them. Two armour-clad figures descended through the destruction, dropping down on the end of a cable.

The first one took off his helmet, revealing dark-skinned features and a wry smile. "Looks like you could use some help."

It was Maxim ras Arbor. The human was wearing a glossy red exosuit and a utility belt loaded with too many weapons to count. A man not only expecting trouble, but looking forward to it.

Rivus frowned at Alvera. "I told you not to bring reinforcements."

"I'd apologise, but given the circumstances, do you really blame me?" She shot him a pointed look. "I wasn't about to let our lives depend on the good grace of someone like Cobus."

Max hoisted his plasma rifle high in one hand and offered Rivus a sidearm with the other. "Admit it, big guy, you're lucky we came. The *Ranger* is probably the only ship that can get through Rasnian patrols undetected. Or get back out again, once they've got half the planet's guns pointed at our asses."

"You!" Cobus popped his head over the top of the wooden bench, his face ashen. "You dare show your face on this planet, in this system, after what you've done? I put a death warrant on your head so large your own brother would be tempted to hand you over."

"I'm flattered you'd go to all that trouble." Max curled his lips into an easy smile. "Feels good to be back. Even better to know you've missed me so much. As for your death warrant, well, it was probably tempting, but if there's one thing my little brother wants to see more than me getting what I deserve, it's you getting what you deserve."

The second figure unclipped himself from the end of the cable and took off his own helmet, revealing the same hard-edged features as Max. He wore his Coalition powersuit like a mark of honour and joined Max's side with a grim, determined look on his face. "Sem ras Arbor. Nice to meet you, Governor. It's been a long time coming."

"A Coalition lapdog. How charming." Cobus bared his teeth. "I hope the two of you realise what you've done. You won't be able to set foot in any Rasnian-controlled system for the rest of your sorry lives, not without being arrested and executed for treason."

"That depends on who's left standing at the end of all this, doesn't it?" Max cast his eyes over the wooden bench. "Speaking of which, it looks like your own allies are already abandoning you."

Rivus looked over. Max was right—Ojara was gone. She must have scarpered out during the chaos of Max and Sem's entrance. Only Cobus remained, pale-faced and wild-eyed as he took in the situation unfolding in front of him.

"It's over, Governor," Rivus said. "We're leaving. If you have any sense left at all, you'll let us go. Save your strength for the curators. You're going to need it."

Cobus watched them with a furious gaze but said nothing as they made their way over to the cables that Max and Sem had left dangling from the *Ranger* above. Rivus clipped himself in and braced as the cable retracted, pulling him off the floor and through the shattered remains of the roof with a gentle whirr. The brisk mountain air swept over his plates as he rose higher and higher until the doors of the cargo hold opened to greet him, inviting him into the sanctuary of the *Ranger*.

Alvera was right behind him, landing easily and unclipping herself in a fluid motion. "What do we do now?" she asked, loosening the collar of her exosuit. "This was always a long shot, but attacking the Omega Gate would have been a hell of a lot easier with the Rasnian fleet at our backs."

"We have other allies," Rivus said. "Krychus and the rest of the dachryn worlds are mobilising their ships to rendezvous with us at Alcruix. The iskaath have promised us numbers too. Whatever happens, we'll work with what we've got. We'll make every ship count. We'll win because we have to."

Alvera smiled. "You've taken well to this Supreme Commander thing."

"Didn't have much of a choice. None of us did. We can't do anything except—"

The shrill cry of an alarm drowned out the rest of Rivus's words. His plates stiffened. That damned noise was becoming far too familiar for his liking. It seemed they couldn't go so much as a few hours without something else going wrong.

Alvera scowled. "Better head up to the flight deck and find out who's trying to kill us this time."

Rivus followed her as she led him through the unfamiliar ship, past gleaming walls and sophisticated holographic displays. The wide corridors and open-plan rooms seemed strange and out of place in their emptiness, like the ship was hollow without its crew. Monitoring stations without anybody to attend them, a mess hall with empty benches. Then he noticed the signs of violence. Bullet holes peppering reinforced glass. Walls blackened from the scorch marks of a plasma rifle. The smell of disinfectant rising from discoloured patches on the hard floor underfoot.

"What happened here?" he asked.

Alvera's face looked like it was made from stone. "Ojara," she said shortly. "I can't think about it right now, not with everything else. But she'll answer for it. As soon as I get the chance."

She pressed forward, keeping her eyes locked firmly ahead until they reached the bridge where Max and Sem were sitting.

The navigation console was lit up with angry red flashes, and both men were tapping furiously at the interface.

Rivus looked out of the viewport. Ras Prime was disappearing behind them, along with the distant glow of Rellion in its orbit. All around them was darkness and the faint light of far-off stars. They'd managed to break atmo and get past the Rasnian blockade. Whatever threat they were facing, it wasn't coming from Cobus.

"What's going on?" he asked, trying to make sense of the information flying across the interface.

Max grimaced. "Nothing good. Hundreds of unknown signatures appeared out of nowhere."

"Curator ships?"

"Having a hard time thinking who the fuck else it could be."

Alvera frowned, leaning over for a closer look. "Are they preparing for an attack?"

"The opposite. They're moving into a defensive formation." Sem swiped through a series of holographic screens. "They're holding position, for now at least."

"Holding position where?"

"See for yourself." Sem enlarged one of the holographic interfaces.

Rivus surveyed the blinking lights scattered around the screen. It didn't take long for the patterns to fall into place. "They've surrounded every space tunnel leading out of this system."

Alvera's face was deathly pale. Rivus could see the horror in her eyes, the same horror that was burrowing its way under his plates. Without the tunnels, they had no way out of this system. No way back to Alcruix, or to the alliance they'd started building there.

The curators had come for them. They were trapped.

FIVE

RIDLEY

Ridley stood at the open hatch of the skimmer and filled her lungs with the dry scent of the desert sand. She'd never thought she'd miss the heat of Jadera, but now she was back, she realised it was the closest she'd ever felt to coming home. It felt like a betrayal, the way she'd missed the rusted, sand-swept buildings far more than she'd ever missed the neon-lit alleyways of New Pallas. But maybe it shouldn't have been a surprise. Jadera was where she'd first met Drexious. Where she'd first met Halressan.

Stop it, she chided herself. She couldn't afford to dwell on the things she'd left behind. There was too much at stake. She'd have plenty of time to regret the decisions she'd made after all this was over—if she survived long enough to see it.

"For the record, I think this is a terrible idea."

Ridley stepped away from the hatch and retreated into the

cool shade of the skimmer. Drexious was huddled on the far side, his tail skimming anxiously.

She sighed. "For the record, you've already told me that."

"That was *before* you convinced the Idran-Var to come with us. Now we have some heavily armed, heavily armoured backup, and I *still* think this is a terrible idea."

Ridley couldn't help the smile that crept onto her lips. For all Drexious's bluster and cynicism, he was still here. Their friendship might have been born out of betrayal and a near-successful attempt on his part to bury her alive, but it had somehow kept them together throughout all that had happened these past few months.

Unlike *some* people Ridley could mention.

She gritted her teeth as the unwanted thoughts flooded her head again. The softness of Halressan's lips against her own, the grip of her hands in her hair. Wanting it so much. Wanting it *too* much. Leaving it all behind because...because what? Because Ridley had deluded herself into making the same mistake she always did—thinking she *mattered*?

"We have a situation." One of the Idran-Var, a human woman named Zal, came over to them. Her russet-brown hair fell across her face as she walked, half obscuring the blinking green cybergraft she wore in place of her left eye. As far as Idran-Var went, she was amiable—almost friendly—but there was part of Ridley that still felt uneasy around her.

"What is it?" she asked.

Zal took out a holopad, powering on the display with a flick of her thumb. "This is a real-time display from the airspace around Jadera Port. All those lights? My guess is curator drop-ships. A lot of them have the same kind of signatures we encountered back on Ossa."

"How did they make it this far into the Rim Belt already?" Drexious asked, his scales rippling. "The Omega Gate is back in the heart of the allied systems."

"The curators have done this before," Ridley said. "They know how to get this right. If they spread outwards from Ossa, the Rim Belt and border planets would have more time to prepare. They're hitting systems at random, jamming communications on a system-wide scale."

"Impressive tactics," Zal said. "It's the kind of thing we might have done when the time came to launch our invasion on the allied systems."

Drexious sent her a sideways glance. "See, when you say things like that, it makes me wonder how much you're really on our side."

A rumble of laughter resounded through the skimmer as another Idran-Var approached out of the shadows. She was a huge, hulking dachryn with blood-red plating and orange eyes that shone with sharp amusement. "You don't have to worry, jarkaath," she said. "We Idran-Var like more of a challenge. You wouldn't be worth the effort."

"You'd be surprised how hard it is to kill someone who values brains over brawn," Drexious shot back. "I wager I'll make it longer through this war than you, bonehead."

"I'll take that bet. You won't be around to pay up, but the satisfaction will be more rewarding than the credits."

Zal let out a sigh. "Settle down, Venya. Save your energy for the curators—*var'veth* knows we're going to need it."

The huge dachryn shuffled off with a parting grin at Drexious. Zal turned back to the holopad, her mouth pressed into a thin line as she studied the flashing markers.

"That bad?" Ridley asked, trying to sound more cheerful than she felt. "I thought you Idran-Var weren't afraid of anything."

"Take a look for yourself." Zal spread her fingers through the holographic feed, enlarging it until it became a green and gold shimmer of flickering images around them. The flashing dots turned into ships hovering above the illuminated projection of Jadera Port. Streams of data transformed into prowling shapes armed with weapons. The tactical markers were no longer pinpoints of light, but places Ridley had once walked. The market stalls burned. The main square was littered with bodies of the merchants she'd bartered with.

"We Idran-Var appreciate a good fight," Zal said. "But looking at these readouts...we'd be walking into a massacre. I don't want to lose half my squad trying to rescue someone who's probably already dead."

"You don't know Skaile. There's no way she's dead."

"I've known a lot of stubborn assholes who believed nothing could kill them. Then Ossa happened." Zal's face darkened. "You see the azuul? Those big ugly things that look like wrecking balls made from bleached leather? They'll toss an Idran-Var around like we're a bouquet of siolean sunreeds. Then there's the velliria—metallic insectoids that emit some kind of ultrasonic signal that messes with your brain and paralyses you. You can't run, can't move, can't do anything but wait for them to kill you. As for the rest—"

"We need to try," Ridley interrupted. "Without Skaile, we don't have a hope of convincing the rest of the Rim Belt to fight."

Zal shook her head, the tousled waves of her red-brown hair bouncing around her face. "A head-on assault will get us all killed. When I agreed to help, I didn't agree to that."

"What if..." Drexious began, then cut himself off with a hiss. "Shit, I can't believe I'm saying this. What if there was another way in? What if we could reach the Queen's Den without landing in the port itself?"

Ridley spun around. Drexious had a look on his face she knew all too well—a look he usually wore when he'd been caught scheming.

"I'd call bullshit," she said, narrowing her eyes. "And ask why you never thought to mention this before."

"I didn't think it was necessary before. I hardly knew we'd be turning up to a warzone, did I?" He jerked his lean, scaled shoulders into a defensive shrug. "I was going through some of the holopads we found on Skaile's shuttle and came across schematics for an escape tunnel. It runs right under the sand-flats and comes out at the base of some old rock formation about fifty klicks away."

Zal gave him a measured stare. "This information would have been useful earlier."

"It would have also been useful for sneaking into Skaile's vault and clearing out all her treasures," Drexious countered. "Which is what I was planning to do with the information once all this was, well, *over*. But seeing as that's not about to happen any time soon, I'm telling you now. Better late than never, right?"

Ridley rolled her eyes. It was always the same with Drex-ious. Always an angle he was trying to play, a scheme he was trying to hatch. It was the sting in their friendship's tail, a barbed reminder that no matter how much he'd look out for her, he'd always look out for himself that little bit more.

Maybe he had more in common with Halressan than she'd realised.

"Send Zal the schematics," Ridley said curtly. "Hopefully this will give us a way in without bringing the curators' forces down on us."

Zal swiped through the images on her holopad, pausing at the file Drexious had sent over. She stared at it for a few minutes before giving a nod. "Seems solid. We go in, get Skaile, and get out while we still can."

"Assuming Skaile is still alive," Drexious pointed out. "If not, I'd still like to get my claws on those treasures of hers."

Ridley glared at him. "She's alive. She has to be."

He grinned back, all teeth and tension. "Careful what you wish for."

A shudder ran through her at his words. It left her cold, like a shadow had blocked out the furious heat from Jadera's sun. Ridley could almost feel the ghost of Skaile's fingertips pressing into her shoulder. Drexious was right. She couldn't forget what was waiting for her if Skaile was alive somewhere in the ruins of the Queen's Den.

She could only hope it would be worth it.

———

The rocky outcropping in the middle of the shifting golden sands stood alone and untouched, like it had been waiting for them to arrive. Ridley allowed herself a breath of relief. If the curators hadn't found the underground passage yet, they still had time.

The air smelled musty and thin as she followed Drexious through the narrow mouth of the escape tunnel into the depths of the cavern. The harsh light from above grew fainter with every steep step she stumbled down, until only darkness surrounded her.

She reached for the torch on her envirosuit and switched it on, illuminating the cramped, crowded tunnel they'd piled into. There wasn't much to see—just their own shadows stretched tall against the stone walls and the glint of something in the distance.

"Are those tracks?" Ridley said, peering through the gloom.

Drexious craned his long neck forward, his bronze eyes gleaming in the light of her torch. "Must be some kind of high-speed rail system connecting the escape tunnel to the Queen's Den. I see some kind of platform further along—hopefully we can get it moving."

Ridley followed him, keeping her eyes trained on the thin rails protruding from the ground. They were covered in grime and sand but still emitted a dull sheen under the torchlight. She used her boot to gingerly scrape off some of the filth. The tracks looked like they hadn't been used in years, but there weren't any signs of damage or disrepair.

"Here." Drexious leapt onto the platform, landing nimbly on all four limbs before straightening himself out again. "We still have power. My guess is it's connected to one of the solar farms on the surface. Controls are pretty basic, but there's only two directions this thing can move in."

"There's not much room," Zal said as she approached, casting her eye over the platform. "Probably best if you two wait here. I'll take Venya and a couple of my squad to pick up the target."

Ridley arched an eyebrow. "You need me. Skaile won't just go along with what you tell her."

"I need fighters more."

"You don't know Skaile, or what she's capable of. She'll melt your fighters inside their armour until they pour out the cracks." Ridley folded her arms. "I might not be good with a gun, but you'll need more than bullets to match the Outlaw Queen. I *know* her. I know the way she thinks. You have to take me with you."

Zal set her mouth in a hard line. "And the jarkaath?"

"The jarkaath is holding the start-up codes to launch this thing," Drexious said, waving the holopad in his claws. "And while I'm usually the first to accept any offer that takes me out of Skaile's path, the temptation to relieve her of whatever valuables she's left behind is too much to pass up."

"Fine." Zal signalled to the rest of the Idran-Var. "Venya, you're with me. The rest of you wait here and hold position until we get back." She fixed Ridley with an appraising look. "I hope you know what you're doing. If Skaile's holdout is compromised, we're likely to be heavily outnumbered."

"Outnumbered, maybe. But not outmatched." A nervous flutter ran through Ridley's chest. "At least, not if Skaile's still alive."

"I guess we're about to find out."

The cart lurched into motion with a violent jerk and a shrill screech of metal. Ridley braced herself against the guardrail as it shot forward, whistling past the tunnel walls at a speed that cooled her flushed cheeks with the passing breeze. The platform rattled violently beneath her feet. It was all she could do to keep her head steady and eyes focused.

It was just short of the half-hour mark when the cart began to slow down. Ridley spotted magnetic brakes catching them as they passed, reducing their speed to a slow crawl as they trundled through each section. Without the breeze, the air felt warm and musty again. But there was more to it than staleness —something thick and noxious tickled the back of her throat.

Smoke. The Queen's Den was burning.

Drexious leapt from the cart, his tail swishing from side to side as he moved methodically down the side of the tunnel. His jarkaath eyes were sharper than hers, better equipped to spot any cracks or crevices in the rock that might lead to a passageway.

"Here," he said after a moment. "I found some steps."

Ridley rushed over and squeezed into the narrow opening. The steps were roughly cut and steep, leaving the palms of her hands sore and coated with sand as she pushed herself up. Blood pounded in her ears. Her heavy breaths echoed off the walls around her. Other noises poured through the rock, muffled and out of reach.

"You see that?" Drexious's voice was soft at her ear. "There's a crack of light up ahead. Must be some kind of access hatch."

Ridley saw it. A halo of pale, dusty light around a grate. She heard sounds from above too—the clatter of bullets against stone, a grunt of pain. They were directly below the Queen's Den, separated by only a metre of rock. Directly below whatever fighting was going on.

The darkness was all-consuming as she reached out her hands and felt for the hatch release panel. Her fingers brushed across something smooth and metallic rising from the surface of the grate. A handle. It was stiff, groaning as she twisted it, but even as the muscles in her forearm twitched under the strain, Ridley felt it slowly sliding into position.

"Don't you want to wait for—"

Ridley pushed up and hauled herself through the hatch.

It took a moment for her eyes to adjust to the light and colour. Jadera's underground was dimly lit, but compared to the escape tunnel, the spotlights seemed garish. Ridley rolled away from the open hatch, shielding her face as she waited for the glare to abate and her vision to return to normal.

Almost immediately, she wished it hadn't.

The chamber's walls were splattered with blood. The stone was soaked, boasting gory murals crudely painted with haphazard strokes, each more grotesque than the last. Bright red, oily blue, everything in between. It dripped from the ceiling to the floor, thick with sinew and bone.

Ridley choked down an involuntary retch, her throat dry and burning. She couldn't identify which of the curators' mindless thralls lay scattered around them. The bodies—what was *left* of the bodies—were mangled and torn, strewn across the floor in the kind of violent pattern only the devastation of a flare could create.

Skaile's arms hung loose at her sides as she breathed raggedly. Blood trickled down the hollow of her neck from a deep gouge in one of her headtails. The pearlescent dress she wore was torn and frayed against her red skin, stained with the same colours as the walls. This was who Ridley had come here to find: the Outlaw Queen, standing on the remains of her enemies.

Skaile turned her head. The black of her eyes was as cold and tenebrous as ever, but the corner of her lips curled into a familiar smile. "My dear outlander," she said, her voice dry and rasping. "Of all the creatures I've killed today, how many do you imagine I pictured with your face?"

Behind her, Drexious let out a groan.

Ridley ignored him. "All I did was steal a ship. Is that worth holding a grudge over?"

"You could have stolen trash from the junkyard for all the difference it would have made." Skaile's voice dropped an octave. "Nobody steals *anything* from me."

"Really? Because it seems Drex and I are getting pretty good at it."

"Just the two of you this time?" Skaile cast a withering glance over them both. "Where is our fearless hunter? Too selfish to stick her pretty little neck out for you, no matter how many times you'd put yours on the block for her?"

Ridley flinched. The words cut too close. It was hardly a reminder she needed—not now, not *ever*. Halressan was out of reach. There was no going back, no matter how much her heart hurt to think about it. She'd made her choice. They both had.

Skaile smirked. "I thought as much. What I don't understand is why in Fyra's name you would risk coming back here. Have you ever taken me for the forgiving sort?"

"Forgiving? No. But you're nothing if not pragmatic." Ridley looked around the room, her stomach seizing at the grisly slaughter. "You're injured. You can't hold these things off forever. Do you want to be here when the next wave of reinforcements arrives? Or do you want to come with us and get off this planet while you still can?"

Skaile threw back her head and laughed. "You think I

couldn't have escaped if I wanted to? I'm here because I choose to be. If more of those beasts come through that door, I'll tear them apart like I did the others. Jadera is *mine*. I won't relinquish my rule over it easily."

"There's not going to be anything left to rule over," Ridley said. "The port is burning. The marketplace is in ruins. The curators won't stop until they've wiped out every trace you were ever here. It's over, Skaile. Better to admit it and escape with your life than get yourself killed for a planet you've already lost."

"I have lost *nothing*," Skaile said, her voice dangerously quiet. "If you think for a moment—" She broke off, snapping her head towards the tattered remains of the curtain hanging over the chamber's entrance. "More of them coming. Make yourself useful if you're staying. If not, get out of my way."

She'd barely finished speaking when the curtain blew back and something whirred through the air between them.

"It's a grenade—get down!"

Ridley scrambled behind an overturned table and pressed herself flat as an ear-splitting blast roared above her. The sound reverberated around her skull, rattling her brain so much she almost vomited.

Somewhere far away, Skaile was screaming. Ridley could barely make out the words. Everything seemed to be coming from a distance, smothered by the fog around her eardrums. Her limbs felt dead and useless as she pulled herself upright.

She peered over the top of the fallen table to see smoke pouring into the room. It billowed towards her, burning her lungs as she tried to cough it out. Through the black cloud, swirling shapes rushed towards them. Ridley recognised the hulking, leathery azuul with their white hides and bulbous yellow eyes. But there were others too, creatures that Zal hadn't told them about. A lithe, gangling horror with a lustrous blue coat and scythe-like tusks protruding from its jaws. A creature with a huge, shell-like crest and no discernible eyes skittering wildly on its pointed legs as it wielded a plasma rifle between its bony fingers.

A skittering of wings rattled the air above her. A huge, insectoid alien hovered above the chamber's entrance, emitting a low hum from the vibrations of its metallic wings. Talon-like claws shot out from the end of each appendage, and its jaws were slick with saliva.

"Ridley, get away from there!" Zal's voice was hushed but sharp with urgency as she hauled herself out of the hatch. "If that velliria emits its paralysing signal, we're screwed. We need to go now."

"But Skaile—"

"If she's stupid enough to get herself killed over this dump, she's not worth saving in the first place."

"I heard that," Skaile said, her eyes dark and unamused. "Tell me, Idran-Var, which one should I kill first? The blue furball, or this buzzing nuisance that thinks it's a sandfly on growth stims?"

"You don't understand," Zal snapped. "The signal it emits—"

The violence stirred the air before it happened, like a rush of energy that skimmed over Ridley's skin. It swirled around Skaile like a vortex—raw and furious, waiting to be unleashed. It steamed off her like a red-tinged vapour, making the air shimmer.

Skaile stretched her lips into a vicious grin and let loose her flare.

Everything happened at once, so fast that Ridley couldn't make sense of it all. A loud pop echoed above her. Something exploded in a starburst of blood and tissue, splattering the already-drenched walls. A thump of metal and flesh hit the slick stone floor. The velliria was gone, reduced to torn parts atop the piles of carcasses surrounding them.

At the same time, Venya charged forward. Her huge, hulking crest was hidden behind her Idran-Var helmet as she barrelled through the middle of the room, knocking the tusked alien to the floor with a powerful headbutt. The tremble of the ground under each step she took rattled Ridley's bones. She was like a mountain made from steel. Each heavy strike she landed on the tusked alien echoed around the room with a sickening crunch—hammer blows reinforced with the full might of her considerable weight.

Zal leapt forward as well, less ferocious than Venya but with a nimbleness and guile that Ridley couldn't help but be mesmerised by. She slid under the towering legs of the azuul and spun around on her knees to aim a wrist launcher at the back of the creature's thickset shoulders. A barbed cable shot out and sank into the azuul's bulging neck, crackling with violent sparks of electricity as it wound itself deeper into the brute's hardened skin.

Ridley watched, her fingers twitching like they were begging for a weapon to hold. *I need fighters*, Zal had said. But Ridley had never been a fighter. A survivor, maybe. Someone who found a way to keep existing in places she had no right to. Someone who could rig a trap, but couldn't face the finality of wrapping her finger around a trigger and squeezing.

"Enjoying the show?" Drexious slid in beside her, crouching down behind the cover of the overturned table.

Ridley glanced at the carbine he was clutching between his claws. "Where did you get *that?*"

"Sneaked into Skaile's armoury while she was busy making aliens explode. Do you like it? Jarkaath military grade—fits my grip perfectly. You wouldn't believe how hard it is to get a decent hold on standard-spec rifles."

"You didn't bring anything for me?"

Drexious let out a low, cackling laugh. "With your aim? I don't think so."

Heat rushed to Ridley's face. "I can't let everybody else risk their lives while I hide here and wait for it to be over."

"Then don't hide. But you waving a gun around will only do more harm than good." His eyes twinkled. "If you want to make yourself useful, go get what we came here for."

The frantic hammering of Ridley's heart picked up again as she pulled her head above the parapet of the table. Zal and Venya were still locked in a bloody tangle with the curator thralls. Their armour was stained with grime and blood as they fought side by side, moving together as more of the alien creatures tore through the curtain into the chamber.

Skaile was in the middle of it all, alone and exposed. She dropped to one knee, her face twisted in pain. The shimmer of her flare was fading, and the rich red of her cheeks had taken on a pale, sickly tinge. Whatever energy she had left, it wouldn't last much longer.

"Go," Drexious said. "I'll cover you."

Ridley pushed herself back to her feet and hobbled across the blood-soaked floor of the chamber. The whistle of bullets and the clang of metal on metal filled her ears as she walked through the middle of the carnage. All this fighting, all this violence... She wanted no part of it. All she had to do was navigate its midst and come out on the other side unscathed, like she always did.

Skaile was shaking when she approached. Whether it was from adrenaline or exhaustion, Ridley didn't know. In that moment, however fleeting, it was a vulnerability they shared. A vulnerability that gave her the courage she needed to reach out, palm open, and offer her hand to Skaile.

"I came here for you," Ridley said. "I need your help."

Skaile sneered. "Even like this, I could still crush you."

"I know. But I don't think you want to."

Skaile braced both arms across her knee, glaring at Ridley's outstretched hand. The gash in one of her headtails was still streaming with blood. Her face was a hardened mask that gave away nothing but the heat of her displeasure. It was a long shot. It had always been a long shot.

Then, by some kind of miracle Ridley could hardly believe, the Outlaw Queen swallowed whatever reluctance she'd been grappling with and slipped her hand into Ridley's, hauling herself to her feet with a withering scowl.

"This doesn't make us even, outlander," she said, each word a quiet warning. "It doesn't make us friends either."

Another explosion echoed through the rock above their heads, jolting Ridley back to the carnage still unfolding around her. Streams of debris poured down from the ceiling, sending dust pluming around their feet. It might not be long before the Queen's Den was buried under the weight of the desert, along with anyone left inside.

The azuul was bleeding heavily, its neck black with scorch marks, but it was still fighting Zal and Venya tirelessly, flailing its rippling limbs with mindless rage. The thunder of footsteps from above grew louder with each passing second. It wouldn't be long until the next wave of curator thralls reached them.

"We need to go," Ridley shouted, motioning towards the escape tunnel. "If we make it back to the underground tracks, we might be able to put some distance between us and these monsters."

The circle of green light from Zal's cybernetic visor blinked rapidly as she ducked out of the way of the azuul's heavy blow. "It's about time."

Ridley turned back to Skaile. "What do you say? Ready to leave this place behind?"

The Outlaw Queen's indiscernible gaze lingered over the bloodied remains of her chamber. The place that had been her centre of power, that had boasted her rule and riches in smuggled artefacts and stolen silks. The place where so many had come to beg and barter and die. The place she would have to abandon if she ever wanted that power back.

Skaile drew her lips into a grim, laughless smile and turned back to Ridley. "For now," she said. "Only for now."

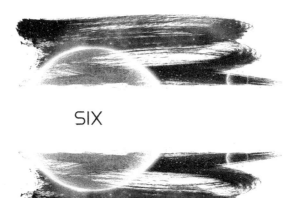

SIX

KOJAN

Under different circumstances, Kojan might have been more sympathetic to Kitell Merala's first experience of Kaath. It wasn't pleasant spending day after day sweating in the confines of an envirosuit, unable to eat anything that wasn't processed into mush and delivered through a straw. Not to mention the stifling heat and near-suffocation.

As it was, it was difficult not to take at least some amusement from the siolean's discomfort, especially when he'd spent most of the journey reminding Kojan that *he* was the one in charge, *he* was the one piloting the ship, and *he* wasn't interested in any opinions or unsolicited advice.

Privately, Kojan thought *he* was doing the best impression of a pompous ass.

The yellow-tinged sky was already brightening from the morning sun. Most of the iskaath had returned to their homes to sleep, but Kite was still sitting around the smoking embers of the fire, trying to itch himself through the protective layers of his envirosuit.

"You know those things have decontamination protocols in them, right?" Kojan asked. "You only need to run them once a day to keep the suit clean."

Kite glowered at him through his transparent visor. "I'm aware of the decontamination protocols. But even if I ran them six times a day, I'd still feel like I've got this layer of filth over me that I can't scrub off. I'm not sure how much longer I can stand being stuck in this thing."

"You'll get used to it."

"Easy for you to say when your cybernetics negate the need for you to wear one." Kite let out a heavy sigh and stared at the remains of the fire. "I'm beginning to think this entire mission was a waste of time. We can't get close enough to any of the factories to investigate, let alone put any measures in place to stop an attack. You'd expect the iskaath to be more receptive to outside help."

"The iskaath have had to make do without outside help for millennia," Kojan pointed out. "The Coalition never took an interest in them before. They didn't even have an ambassador. I don't blame them for being slow to trust."

"Technically, the jarkaath ambassador acted for both—"

"Come on, Merala. We both know the jarkaath don't give a damn about anyone on this planet. If the intel we got is right, they knew about the possibility of an attack and decided to sit on the information."

"We still haven't been able to confirm if there's even going to *be* an attack." Kite grunted. "It's not that I don't want to help. It just feels wrong to be stuck here waiting for something that might never happen when the curators are out there destroying our worlds."

Kojan sighed, his irritation trickling away at the note of helplessness in Kite's voice. He knew too well what it felt like to be on the fringes of the fight, unable to help the people who needed him most. He couldn't think about New Pallas anymore, not without despair rising in his chest. If they were forced to abandon them, would he ever be able to forgive himself?

The sound of soft footsteps disturbing the undergrowth tore Kojan from his thoughts, and he looked up to see Cyren approaching, her mottled skin dancing with green speckles under the sunlight. She lowered herself onto one of the logs beside them, curling her long tail and leaning forward with a satisfied glint in her eyes.

"I have a way in," she said. "One of our youngsters who left the nest two summers ago works maintenance in one of the nearby factories. He can get you in through the sewers."

"The sewers? Charming." Kite grimaced. "This better not be a waste of time. We're already playing catch-up."

"Time is against us," Cyren agreed. "That's why I've told Lyriax to expect you at solar noon. He'll get you into the factory. Once you're there, keep watch for anything suspicious. If you see anyone in a mask, you'll know it's a jarkaath. This is the one place in the galaxy where our positions are reversed. This is *our* home. They would do well to remember that."

Kojan squeezed her arm, her mottled scales cool beneath his fingers. "We'll stop them. The iskaath will get to choose their own future like Eleion wanted. I promise."

As soon as the words left his mouth, he regretted them. He couldn't promise the iskaath anything. He didn't have that right. Even if he did...well, he knew only too well the cost of such things. Alvera was a living reminder of that.

"You'll try," Cyren said gently. "That much I know, and that is more than anybody else has given our people."

Kojan turned back to Kite, a fluttering mix of nerves and adrenaline churning in his stomach. "Well? Are we doing this?"

"I doubt I could stop you even if I'd changed my mind," Kite said dryly. "It's worth checking out, at least. If we don't find anything, that's our cue to leave this planet and get back to the fight. And if we do, well..." A slow grin unfurled across his face. "I doubt these jarkaath terrorists are expecting a legionnaire."

———

The sun hung directly overhead by the time they arrived at the factory, turning the air thick with moisture. Out of the shade of the forested swampland, Kaath was stiflingly warm. The rustling of leaves and chirping of insects had been replaced by the grumble of the factory's innards and the chuffing of fumes billowing out from its huge chimneys.

A sharp, acidic smell burned Kojan's nostrils as they followed the artificial feeder streams towards the sewer entrance. Brown water swirled next to them, coated with a layer of yellow foam.

"And that's supposedly already treated?" Kite said, grimacing behind the barrier of his visor. "Can't wait until we get to the unprocessed stuff."

"You do realise this is where they refine that high-spec fuel that powers your fighter, right?" Kojan pointed out. "I think you could do a little less complaining."

"Just because I like what it does, doesn't mean I need to see where it comes from."

Kojan opened his mouth to reply, then snapped it shut, a knot of guilt pulling tight. How many surfacers on New Pallas had died mining the resources used to fuel the ships he'd spent half his life flying? How many years had he never considered the cost, just like Kite? He was as bad as the rest of them. New Pallas deserved better. The iskaath deserved better. Maybe this was his chance to make some of it—even a fraction of it—right.

"That looks like our way in." Kite pointed at a lone iskaath skulking in the shadows of the factory walls, his scales silvery with their juvenile coating.

When the iskaath saw them, he let out an agitated hiss. "Was beginning to think you weren't coming. Doesn't look right for me to be waiting around in the open like this."

"Lyriax, I presume?"

"That's me." His eyes darted around nervously. "Cyren told me you're trying to stop some sort of attack on the factories. If that's true, we better go inside."

Kojan nodded. "Lead the way."

He followed the young iskaath through a sliding panel next to the huge pump that the stained, brown-coloured water was pouring out of. The floor underfoot was corrugated and rough, offering plenty of grip under the soles of his boots. Kojan couldn't help but feel grateful. Inside the tunnel of the sewers, the river of waste was fast-flowing and relentless, surging against the walls. A misplaced step would be more than unpleasant.

He continued forward, struggling to keep pace with Lyriax's hasty stride. Every few metres, the iskaath looked back like he was checking they were still there. The spindles along his spine quivered as he walked, and Kojan felt a prickle in the air between them.

Kite seemed to have sensed it too. "Something is off. This kid is seriously wound up."

"He's bound to be nervous," Kojan said. "These factories are the lifeblood of the iskaath economy. He's risking a lot by helping a couple of outsiders break in."

"It's more than that. He's on edge, like he's waiting for something to happen."

Kojan said nothing. Kite wasn't wrong; there *was* something off about Lyriax. It was more than nervous jitters. Kojan had spent enough time around Eleion to recognise the agitation in the restless swing of Lyriax's tail, the way his scales rippled with anxious energy. Every part of the young iskaath's body was on high alert.

"So Cyren told you why we came here?" Kojan asked casually. "Do you know anything that could help us?"

Lyriax stiffened. "Why would I... No, I don't know anything. Cyren said she needed help getting a couple of off-worlders into the factory to help stop an attack, that's all."

"Bit of a risk for you, isn't it?"

Lyriax shrugged. "It's Cyren. She's the nest healer. She's taken care of me and my clutchmates more times than I can count. Figured I owed her at least one."

"I understand. She saved my life the first time I came to Kaath, then took a bullet while helping me escape. Between her and Eleion..." Kojan trailed off. "Well, I owe her more than one."

Lyriax stopped dead. He turned around slowly, his clawed feet scraping on the floor. His eyes had a horror-struck look to them as he stared at Kojan. "That was you? You're the human that Eleion brought back to the nest?" The scales on his cheeks rippled as he let out a puff of air. "This can't be happening. Cyren didn't say anything about... You were meant to be some interfering legionnaires, not one of the nest!"

Something twisted in Kojan's gut. "What are you talking about?"

"This wasn't how it was supposed to happen," Lyriax said desperately, flicking his tail from side to side. "You shouldn't be here. I would never have..." He broke off, flustered. "You need to leave, now. Before it's too late."

"Sounds like a good plan," Kite said grimly. "Come on Kojan, let's go."

"I'm not going anywhere."

"Have those fumes gone to your head? This traitor is clearly working with the jarkaath terrorists. We should count ourselves lucky his conscience decided to rear its head before we got ourselves killed."

Kojan ignored him and turned back to Lyriax. "I don't understand. You're an iskaath. Why would you help them?"

"For exactly the reason you said. I'm an *iskaath*." His voice strained over the word like it was about to break. "Those implants will destroy everything we are. Our people didn't spend millennia suffering under jarkaath ridicule and scorn just to end up *becoming* them at the end of it all." A low, angry hiss tore from the back of his throat. "I'm not the only one of my kind who feels this way. That's why we're doing this. These factories are creating abominations—implants that will change the nature of our species. It's not something a human could ever understand."

Kojan laughed bitterly. "I understand better than you think. You see this?" He gestured to the cybernetic casing running from his brow to his jaw. "I know what it's like to have your body created and carved out for you before you had the chance to agree to it. I've seen the kind of damage that can be done when you force tech into someone's head. I wish somebody had given me the choice to decide if I wanted it or not. But that's what it is, Lyriax—a choice. That's what Eleion was fighting for, what she gave her life for. Not to become a jarkaath, but to let the iskaath choose what kind of life they wanted for themselves."

"No iskaath could possibly choose—"

"*We always come back to the nest.* That's what Eleion told me once. She loved being out there amongst the stars in that shitty old cargo runner of hers. But what she loved more was coming home." Kojan's throat constricted at the memory, and he fought to swallow the pain. "Don't make the same mistake we did on Exodus Station, thinking that some wires and circuits can change who you are. Your people are already more than any implant could make them. It won't turn them into jarkaath— even if they wanted it to. All it will do is give them the chance to find a place for themselves in the galaxy."

"And if that place lies away from Kaath?" Lyriax asked.

"Then you let them go, like Cyren did. And you make sure when they come back, you make every damn second count."

Lyriax didn't say anything. The quills on his neck had softened, drooping down against his silver-coated scales. Kojan saw the anger disappearing from the stiffness of his body, evaporating like the Kaath morning mists.

After a moment, Lyriax let out a quiet, pained stutter from the back of his throat. "Eleion wasn't the first of my friends to leave and never come back," he said softly. "I never understood why they chose to go and get themselves killed out there in a galaxy that didn't want them. And now you want to help more of my people do the same. Do you really believe this is what's best for the iskaath?"

"I have no right to say what's best for the iskaath," Kojan replied gently. "All I know is I trusted Eleion with my life. I trust what she wanted for her people. She was willing to sacrifice everything for this."

"And you're willing to sacrifice everything to make sure it wasn't for nothing." Lyriax closed his eyes, his nostril slits rippling. "She knew what she was doing when she brought you here. You know what it means to be one of the nest. I never thought it was possible for an outsider to understand."

"Please help us stop this. This isn't the way."

Lyriax shook his head. "Even if I wanted to, it's too late. You should listen to your friend and leave. In a matter of minutes, a jarkaath black ops group is going to fly through this tunnel carrying a significant deposit of mavacite. You don't want to be here when they arrive."

"Mavacite?" Kite frowned. "The metal? What's so dangerous about that?"

"It's highly combustible when it comes into contact with certain chemicals," Lyriax said. "Chemicals like the untreated refinery by-products in the waste processing plant at the end of these tunnels. All the jarkaath have to do is fly in, dump their deposits and try to outrun the explosion. It will level the entire factory."

Kite took a furious stride forward. "And what was your part in all this?"

"I gave them schematics. I mapped out the route to the processing plant for them. I provided them with identification codes so their speeders would make it through the sewer doors." Lyriax lowered his head. "When Cyren started asking questions, I told them about that too. They said to lure you in here, to make sure you were trapped when the explosions went off. That was before I knew—"

"That Kojan here was an honorary family member. Yes, yes, how touching." Kite drew his lips into a snarl. "Good to know you're only *mostly* a murderous traitor."

Kojan stiffened. "Merala, that's enough."

"I agree. We are *done* here. I'm not standing around any longer waiting for a bunch of jarkaath terrorists to blow us to pieces. I'll give the Supreme Commander my report and he can take it up with the government."

"I told you already, I'm not leaving."

"And I told *you* already, this is my mission," Kite snapped. "I'm the one who decides when we're leaving."

"You can decide for yourself. I didn't come this far to let these bastards win. Eleion deserved better than that."

"Did you hear nothing the iskaath said? They're already on their way. It's too late."

"Not if we stop them before they get to the processing plant." Kojan turned back to Lyriax. "You work maintenance, right? You must have some kind of vehicle to get around these tunnels. The factory spans ten klicks."

"Tramways and skiffs mostly," Lyriax said. "Nothing with the kind of speed or firepower you'd need to take out a jarkaath on a speeder."

"No grav bikes?"

"In the security garage outside. But trust me, human, all you'll do with a grav bike is get yourself killed. They're all raw power and muscle, with volatile controls and a nasty temper if you don't know how to rein it in. They're built for iskaath. A human couldn't possibly fly—"

"Watch me."

Kojan pushed past the two of them and started back towards the sewer entrance, moving as quickly as he dared along the narrow walkway. The frothing brown river below seemed more ominous than ever now he knew the jarkaath's plans. If the black ops team made it to the processing plant and managed to release the mavacite, it would set off a chain reaction that would set the sewers ablaze and reduce the factory above to a pile of rubble, along with the cybernetics they were mass manufacturing. He couldn't let that happen. He wouldn't leave that kind of defeat as Eleion's legacy.

Outside, all was quiet apart from the ever-present rumble from the sprawling walls of the factory behind him. There was no hum of engines on the horizon, just the gentle whistling of the wind across the grey concrete work yard. There was still time to stop this.

Kojan pulled up his wrist terminal and opened a line to Cyren. "The intel Drex gave us was right. The jarkaath are planning to hit the factories."

The pause on the other end of the connection seemed to last minutes. "Lyriax knew, didn't he?"

"That's not what's important right now. The jarkaath could make their move at any minute. You have to warn the rest of the factories. Tell them to shut down all access to their sewers. The terrorists plan to dump mavacite into the waste processing plants."

"Mavacite?" Cyren let out a sharp hiss on the other end of the line. "But that would... Kojan, our factories would be decimated. Even if they only hit the sites manufacturing the cybernetics, the impact it would have on our trade, our economy…"

"We won't let that happen. But you have to warn them now, before it's too late. If the jarkaath get inside, it's over."

"What will you do?"

"Try to stop them."

Kojan scanned the side of the factory, looking for the security garage Lyriax had mentioned. Pain jolted through his head as he focused his retinal implants on magnifying his vision. The effects of the quickening still lingered. It wasn't just the damage to his organs or the weakness that had set into his muscles. His implants themselves had become temperamental, rebelling against commands that had once come as naturally as breathing.

Maybe Alvera and the Idran-Var medic were right. Maybe he was pushing himself too hard. But if a bit of pain and cybernetic degeneration was the price he had to pay for helping the iskaath, he would pay it gladly. He had no choice, not after everything they'd done for him.

Inside the garage, Kojan found a row of grav bikes tethered to their charging stations, bobbing gently in the air. It wasn't a ship, but it didn't matter. It was something he could fly, something he could push to its limits.

"Kojan, wait." Kite appeared behind him. "Stop and think for a second before you go rushing off and get yourself killed."

"I have no intention of getting myself killed."

"It's suicide. They have schematics of the whole sewer network. You'd be flying blind on a grav bike. You're as likely to crash into a river of toxic waste as burn in the explosion."

"Thanks for the vote of confidence."

"That's not what I—" Kite shook his head. "You're a good pilot, damn it. I haven't forgotten our little dogfight back at Hellon Junction. I know what you can do. That's exactly why you need to leave this alone."

"What are you talking about?"

"In a matter of weeks, we'll be launching an assault on the Omega Gate. It will take more than regular pilots to lead that kind of operation. We need the best. People like me and you."

"Nice try, but flattery won't make me change my mind." Kojan tried to force a smile, but his jaw was clenched too tight. "I owe a debt to the iskaath."

"You owe a debt to your dead friend. That's what this is all about. But she's gone. Throwing your life away for the sake of her memory won't change that."

Kojan felt the colour drain from his face. "You have no right—"

"I have every right," Kite shot back. "Don't you think there are people I'm grieving too? I lost half my old squad after they got trapped in that temporal net your precious captain triggered at Ulla Waystation. She didn't care what happened to the rest of us when she blew up that jamming rig. That's what happens when you put your personal feelings above the good of everyone else in this galaxy."

Kojan shoved him, blood pounding in his ears as the siolean stumbled back. "You want to talk about personal feelings? If we can't shut down the Omega Gate, if we have to destroy it instead, the tunnel back to New Pallas will collapse. Our entire colony, our *home,* will be lost. Billions of lives. People we promised we'd come back for. So don't talk to me about putting personal feelings above the good of the galaxy."

Kite froze. "And the agitator...your captain..."

"She knows. She'll do it, if it comes down to it. She's the only one of us who can." Kojan rubbed his hand over his eyes. "There is nothing else I can do for New Pallas now. It's out of my hands. But I can still help the iskaath."

Kite stared at him, his black eyes solemn and unblinking. Then he let out a tired sigh. "I am sorry about your friend. And I understand why you want to help her people. But—"

The rest of his words were lost to a muffled drone in the distance. The air around them trembled with vibrations, disturbed by the roar of engines. Even under the fabric of his suit, Kojan felt the hairs on his skin prickle. Time was up.

He ran into the shade of the garage and unhooked the nearest grav bike from its tether. The odd-shaped controls were cumbersome, the seat sculpted for a body nothing like his own. None of that mattered. He could fly it. He could fly anything.

"If you go in there, you're not coming back out again," Kite said.

"If you're right, then I guess this is goodbye." Kojan slid over the seat and hunched his back to reach the controls. His arms were stretched to the point of discomfort, his fingers strained around the grips. "And if you're wrong, well, I guess we'll know who's the better pilot after all."

He twisted the controls and the engine roared into life. All raw power and muscle, Lyriax had said. It coiled beneath him, ready to strike as soon as he unleashed it. It was a thrill that manifested as a flip in his stomach, a jump in his heartrate. This was the one thing in his life he'd chosen for himself. The thing he was meant to do.

Another roar ripped through the air behind him, startling him from his thoughts. He turned around to see Kite sprawled clumsily over the seat of another grav bike, knees bent and elbows out.

When he saw Kojan looking at him, he scowled. *I guess we'll know who's the better pilot after all?* Yeah, like I would ever let that one go."

"You don't have to—"

"I know. But now you've fired one of these up, I'd be lying if I said I didn't want to take one for a run myself." Kite met Kojan's eyes with a steady gaze. "After this, we're done on this planet. We save the iskaath, then we save the galaxy. Deal?"

Across the grey concrete work yard, Kojan saw the faint

shapes of speeders approaching from a distance. They were burning hard, leaving a trail of fumes in their wake. The jarkaath were almost at the sewer entrance. It was time to go.

He gunned the thruster, and the engine answered with a menacing growl. "Deal. Now let's fly."

SEVEN

Rivus

The curators had them trapped.

Every time Rivus looked down at the nav console, more flashing lights appeared, hovering like constellations in miniature. It might have been pretty to look at, had he not known that each one of them represented a curator ship that wanted to kill them.

Next to him, Alvera was breathing heavily. She expelled the air from her nostrils in angry little huffs, never taking her eyes off the holoscreens.

Huff. Another furious breath. *Huff,* again and again.

Rivus winced. "Could you stop that? It's a little distracting."

The lines on Alvera's forehead deepened as she crinkled her brow. "You're one to talk. You've been rumbling like a spare engine for the past half hour."

It wasn't until she pointed it out that he realised it was true. His chest was shuddering with the vibrations of a barely-contained growl. It wasn't a sound audible to most humans, but as he'd learned over the past few months, Alvera Renata was nothing like most humans. It wasn't just her cybernetics—it was like she was made of something both more durable and more combustible than the rest of her species. Something Rivus couldn't decide if he admired or feared.

Alvera leaned forward, her knuckles white as she gripped the back of the pilot's chair. "There's *nowhere* we can go? We can't punch a new tunnel to get us out of this system?"

Maxim ras Arbor shook his head, his eyes weary. "The *Ranger* doesn't have tunnel punching technology installed in its hardware. We can go through existing space tunnels, but we can't make our own."

"But when we came here from New Pallas—"

"The waystation created that tunnel, not the *Ranger.*" Max rolled his eyes. "Look, not that I didn't appreciate the first five times you brought it up, but you need to drop the tunnel-punching idea. The only way out of this system is through one of the existing tunnels."

"The tunnels currently blockaded by the forces that want to wipe all trace of our existence from the galaxy," Alvera said icily. "Yes, that's a much better solution."

"I'm not here to give you solutions, *Captain,* I'm telling you what the situation is. And in summary, we're fucked."

The bridge fell into an uneasy silence. It was difficult to argue with Max's assessment. They were horribly outnumbered. Even in the *Ranger* there was no chance of breaking through the blockade without getting blown to pieces. The curators had cut off every hope of escape.

"Something doesn't feel right about this," Rivus said quietly. "It's like they knew we'd be here."

Alvera's head snapped up. "What do you mean?"

"I mean they know you. They know this ship." He turned towards her, his brow plates shifting. "You're the only living being who has ever seen their hive. The *Ranger* is the only ship that has ever managed to escape their temporal net. You're a threat to them, and they don't like it."

Alvera shook her head. "You don't know the consciousness like I do. We're so insignificant to them on an individual level that we might as well not exist. They don't see us like that."

"I think they might have made an exception."

Alvera pressed her lips into a thin line. There was a shadow behind her eyes that was hard to read. Looking at her was like looking at a black hole—a singularity on the brink of collapse, fascinating and dangerous and capable of things Rivus didn't want to imagine.

"Chase was the exception, not me," Alvera said. "Without her, I'd have been absorbed into the hive. She was the only thing capable of standing against them."

Her voice was raw and aching, carrying a grief Rivus was all too familiar with. The absence of Tarvan still followed him like a ghost. He knew that kind of pain. He knew how lonely it was.

"Is there no way to get her back?" he asked. "No kind of backup?"

"She was more than a programme. She was alive. She was part of me..." Alvera trailed off, her eyes glazed and distant like she'd lost herself in memories. "Part of me..." She snapped upright, her eyes widening. "That's it. That's how we make them see."

"What are you talking about?"

The muscles on either side of her neck twitched. "We came here for the Rasnian fleet. We should never have left without it."

The grief on her face had been hard to look at, but far more unsettling was how quickly it disappeared, replaced by a steely kind of grit Rivus had only ever seen in Tarvan. He was all too familiar with that kind of expression. All too familiar with what came after it.

"What more could we have done?" he said, a chill creeping through his plating. "The humans made their decision."

"Cobus and Ojara made a decision. The Rasnian people never even knew we were there. They're under a system-wide comms blackout. They have no idea what's coming for them. If they did..." Alvera tightened her jaw. "This wouldn't be the first time I overthrew a government that didn't give a shit about protecting its people."

Rivus stared at her. "How could you possibly—"

"Her cybernetics." Max straightened in the co-pilot's chair, his eyes sharp and discerning. "She wants to get into their heads."

"Out of the question," Rivus said. "I know how powerful those implants are, how dangerous they are. I didn't come here to do the curators' work for them."

"And I didn't come here to give up when there's still a way we can win," Alvera shot back. "I don't need to hurt the Rasnians. I just need to make them see." She turned to Max. "Most of your people have some kind of implant, right?"

"Auditory devices with translation software are pretty standard," he replied. "Retinal implants are catching on too."

Alvera turned back to Rivus. "I need to interface with a local communications uplink. I'll be able to send a message directly into the heads of everyone on Rellion and Ras Prime. Cobus's opponents. The Rasnian military. All the people down there who stand to lose everything if the curators win. They'll help us. They'll have no choice."

"If I wanted to use intimidation to bring the Rasnians to heel, I'd have brought the Coalition fleet," Rivus said. "The entire point of coming here was to let diplomacy do its work."

"Diplomacy *didn't* work, that's why we're in this mess."

"Supreme Commander?" Sem ras Arbor had been quiet, but now he lifted his chin towards Rivus. "I was serving in the Coalition fleet when the agitator triggered the temporal net around the waystations. I almost died because of her. You won't find anyone who disagrees with her methods more than I do. But as much as it pains me to admit it, she has a point. We owe it to the Rasnian people to let them know what's coming for them. They deserve to decide whether they want to face it alone or with the rest of the galaxy."

"And the fact you want Cobus out of government has nothing to do with it, I suppose?" Max chuckled. "I thought Coalition soldiers were supposed to be neutral."

Sem scowled. "Coalition soldiers are supposed to protect the people of this galaxy. Cobus is endangering Rasnian lives with his reckless isolationist politics."

Rivus ground his teeth together. It was so much *easier* when someone else was giving the orders. If Tarvan had been here... A stab of pain caught in his gut. No, it was pointless thinking like that. Tarvan wasn't here. Rivus couldn't hide behind his decisions anymore. It was too easy to second guess when you weren't the one in charge. Too easy to let someone else accept the blame.

Whatever happened next had to be his to bear.

He straightened the white cloak around his shoulders. "How do we make this work while avoiding civilian casualties?"

Alvera leaned forward and brought up a holoscreen on the nav console. "There are a dozen suitable uplink towers on Rellion. If you drop me on the roof of one of them, I should be able to interface with the network from there."

"And what are we meant to do in the meantime?" Max crossed his arms. "Rellion has anti-aircraft defence towers all over the moon. Getting you in is one thing, but we'll leave ourselves exposed if we hang around waiting for you."

"I can map a friendly signature into our systems so their missiles won't target us. That should be enough to keep you out of trouble until I'm done." Alvera looked up at Rivus. "Are we doing this?"

He nodded, trying to ignore the unease gnawing in the pit of his stomach. "We don't have much choice. But Alvera—"

"Set a course for those coordinates," Alvera said. "I'll head down to the cargo bay and get ready for the drop. We should have some grav-boosters primed and ready."

Rivus followed her, lengthening his stride to keep pace with her frantic footsteps. By the time they reached the cargo bay, the soft flesh of her face was pale and clammy. She said nothing as she pulled on her exosuit piece by piece, snapping each covering into place with a grim resolve.

She fixed him with a challenging stare, sending a ripple of discomfort over his plating.

"What is it?" she said.

"It's nothing, I—"

"Don't tell me it's nothing. You've been giving me that same look ever since we met on Alcruix."

Rivus closed his eyes. When he opened them again, all he saw was the shadow of his old commander. "You remind me of someone," he admitted.

"Someone terrible, no doubt."

"When he needed to be." The words caught in his throat. "If Tarvan had been here, he wouldn't have taken no for an answer. He'd have brought the might of the legionnaires down on Cobus until he crushed him into compliance. He would have sacrificed half of Rellion to make an example if he thought it would work."

"And you think I'm the same."

"I think Tarvan would have been afraid of you. And the entire time I knew Tarvan, he wasn't afraid of anything."

Alvera's expression was impossible to read. The tug at the edge of her mouth might have been amusement or the twist of a grimace. The deadness in her eyes might have been resignation or buried shame.

Eventually, she spoke. "If I am such a monster, why did you let me stay?"

"Because Tarvan wouldn't let me share his burden. He tried to protect me from it, over and over again. He let himself do terrible things to spare the rest of us. And in the end, he died for those mistakes." Rivus paused, taking a moment to contain the bitter concoction of regret and sorrow on his tongue. "I won't pretend that what you're capable of doesn't scare me. But neither am I willing to let you bear what's to come alone. This is my fight as much as it is yours. And if I can stop you from making the same mistakes Tarvan did..."

Alvera laughed softly. "You think you can protect me, Rivus Itair?"

"You don't need protection. You need somebody on your side. A friend."

She faltered at that, her mouth open as if she wanted to say something in reply but couldn't find the words. Something in her expression softened, and for the first time since Rivus met her, the smile twitching at the corners of her mouth made its way to the creases of her eyes.

Before either of them could say anything else, the intercom in the corner of the cargo bay rustled into life. "We're about to hit atmo," Max said. "We'll make a direct line for the nearest comm uplink tower. You better get in position."

Rivus grabbed one of the grav-boosters and secured it around his waist. The design clearly wasn't meant for a dachryn—the straps barely stretched enough to click into place. He only hoped the jets would hold up under his weight.

Alvera raised an eyebrow as she slung her own pack over her shoulders. "You're coming?"

"There's likely to be resistance on the roof. You could use some backup." He grunted. "Besides, it's not like I'm much use on the ship. I'm sure those ras Arbor brothers can keep a handle on everything until we get back, if they stop bickering long enough to return for pickup."

He'd barely finished speaking when the hatch of the cargo access door slid open and a screaming wind tore around the hold. The blanket of clouds below grew thinner and thinner until the silver cityscape of Rellion appeared before his eyes. Pinprick spires and glittering lights. Sloped glass roofs reflecting the burnt-orange colour of the evening sky. A world no less beautiful for how artificial it was.

"That's our target coming up," Alvera said, edging herself towards the hatch. In the darkness of the hold, Rivus saw the faint glow of the retinal implants behind her eyes as she focused on the buildings below. "Get ready to jump."

Rivus joined her, trying to ignore the way his insides squirmed. He couldn't see the surface of the moon, only shadows where the skyscrapers disappeared far below. The skycar lanes looked impossibly small, like they were made up of glimmering metal insects rather than roaring shuttles. He tugged on the anchors of his grav-booster, suddenly conscious of how flimsy they were.

"Now!" Alvera yelled.

Rivus leapt. For a fleeting, singular moment, he hung there, suspended in time. Then he fell through the air like a meteorite burning towards the ground. His stomach plummeted, dragging his insides with it. The wind whirled around him as he tumbled in a mess of thrashing limbs.

Focus, he thought to himself. *Use the grav-boosters.*

He fumbled at the controls until he found the button to initiate the jets. Something roared behind him and he felt a jolt, like something had hooked onto him, pulling him upwards. The buildings below weren't rising to meet him so rapidly now. He was still falling, but it was steadier now, more controlled.

Alvera appeared in front of him, the glow of the jets burning at the rear of her own grav-booster. She seemed considerably more at ease than him, her limbs loose and relaxed as she zipped forward and pointed an arm towards the large, flat roof of one of the nearby buildings. The satellite on top of the tower was huge, its parabolic face pointing to the stars beyond Rellion's atmosphere.

Rivus leaned forward to match her trajectory. All he had to do was ease off the grav-boosters a little and—

"Watch out!"

He banked sharply to the left as a stream of bullets flew through the air towards him. They whistled as they shot past, dangerously close to the volatile fuel cells in his grav-booster.

Rivus snapped his head back towards the tower. A squad of armoured humans had burst onto the roof, guns drawn. Building security, by the looks of them. *Damn* it. They'd got there quicker than he expected.

He glanced over at Alvera, hovering metres above the roof with a grim look on her face. "What are we going to do?"

She stared down at them. "Clear a landing zone."

She shot forward, her grav-booster roaring behind her. One moment she was flying through the air, the next she was on the rooftop, rolling out of her landing. In one fluid motion, she unhooked the grav-booster from around her shoulders and sent it skittering across the roof towards the security officers, its jets still burning.

She drew a pistol from the holster on her exosuit and held it level in front of her eyes. It was a straight shot. She couldn't miss.

She didn't.

The explosion roared across the rooftop, engulfing the helpless security officers in a blazing ball of fire and fuel. If there were any screams, they were lost in the sound of the blast. It happened too fast for them to react. Too fast for them to escape. Their bodies were already charred ash inside melted armour, smothered by the smoke rising around them.

Rivus turned his grav-booster towards the roof, his body shaking as he met the ground with a heavy thud. The smoke-filled air seared the back of his throat as the rest of the fuel burned out. He didn't need to see what the flames had left behind.

He turned to Alvera. "What did you do?"

"What I had to," she said, her face expressionless.

The words were her own, but the voice belonged to Tarvan. It carried the same cold justification. The same ruthlessness, so sharp it cut deeper each time Rivus heard it. It was like the worst parts of his old friend had been returned to him. The parts Rivus hated himself for not fighting more strongly against when he'd had the chance.

Alvera stared at him, her eyes devoid of anything but utter resolve. "We don't have long. Let's do what we came here to do."

Rivus followed her across the roof, his body growing more numb with each step. He might have drawn his gun and pressed the barrel against her neck if he'd thought killing her would have made a difference. But sooner or later, desperation would force someone into replacing her. Maybe Tarvan had left behind a void the galaxy needed to fill. Maybe it would always need a tyrant.

Someday, it might be him. That was what scared him the most.

Alvera stopped at a small door. The satellite towered above them, blocking out half the sky. She ripped open the covering on the external access panel and tapped at the interface underneath, her eyes focused. Rivus imagined the cybernetics in her head whirring away, working to decrypt the locking mechanism.

After a moment, the door slid open and he followed Alvera into a dimly-lit server room. The only illumination came from a faint blue glow emanating from the humming machines that lined the walls.

Alvera approached one of the consoles, trailing her fingers across the holographic interface. "This should do," she said. "I can connect to the Rasnian communications system from this uplink node. System-wide beams are still jammed, but I'll be able to send a message to everyone on Rellion and Ras Prime, as long as they have some kind of implant."

Rivus watched the feverish gleam in her eyes as she worked away on the machine, her brow furrowed in concentration. Maybe she had already forgotten about the burning bodies she'd left outside. Maybe they didn't matter. Stars, maybe she was *right*. What were a handful of lives in the face of extinction?

"How do you do it?" he said quietly.

Alvera didn't pretend not to understand. "By accepting that everything I've done is already catching back up to me. By accepting there's no escaping the reckoning I'll face at the end of it. By accepting that even if we save the galaxy, there won't be a place for me in it when this is all over."

She flicked on a switch and the blue lights turned gold. A spinning circle lit up on the holographic interface. "Everything's ready, if you are."

He had to be. There was no other choice.

"Do it," he said.

Alvera closed her eyes. For a moment, she looked peaceful. The lines of her brow softened and her eyelids fluttered gently under the glow from the lights. It was like a glimpse into the woman she could have been if this hadn't fallen to her. If she hadn't become the agitator.

Then she opened her eyes, and terror came for him.

It was worse than his visions, worse than the pain that had shot through him during the waystations' countdown. It was like something had forced its way into his brain, burrowing into every crack and crevice until it filled his entire mind with white-hot pain. It invaded parts of him he didn't know existed. It showed him memories that weren't his own.

Alvera. Her grief and rage poured into him, so loud he couldn't shut it out. All he saw were glimpses into a fragmented mind.

This is what's coming for you, she said.

The images in Rivus's head sharpened. He still couldn't make sense of the shapes, but he understood the horror he felt when he looked at them. Except it wasn't *his* horror, it was Alvera's. This was what she'd felt when she'd been trapped in the curators' consciousness. This was the moment of her despair, when she realised nothing would stop what was coming.

They are here to put an end to an experiment none of us knew we were part of, she whispered.

Rivus's mind flashed with a thousand memories. Worlds burning as curator ships hung in the air like floating tower blocks. Cities reduced to rubble as mindless alien thralls came to clean up the remains of a fallen civilisation. Survivors thrashing and screaming as they were carried away.

He was drowning in the depths of Alvera's memories, unable to push them from his head. Her thoughts became his own. It was impossible for him to ignore the things she was showing him. Impossible to deny them.

None of us can stand against them alone, she continued. *If we want to survive, we have to do it together.*

Her voice sounded more desperate now. There was a strain to it that reminded Rivus of a frayed rope on the edge of snapping. His mind flooded with more images. Fleets gathering in orbit. An Idran-Var and a legionnaire standing side by side. The broken remains of Alcruix.

Help us, she said, her voice faint and fading. *Help us to...*

The pressure in Rivus's head lifted. He opened his eyes to the blinking blue lights of the server room and tried to make sense of his blurred surroundings. The hold Alvera had on his mind was gone. It was over.

He stumbled forward, darkness taking hold at the edges of his vision. His legs trembled like they were ready to give way. It was like fighting an exhaustion he couldn't stave off.

"Alvera?"

She was lying on the floor next to the machine, her eyes glazed and half-shut. Her skin was deathly pale, and blood trickled from her nose in a steady stream. No, not just her nose —her ears too. Rivus saw the trail where it had dripped down her neck and along her jaw, leaving faint red streaks in its wake.

"No." He pulled up his wrist terminal to sync with her cybernetics. Her pulse was flagging, her vitals weak. "You don't get to die like this. The galaxy still needs you. You have to hold on."

He fumbled with the interface, trying to signal the *Ranger*. His claws weren't working the way he wanted them to. The flashing text in front of his eyes didn't make any sense. He was losing his grip on his senses, drifting towards the heavy comfort of sleep.

The last thing he remembered was the clatter of his wrist terminal against the floor as he sank down next to Alvera's limp body and succumbed to the pull of unconsciousness.

EIGHT

NIOLE

I *can control it.*

Niole repeated the words in her head, trying to ignore the way her body betrayed her. Under her armour, her skin prickled with energy waiting to be unleashed.

I can control it, she thought to herself again. *I am not ilsar, I am Idran-Var. I can control it.*

Maybe if she said it enough times, she'd start to believe it.

Serric turned his helmet towards her. "I can hear your teeth chattering through your armour," he said quietly. "You're making me nervous."

"*That's* what's making you nervous?" Niole hissed back. "Not the fact we're walking into one of the most notorious prisons in the galaxy, but that you can hear my teeth chattering while we're doing it?"

Serric didn't answer. His flare stirred in the space between them, but it was more subdued than hers. More patient. For all his rage, Serric knew how to restrain himself. He also knew when to strike.

A shiver raced down Niole's spine. Picking a fight in the Bastion was the last thing she wanted to do. The guards were more than capable of handling people like her and Serric. They trained for it like the legionnaires had once trained for the Idran-Var. She didn't want to think about what kinds of countermeasures might be lying in wait for them if they stepped out of line.

The warden's office they'd been brought to was simple and nondescript. Its walls were plain and grey, and the room was empty apart from a sturdy desk and a weapons locker on the back wall.

Then Niole looked up and saw the ocean.

The sight of it almost sent her to the ground in panic. The entire ceiling was made from glass. Water surrounded them, deep blue and full of shadows. The surface was so far above that she could only see a pale, far-off light. All that water, all that weight crushing in around them. If there was a single weakness in the structure, a single crack in the glass...

Niole swallowed. The Bastion had a reputation for being impossible to escape from. It was only now she realised what they were up against.

"Admiring the view?" asked the warden, a middle-aged siolean with bright orange skin and faint red speckles smattered across his brow ridge. "There's a certain calmness about staring into the might of the ocean from down here, wouldn't you agree?"

Niole didn't know how to answer. The question was cordial enough, but it was difficult to return the pleasantries without feeling like she was treading in dangerous water. "It's a bit overwhelming. I'm more comfortable on dry land."

"Indeed? Dry land is in short supply here on Pxen." The warden gave an unsettling smile. "It seems an ill-suited planet for you to have chosen to visit if that's what you're hoping to find."

"We were hoping to find help," Niole replied curtly. Something about the warden made her insides squirm. Under his unctuous words was a hidden barb lying in wait, and playing along would only get her stung. "The Coalition has fallen. The galaxy is under attack. We came here to find people who might be able to help us fight."

"Yes, my guards sent their bodysuit recordings on ahead. They made for fascinating viewing." The warden clasped his hands together. "An alien army. A gateway to dark space. The Idran-Var allying themselves with what's left of the Coalition. I hardly know which part is the most difficult to believe."

"Believe what you want," Serric cut in. "We didn't come here to convince anyone. We came here for your prisoners."

"My prisoners?" The warden raised the ridge of his brow. "I see why you think they might be useful. The *ilsar* imprisoned here are powerful—dangerously so. Anybody capable of controlling them would find themselves with a deadly force at their disposal. And therein lies our problem." The warden shook his head, his headtails rustling over his shoulders. "The prisoners you seek *cannot* be controlled. Each of them ended up in the Bastion for a reason. Unleashing them on the galaxy would be tantamount to a war crime."

Serric folded his arms. "Bit of an exaggeration, don't you think?"

"Ah yes, I forgot who I was speaking to." The warden chuckled. "The Idran-Var have always had a somewhat looser definition of a war crime than the rest of the civilised galaxy. It doesn't surprise me that you'd use these creatures for your own gain."

"We didn't come here for ourselves," Niole insisted.

"Didn't you?" The warden glanced between them. "Don't make the mistake of presuming I don't know what's under that armour of yours. I have spent my life keeping watch over others like you. I know the touch of your flare. I sense the bloodlust that lies ever-present in your minds. If you think I am going to let two *ilsar* walk out of here with an army of violent prisoners, I'm afraid you're gravely mistaken."

He rose from behind his desk and made his way over to a holographic console on the wall. "I have never known an *ilsar* to walk willingly into the Bastion," he said, swiping through the interface. "But now that you're here, I cannot let you leave. Not until the Coalition confirms your story, at any rate."

Niole's insides turned to ice. Comms were down. There was no way the warden could contact the Coalition. And even if he managed to get a message through... She squirmed. Rivus didn't know about any of this. They'd planned it behind his back. Maybe he'd take the chance to be rid of her. Maybe he'd see it as justice after what she did to Tarvan.

She reached for Serric's arm. Their vambraces clinked as they brushed off each other. "We need to get out of here," she said under her breath. "We can't let him take us."

"We're not going to." Serric's voice was as hard as steel. "But we came here for a reason. I'm not leaving without those prisoners."

"Serric..."

It was already too late. Before Niole could brace herself against what was coming, Serric unleashed his flare. A burst of blue-green energy exploded from his arms, catching the warden square in the chest and sending him into the wall with a sickening crack. Niole half expected to see a shower of blood splatter across the ceiling, but the warden's crumpled body remained intact, his chest rising and falling with shallow breaths.

Serric grabbed her arm. "Come on. We need to find our way to the prison block."

She followed him back through the corridor, her heart

jolting when they passed the elevator they'd descended in. Freedom was right there, only metres away. It would have been so easy to step in and shoot back up through the ocean depths in the transparent tube. Nobody was there to stop them.

Serric kept running, leading her deeper into the complex, away from the possibility of escape. In front of them, the corridor opened out into a huge atrium, like a crystalline bubble surrounded by the blue of the ocean. Niole might have been able to marvel at the beauty of it if it wasn't so terrifying. Water was all around them, held back by only a few feet of reinforced glass.

"We're trapped."

Niole turned to Serric. He wasn't looking at the atrium. He was looking at the armed guards blocking off every doorway and corridor that led out of it. Sioleans with skin the same shade of blue as the depths outside took up position around them, their rifles pointed and steady. There was no way out.

The crack of a rifle echoed around the dome. Niole flinched as the bullet ricocheted against her armour with a clang, the impact sending her staggering back on her heels. But there wasn't a mark on her chest plate. The bullet had deflected off and lodged itself in the floor halfway across the room.

"Rest assured, my *ilsar* friend, that was merely a warning."

Niole spun around. The warden stood at the mouth of the corridor they'd come through, flanked by two sioleans in power armour. She couldn't see their faces behind their white helmets, but there was something in the way they held themselves that sent a cold trickle of fear down her spine.

Serric grunted. "You want to talk warnings? Here's one of our own: you'll need more than bullets to take down an Idran-Var."

"You're correct, of course." The warden bowed his head. "This is the Bastion. Our business isn't in taking down Idran-Var. But we've become rather adept at subduing *ilsar*."

Niole froze. Something wasn't right. The warden was too confident. He had been since the moment they'd arrived. It didn't matter that they were Idran-Var. That part of them didn't concern the warden, not when he knew how to defeat the other part of them. The part she'd spent half a lifetime trying to leave behind.

"Be careful, Serric." Her words sounded thin to her ears. "He's going to…"

It had already started.

The anti-radiation drugs Tarvan had pumped into her veins back on the *Lancer* had coursed through her like poison, dulling her senses and withering her from the inside out. But this was something else. The sensation washed over Niole like a haze, leaving her mind clouded. She buckled from its weight as it drained her more and more with each breath.

"Gas," she muttered, not knowing if Serric could hear. "He's using some kind of anti-rad gas."

"Very astute." The warden clasped his hands together. "It's a unique compound our siolean scientists created. Odourless, colourless and highly penetrable. I'm afraid even the seals on that impressive Idran-Var armour of yours won't be enough to keep it out. The effects don't last as long as a proper course of injections, but it will slow you down long enough for us to relieve you of your armour."

"We're not the only ones it will slow down," Serric said, his voice strained. "Your guards will be affected too."

The warden's smile didn't falter. Beside him, the two guards removed their pristine, gleaming helmets.

Niole recoiled. The guards' grey skin was dry and cracked. A dull film coated their eyes. They had a pallor that seemed lifeless, drained of the radiation that gave them colour, that gave them *power.*

It was like looking into the reflection of who she'd been only a few short months ago. She'd withered under the effects of Tarvan's anti-rad drugs, shrinking into herself like her body was a shell to retreat into. But the guards carried themselves like their spines were reinforced with steel rods. They stood poised and unflinching, ready for a fight.

"Fyra," she whispered. "They *chose* this."

Serric blanched at her words. "Nobody could choose that."

He didn't understand. He'd never feared it like she had. Never run from it like she had. For years, Niole had deafened herself to the impulses that sang to her from beneath her skin. If someone had offered to take it all away, she might have given it up willingly like these guards had.

But not now. Never again.

The gas was already doing its job. Even as Niole tried to summon her flare, it slipped away from her. An emptiness seeped through her, turning her insides numb. It wrapped itself around her, leeching what little life she had left in her limbs.

Serric crashed to his knees. The sound of his armour hitting the floor jolted Niole from the haze that had set in around her eyes. Across the room, the two flareless guards approached, their faces grey and expressionless. There was nothing behind the black of their eyes but a void. They'd given up everything to become what they were.

Niole looked down at the vambrace Rhendar had given her. The metal had a different sheen to it than the rest of her armour. He'd given it to her before she'd ever stepped foot on Alcruix, before she went to the Forge to claim what was hers. He'd known what she was capable of before she did.

A memory filled her mind. Bloodstained lilac grass on a border planet. A hand offering her a place in the galaxy.

We're not what they tell us we are, Rhendar had said. *We're more than the sum of flesh and matter inside these metal shells.*

She was not *ilsar*. She was Idran-Var.

Niole charged towards the closest guard. Bullets pinged off

her armour and fell to the floor. Bullets couldn't stop an Idran-Var. She knew that better than anyone.

She crashed into the guard in a flurry of limbs, hauling him to the floor. Even in his power armour, his strikes were useless. They bounced off her helmet harmlessly. He couldn't hurt her. None of them could.

The guard shifted his weight, pinning her against the floor. Every motion, every struggle of movement, left Niole with a little less air in her lungs. Her arms and legs were deadened with fatigue. Her stomach was churning. Bile rose at the back of her throat.

They were draining her of all that she was. But she'd survived that once already. She'd survive it now too.

She reared her head back and sent her helmet crashing into the guard's face. The metal crunched against the brittle edge of his brow ridge, and his grip on her shoulders slipped enough for her to slide away. She caught sight of a sidearm fastened to his leg strapping. If she could just reach it...

Her fingers tightened around the gun, and she yanked it loose from the strapping. The guard was still scrambling to pin her down when she pressed it calmly against his ribs. "Stop," she said quietly.

The guard froze. It was all Niole needed to wrench herself free from his grip and pull herself to her feet, the gun warm and ready in her hands. She kept it trained on him as she side-stepped over to Serric. He was still on his knees, hunched over like he'd been beaten.

"How are you doing this?" Serric's voice scratched against her ears. His flare, always eager to surge against her, was silent. All she could feel was the remnants of what had been taken from him, like an echo of something that no longer existed.

Niole grabbed his arm and slung it around her shoulder. "We're not *ilsar*. We're Idran-Var." She turned to the warden. "The prison block. How do we get to it?"

The warden's orange skin darkened to an angry, ruddy complexion. "I won't let you—"

Niole levelled the gun at his head. "If you won't tell me, I'll shoot you and ask someone who will."

Her finger danced on the trigger. If he called her bluff, she'd have to pull it. If she didn't, he'd call more flareless guards to overwhelm them. They'd strip them of their armour, and without that... She shuddered. No, there was no other choice. The warden would let them go, or he'd pay with his life.

A film covered the warden's eyes as he stared back at her. The anti-rad gas must have affected him as well. How conditioned was he against it? Would he be able to hold out longer than she could?

Each passing second numbed her grip more and more. The room swayed gently in front of her eyes. If she lost focus, if she let the gun slip...

"So be it." The warden's voice rang out across the atrium. "If you want the Bastion so badly, it's yours. My life isn't worth trying to stop a few rogue *ilsar* being set loose in the galaxy." He gestured to one of the tunnels, and the guards on either side of the entrance stepped away. "The prison block is a separate compound, accessible only from the ocean floor. This corridor leads to the submersible bay. You'll find the coordinates and airlock access codes are already programmed in."

"How generous of you."

"Is that what you think?" The warden raised his brow ridge. "I'll be calling my guards back here. By the time you reach the prison block, there will be nobody left to protect you. It will just be the two of you and the prisoners. I hope you've both thought long and hard about what you wanted—Fyra knows you'll get it."

The echo of his words rang in Niole's ears as she stumbled, half-dazed, towards the tunnel that led to the submersible bay.

Her mind was muddled from the gas, and Serric's weight against her was the only thing keeping her from falling.

A dozen submersibles waited for them in the bay, bobbing gently in their pools. Each craft was sleek and streamlined, with powerful twin engines and curved wings that arched like the crest of a wave. Niole opened the hatch of the closest one and slid in across the leather seats, helping Serric in after her. The instruments made the small cockpit glow with a green light, but everything past the pane of the viewport looked murky.

Serric reached out and tuned some of the dials on the console. A joystick slid out of the casing in front of him, and he grasped it with both hands. "I think the gas is wearing off. Starting to feel more like myself again."

Niole felt it too. The fog around her skull was lifting. She felt the burn of her muscles again, the beat of blood around her body. Her flare uncoiled itself from somewhere deep under her skin. It was like coming up for air after almost drowning.

Serric fired up the engines. Their rumble was muted, muffled by the water surrounding them. The sub sank further into the pool, leaving behind the bright lights of the docking bay. Ahead, the tunnel was so dark Niole couldn't make out which way it was leading them. The beams of light from the nose of the sub scattered away some of the shadows, but there was still too much out there in Pxen's depths that she couldn't see.

Maybe that was a good thing.

"About what happened back there..." Serric said, breaking into her thoughts. "You handled it well. Better than I did."

A rush of warmth raced through Niole's headtails, chasing away the fear and tension. "I'd already been through it before," she said lightly. "I knew what to expect."

"Still, it's thanks to you we've made it this far. When I realised what was happening..." Serric's hands trembled on the sub's controls. "I always guessed at what they did here. Always hated the thought of them ever doing it to me. When I felt myself losing it—"

"Don't think about it. Like you said, the gas is already wearing off." Niole reached out and put her hand over his arm. Even with the armour separating them, she felt the pulse of his flare. Weakened, but no less persistent for it. It was the part of him that made him all that he was. The part of him that had brought her back when she'd lost herself. He'd offered it to her when she'd needed it most. Maybe she could return the favour.

She let her flare rise up and skim over the surface of her skin. She pushed it towards him gently, guiding it through his armour. She felt him open up to it, pulling it inside him with such force it was like he was pulling her along with it. His own flare reared up in response, catching her off guard with its quiet ferocity. It would be so easy to lose herself in it. So easy to—

"Niole." He didn't need to say anything else. It was a rebuke —a soft-spoken one, perhaps, but a rebuke nonetheless.

She pulled her arm away and stared out the viewport, grateful that her helmet hid the flush of her headtails. Serric was right. She couldn't allow herself to become distracted. She'd let herself get carried away, too swept up in the rush of relief at her flare returning to her. She had to focus. They both did, if they wanted to get off this planet alive.

Outside the viewport, Pxen's water was full of shadows. Niole could barely make out the distant grey shingle of the ocean floor. The only living creatures were long, skulking beasts with angular heads and needle-like teeth glinting in the dim light. It made her want to wrench the controls from Serric and send them straight for the surface.

The Bastion's prison block loomed into life out of the grey-green gloom around them. There was no glass here. No transparent elevators or ornate atriums to impress visitors. Just steel blocks and reinforced doors, like a lockbox dropped on the ocean floor.

"I see the airlocks," Serric said as the instruments flashed in front of him. "All the docking ports are empty. Looks like the warden meant it when he said he was going to evacuate his people. Should mean less resistance for us inside."

Niole wasn't so sure. It was too easy. Even if the warden had feared for his life, there was still no reason for him to have given them the keys to the prison so readily. He could have put the submersible bay on lockdown, changed the airlock codes. But he'd seemed all too eager for them to reach their destination.

The sub's hatch clicked into place as they slid into the docking port. Niole held her breath as the mechanism whirred and whined above them. After a moment, a hiss of air rushed over her headtails as the latch opened.

They were in.

Serric's expression was unfathomable behind the diagonal slits of his visor. "Ready?"

She had to be. There was no other choice. "Let's go."

Serric hauled himself through the hatch and Niole followed. The temperature had plummeted. Droplets of water trickled down the industrial-looking walls. The air recyclers in the ceiling blew out dust and grime. There were no comforts here, just the bones of a building that had only one purpose: to hold people like her.

Serric made his way towards a holographic access panel and keyed in an override request. A moment later, the adjoining door opened with a low groan.

Too easy, Niole thought to herself again. This was meant to be the most impenetrable prison in the entire galaxy. Where was the security?

The room led to a corridor so dimly lit that she couldn't make out where it ended. There were no signs of life. No holoscreens showing the news feeds. No personal lockers or storage crates. No signs to a mess hall or bathroom. It was like the entire place had been gutted and stripped bare of everything apart from its reinforced metal carcass. The whole place smelled damp. Puddles pooled on the floor, forming where water had dripped down from cracks in the ceiling.

"I guess maintenance isn't a priority over here." Serric's tone was light, but Niole didn't miss the chill that had crept into his words. He must have felt it too, the foreboding that had crept in as they slowly moved through the corridor, one clinking foot-step after another. Something was wrong. Something was *very* wrong.

The door back to the airlock made a deep, rattling clunk behind them. *Too late*, Niole thought. She knew what a locking mechanism sounded like. She knew the feeling of an escape route being shut off. She knew that whatever was coming now, there was no way out.

"Don't worry, my *ilsar* friends. You're exactly where you belong. Exactly where you've always belonged."

Niole froze. Somewhere above her, a voice crackled with static. The warden's voice.

"I told you the Bastion was yours if you wanted it so badly," the warden continued, his voice tinny over the intercom. "I hope you like the look of these walls. They're the last thing you'll ever see."

Serric spun around. "What game are you playing here, warden?"

"No game," the warden replied. "Just enacting a little contingency."

Contingency. The word felt like a blade in Niole's gut. The same word Rhendar had used back on Alcruix. It had terrified her then. It terrified her now.

"What have you done?" she asked, hoping her helmet obscured some of the tremor in her voice.

"Only my duty," the warden said coldly. "The Bastion was built with self-destruct protocols to account for the possibility that it may one day come under siege. I enacted those protocols around thirty seconds ago."

Niole's mouth was too dry to speak. Fyra, they were already dead. They just hadn't realised it yet.

"What protocols?" Serric demanded, his voice little more than a snarl. "*What protocols?*"

The warden didn't answer. He didn't have to. Niole already knew what was coming. The drips through the cracks in the ceiling had become a trickling stream. Somewhere past the end of the corridor, she heard the gurgle of rising water. The beams on the walls juddered with a force they would soon no longer be able to contain.

The crushing weight of Pxen's wrath was coming for them, and there was no way out.

NINE

RIDLEY

There was no ambush waiting for them at the end of the escape tunnel. When they spilled back into the hot Jaderan sun, all was still and quiet. Nothing moved except the faint film of sand skimming over the surface of the dunes with the desert wind. It might have been peaceful, if it hadn't been for the blood.

The Idran-Var they'd left behind to guard the tunnel entrance had been slaughtered. Ridley stared at the scattered mess of bodies, nausea rising in her stomach. Pieces of armour had been picked off and strewn around like discarded junk. The bloodied remains had been left to rot under the violent heat like they were nothing more than carrion for the desert crows.

I did this, Ridley thought, her insides cold. *They came here because of me.*

Zal knelt over one of the fallen Idran-Var. Her hair had

fallen across her face, half-hiding the faint streak of tears down one cheek. "A velliria," she said, her voice tight. "Nothing else could have incapacitated them long enough for their armour to be removed."

"They fought until the end," Venya said, her face plates shifting fiercely. She scuffed the sand with a heavy boot and scanned the dunes. "Ship's gone. The curators must have taken it."

"They didn't go far." Zal pushed herself back to her feet and looked out over the stretching sea of sand. Her cybernetic eyegraft whirred in its socket, glowing green and bright even in the glare of the sun. "You see that plume over there in the distance? It's coming from the wreckage."

Ridley shielded her eyes from the sun and squinted. She didn't have Zal's cybernetics, but she could still make out the faint wisps of smoke billowing into the sky.

This was her fault. This had been her mission, her plan. All because she needed to feel useful. All because she needed to *matter*. Now they were stranded on a hostile planet, surrounded by the bodies of those she'd asked to follow her here.

"You call this a rescue operation?" Skaile's voice was low and silky, her flare wisping red around her arms. "I'd have been better off if you'd left me in the Queen's Den."

Zal turned to her sharply. "My people died getting you out of there. Right now, I'm not convinced their sacrifice was worth the trouble you bring. So I suggest you keep quiet and show some respect before I change my mind and leave you on this rock to rot."

"Leave me?" Skaile bared her teeth. "You're stuck here as much as I am, Idran-Var. And if I were you, I'd be careful not to make threats you can't follow through on. That armour might be able to stop bullets, but it won't stop me if I decide I'd like to see the colour of your insides."

Venya shifted her weight forward in the sand, her claws tightening around the grip of her rifle.

Skaile glanced at her. "Oh please. I could separate that obtuse dachryn head of yours from your body before you even had time to consider pulling the trigger. Just try me."

"I hope this plays out like you think it will," Zal muttered, spinning her cybernetic eye towards Ridley. "Because from where I'm standing, you got most of my squad killed over a loose cannon."

Shame flooded Ridley's cheeks. Zal was right. If Skaile turned on them, those Idran-Var had died for nothing. Their blood was on her hands.

Fear and guilt wormed into her stomach. Was this how Alvera felt every time she made a decision that got somebody killed? Was there a place inside her where she kept the horror and shame? Maybe that's how her old captain had fallen so far, rotting from the inside out. Maybe that same rot was taking hold in Ridley, waiting to see how far she'd let it spread.

"Let me talk to her," she said. "Maybe I can—"

Her words were lost to the scurrying of claws against stone coming from the tunnel behind them. Drexious burst from the entrance, the spindles on his lean neck quivering as he lowered himself onto all fours. "They're coming."

Zal stiffened. "How many?"

"You think I stayed to count? Too many. Enough to make easy work of the five of us."

Zal grimaced. "We need to move. Let's head towards the wreckage and see if there's anything we can salvage."

"You want to take your chances in the dunes?" Skaile let out a velvety laugh. "You forget, Idran-Var, this is my planet. I set up on Jadera for a reason. This desert has as many tides and currents as an ocean. If you go out into those sands, your armour will drag you under the surface like a sinking stone. You'll be buried, unable to move, unable to dig yourself out.

Trapped all alone as the precious air in your reserves slowly runs dry."

Zal glared at her. "You have a better idea?"

"We're dead either way. Far better to stay here and make them work for it than let the desert do their job for them." Skaile's black eyes glittered in the sunlight. "At least this way, we can have some fun taking them down with us."

Venya grunted. "Hate to say it, but she's right. I'd rather die fighting than drowning in sand."

Zal pulled her helmet back over her head. "All right then. Venya, you take point behind that outcropping of rocks there. Use the tunnel entrance as a pinch point and stop as many as you can before they overwhelm us. Drex, you move off to the side and help her by flanking them."

"Forget your pathetic attempts at strategy and let me do what I do best," Skaile cut in. "I'll tear apart every living thing in one burst from my flare."

"And take the rest of us along with you?" Zal said dryly. "Save your suicidal bullshit for when we're beaten. Until then, we fight like we expect to win." She turned her glowing visor towards Ridley. "That means you too. You said you're not a fighter, but you'll have to learn fast. Stay behind the cover of the rocks. Point and shoot when there's an opening. Try not to hit your friends. Our armour can handle friendly fire—theirs can't."

Ridley's mouth felt as dry as the desert around her as she accepted the rifle Zal gave her. Droplets of sweat trickled down her temples as she crouched behind one of the rocks. She blinked away the blurriness from her eyes and focused on the mouth of the tunnel. *Point and shoot*, Zal had said. She made it sound so easy.

"Here they come!"

Ridley didn't know who shouted the warning. It didn't matter. Her hands had turned to stone, her fingers petrified in place around the trigger. She couldn't move. Gunfire rang around her ears, but she didn't flinch. It was like her entire body was frozen in place, trapping her as an unwilling observer.

A pair of towering, leathery-skinned azuul were the first to emerge. Their thick hides absorbed Venya's spray of suppressing fire like the bullets were nothing more than insects irritating their flesh. It wasn't until Skaile released the cruel lash of her flare that they slowed their advance. One of them fell to its knees, writhing under the torture of whatever Skaile was doing to the flesh and tissue underneath that formidable white hide.

"That's enough, Skaile!" Zal yelled. "We'll take care of the azuul. Save your strength for the velliria."

If Skaile heard her, she gave no indication of it. Her mouth was drawn into a half-grin, half-grimace as she unleashed more of her flare from her outstretched arms. The muscles and tendons in her neck swelled beneath her skin at the effort. The azuul wouldn't last much longer, not against that kind of furious energy.

A sharp pop filled Ridley's ears, and she looked away. One down. How many more were left?

Skaile glanced over, breathing heavily. "Are you planning on using that thing at some point, or are you going to let me do all the work?"

Ridley balanced the weight of the rifle in her hands. It was heavy, built for someone stronger than her. Someone who knew how to use it. But Skaile was right. She couldn't sit this one out. Her friends were fighting for her. It was time for her to fight for them.

Her first shot missed its mark, the bullet lodging somewhere in the rock above the tunnel entrance. She willed her shaking arms to settle. *Point and shoot*, Zal had said. *Point and shoot.*

She pulled the trigger again and jolted in surprise as the bullet clipped one of the thralls emerging from the tunnel. The alien turned towards her with six beady eyes, its huge, blade-like tusks hanging from its gaping mouth. Dark green blood poured from the wound in its narrow shoulder. The wound she'd inflicted.

The creature let out a low, whistling mewl as it advanced towards her, its long, backwards-looking legs powerful and nimble across the sand. Ridley squeezed the rifle tighter in her hands, her fingers already tense and sore. She couldn't miss again. She had to shoot it. Had to kill it. Even if it meant pulling the trigger again.

She let go of her breath, and the bullet hit its mark.

A strange numbness washed over her when the thrall fell to the ground in a crumple of fur-coated blue limbs. Maybe it was a good thing that she didn't feel any guilt or remorse at the blood pooling beneath it. Or maybe it was one more thing that would catch up to her later.

"Velliria!"

The panic in Zal's voice jerked Ridley back to her senses. She snapped her head towards the tunnel, peering through the shadows to find the velliria. Its wingspan stretched across the full breadth of the tunnel's mouth. Metallic appendages and vice-like jaws sprang from its face. Bulbous sacs sat along its curved back, coated in a chrome sheen.

"Venya, fall back. You're too close. It's going to—"

The rest of Zal's words were lost to the high-pitched scream that erupted through Ridley's skull. It wasn't so much *noise* as a sensation, something jagged and buzzing with the force of a thousand volts. It lit up her nerves and synapses, leaving her unable to do anything but writhe under the agony of it.

The edges of her vision were already turning black. Sand and stone bled together in a blurry mess. She could barely make sense of the shapes in front of her, not until Venya clattered to the ground in a thunder of armour, stiff and unmoving.

Something trickled from Ridley's tear duct. She dabbed at it and brought her fingers away tinged with red. The velliria's signal was in her head, crushing her blood vessels in its merciless grip. How long before she haemorrhaged and bled out? How long before the curators left their remains for the scavenging desert wildlife like they'd left the Idran-Var?

"Skaile…" It took all Ridley had to spit the word out. It barely made a sound between her dry, cracked lips. "Please, do something."

But Skaile was limp against the rock, her headtails drooping across her shoulders. Blood streamed from her nose and the corners of her eyes. The remnants of her flare faded into nothing.

Ridley pressed herself against the rough surface of the rock. Was this the end? Was there nothing left to do but close her eyes and wait to die?

The sounds of fighting had faded. All she could hear now was a muffled drone that echoed in her eardrums like the buzz of an insect. The velliria coming to finish her off, perhaps.

The noise grew louder. It wasn't so much a drone now as a far-off rumble. A roar that Ridley recognised despite the stupor she'd slipped into. Not the buzz of an insect at all. Something bigger, something more powerful. Wings of steel, powered by fuel and fire.

Ridley opened her eyes and jerked herself upright.

It was a *ship*.

The rumble grew louder. Vibrations ran through the rock behind her back, sending trickles of sand sliding down its cracks and crevices. A faint, blurry shape appeared against the sky. It was coming low and fast.

It was coming for them.

Ridley held her fists over her ears as the ship roared overhead. Something exploded in the ground next to her, sending a pillar of sand erupting into the air. The smell of scorched flesh burned the inside of her nose and she gagged, trying not to choke on the bile in her throat. Who had been hit? Was it one of the curator thralls, or had Skaile or Drexious been caught in the blast?

She didn't have time to think before the ship circled back for another attack. It skimmed close to the ground, its engines roaring as it approached. Ridley closed her eyes and huddled against the rock as the next plasma missile hit and sent another explosion of sand into the air.

When the barrage was over, she rolled over and saw Zal pushing herself to her feet, her armour encrusted with dried blood and sand. On her other side, Skaile was stirring, uncoiling her long limbs like she was awakening from sleep. Drexious limped his way over to Venya, a chunk missing from his tail. They were alive. Shaken and wounded, perhaps, but alive.

"Don't start celebrating yet. More will be coming." Skaile turned her face towards the sky, the flat slits of her nostrils widening as she gave a disgruntled snort. "Anyone get a read on that ship?"

A green hologram blinked in front of Zal's visor. "Signature is registered to somewhere called Nova Station."

"The Belt Cabal." Skaile let out a breath. "About time those bastards showed up. I sent a call to arms the moment those curator ships blockaded the port. I need to remind each and every one of those pirate crews what's expected of them when I make a request like that. They'll not forget so easily a second time."

"Better late than never, as far as I'm concerned," Drexious said. "They're our only ticket out of here."

Ridley focused her eyes on the approaching ship. It was coming in slower now, opening an access ramp from the metal belly of its hull. The air around it shimmered as it hovered above the dunes, kicking up the sand in whirling clouds. She'd never seen a more welcome sight in her life.

A sharp click of heels echoed against the surface of the ramp as it touched down in the sand. Then a pair of boots came into view, followed by form-fitting jumpsuit legs and the familiar garish colour of an overpriced vaxadrian leather jacket.

Ridley froze, her heart thumping against her ribs. It wasn't the Belt Cabal.

Halressan locked eyes with her, steel-gazed and smiling. "Hey, babe. How about this for a grand entrance?"

———

The stolen Belt Cabal ship wasn't anything like the *Ranger*. There was no bridge as such, no operations room or combat centre. It was a pirate craft, filled with hidden compartments for smuggling and a spacious lounge area for... Ridley wasn't sure what it was for. The walls smelled of spiced smoke and there were sticky patches on the floor she hoped were the result of broken liquor bottles and not anything more intimate.

Ridley found herself a plump armchair across the room from Halressan. She could barely bring herself to look at her. Too many emotions warred within her. The fog of confusion, the sting of betrayal, the rush of heat at the memory of Halressan's mouth pressed against hers, her tongue warm and insistent as they explored the taste of each other.

Stop that, she chided herself. *That's what got you into this mess in the first place.*

Still, no matter how hard she fought against it, it was impossible to keep her eyes from drifting. Halressan was lounging back on the couch, one leg crossed over the other. A slight smile tugged at the edge of her mouth, and her pale skin was flushed pink at the cheeks. She looked pleased with herself. *Too* pleased.

"Why did you come back?"

The words left Ridley's mouth more coldly than she'd intended. Halressan opened her mouth to reply, then closed it again, her grey eyes flickering with uncertainty.

Fyra had been sitting in the corner, watching quietly as everyone had awkwardly found their seats. Now she stood up, crossing the room with a kind of grace Ridley couldn't help but admire. She was outfitted with sturdy knee-high boots and a long-tailed blue-and-gold tunic that looked suspiciously like it had come from the wardrobe of a Belt Cabal captain.

"I believe I can answer that," Fyra said, looking in Halressan's direction. "Your friend is terrible company."

Drexious chortled, prompting an icy glare from Halressan. "That's not exactly how I would describe it," she said forcefully. "We just came to the decision that the rest of our lives would be better spent *doing* something rather than waiting for the end to come, even if that planet was paradise."

"You were moping," Fyra said. "Constantly. And when you weren't moping, you were pining. I was half-tempted to put myself back in cryosleep to get away from it all. Coming here to get myself killed in a war that was never mine to fight was the next best option."

Ridley couldn't help the way her heart skipped at the spots of red that appeared on Halressan's cheeks. Was it possible that Halressan had changed her mind, not for the galaxy, but for *her*? Even if it was true, was it what Ridley wanted, or was she heading back down a path too dangerous to tread?

She shook her head. It didn't matter that Halressan had come back. Ridley had a job to do. Stolen glances and a quickening pulse wouldn't change that—*couldn't* change that.

"How did you know where to look for us?" she asked, fighting to keep her voice steady.

Fyra motioned to the terminal she'd strapped around her wrist. Another thing stolen from the Belt Cabal, no doubt. "We picked up your distress call."

Skaile bristled. "It wasn't a distress call."

"That's what it sounded like to me."

"And who the fuck are you, exactly?" Skaile pushed herself to her feet, swaying slightly. Her eyes had a filmy glaze over them and the gash in one of her headtails had reopened, sending a stream of blood down the side of her neck. Even so, the air around her shimmered with a faint red haze. Ridley knew all too well that Skaile wasn't the kind of person to let injury or exhaustion get in the way of picking a fight.

Halressan barked out a laugh. "Go on, Skaile, try it. I'd love to see you put on your ass."

"This is Fyra," Ridley said, hastily stepping between them before Skaile decided to tear a hole in the bulkhead and send them all into the vacuum. "We met her on that planet on the edge of dark space, the one you tracked us to. She—"

"Fyra?" Skaile interrupted, arching her brow ridge. "Like the siolean goddess?"

Fyra made a sticking sound at the back of her throat. "Like the siolean *general*."

"Never heard of you."

"That reflects more on your own ignorance than it does on any of my achievements."

Ridley groaned. And she thought *Halressan* would be the problem. "It's a long story," she told Skaile. "One you'll probably need a drink for. In the meantime, let's just say Fyra was around the last time the curators descended on the galaxy to kill us all."

Fyra's expression was sombre as she nodded along with Ridley's words. "I already fought my war," she said. "I had no desire to join another. But it's not easy to ignore the truth once you've learned it." She hardened her mouth into a grim line. "I fear this fight will come for me, whether I want it to or not."

Skaile stared at her, her expression stony and unyielding. Then she turned to Ridley. "You have a lot of explaining to do, outlander."

Halressan flicked her eyes over towards Zal and Venya. "Yeah, like what you're doing messing around with a couple of Idran-Var."

Her accusatory tone made Ridley stiffen. "They're on our side."

"The Idran-Var aren't on anybody's side but their own," Halressan said, bitterness dripping off every word. "I know that better than most."

For the first time since they'd boarded the ship, Zal looked up from the floor, fixing Halressan with an interested gaze. "You were one of us?"

Halressan shrank back in her seat. There was no colour in the paleness of her cheeks now, just a defiant, desperate look in her eyes. "Yeah, I was one of you," she said. "Until I decided I didn't want to be anymore."

"Nothing wrong with that," Zal said indifferently. "This life isn't for everyone."

"Except it wasn't enough for you to let me go, was it? You had to send your people after me, all because you wanted your precious armour back."

"Why would we come after your armour?" Zal frowned, her cybergrafted eye blinking rapidly in the dim light of the lounge. "You earned it—it was yours to keep."

"Bullshit." Halressan glared at her. "The Idran-Var put a bounty on my head."

"The Idran-Var have no need for bounties," Zal said. "If we have a score to settle, we settle it ourselves."

"Then how..." Halressan trailed off, her words disappearing into the air. She turned towards Skaile. "No. No *fucking* way."

Skaile shrugged. "I suppose you had to find out sooner or later."

"*You* did this?" Halressan leapt to her feet, her hands balling into fists. "All this time I've been running from the Idran-Var, it was *you* who put the price on my head? You who sent them after me, claiming my armour was stolen?"

"It was in my interest to keep you looking over your shoulder at the life you'd left behind," Skaile said. "People are easier to control when they're running from something. When they're desperate."

"Like you are now, you mean?" Ridley shot back.

The humour on Skaile's face faded. "Careful, outlander. Don't forget who you're talking to."

"And don't *you* forget that the only reason we didn't leave you for dead back on Jadera is because we need you," Ridley said coolly. "If you won't help us, there's no reason to keep you around."

Something twitched on Skaile's face. Ridley wasn't sure whether it was a tug of amusement or a tremor of barely-controlled rage. The Outlaw Queen's red skin was bruised and sallow, her eyes bleak with exhaustion. Anyone else would have collapsed by now. But Skaile commanded power like nobody Ridley had ever met, except perhaps Alvera. And as much as she hated to admit it, she needed that power.

Skaile let out a brusque laugh. "You think I'm going to help you?"

"I know you are." Ridley fixed her with a hard look. "You told me once that the day our positions were reversed, the day you owed me your life, was the day I could call in a favour. It's time to pay up."

Skaile took a step towards her, and Ridley feared she'd pushed too far. Even injured, Skaile could snap her neck without breaking a sweat. It would be over before she realised what had happened.

But all Skaile did was lower herself into a deep, mocking bow, her eyes glinting with amusement—maybe even the faintest suggestion of respect. "Let it never be said that the Outlaw Queen doesn't keep her word," she said, her voice dripping with disdain. "So tell me, outlander, what is it you want from me?"

Fear and exhilaration surged in Ridley's chest. She swallowed, her mouth almost too dry to answer. "You said this ship came from Nova Station. That's the Belt Cabal's base of operations, right?"

"Why?" Skaile looked at her warily.

"That's what I want from you, Skaile. I want the Belt Cabal." Ridley grinned. "Give me a pirate army."

TEN

ALVERA

Consciousness returned to Alvera in the form of an ache creeping through the base of her skull. The pain trickled its way through her head, growing sharper and more insistent as it reached her temples.

She cracked open one eye. Flashing sensors from the comms relay danced blurrily in her vision until she blinked the haze away. She was propped up against the wall, her legs stiff. Something clogged the inside of her ear, and when she scratched at it, her fingernails came away with flakes of dried blood.

Shit. Something had gone wrong.

The room was quiet apart from the hum of the servers. There didn't seem to be any signs of a system overload or sabotage. What had caused her to black out? Was it the fact that Chase was no longer there to help her?

Alvera caught sight of a large, hunched-over shape on the

floor by the adjacent server tower. She recognised the white gleam of his power armour, the gold trim of his cloak.

"Rivus!"

She forced herself to her feet and hobbled over, each movement stiff and strained. He didn't have any signs of injury, but his plates were rigid and unmoving, his breathing shallow. Dark blue blood encrusted the plates of his jaw. Whatever had happened to her had affected him too.

Alvera fell back on her knees. Rivus's huge dachryn frame was too heavy to drag out of there by herself. She had to get back to the rooftop and signal the *Ranger*. Maybe Max could go back for him, if there was enough time. If there wasn't...

"Thinking of leaving him behind? It's what you're best at, after all."

Alvera froze, her blood turning to ice in spite of the server room's stifling heat. She knew that voice. It had a way of burrowing under her skin, of bringing to the surface all the parts of herself she tried to keep hidden.

Ojara stepped into the room, her mouth drawn into a thin smile. She had donned an armoured tunic over her dress, the material glinting under the lights. "I knew you would do something like this," she said. "For all your attempts at moralising, we're not so different after all."

Alvera gritted her teeth. "Something like what?"

"Forcing your way into people's heads. Controlling them."

Alvera fought to calm her nerves. She couldn't afford to get drawn into this game. Talking to Ojara was like fighting a noose around her neck—the more she struggled, the tighter it pulled. "I've never cared about controlling people," she said. "I wanted to give them a choice."

"A choice to do what you wanted them to, you mean." Ojara clasped her hands. "It's not all that different from the quickening, is it? The ability to make a choice loses its power when you attach consequences to it."

"The quickening was an atrocity."

"One that *you* created."

"I didn't mean for—" Alvera broke off, shame rising in her throat, catching there like shards of broken glass. What could she possibly say to justify the things she'd done? That was a different life. She'd been a different person back then, one that was more like Ojara than she ever wanted to admit. "I made a mistake. One I don't deserve forgiveness for. But you...you used it on Kojan. Your own son."

"Why wouldn't I?" Ojara replied, unperturbed. "Unlike you, I never lost sight of the value of control over another human being. Control is power."

"That's why you hated the people of New Pallas so much, isn't it? You couldn't control them."

"Nobody could control them," Ojara snapped. "They ran free, like vermin. Like an infestation." She smoothed out her expression and reaffixed the smile on her face. "But that hardly matters now. Their fate is sealed."

The accusation was a like a blade twisting. "I got a message back. There's still time..."

"Time before what?" Ojara fixed her with a shrewd look. "Before you make the decision to destroy the Omega Gate? What happens when it's gone and the tunnels collapse? What happens to your precious New Pallas then?"

Alvera stepped backwards, dazed. "How could you possibly know—"

"*And if we don't manage to get control of it?*" Ojara said, injecting her voice with disdain. "*If all that we're left with is the choice of destroying it, even if that means destroying New Pallas's hopes of survival?*"

Alvera stared at her. "Kojan... You didn't just trigger the quickening. You put a damn bug in his head!"

"Clever girl," Ojara said, soft and mocking. "Though not

clever enough, it seems. You missed it when you removed the quickening from him. So sloppy. So careless."

Alvera's head grew heavy. She should have known there was some other trick. There always was with Ojara. She'd been so preoccupied with stopping the quickening that she hadn't considered the possibility there was another layer to her scheming. Ojara knew *everything*. She'd had time to prepare, time to manipulate their plans to her advantage. And Kojan...

Alvera swallowed. "What have you got planned for him?"

"What makes you think I have something planned?"

"Control is power, Ojara—you said it yourself. Kojan escaped from your grasp, and you can't stand it. There's no way you'll let him go."

Ojara smiled. "I arranged a reunion between my son and an old friend. Someone you both know very well."

"Shaw?" Alvera stilled. "You sent Shaw after him?"

"One hardly sends Shaw anywhere these days." Ojara shrugged. "I'm afraid after what you did to him, he's become little more than a rabid animal. Still, even rabid animals have their uses." She drew her lips back into a sneer. "All I had to do was point him in the right direction and let him off the leash."

Alvera charged. She landed on Ojara with a clatter of limbs, dragging her to the floor. Her knee smashed off one of the tiles with a sickening crack, but the pain was dull and distant through the rage that had descended across her mind. Ojara would pay. For Kojan. For the crew of the *Ranger*. For everything.

She wrapped her hands around Ojara's bare, exposed throat. She barely felt Ojara's skin under the numbness of her own. All she could focus on was squeezing her fingers like they were made of steel. This was the last time she'd give Ojara the chance to hurt anyone. The last *fucking* time.

Ojara thrashed and spluttered beneath her. A vein pulsed in the middle of her forehead as her pale skin turned blotchy and purple. Alvera squeezed tighter. There was no going back now. No letting go. Not until she'd drained every last worthless breath from Ojara's lungs. Not until she was certain beyond doubt that she'd finished the job.

"Alvera, that's enough." A strong pair of arms wrapped themselves around her and prised her away.

"Get off me!" The words left her mouth in a snarl as she thrashed to break free from the vice-like grip around her ribs. Her arms were pinned helplessly to her sides, her fingers ripped free from Ojara's throat.

"Alvera, listen to me."

She recognised the voice now. Deep in timbre, each word coarse and rumbling. Rivus.

"What we're fighting is bigger than one person," he said. "Don't do this. Don't lose sight of what we came here for."

"You don't know what she's done."

"This isn't about her. It's about you." Rivus pulled her around to face him. "If you kill her, if you murder her in cold blood, you'll never come back from it. I can't let that happen. We need you. This war needs you."

His words washed over her like ice water. She could almost see herself—face red, mouth contorted. Eyes wild and crazed, filled only with rage and bloodlust. How had it come to this? How had *she* come to this?

Ojara lay metres away, her body limp. Her eyes were red and glazed, her throat marred with angry red lines. But there was a ragged rise and fall to her chest. She was still breathing. Still alive.

Alvera turned away, unable to look any longer. "Kojan," she said thickly. "I need to warn him. Shaw's coming for him."

Rivus stilled. "He's with Kite. I sent them to Kaath together."

"Then we need to get a message to them."

"This whole system is under a comms blackout, remember?

Short-range signals only. If we want to warn them, we need to get out of here."

Ojara was still lying on the floor, weak and unmoving. It wouldn't take long for Alvera to finish what she'd started. Rivus had loosened his grip on her arms. She could slip through and be across the room in a matter of seconds. Maybe she'd lose what little humanity she had left, just like Rivus feared. Maybe it didn't matter.

An aching pain crept through her. Ridley was right. She'd failed her, failed the *Ranger's* crew. Killing Ojara wouldn't change that. It wouldn't make it any easier to bear. All she could do now was fight for the people who were left. She could still save Kojan.

"Signal the *Ranger*," she said. "Tell them we're getting out of here."

———

Being back on the bridge felt like being back in control. After everything that had happened, returning to the *Ranger* was like coming home.

Sem ras Arbor was waiting in the pilot's chair as Alvera approached. He was shorter than Max, but they shared the same brown skin and dark eyes. He had a sunken look about him, an expression that spoke of the suffering he'd been through. The suffering Alvera had inflicted on him. He'd almost died in the trap she'd triggered around the waystations. He'd spent weeks waiting for help that never came, watching his friends fall as food and oxygen grew scarcer by the day.

Just one more person she'd never be able to earn forgiveness from.

He met her eyes with a hard, impenetrable gaze. "Whatever you did down there seemed to work. The people are demanding answers. The First Admiral of the Rasnian fleet contacted us by vidlink while we were waiting on your signal. We're getting our armada."

"What about Cobus?"

"Fuck Cobus," Max said smoothly. "First Admiral's words, not mine."

"Can't argue with the sentiment," Sem muttered. "In any case, they're helping us get out of here. The fleet is gathering as we speak, ready to launch an attack on the curator ships guarding the tunnels. Half of them will cover our escape, then pull back to defend the Rasnian systems. The other half are joining us for the assault on the Omega Gate."

A flutter leapt in Alvera's chest. Her plan had worked. The horrors she'd shown the Rasnian people had been enough to spur their military into action. She'd come out of this with more ships at her disposal than she'd dared hope for. Maybe this was where the tide turned. Maybe this was where they started to fight back.

The comms console pulsed with an incoming vidlink request. A moment later, the transmitter flickered into life, displaying a stern-faced man with pale, freckled skin and close-cropped white hair. "This is First Admiral Joran," he said tersely. "I see you made it back to your ship, Captain Renata?"

Alvera nodded. "I'm grateful for your assistance, First Admiral. The situation is far from ideal."

"You have a gift for the understatement, Renata. I trust it comes with a plan to get us out of this mess."

"The Omega Gate is the key. We shut it down, we stop the curators."

"So I've heard." Joran knitted his brows together, deepening the creases across his forehead. "I'm yet to see any evidence to support this plan of attack, but as you so astutely put it, the situation is far from ideal. As far as I see it, we have no other choice but to give it our best shot and hope it's enough to send these bastards back to where they came from."

"That's the idea."

"Our vanguard is ready to move on the nearest tunnel. We'll do as much as we can to cut a path through their ships and give you an opening. Once you're through, our forces will follow." Joran's mouth twitched. "See you on the other side, *Ranger*."

The wavering holoprojection disappeared as he cut the feed, leaving the bridge in silence. The *Ranger's* engines thrummed gently in the background as they waited. Nobody seemed to want to be the first to speak.

Rivus gave a deep sigh. "We should get into position. When this starts, we might not have much of a window to break through the curator blockade. We need to be ready to take any opening we can get." He hesitated and turned towards Alvera. "This is your ship. If you'd prefer to—"

"No, go ahead." She waved a hand. "Large-scale space battles aren't exactly my area of expertise."

"All right," Rivus said. "Sem, let's line up our approach. We want to be right on the tail of the Rasnian fleet."

The muted hum of the engines grew into a gentle roar as Sem worked the controls to take the *Ranger* forward. Alvera's heart twinged as she remembered how it had felt standing here a year ago, waiting with breathless anticipation as Kojan prepared their launch from Exodus Station. If things had been different, Kojan might still have been there. Her failings had pushed him away. He was gone. Out of reach, oblivious to the danger Ojara had sent after him.

Sem tapped the nav console and let out a low whistle. "Damn, they've got the *Dissector* leading the vanguard. It's the flagship of the Rasnian military fleet. If that can't punch through the curator lines, I don't know what can."

Alvera cast her eyes over the blinking green lights on the console display. The curator forces were still holding formation around the tunnel. Steady, patient, like they were waiting for them to make their move.

They were about to get their wish.

"Vanguard is preparing to launch," Sem said, his voice calm and steady. "Max, check our weapons systems are primed."

Max rolled his eyes. "Already taken care of, little brother."

"Check again."

Alvera felt the shuddering of the hull in her throat. The tunnel was getting closer and closer with every passing second. All they had to do was break through the curator forces defending it without getting shredded in the process.

"Picking up movement," Max said, bringing up one of the holofeeds. "They're sending out fighters."

"Understood," Sem said. "Everyone better get strapped in."

Alvera sank into one of the auxiliary flight chairs at the side of the bridge, pulling the harness over her head and clicking the fastenings into place. She tried to steady the pounding of her heart. This was hardly her first fight. She knew what it meant to stare down the possibility of death. But this time was different. If they lost here, they lost everywhere.

"Tactical feeds?" she asked.

A blue-and-gold hologram appeared on one of the displays in front of her. This was what they were reduced to—not living beings inside steel-bellied ships, but flashing markers on a screen. It was hard to imagine the loss of life when all it meant was a pulsing light disappearing from the board. Hard, at least, until she remembered that *they* were one of those pulsing lights as well.

Rivus shifted next to her, fixated on the feed. "The bulk of their forces are holding steady, but we're about to be swarmed with fighters," he called to Sem. "Keep close to the Rasnians for cover and pick off any exposed curator ships. We're here to cut through their defences, not destroy them."

"We'll do our best. Here they come now—brace for acceleration!"

The knot in Alvera's stomach pulled tighter as the *Ranger*

lurched forward. Sem let out a string of Rasnian expletives from the pilot's chair as he frantically scrambled with the controls. Beside him, Max's brow was heavy in concentration as he worked to adjust the targeting parameters.

"Their fighters are fast," he said grimly. "We better break for the tunnel now."

"We have to wait for the fleet to advance," Sem said. "The *Ranger's* point-defence system is good, but it can't work miracles. If we don't have the cover of the larger Rasnian ships..." His face took on a sickly grey tone. "Shit. Oh shit. They've got reinforcements."

Alvera leaned forward, straining against the harness as she fought to get a better view of the holoscreen. The feed was lighting up with more and more pinpricks of blue. They gathered in clusters around the site of the tunnel, moving steadily and with purpose.

"More fighters?" she asked, her throat dry.

Sem shook his head. "Dreadnoughts. Big ones. This isn't a blockade anymore. It's an invasion."

"It doesn't change the plan. We still have to get out of here."

"And abandon the Rasnian systems?" Sem's eyes burned with resentment. "How long do you expect them to hold out against that kind of force?"

"As long as they have to," Rivus interrupted, before she could reply. "Alvera is right. We can't do any good by staying here. We need to take out the Omega Gate. That's the only hope the Rasnian systems have now."

Sem turned back to the nav console, his jaw locked. "I don't like this."

"Neither do I," Rivus said. "But we don't have much choice."

The hull rocked with a heavy impact. Alvera closed her eyes and imagined the fighters swarming around them, pinning them down while the massive dreadnoughts slowly brought themselves into position.

"Dreadnoughts have launched their first set of missiles," Max said. "Our point-defence system is responding."

"So are the Rasnians." Sem swiped through the console. "The *Dissector* returned fire at the nearest curator dreadnought. That's one ship that won't go down without a fight."

"It's not enough," Max said. "Curator ships are appearing out of nowhere—they must be punching their own tunnels. The fleet will be torn apart."

"It already is," Rivus said, his green eyes glinting with reflections from the holoscreen.

More blue lights blinked into life. More gold lights sputtered out, disappearing without a trace. It was all so far away. All so impersonal. Just a dead spot in the middle of a screen. But Alvera didn't have to try hard to imagine what was happening out there. Huge torpedoes ripping through a hull, leaving a hole exposed to the vacuum. Flight crew and soldiers sucked into space, suffocating as they drifted out of reach. Fiery explosions turning steel into space dust, obliterating everyone inside.

Sem was shaking. "We brought the curators here," he said bitterly. "They followed the *Ranger*. We did this."

"They'd have come here eventually," Max said, but the dismissiveness in his voice didn't match the shadow behind his eyes. "We warned Cobus this would happen."

The light from the comms console blinked into life again, and First Admiral Joran reappeared, his holographic face drawn and grim. "I hate to say this, *Ranger*, but the situation has changed."

Alvera forced a smile. "Had a feeling you were going to say something like that."

"You see how it is. There's too many of them to engage in an all-out assault." Joran shook his head. "I'm not a man who likes to go back on his word, but we need every ship we have to protect the Rasnian systems."

"You're doing what you have to do to protect your people. I understand."

"I thought you might." Joran gave a heavy sigh. "Renata, I might not be able to give you the ships you need, but I can at least give you a shot at getting out of here. I'll order our forces to concentrate fire on the dreadnought nearest the tunnel entrance. We'll do our damn best to bring it down, but even if we don't, it should draw their attention towards us. That's when you make a run for it."

Rivus ground his plates. "You'll likely suffer heavy losses."

"I fear that will be the case no matter what we do," Joran said. "We'll hit them, then retreat as quickly as we can. You won't have long to make the tunnel, so be ready. And when you launch your assault on the Omega Gate, give them hell from the Rasnian systems."

Alvera wrapped her fingers around her harness. "Understood."

The connection lingered for a moment under the dim lights of the bridge. Then it was gone.

"Sem," Rivus said, his voice low. "I know how much you want to stay and help. I didn't want to leave Ossa either. But if we want any chance of saving the human systems, saving the *galaxy*, we need to make this window. We need to get through the tunnel."

Sem nodded. "I've always believed in the Coalition, believed in being part of something more than just the Rasnian systems. That's why I signed up." He clenched his jaw. "Don't worry, Supreme Commander. I'll get us through that tunnel."

Alvera's stomach churned as Sem sent the *Ranger* hurtling forward again. The roar of the engines filled her ears. Her mouth ached from the pressure of grinding her teeth together, but she couldn't bring herself to relax. Not when so much hung in the balance.

"We've got a clear run. The curator ships are too busy

with..." Sem trailed off. "The *Dissector*. It's hit. Those curator dreadnoughts have torn a hole right through it. If we don't help them—"

"Joran knew what he was doing," Rivus said. "The only way the Rasnian systems survive is if we get out of here and find a way to shut down the Omega Gate. Take us through the tunnel."

"I... Yes, Supreme Commander."

Alvera pressed herself back into her chair. Everything felt so far away. The rattle and clunk of the point-defence system as it adjusted its targeting. The drifting, fiery carcass of the *Dissector*, another fading blip on the holoscreen. The lurching of the ship around her.

Then it all disappeared. The viewports lit up with a white glare, and the *Ranger* leapt forward. The tunnel was luminous around them, swallowing the darkness as it took them away from the Rasnian systems. Away from the curator ships that had come to kill them. Away from those who stayed behind to buy them a chance to escape.

All of us go, or none of us go. The words seemed like a cruel joke now.

"What now?" Rivus asked, his eyes keen and piercing and he surveyed the nav console. "Do we return to Alcruix and wait for the rest of our forces to gather?"

Kojan. Ridley. The Idran-Var. They were all out there, trying to find a way to make a difference in this fight. It felt too much to hope for that they'd found more success than she and Rivus had.

Especially when one of them was walking into a trap.

"We return to Alcruix," Alvera said. "But first, check if our comms are back. I need to send a message."

ELEVEN

KOJAN

There wasn't much that Kojan hadn't experienced when it came to flying, but piloting a grav bike through the narrow tunnels of the factory sewers was something else entirely. There was no margin for error, no promise of forgiveness from the tight walls and protruding beams that jutted out like obstacles in his way. The slightest lapse in concentration would send him spiralling into the river of waste frothing below.

He squeezed his fingers around the controls and pulled into a sharp turn to skirt around a platform. The bike answered with an angry snarl from its engine as it hurtled forward, brushing past the edge with millimetres to spare. It was too easy to get lost in the thrill. The speed, the precision, the life-or-death stakes. But this wasn't some joyride or street race. The blinking lights of the jarkaath speeders in the distance were all Kojan needed to remind himself of that.

"Looks like security got Cyren's message," Kite said, his voice crisp through Kojan's auditory implant. "They've locked down every factory across the planet. Shame they couldn't have done it five minutes earlier."

"Doesn't change what we came here to do."

"Except if we fail, we no longer have a way out. If those jarkaath make it to the waste processing plant and dump the mavacite, this whole place will blow up around us."

Kojan grimaced. "You think I don't know that?"

"I thought I'd better remind you now. There might not be time for an 'I told you so' later."

Kojan ignored him, pushing the grav bike into a steep dive until he was skimming dangerously close to the toxic river below. As they'd followed the jarkaath deeper into the heart of the factory, they'd passed several treatment checkpoints along the way. The section they were following now was no longer just foul-smelling—it was corrosive and deadly. Steam rose from the surface of the green-brown liquid. If they crashed, they'd be eaten by acid in a matter of minutes.

"We're getting close," Kojan said.

"So are they. If we don't stop them soon, we'll be too late." Kite's voice had lost its humour. "Remember, these jarkaath never expected to get out of here alive. They won't be afraid to take risks. Watch how you engage them, and don't—"

"You know, for five minutes there I almost forgot you were a legionnaire."

"Mock me all you like, but there's a reason my squad has more commendations than the next dozen combined. I know what I'm doing."

"Yeah, well, that makes two of us." Kojan gunned the thruster. "So how about we go do it?"

Without waiting for a reply, he leaned forward and pushed the bike's engine as hard as it could go. The musty tunnel air skimmed over the surface of his envirosuit like a fierce wind as he hurtled along the toxic river, banking to one side and then the other as he navigated the bends. He was on the back of the jarkaath now. A few more seconds and they'd be in range.

Kojan ran his fingers over the weapon controls. The grav bike wasn't designed for a firefight—just a single plasma cannon with no automatic targeting—but a well-timed bolt would be more than enough to cause the jarkaath problems. The swirling acid waste below would take care of the rest.

Four sets of flashing taillights gave the tunnel ahead a faint red glow. Kojan was close enough now that the scream of their engines filled his ears.

He lined himself up behind them and squeezed the trigger.

The searing hiss of the plasma cannon pierced through the air, and a yellow-orange bolt shot out faster than Kojan could blink. He didn't have time to see where it hit—all he could do was tug the bike to one side to avoid the fireball that followed.

Heat licked at his envirosuit as he shot past the smoke and flames. It was impossible to tell what had happened to the speeder and the unfortunate jarkaath who'd been piloting it. Maybe the shot had sent them crashing into the tunnel wall. Maybe they'd ended up in the bubbling sewer below. It hardly mattered. There was one less for them to worry about.

"Nice shot," Kite said.

"You could try to sound a little happier about it."

"I'd sound a *lot* happier if the rest of them hadn't been alerted to the fact we're right on their tails."

He was right. Up ahead, the three remaining jarkaath had manoeuvred into a line across the tunnel. That was when Kojan noticed their rear cannons.

"Shit."

He pulled on the grav bike's controls as a flurry of plasma bolts hurtled towards him. A second later, something hot tore along his arm and he glanced down to see a blackened scar along the sleeve of his suit.

"You all right up there?" Kite asked.

"Barely. The size of these tunnels doesn't leave much room to manoeuvre at the best of times, let alone under gunfire."

"I told you—"

"*I know.*" Kojan clenched his jaw. "Save it for when we get out of here."

A dull ache throbbed in his arm as he pushed harder on the controls. The plasma bolt had left a sting, despite the barrier of his envirosuit. Part of the protective coating had melted away, exposing raw, red skin underneath. Kojan ignored the pain. He could worry about that later—if they stayed alive long enough for there to be a later.

Up ahead, one of the jarkaath fumbled with something on the side of his speeder, his claws working at a catch on a container attached to the sidepod.

Kite's voice rang through his implant, fraught with urgency. "He's going for the mavacite!"

Kojan fired another round of plasma bolts, but it was too late. He could only watch as the bottom of the container slid open and a stream of silver shavings fell out.

The mavacite floated on the surface of the sewage in a thin, glittering layer. Then it started glowing white, sparks leaping furiously from the shards as it fizzled and frothed.

"Look out, it's going to—"

Before Kite had time to finish, the sewage around the mavacite swelled into a huge bubble and burst. The toxic waste splattered across the tunnel walls, steam rising from the places the acid had hit metal.

There was no time for Kojan to pull up or turn back. He could only go through.

The mavacite continued to spark and burn, aggravating the murky liquid around it. A jet of steaming sewer water erupted, hitting the tunnel roof with such force that the droplets showered back down like rain.

Kojan swung to one side to avoid the spray. Another jet spurted up from below, catching the side of his bike. The metal fizzled as the acid ate a hole though one of the footrests. A few millimetres more and it would have been—

"Fuck!" Kite cried. "My leg got caught in the spray, burned right through my suit."

"How bad?"

"I'll live. For the next few minutes at least." His voice was strained. "Looks like the mavacite reacts to even the smallest traces of those chemicals the iskaath are working with. If it's this volatile when introduced to residual amounts, we're in for a grim end if they manage to dump it in the processing plant."

Kojan shivered. "We can't let them get that far."

"Then let's take this bastard out before he does any more damage."

Kojan leaned forward and aimed at the jarkaath's speeder. The plasma cannon screamed, and another flurry of bolts erupted from the barrel. Some of them flew past as the jarkaath jerked the speeder to the left, but one clipped the back of the engine. The speeder lurched into a violent spin, streaming smoke in a spiral behind it as it crashed into the sewage.

If the jarkaath screamed, Kojan didn't hear it. He didn't *want* to hear it. He didn't want to imagine sinking into that toxic river, acid burning through his flesh, stripping it from the bone. If the jarkaath was lucky, it would be over quickly.

"Two to go," Kite said. "We might survive this after all."

Kojan tightened his hands around the weapon controls again. He was on top of the second jarkaath. All he had to do was line up another shot and—

Too late, he realised his mistake. The jarkaath slammed on her speeder's brakes so sharply that he overshot, hurtling past her before he could pull the trigger.

Kojan glanced over his shoulder. The jarkaath had fallen behind him, but she was still level with Kite, her speeder and his grav bike locked together in a deadly tussle. As he watched, she threw her speeder towards Kite with a heavy shove, knocking Kite's bike dangerously close to the wall.

Kojan loosened his grip on the thruster controls. If he dropped back, maybe they could flank her and send her off course.

"What are you doing?" Kite yelled.

The volume of his voice sent a jolt of pain through Kojan's implant. "Helping you, you idiot."

"Does it look like I need help? You're the idiot. Stay on the leader—I've got this."

"I was trying to—"

"Go!"

Kojan scowled and pushed the bike forward again. As little as he wanted to admit it, Kite was right. He should never have taken his focus off the last remaining jarkaath. Now he was playing catch up again, and time was running out.

The tunnel snaked to the right, and Kojan leaned into a steep turn as he followed the frothing green-brown river past the bend. They couldn't be too far off the central processing plant. Any moment now, the last jarkaath might dump his container of mavacite over the pool of raw chemicals, starting a chain reaction that would see the entire factory erupt.

Something roared behind him, rattling his teeth. A second later, Kite emerged from a cloud of smoke, the jarkaath nowhere to be seen. Kojan let out a short breath and whipped his head back around to concentrate on the last speeder.

Then something rocked the rear of his bike.

The shot sent Kojan wildly off course, the bike rearing beneath him as he scrambled with the controls. It took all the strength he had to wrestle it upright and avoid a head-on collision with the wall.

"Shit, where did that come from?" Kite snarled. "I only counted four of them. Who is—"

The scream of another plasma bolt drowned out the rest of Kite's words. Kojan pulled his bike into a dive, but it was too late. He smelled leaking fuel coming from somewhere behind him. The controls rattled uselessly in his hands. There was only one way this would end, unless...

He spotted the faint outline of a gangway spanning the sewer. It was his only chance.

His hands trembled around the broken controls as he lifted one foot onto the cushioned seat of the grav bike. The bike shuddered, threatening to toss him into the steaming river below. One violent lurch, one loose step, and he'd be gone.

The gangway was in sight. Kojan counted the seconds in his head, marking each passing rivet in the wall with a mental note. It was all about timing now. Timing, and a hell of a lot of luck.

He leapt, waiting for his stomach to plummet as the fall began. He was vaguely aware of Kite shouting something through his earpiece, but too much blood pounded through his head for him to hear it.

Then the hard metal edge of the gangway hit his chest, knocking the air from his lungs.

Kojan gasped, frantically scrambling for some kind of grip. He locked his fingers around the gaps and held tight while his legs dangled below. His chest ached from where he'd collided with the gangway, but he gritted his teeth against the pain and hauled himself up, one elbow after another.

He rolled onto his back, staring up at the tunnel roof. He was alive. His grav bike was likely melting in the middle of the toxic river, slowly disintegrating under the burning acid, but he'd bought himself time. The rest was up to Kite now. If he failed, Kojan would soon know about it. The roar of the explosion. The rattling walls. The sewer surging as the whole place came crumbling down.

He pulled himself up with a groan. The speeder that shot

him down had circled back. This wasn't one of the terrorists. This was something else.

The speeder stopped next to the platform, and the rider climbed off. No tail. A heavy exosuit. A tinted helmet concealing their face. Whoever it was, they just stood there, surveying him with a chilling kind of detachment. Then the helmet retracted, and Kojan's blood turned cold.

Shaw.

The man who'd killed Eleion. The man warped by Ojara's poison, then left for dead by Alvera. However hateful he'd been before all this, he'd still been human. Kojan wasn't sure what he was now.

Shaw stretched one side of his mouth into a sneer. Burned, blistered skin peeled back over what was left of his jaw, revealing the metal plating underneath. A gaping hole stared out at him from where one eye should have been, glowing red with the light from his retinal implant. Kojan had never seen anything so wretched, or so dangerous.

"You risked a lot coming here, Shaw," he said. "In a matter of minutes this whole place could be exploding from the inside."

Shaw curled his lip back further. "You think death scares me? It would be a mercy. I welcome the thought of freeing myself of this existence your precious captain bestowed on me. The only thing that could make it sweeter is watching you suffer alongside me."

"You already did that back on Nepthe."

"What, by killing the lizard bitch?" Shaw grunted. "She was in the way. I was after Alvera. She's the one who did this to me. And *you* brought her back."

"That's what this is about?" Kojan braced himself against the barrier, holding his bruised ribs with one hand.

The torn, half-metal snarl on Shaw's face tightened. "You started this. I was meant to be Ojara's right-hand man. I was meant to be her enforcer. But when you escaped the *Ranger*, she lost confidence in me. She sent me off to Ras Prime on escort duty with your slete-loving captain. And we both know what happened next." He gestured to his face.

"I told you what would happen," Kojan said. "I warned you what Ojara does to people she no longer has use for."

"But she did still have a use for me." Something gleamed in Shaw's eye. "She offered me revenge. She led me right to you."

Kojan stilled. "What are you talking about?"

"The quickening wasn't the only thing she did to you. Ever since she let you go, she's had you right where she wanted you. Watching you, listening to your conversations, following your every move." Shaw drew his half-formed lips into a smile. "I wonder if she's watching now, waiting for the moment she's finally rid of you."

Horror pooled in the pit of Kojan's stomach. All these months he'd been carrying Ojara with him like some kind of disease. No wonder Shaw had such an easy time tracking them down. He'd given her everything. He'd been playing her game, dancing to her tune without knowing he was doing it.

"It's over," Shaw said. "Your lizard bitch isn't here to save you this time. It's just you and me."

Kojan looked back up the tunnel. Kite must have reached the processing plant by now. Had he managed to shoot down the last jarkaath in time? If he was to die here, at least he could die believing they'd saved the factory. Believing they'd saved Eleion's legacy. Maybe that was enough.

Shaw stepped towards him. His metal-encased legs made the gangway shudder, the vibrations rattling their way through Kojan's limbs.

The edge of the platform was only a metre away. Each of Shaw's footsteps sent Kojan inching further and further back, until there was nothing behind him but empty air and a steep drop to the acid river below. Maybe the fall would be more merciful than whatever Shaw had planned for him. It wouldn't take long for the caustic sewer water to burn through his flesh and bones. At least it would be over quickly.

Shaw paused, the red glow from his empty eye flicking towards the river. "Your trauma regulators won't save you from that."

"I know."

"What's your game then? You want to take the easy way out instead of facing what you've done?"

Kojan chuckled. "Like I'm going to be lectured by you on the concept of facing what I've done. No matter what happens here, at least I played my part in helping the people of this galaxy. That's what I'm leaving behind. What about you? Nobody will mourn you when what's left of you finally falls apart. Ojara won't stop to think of you for a single second before she finds her next beast to put on a leash."

Kojan slid his foot back and felt his heel go over empty air. This was it. There was nowhere left to go. His ears filled with the echo of his own breathing. Everything on the outside was muffled and distant. If he strained hard enough, he could hear the sloshing from the chemical river below. He could hear the gentle rumble of Shaw's idling speeder. He could hear the far-off growl of an engine pushed to its limits.

Shaw took another step forward. "Your mother wanted me to tell you something before I killed you. She wanted me to tell you that you chose this. You could have been part of something bigger. You could have been part of her vision for this new galaxy, her vision for humanity. Instead, all your pathetic life amounts to is—"

"A constant disappointment?" Kojan raised an eyebrow. "So she keeps reminding me. But me failing her is not a flaw. It's a choice. And as for her vision, well, that's always been far too narrow to see the full picture." He drew the side of his mouth into a grin. "Lucky for me, you seem to have picked up her bad habits."

Shaw glared at him. "What's that supposed to—"

Kojan twisted around on the balls of his feet, spinning himself to face the edge of the platform. Acid bubbles and hot steam rose from the churning river below. A roar echoed around the bend of the tunnel. Timing was everything.

He jumped.

Even as the acid rushed up to meet him, he felt no fear, just a stab of adrenaline in the middle of his chest. His heart thumped against his aching ribs. Death was only metres away, but he wasn't afraid.

He knew how good a pilot he was. And as hard as it was to admit it, Kitell Merala matched him in every way that mattered.

Kojan landed on the back of the grav bike with a thud. The impact sent pain shooting up his spine, but there was no time to think about what damage it might have done. He grabbed the harness of Kite's envirosuit and pulled himself close, wrapping his legs around the rear struts of the bike as tightly as his muscles allowed.

In front of him, Kite leaned forward and gunned the thruster. "Make sure he can't follow!"

Kojan grabbed the sidearm strapped to Kite's leg. Shaw's speeder was still hovering next to the gangway like a target bobbing in the breeze.

He curled his finger around the trigger. A flash lit up the tunnel, and as he turned back, he heard the roar of an engine exploding and Shaw's scream of rage dissipating into the wind.

"Nice shot," Kite said.

"Nice flying. For a moment there, I didn't think you were coming back."

"You seemed pretty confident of my timely rescue, what with the way you leapt off that platform."

"I heard you coming. I know my engines." Kojan let out a

long, heavy breath. "Since we're both alive, I assume you managed to take down the last jarkaath before he dumped the mavacite?"

Kite snorted. "Like it was ever in any doubt."

"Then I think it's time we got out of here."

The tunnel walls swept by in a blur as Kite took them back through the maze of sewers. All the adrenaline and exhaustion of the past few hours set deep into Kojan's bones, making his limbs leaden and heavy. It was all he could do to keep himself upright.

After a while, the artificial light of the tunnel gave way to something brighter. The water lost its acidic green tinge and returned to a dull brown. Sunlight glittered over the surface like broken glass.

"They lifted the lockdown," Kite said. "That must be good news."

Kojan pulled up his wrist terminal as they shot out the sewer exit. His comms log was filled with unopened messages, most of them with a local signature.

He tapped the interface and opened a channel to Cyren. "I'm here. We lost signal in the factory."

She let out a worried hiss. "Thank the stars. I feared the worst."

"It was close. The jarkaath managed to breach the factory through the sewers, but we took them out before they reached the central processing plant."

"That is welcome news, especially in light of the reports coming in. Not all of our factories were as lucky. Most were able to secure their entrances and exits, but we lost three that didn't manage to lock down in time. You can only imagine the damage, the lives lost. It's catastrophic, yet compared to what might have been..." Cyren gave a pained hiss. "Thanks to you, our largest manufacturing site still stands. Thousands of lives have been saved. The iskaath owe you a great debt."

A hard lump caught in Kojan's throat. "You owe me nothing."

The line crackled, then Cyren spoke again. "There's something else. Your captain has been trying to contact you. She asked me to pass on a message if I was able to reach you."

"What was the message?"

"Shaw is tracking you. Watch your back."

Kojan laughed, his throat hoarse. "A little late, but I suppose it's the thought that counts. We met back in the factory. Seems like he's been trailing me ever since Nepthe."

"This man, this...Shaw." Cyren's voice trembled. "This is the man who killed my daughter?"

"Yes."

"Did you... I mean, is he..."

Kojan swallowed. "No, not yet. But one way or another, he'll get what's coming to him. It's only a matter of time."

"I fear that may be true for all of us," Cyren said. "There was another part to Alvera's message. She said if you made it out of there alive, you were to return to Alcruix with all the help you could bring with you. She said it was time."

Kojan's spine tingled. "We're going after the Omega Gate."

Kite glanced around from the front of the grav bike, his eyes gleaming through his visor. Kojan nodded back. Save the iskaath, then save the galaxy. Kite had held up his part of the bargain—now it was time for him to do the same.

"Tell Alvera we'll see her soon. And Cyren?" Kojan allowed a slow smile to creep over his face. "It's been too long since I've flown the *Ranger*. Tell her to make sure my ship is ready for me."

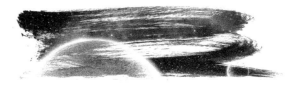

TWELVE

NIOLE

The water was already up to Niole's knees. It sloshed around her, angry and black against the sheen of her armour. Moving her metal-clad legs became more of a struggle each passing minute.

Serric was further up the corridor, the spotlight from his gun illuminating the waves as he pushed forward against the oncoming current. Reflections from the overhead emergency lighting bounced off his helmet, but otherwise he was little more than a shadow drifting out of reach.

"Serric, wait!"

He turned back, the diagonal slits of his visor glowing blue. "We need to find the prisoners."

"We need to find a way out of here. How long do you think our armour's oxygen reserves will last once this whole place goes under? We have to find a way through the airlock door and get back in the sub."

"And leave here with nothing?"

"And leave here with our lives." Niole waded up to him and put a hand on his shoulder. Serric flinched at the touch, his expression unreadable past the steely façade of his helmet.

"Five more minutes," he said stiffly. "Then we make the call."

There was little Niole could do but follow him. All the monitoring stations and security consoles were quiet and lifeless, drained of power from the shutdown protocols the warden had enacted. Water gushed in from openings in the ceiling and pipes in the walls, filling her ears with an ever-present reminder of the time that was running out.

"Look," Serric said, motioning to something further down the corridor. "You see that?"

A faint glow danced off the water up ahead. It was brighter than the emergency lighting, shimmering against the surface in shards of blue and red.

"They shut down all non-essential systems," Serric said. "If there's something down here that still has power, it's because they want to keep it secure."

"The cells?"

"Can't be anything else."

Every step Niole took was awkward and weighty, her armour too heavy to drag through the current with any semblance of speed or grace. Her submerged footsteps hit off the metal floor with a distant clunk, muffled by the weight of the water.

The glow was getting closer now, casting red-blue lights over the grim walls. It was coming from a window up ahead.

Niole caught her breath. There, standing in the centre of a sterile cell, was the gaunt, grey-skinned figure of a young siolean.

The siolean didn't move as they approached. She just watched them with blank, lifeless eyes. Niole counted fewer than a dozen headtails on her, dry and cracked, coiling as if they belonged to someone three times her age. Her withered skin was awash with colour under the red and blue lights of the cell, but it was nothing more than an illusion. Niole could see the dullness of her cheeks, the sallowness left behind where her pigmentation had been drained from her, leaving her faded and grey.

Something painful seized in Niole's chest. It was too much like a mirror to what might have been. A reminder of her own suffering.

"I doubt she'll be much help," she said quietly. "There's no life left in her."

"We've not tried," Serric said. He placed both hands on the side of his helmet. A faint, mechanical hiss cut through the air as the seals disconnected, and Serric slowly lifted the helmet up over his headtails.

Inside the cell, the siolean let out a bloodcurdling scream. She thew herself at the window, slamming her fists into it over and over until she left bloodied marks smeared down the inside. Then she threw herself into it head first, cracking her skull against the glass.

Niole jumped back, her heart hammering. "What is she doing?"

Serric stepped away, disgust falling across his features. "Bastards," he snarled. "It's not enough to take their flares away, is it? They have to break them. They have to take their minds too. They have to destroy every part of them, until all that's left is…"

He didn't need to finish. Niole understood. "Do you think all of them are like that?"

"No, not all of us."

Niole froze at the sound of the new voice. The words were soft-spoken, obscured through the thickness of a cell window. She turned to Serric, who was standing stiff and still, his hands tight around his rifle.

"Down this way," the voice called. "You don't have to worry. I'm not exactly in a position to do you any harm."

Niole followed Serric through the water as he led the way further down the corridor. Before long, they came across another window, identical to the first. The cell was featureless and bare, illuminated by the same red-blue lighting. Sitting on the floor, head dipped low and legs crossed, was another siolean.

He didn't look up as they approached. His headtails fell across his shoulders, so stiff they looked like they might break. His skin was no longer grey, but a stark, pallid white. The speckled markings across his face were dark in comparison, circling his eyes like shadows.

After a moment, he lifted his head. His neck was thick and muscular, and his long white arms were full of sinew as he folded them across his bare chest.

He stared at them both, his eyes black and curious. "I suppose you're the ones who initiated the flooding?"

Serric bristled. "The *warden* initiated the flooding."

"But you forced his hand, didn't you?" The siolean flicked his eyes between them. "That's the reason we're all about to drown, isn't it?"

Coming from anybody else, it might have sounded like an accusation. But the siolean's voice was oddly devoid of anger or resentment.

Niole took off her helmet and clipped it to her belt. "We didn't mean for this to happen. We were trying to find a way to get you out of here."

"A little late for that, don't you think?" The siolean loosened his pale, broad shoulders. "These cells may hold for now, but as soon as the water level rises enough to flood the ventilation shafts…" He motioned to a small white grate on the ceiling. "Still, it will be a kinder death than most of us down here deserve. Myself included."

Niole shivered. "Who are you?"

For the first time, a small smile tugged at the edge of the siolean's mouth. "That's what you want to ask me? Who I am?" He paused, tilting his head to one side. "Would you not rather know what I've done?"

Serric shrugged. "We wouldn't be here if we cared about what you've done."

The siolean unfurled his legs and slowly pushed himself to his feet. At his full height, he towered over them both. The lights from inside the cell danced over the bare skin of his arms and torso, highlighting deep, gnarled scars Niole hadn't noticed before. Suddenly she was grateful for the thickness of the glass between them.

"My name is Jasvan," he said. "And if you don't care about what I've done, I wonder what you do care about. Why are you here?"

"Looking for people like you," Serric replied. "We know first-hand the strength of an *ilsar*. We need that strength."

"You need a weapon, you mean." Jasvan kept his expression neutral.

"It's not like that," Niole said quickly. "It might seem difficult to believe from down here, but the galaxy is under attack. Millions are already dead. Entire systems are falling. We have a shot at fighting back, but we need all the help we can get. Help from people like you."

"And if I refuse, you'll leave me here to drown, I imagine?" Jasvan raised his brow ridge. "That's not much of a choice, Idran-Var."

Serric placed a hand against the window of the cell. "It would be enough of a choice for me, if I were in your position. Even before the warden flooded this place, you were already as good as dead. They've drained you of all that you were. They've taken everything from you."

Jasvan gave him a measured stare. "Have you not considered the possibility they were justified in doing so?"

Blue-green vapour rose from Serric's armour as his flare swirled around him. "I guess we'll find out, won't we?"

His flare pulsed around her like a heartbeat. Niole let it seep through her skin, shuddering at the rush flooding her headtails. Opening herself up to Serric might lead her somewhere she couldn't come back from. Somewhere she didn't *want* to come back from. Maybe that was why she kept doing it. She could think of worse places to lose herself in.

"Focus," Serric said, his voice little more than a murmur. "It belongs to you, Niole. It always has."

She pressed her hands against the window, bracing herself against the glass. It wasn't alive. She couldn't feel the beating of blood, the twitching of nerves and synapses inside it. But that didn't mean she couldn't break it.

Serric let out a long, steady breath. Beads of perspiration trickled down his brow ridge as he pressed his hands against the window too. His whole body was aglow, enveloped by a brilliant blue-green aura as the tendrils of his flare bled into the glass.

He turned towards her. "Ready?"

Niole didn't trust herself enough to speak. She could only nod.

Something crackled through her body like a bolt of lightning. She sensed the molecules the pane was made of, the chemicals that had melted and solidified to create it. Every part of her was inside the cell window, pulling it, tearing it apart. But it wasn't just her—it was Serric too. She felt him alongside her, the ache of his muscles, the frenzied thumping of his heart.

The glass couldn't stand against them. Nothing could.

The window splintered. Lines spread around Niole's hands, spiralling out in fractals. It was like the whole window was covered with a thick white frost.

Then it shattered.

Niole leapt back as a thousand shards of clinking glass landed in the water around them. The water surged into Jasvan's cell, washing up against his chest, but he didn't flinch. He skimmed his hands over the surface of the water, as if he couldn't believe it was there.

After a moment, he looked up. "I'm impressed."

His voice sounded different without a barrier between them. So thin, so empty. Niole reached for him with her flare, but she found nothing. Just the absence of the place Jasvan's own flare should have occupied. It was *wrong*. Wrong on a visceral level she couldn't explain.

"How did they administer the anti-rad meds?" Serric asked, a disturbed look on his face.

"Injections six times a day. Plus a constant stream of gas in our air supply, just in case."

"No implants?"

Jasvan snorted. "What did they need implants for? It's not like we were going anywhere. They even removed our translator devices. No sense wasting precious credits on implant maintenance for an *ilsar* who will never see the light of day again." He watched them carefully. "I was meant to die here. We were all meant to die here. I'm not sure the two of you fully understand what you risk by changing that."

Serric's expression hardened. "Is that a threat?"

"Call it a warning." Jasvan shrugged. "I've made my peace with who I am, with what I am. There are others in here who lack that kind of self-awareness. I'd keep that in mind, if I were you."

Niole pulled Serric to the side, glancing down the corridor towards the rest of the cells. "We don't have time to assess every prisoner before we let them loose. Jasvan seems stable enough, but if more of them turn out to be like the girl back there..."

Serric nodded grimly. "Thirty seconds on each cell. If something feels off, we leave them and move on."

"Leave them to drown, you mean." Niole couldn't help the bitterness on her tongue. "Jasvan is right. We caused this by coming here. Whatever they've done, these sioleans are going to die because of us. And you know what the worst part is? Things are so desperate I can't even bring myself to feel bad about it."

"It's war, Niole. If we don't stop the curators, these sioleans won't be the only ones to die."

"I know. I just wish I wasn't getting so used to it."

She followed Serric through the water as the black waves crashed against her. Each cell brought with it a new exhaustion. Time and time again, she pressed herself against the glass, pushing her flare into it until it cracked and shattered. Time and time again, she reached for Serric, until diving into his presence started to feel like returning home.

"Can't go...much longer," Niole said, after another cell window shattered beneath her hands. Each breath came shallower than the last, burning her lungs with the effort. "How many more?"

Serric cast his eyes over the six prisoners they'd managed to gather. "This will have to be enough. We're out of time."

He was right. The water was splashing around Niole's shoulders now. She pulled herself along using one of the pipes jutting out from the wall, but it was difficult to keep her head above the water. Her limbs felt like they'd turned to lead. The airlock seemed so far away now, so out of reach.

A wave crashed over her head and she spat out a mouthful of ocean water, the salt stinging her tongue. She was falling behind the others. She saw their shadows in the distance, vanishing into the darkness. Maybe they'd leave her behind. Maybe her armour would drag her to the bottom and that's where she'd stay, buried under Pxen's inescapable weight.

"Need some help?" Serric swam to her side, his turquoise skin dripping wet. He slung one of her arms over his shoulder, lifting her above the waves.

"I keep going under," Niole said, gulping down more seawater as she spoke. "Maybe I should put my helmet on."

"Not yet. We only have a finite supply of oxygen in our suits' reserves. The minute your helmet goes on, that oxygen starts depleting. We need to save it for when we really need it."

Niole pulled herself forward, one hand draped around Serric, the other scrabbling for support along the pipe. His face was so close that the heat from him warmed her skin, even as her teeth chattered. She reached out with her flare, trying to take some comfort from the energy radiating off him, but it slipped out of her grasp, leaving her adrift.

Serric furrowed his brow ridge. "What is it?"

"Something is wrong." She coughed up more water. "It's more than exhaustion. I feel drained. I've not felt like this since…" She trailed off. "Serric, someone is sapping my flare."

He stiffened. "That's not possible. There's no way any of them could recover from the anti-rad drugs so fast. And even if they had, the strength they'd need to drain you…"

"There's something different about Jasvan," Niole said. "His skin isn't grey like the rest of them—it's pure white. And did you see the way he looked at you when he asked if you wanted a weapon?" She shivered. "Maybe we made a mistake not asking about his past. They did something to him. Something that changed him."

They caught up to the rest of the group. Jasvan stood out from the others with his stark, ashen skin and thick headtails. He bobbed up and down with the water, his arms cutting through the waves like white blades.

"You bastard," Serric snarled. "What do you think you're playing at, drawing off her flare like that? You could have killed her!"

Jasvan met Serric's glare with a steady gaze of his own. "Getting through this airlock will be harder than breaking some glass. You need my help. And for that, I needed some of my old strength back."

"I don't give a fuck what you need! Leave her *alone*."

Jasvan ignored him and set his eyes on Niole, unsettlingly calm. "You asked for my help, and I took what I needed from you in order to provide it," he said. "To me, that is a fair exchange. If it has left you weak, then I apologise. But I have the feeling you have survived worse than this already, *ilsar*. It's not difficult to see the traces of what they did if you know where to look."

"I'm Idran-Var, not *ilsar*," Niole said coldly. "As for the rest of it, you're right. I've already had my flare taken from me once. Believe me when I say I won't let it happen again."

Jasvan gave a slow, solemn nod. "I'll take your warning under consideration. Now, should we proceed with getting through the airlock door before we all drown?"

"If we destroy the door, the water will flood the chamber before we have time to get into the submersible," Niole said. "We need to do this carefully. Create a small hole, just big enough for us to fit through. The chamber will still flood, but not as quickly. It will give us the time we need to get into the sub before the whole room goes under."

Serric looked at her pointedly. "That kind of precision isn't easy. It will take time. Time we don't have."

Niole turned her eyes to the ceiling. There was less than a metre of space left. In a few minutes, they'd be completely under. "It's time we put our helmets on."

One of the siolean prisoners snapped his head towards her. "That's it? You're suiting up in your fancy armour and leaving the rest of us to drown?"

"We're going to break through that airlock door to save us all," Serric shot back. "Can't do that if we're dead."

"And what are we meant to do in the meantime—hold our breath?" The siolean sneered. "You got us into this mess, and you'll get us out of it. I'll take that armour off your dead body if I have to."

He lunged towards Serric, grabbing him around the neck and hauling him below the surface of the water.

Niole tried to shout, but all she got was a mouthful of salty water. She spluttered out as much as she could, her lungs burning. Her headtails brushed against the ceiling, and she unclipped her helmet, jamming it down over her head and slapping the seals shut before her armour let in any more water. Her neck was almost completely submerged now. They were out of time.

Below the surface, she saw a violent stream of bubbles where Serric was struggling with the siolean prisoner. Serric wouldn't be able to fight him off with his armour weighing him down. The siolean would hold him until his breath gave out and the ocean water filled his lungs.

Then a blinding flash of light filled her vision, and the thrashing stopped.

It took a moment for Niole's eyes to refocus, but when they did, her heart stopped. The siolean was lying face down, his body split cleanly in two and his blood clouding the already-murky water.

Jasvan shrugged. "You mentioned precision? We better get started." He took one last gulp of air and sank below the surface, as supple and lithe as one of Pxen's ocean creatures.

The rest of the siolean prisoners exchanged a look, their gaunt, grey features tight with worry. Then, as if they had reached some unspoken agreement between them, they filled their lungs in unison before following Jasvan down below.

Niole glanced at Serric. He'd managed to pull his helmet on before it was too late. The diagonal strips of his visor lit up the water with a blue glow.

"Ready?" he asked, his voice distorted from under the waves.

She nodded. "Let's go."

She let go of the pipe she'd been clutching onto and allowed herself to sink. There was something calming about not fighting it anymore. The weight of her armour did most of the work, carrying her down in a swift, straight drop. Her boots hit off the floor with a thud, the sound of it echoing around the inside of her helmet. A moment later, Serric landed beside her.

Jasvan was already getting to work on the airlock door, his bare shoulders surrounded by the white glow of his flare. Pulses bounced from him like ripples through the water. Niole had never seen anything so measured, so precise. If Serric wielded his flare like a blade, then Jasvan's was a needle, capable of finding a weak spot with deadly accuracy.

Niole dragged her limbs through the water like she was moving in slow motion. The siolean prisoners wouldn't last long. They needed to do this now.

The water bubbled eagerly as she summoned the rest of her remaining strength. Jasvan had sapped most of her energy, but already some of it was returning to her, uncoiling from somewhere deep underneath her skin, swelling until it was ready to race through her once more.

She released the flare from her hands and pushed it towards the door, following the invisible trail Jasvan had left behind. She could feel the places he'd touched, the parts he'd already weakened and broken through. It was so meticulous, so *controlled*, that Niole couldn't help but shudder. Whatever reason Jasvan had for ending up in the Bastion, it wasn't because he had trouble reining in his flare. Whatever he'd done, he'd meant to do it.

A sharp movement caught Niole's attention. One of the sioleans was convulsing, his eyes wide and bulging as his body jerked uncontrollably. His hands clutched at his throat like he was fighting off some invisible enemy, unable to keep the water from pouring into his lungs. Then, as quickly as it started, the thrashing stopped. His body was still again, his face blank and lifeless as he floated aimlessly away with the current.

They were out of time.

Jasvan eased another tendril of white light into the wall. Niole joined her flare with his, pushing as much energy into it as she dared to give. Serric was there as well—she sensed his surging, volatile presence alongside her. The inner workings of the door were straining under the pressure of their combined flares. She felt the empty chamber on the other side. Any moment now, and—

The force of the current caught her by surprise. It dragged her forward, sucking her through the hole she'd helped create. The water churned around her, so violent she couldn't see anything past her own flailing limbs. She tumbled forward, not knowing which way was up, crashing off the metal innards of the door.

She spilled into the airlock chamber in a crash of limbs, her body bruised and battered inside her armour. The water was already rising fast. The submersible bobbed on top of the waves, rocking back and forth as more and more water gushed in from the hole they'd made.

Serric came through next, carried by the current with such force that he slammed against the wall with a violent crunch. The siolean prisoners followed, their grey faces pale as they coughed up water and bile. Jasvan was the last through, his ashen face fraught with exhaustion.

"Get to the sub," he said hoarsely. "I'll buy us the time we need."

Serric was already on the move. He clambered up the ladder on the sub's curved hull and pulled open the access hatch. One by one, the sioleans followed him, each slipping through the narrow entrance to safety. A rumble filled Niole's ears as the sub's engines whirred into life.

The water was filling up the chamber too quickly. There wouldn't be enough time for Jasvan to cross the floor and get into the sub before the room was submerged entirely.

"Move!" she yelled. "We need to go right now!"

Jasvan threw out his arms, summoning a shimmering white wall of energy around him. It stretched from the floor of the chamber all the way to the ceiling, from one end of the room to the other. Niole had never seen anything like it. His flare held as steady as a barricade, blocking the water from encroaching any further. Waves crashed against it like it was made of steel, the spray showering to the ceiling. But still, Jasvan held strong. The muscles across his shoulders twitched furiously as he spread his arms wider to contain the water.

"What are you waiting for?" he grunted.

Niole splashed her way over to the ladder and hauled herself up. The cockpit below was already cramped, with Serric in the pilot's seat and the three other sioleans crushed together in the back.

"What's taking so long?" Serric asked as she slid into the seat beside him. "Is he coming?"

"For our sake, I hope so." The water had already risen above the windows, and Niole couldn't see any sign of Jasvan. "If this is what he can do an hour after coming off anti-rad drugs, the curators won't know what's hit them."

A moment later, a stream of water splashed down from the hatch as Jasvan dropped through, landing awkwardly in the confined space. His back rose up and down with heavy breaths. He was alive. They'd made it.

Some of them, at least.

As the sub shot forward into the cloudy gloom of Pxen's ocean, a cold stab of guilt shot through Niole's chest. Four. That's how many *ilsar* they were taking with them after all this.

Jasvan and the three surviving siolean prisoners. How many hundreds more had they left in watery graves, only because they'd deemed it necessary to come here?

Then she thought of Jasvan. The way he'd cleaved in two the siolean who'd attacked Serric. The way he'd held that wall of water back with a flare so powerful it had left her numb watching it. She imagined what he might be able to do to the curators, and a shiver that wasn't entirely unpleasant danced down her spine.

Maybe Serric was right. Maybe, despite all those pitiful, condemned *ilsar* they were leaving behind, coming here had been worth it after all. Maybe she was learning how to balance that kind of sacrifice for the chance of victory.

It's war, Niole thought.

She was finally beginning to understand how much of herself it might cost her.

THIRTEEN

RIDLEY

R idley wasn't sure if such a thing as a smuggler's paradise existed in this galaxy, but if it did, it would look a hell of a lot like Nova Station.

It was like the Queen's Den on stims. Everywhere she turned there was another bar, another club, another strip joint. The halls were lit with neon displays and holographic ads in so many colours it made her head spin. The air was thick with sweet-smelling smoke and fried food and spices. Her ears throbbed with the low, pulsing bass beneath the chatter and buzz of the galaxy's most wanted.

It was a place Ridley could easily get lost in. But as much as Nova Station tempted her, she was here on business.

"When are you going to ask them for their ships?" she whispered, leaning in towards Skaile. "We've been at this for hours and all we've done is make small talk."

Skaile sipped a mouthful of sparkling pink liquid from a

crystal flute. "All *you've* done is make small talk. It's not my fault you won't have a drink."

"We're not meant to be drinking. We're meant to be negotiating."

"It's the same thing." Skaile arched her back and repositioned herself on the leather couch. "Out here in the Rim Belt we have a certain etiquette we like to follow."

Ridley snorted. "I've seen your idea of etiquette. It usually involves less liquor and more threats."

"And that works on Jadera. On Nova Station, however, a defter touch is required. People come here to decompress after a long run. To let off steam after getting out of a tight spot. You can't go in making demands of them without letting them loosen up a little first." Skaile curled her lips. "You might want to loosen up a little yourself. Go find that pretty little bounty hunter of yours and—"

"I get the point." Ridley gritted her teeth. "All I'm saying is we don't exactly have time to spare. You saw what happened on Jadera. Pretty soon, that will be happening everywhere."

"I agree," Fyra cut in, her eyes darting towards the gathered Belt Cabal leaders on the other side of the room. "Every moment you spend here is a moment wasted. You'd be better served preparing for the fight to come."

"I'm working on getting us an army, which is more than I can say for you," Skaile retorted, a wisp of red unfurling from her skin. "The only reason we're in this fight is because your people couldn't finish them off all those years ago."

"My people?" Fyra stood up, bristling. "Are we not both sioleans? Do not talk to me about the failings of *my people*. All I'm trying to do is stop you making the same mistakes we did. If you will not learn from us, you will lose like us." She stormed away before Ridley could call after her, shoulders stiff and headtails quivering.

Skaile slugged the rest of her flute and grimaced, as if the taste had turned sour on her tongue. "She's a judgemental bitch."

"She's lost more than any of us."

"She lost it a couple of hundred millennia ago. I lost Jadera *yesterday*." Skaile scowled. "You're putting too much hope in the fact she's fought these things before. She couldn't beat them back then, and she's not going to be any use now. She's a relic you should have left buried."

"We'll see." Ridley pursed her lips. "In the meantime, how about you focus on getting us the ships we need? If you want to survive long enough to retake Jadera, that's what will make it happen, not whining about Fyra."

Skaile allowed a smile to dance across her lips. "I was about to say you've changed, outlander, but that's not true at all, is it? You are who you've always been. What's changed is that people have started listening to you."

"Even you?"

"Even me." Skaile turned her gaze to where the Belt Cabal leaders were gathered. "Those poor excuses for pirates probably won't take you seriously, but they've never been able to see what's good for them without a little...persuasion." She rolled her wrist, releasing a shimmer of red into the air. "But that's why I'm here, isn't it? *Less liquor and more threats*, as you so eloquently put it."

"So we're going to go talk to them?"

"*I'm* going to go talk to them. Trust me, outlander, these are my kind of people. They won't respond well to your brand of self-righteousness. Go for a walk. I'll come see you when I'm done." The corner of her mouth quirked. "If I can find you, that is. Nova Station is full of distractions. You should find yours."

Heat rushed to Ridley's cheeks as Skaile stood and left the table, sauntering easily through the crowd as she made for the booth with the Belt Cabal leaders. Ridley watched as she chose a spot in the centre of them and signalled for another glass of sparkling liquor, her smile sharp and dangerous every step of the way.

She let out a sigh. Skaile's parting jibe had burrowed its way under her skin. Halressan *would* be a distraction. She had been a distraction since the moment they'd met. A beautiful, dangerous distraction, one that made Ridley want to run as much as it made her want to jump into Halressan's arms and bury herself there.

Her wrist terminal pinged. *You done yet? Café across the plaza, upper level. I'll get the drinks.*

Halressan's words blinked from the holographic interface as if Ridley had summoned them. They made her stomach flutter until she'd wound herself so tight she felt nauseous.

The smart move would have been to wipe the message and head back to the ship. Maybe the Idran-Var had received word about how preparations were going for the assault on the Omega Gate. She could talk things over with them and Fyra. She could fill her head with strategy and tactics, leaving no room for anything else.

Ridley always made the smart move. That was how she'd survived for so long. Changing things at this point would only bring her trouble she didn't need.

Her fingers hovered over the interface. She hadn't realised how much they were trembling, how dry her mouth had become, how the fluttering had migrated somewhere deeper, somewhere full of yearning. Her whole body felt like it was ready to burst under the slightest touch.

Screw the smart move.

Ridley sent back a hastily-crafted acknowledgement and jumped to her feet before she had time to change her mind. She couldn't turn back. She didn't *want* to turn back. She was long past caring about what this might cost her.

The café Halressan had directed her to was buzzing with music and chatter. Ridley let the sounds wash over her as she slipped her way through the tables. Something about the hum of voices and snippets of strange language made her skin prickle with delight. She sidled past humans playing card games, a dachryn and siolean engaged in deep conversation, even a couple of iskaath perched on barstools, their long jaws hidden behind breather masks. It was all so relaxed, so *normal*. She could almost trick herself into forgetting there was a war going on.

She climbed the spiral staircase that led to the upper level. The room was cast in a soft glow from the crystalline chandeliers hanging from the roof, their colours gently changing every few minutes. A long balcony stretched from one end of the room to the other, overlooking the plaza below. And there, sitting at one of the private tables dotted along it, was Halressan.

Ridley froze. It all seemed too real now she was here. All the hurt and resentment she'd been pushing away was as raw as ever, like an old wound ripped open. The sight of Halressan turned her stomach into knots, pulling tighter as Ridley allowed her eyes to linger on all the things she'd missed these past few months. The shine of Halressan's frost-blonde hair under the lights. The cold, pale colour of her skin. The sharpness of her cheekbones, the angle of her jaw...

Halressan turned towards her, catching her off guard. "Hey, babe. Wasn't sure if you'd show."

And her eyes. Those steely eyes Ridley couldn't help but drown in.

She lowered herself into the seat opposite, her body stiff. "I wasn't going to. In fact, I'm still not sure why I'm here."

"To hear what I have to say, maybe?" Halressan shrugged. "If not, then the food is pretty good too. Hope you don't mind, but seeing as I've not had a decent meal in months, I took the liberty of ordering us a couple of things." She twitched the corner of her lips. "Skaile's paying, of course."

"Does she know that?"

Halressan smiled.

It took all the strength Ridley had to keep the mask of composure steady on her face. Halressan made it all too easy to fall back into this again, to give in to the softening inside her and pick up like nothing had ever happened. Like they hadn't torn themselves apart back on that beach. Like they hadn't done their best to rip each other's hearts out. But keeping her distance had never been easy for Ridley. Her body wanted to lean in without her knowing it. Pulling herself away was a physical effort.

Ridley cleared her throat. "Is that what you came here for? The food?"

"I was more interested in the view." As soon as she said it, Halressan froze. Her cheeks turned pink and she let out a wry grin. "Would you believe me if I said I didn't mean that how it sounded? I was talking about the vantage point. I can see everything from up here. I wanted to keep an eye on you...on the situation. Just in case."

Ridley scoffed. "And what would you have done if things went to shit? Taken on the entire Belt Cabal by yourself?"

"If that's what it came to." Halressan shifted in her seat. "Look, the way things went down between us...that wasn't what I wanted to happen. I never—"

She broke off as a long-limbed jarkaath approached the table to lay down two steaming platters of food. Ridley couldn't help but feel grateful for the interruption. She wasn't sure she was ready to hear what Halressan had to say. Wasn't sure she could deal with what it might mean for her—for them both.

She picked up the glass of wine the jarkaath had poured and took a sip. It was smooth and buttery and warmed her insides as she gulped it down. The toasted flatbread was fragrant and crunchy, coated in a spicy paste that soon had her tongue pleasantly burning. Ridley couldn't remember the last time she'd savoured the taste of a meal.

On the other side of the table, Halressan pushed a torn-off piece of bread across her plate, using it to scoop up some fried grains. She stared down at her food with a furrowed brow and her mouth pressed into a line. There was a part of Ridley that wanted to reach out a hand to comfort her. Another part wanted to throw the remains of her flatbread in Halressan's perfect face.

"Why did you come back?" Ridley asked, the words leaving her mouth more bluntly than she'd meant them.

Halressan looked up. "You know the answer to that already."

"It would still be nice to hear you say it."

The faintest trace of a smile crept over Halressan's lips. "You want some grand, sweeping declaration that I can't imagine life without you?"

"I want the truth."

"That *is* the truth." Halressan's pale cheeks turned flaming red. "Shit, it's not enough that you left me behind there, you have to humiliate me as well? I couldn't stand it, all right? The moment you left, it was like part of me was broken. Like I was missing something I didn't know I had. And I hated you for it."

"You hated *me?*" Ridley echoed. "You were the one that changed everything back on that beach. You saved my life, you *kissed* me, and then you threw it all away like it was nothing! All because I wouldn't stay in some selfish fantasy with you while the rest of the galaxy burned."

"I don't give a—" Halressan winced and lowered her voice. "I don't give a fuck about the rest of the galaxy. Never have done. The only person in it I've ever cared about is you. That's why I came back. Because no matter how scared I am, no matter how much I really, *really* don't want to die, I'd rather spend a few final days by your side than live out the rest of my life in that paradise without you."

Ridley couldn't speak. It was like her tongue had dried up in her mouth, leaving her without words. All the hurt and anger she'd been clinging to slipped through her fingers, leaving her with nothing but the painful realisation that for the first time in her life, she knew how it felt to be truly *wanted* by someone.

"I never wanted to say yes to anything as much as I wanted to say yes to you on that beach," Ridley said, the words leaving her throat raw and aching. "If I could have stayed with you, I would have. But I can't close my eyes and turn away while the rest of the galaxy suffers."

"I know. I always knew that, from the moment I met you. That's one of the reasons I—" Halressan clenched her jaw. "What I'm trying to say is if this is something you need to do, then I'm with you. I won't pretend I'm not scared, or that I like the idea. But if there's any motivation I need for joining this fight, it's making sure both of us get out of it alive."

Ridley reached for her hand. The rest of the food sat between them, untouched. Fragrant spices wafted through the air, but any hunger she might have felt was lost in the desperate need rushing through her body. She wanted to get closer to Halressan, to press her lips against the crook of her neck, to bury her face in her hair and inhale every part of her.

Halressan threw back the rest of her wine, her cheeks flushed and eyes glinting. "Come on, I need some air. Or whatever passes for it on this cesspit of a station."

She took Ridley's hand and pulled her to her feet. The movement made Ridley's head spin. Or maybe that was the wine. Or the fact they were walking out of the café with their fingers still interlinked. The beat of Halressan's blood pulsed under her fingertips. Her skin was softer than Ridley had imagined, and the sensation of it sent an ache around her whole body, begging to be released.

When she turned to look at her, Halressan was staring back. The hard flint of her grey eyes had been replaced by something else, something smouldering underneath.

"Fuck it," Halressan said.

The next thing Ridley knew, Halressan's hands were on either side of her face, fierce and strong and gentle all at once. She pulled her in close, and Ridley offered no resistance as their lips met, crashing together with a beautiful kind of violence she'd never imagined tasting so sweet. The lingering flavours of wine and spice on her tongue were nothing compared to the taste of Halressan, full of hunger and want.

Ridley didn't care that they were still in the middle of the crowded plaza. Everything melted away but the electricity lighting up her nerves and the warmth pooling in the pit of her stomach. Every brush of Halressan's lips sent another wave of pleasure through her, until her cheeks were burning. She wanted to drown in it. She wanted to dive into her and never resurface. She wanted to—

A ping from her wrist terminal cut through the air.

Halressan pulled away, her eyes bright and feverish. "Don't you dare think about answering that."

"It might be important."

"Riddles, I swear, if you answer that I'll—"

Ridley ignored her and tapped the holographic interface. The incoming connection request wasn't from Skaile. It was from Kojan.

Adrenaline rushed through her as she set up the link. "Hey, Kojan. You better be calling to tell me you're still alive."

A dry chuckle came through the line before he flickered into view, tired-eyed and smiling. "It was a close call. That's all there ever seems to be these days."

"And the iskaath? Did Drex's intel pay off?"

A shadow fell across Kojan's face. "Yeah, it did. We lost a couple of factories, but things could have been a lot worse. The remaining factories are ramping up production of the trauma regulators. The iskaath are getting them fitted as we speak so they can join the fight."

Ridley shivered. "It's going to happen soon, isn't it?"

"Alvera and Rivus are ready to move. I'm heading back to Alcruix now with the iskaath forward fleet. As soon as everyone else is gathered, we're hitting the Omega Gate."

"Then I don't have much time." Ridley glanced over to the club where she'd left Skaile. "Thanks for the update, Kojan. If all goes well, I'll be seeing you soon."

He nodded. "Good luck out there, and whatever you're doing, stay safe."

"I'll do my best."

Ridley powered down her wrist terminal. All the warmth flooding her body had deserted her, leaving her numb. The reality of what they were up against left little room for warmth. Little room for hope.

Still, when Halressan reached out to clasp her fingers gently around hers, Ridley couldn't help but feel a kernel of comfort somewhere in her chest, no matter how small it was.

"I always imagined I'd be better dressed on our first date," Halressan mused, looking down at her leather jacket. "I should have stolen a dress or two when I raided Skaile's wardrobe. Do you know how long it's been since I had an excuse to wear a dress?"

"Our first date?" Ridley smirked. "Is that what this is?"

"Isn't it?" Halressan frowned. "Unless you count getting buried alive on Sio. Or almost getting spaced by the Idran-Var. Or crash landing on a planet inhabited only by frozen sioleans. Things were going pretty well this time around, at least until we got interrupted by your pilot friend."

"Speaking of interruptions..." Ridley gestured over Halressan's shoulder. "Look who's heading this way."

Drexious was moving quickly, slipping his lithe shoulders

one way and the other to navigate his way through the bustle, his bronze eyes sharp and alert. "Finally," he said when he reached them. "I've been looking for you everywhere."

Ridley rolled her eyes. "Why do I get the feeling you've landed yourself in some sort of trouble again?"

"Because you have a habit of assuming the worst of people."

"Not all people. Just you."

Drexious snickered. "In any case, you're wrong this time. There's no trouble. Well, no *new* trouble, at least. But I couldn't shake the feeling that I had eyes on me, and I remembered there are still some among the Belt Cabal who might have an old grudge or two they want to settle. So I figured I'd come and find you. What is it you humans like to say...safety in numbers?"

"You made it just in time," Ridley said. "We're going to find Skaile."

Drexious let out a huff of breath. "Skaile? Isn't she in talks with the Belt Cabal? Isn't that who I *just said* I was trying to avoid?"

"Don't worry about it," Halressan said, giving him a nudge. "You might be a lying, thieving bastard, but you're *our* lying, thieving bastard. Anyone who wants a piece of you will have to go through us first."

Drexious narrowed his eyes. "You're in an unnaturally pleasant mood. I'm not sure I want to ask why."

"I figured since we're all likely to die horrible deaths very shortly, I might as well give the whole heroic thing a shot. Not likely to get another chance at it."

"Such a defeatist attitude, my dear hunter," a silky voice said from behind them. "I always thought you had more steel. Or did you lose that along with your precious armour?"

Ridley turned around to find Skaile behind them, a mocking smile playing at the corners of her mouth.

Halressan bristled. "Save it, Skaile. I'm not in the mood."

"Oh, but as it happens, I *am*," Skaile replied, her eyes gleaming. "You see, the three of you owe me now. Not that you didn't before, what with the ship you stole, but your debt to me just increased exponentially."

Ridley's heart leapt. "You got the ships?"

"Of course I got the ships." Skaile snorted. "I told you these pirates were my kind of people. They're fools, but even fools can be made to see what's good for them, with a little persuasion. They're sending out word as we speak. Before the next sleep cycle is over, the biggest combined fleet of pirates, mercs and smugglers the galaxy has ever seen will be heading for Alcruix."

Something loosened in Ridley's chest. They'd done it. They'd got the Rim Belt on side. When she returned to Alcruix, she wouldn't be empty handed—she'd be bringing a fleet with her. Whatever happened next, she'd played her part. She'd *mattered*.

"Thank you," she said. "I mean it. These ships could be the difference between us winning and losing this fight."

"I hope so. It won't be easy to get what I'm due from you if we're all dead." Skaile bared her teeth. "And I will get what I'm due, outlander. You can count on that."

"I'm well aware." Ridley turned to Halressan and Drexious. "We should get back to the ship. Tell Fyra and the Idran-Var what happened and get us ready to go. I'll be right behind you." Ridley waited until they were out of earshot, then turned back to Skaile. "What did it cost you?"

Skaile drew her lips into a smile. "Always so perceptive, aren't you?"

"I've had a lot of practise. Now tell me—what did it cost?"

Skaile looked away, the amusement gone from her face. "Jadera," she said quietly. "It cost me Jadera."

Ridley let out a breath. "Do they know—"

"That the planet is lost? Of course they know. The rumours

arrived on the station before we did. But if we win this war, Jadera will be waiting for somebody to rebuild it. And I agreed to surrender it to the Belt Cabal."

"They believed you?"

"Why shouldn't they? I follow through on my promises as much as my threats. If I went back on this, with all the Belt Cabal faction leaders as witnesses, my reputation would never recover." Skaile shook her head. "If we survive this, the Belt Cabal will have Jadera."

"I'm sorry."

"Sorry? And I thought you were perceptive." Skaile chuckled. "Those fools will find no power on Jadera, because I *gave* them it. They didn't ask for it, they sure as shit didn't take it by force—if they ever set foot in that port, it's only because I allowed them to."

"I'm not sure I understand."

"Then listen closely, outlander, because sooner or later you might find yourself in the same position." Skaile's eyes took on a fervent shine. "There is not a single person in this galaxy capable of wielding power over you if you have nothing you are afraid to lose. Jadera only mattered as long as I wanted it to. I made it what it was, and I took that with me when I left. When the Belt Cabal arrive, all they'll find is a few prefab buildings on a dusty rock. It's only a place, after all. But its power...that belongs to me."

Ridley nodded slowly. "You mean to say you'll start over."

"I already have." Skaile gave her a sidelong glance. "And whether or not you've realised it, you have too."

Her words struck something inside Ridley. Skaile was right. She wasn't the same person she'd been back on New Pallas, or on the *Ranger*, or on Jadera. Starting over was her speciality. Every time she'd left a place behind, it was because she'd survived it.

Ridley had never thought of that as power before. Not until now.

As her feet carried her back towards the docking bay, something lightened in each step. Surfacer, slete, outlander—none of it mattered anymore. She was the sum of all of those things and none of them. She'd existed in places nobody else could. She'd survived in places nobody else could.

All she had to do was survive this one too.

FOURTEEN

Rivus

The worst part about being back on Alcruix was the way it was so utterly Idran-Var. Every step Rivus took through the base was a reminder of how much of an outsider he was, how little he understood them. He heard it in the mechanical tones of their voices. He saw it every time he glimpsed his own reflection in their armour. Whatever it was he was doing here, one thing was clear: he was not one of them.

It had been easier to ignore during the summit. Back then, he thought they were all on the same side. Back then, he thought they were all working towards the same goal. But now, standing opposite an unrepentant Rhendar, Rivus was beginning to wonder why he'd ever believed this alliance could work.

"It is unacceptable," he said again, trying to steady the rage in his voice. "When I agreed to work together for the good of the galaxy, it wasn't an invitation to stage an attack on a Coalition world."

"There was no attack on Pxen," Rhendar replied. "The destruction of the prison was unfortunate, but out of our control. You only have the Bastion's warden to blame for that."

"The warden was following siege protocols to prevent a mass breakout. If you wanted to do this the right way, you'd have come to me. I could have sent a legionnaire with an encrypted warrant for the prisoners."

"Or you could have refused entirely," Rhendar said evenly. "That wasn't a chance I was willing to take."

"So instead you sent two *ilsar* to make your demands? Were you trying to provoke them?"

"I sent two Idran-Var," Rhendar said, his voice taking on an edge. "Both of whom risked their lives to return here with a strike team that might be capable of breaching the Omega Gate."

"And left everyone else to die, by the sounds of it." Rivus glanced at Niole. She was staring blankly ahead, her jaw tight. Serric stood next to her, curling his lip in a derisive sneer that made Rivus want to march across the room and beat him bloody.

"Nobody wanted that to happen," Rhendar said. "If there's blame to be had, it's on me for authorising the mission in the first place. But let's be clear, Supreme Commander—when I agreed to work together for the good of the galaxy, it wasn't with the understanding that the Idran-Var answered to you or anyone else. This fight belongs to all of us. I won't ask your permission to play my part as I see fit."

Rivus turned away, fighting to quell the snarl rising in his throat. He couldn't look at any of them—not Rhendar, not Serric, and certainly not Niole. She was a reminder of all the things he'd lost. Ossa. The legionnaires. Tarvan. *Her.*

After a long, drawn-out breath, he managed to force himself to speak calmly again. "These prisoners from the Bastion...you want to use them to *board* the Omega Gate?"

"You know as well as I do the nature of the enemy we're up against," Rhendar said. "We have no idea if our ships' weapons will be able to damage the external defences. If our only choice is to find a way to shut it down from the inside, we'll need a force capable of fighting through whatever stands in their way."

"Led by one of your Idran-Var, no doubt."

"You have someone else in mind?"

"Actually, I do." Rivus ground his plates together. "Nobody knows the curators and their capabilities better than Alvera Renata. She's been in their mind. She understands them in a way nobody else does. If there's a way to disable the waystations from inside the Omega Gate, she's our best choice at finding it."

For a moment, he thought Rhendar might argue. It was impossible to read any kind of expression behind the grim metal mask that covered his face. But all the Idran-Var war chief did was give an assenting grunt. "A sensible choice. One I'm inclined to agree with." He tilted his head. "Look at that, Supreme Commander. Turns out we can agree on how to get things done."

"This time, at least," Rivus said. "Let's make sure things stay that way, shall we? In the meantime, I'll go find the captain. She'll need to be briefed on the specifics before you leave."

Rhendar nodded. "Meet us in the war room in an hour. We'll be ready to go through the plan of attack."

Rivus felt their eyes on him as he turned and walked stiffly out of the room. Every minute he spent in their presence was like waiting for a trap to spring. Every exchange was a battle he was running out of strength to fight. His only ally in this place was Alvera, and he'd just volunteered her for a suicide mission.

He pressed his claws against the medbay access panel and waited for the door to slide open. Alvera was hunched over a holographic interface, her forehead creased. Next to her, another human lay flat on a medical trolley with several wired nodes stuck to his face. It took Rivus a moment to recognise him as the pilot who'd come to warn him about the terrorist plot on Kaath.

"Is everything all right?" he asked. "Kite told me the mission was a success. I didn't realise—"

"He's fine," Alvera said tersely. "Just checking Ojara didn't leave any other surprises in his cybernetics. I wiped the bug she put in his retinal implants, but I'm not taking any chances this time." She flicked her eyes to the monitor. "The scan is almost finished."

"Does it look clear?"

"Yes, but that's what I thought last time." She tapped in a series of commands over the interface. "All done. Let's bring you back, Kojan."

The gentle whirr of the medbay door sounded from behind him. Rivus turned around to see Kite walk through, carrying a tray of steaming ceramic bulbs. The rich, bitter smell made his stomach grumble. He'd been so wrapped up in debriefs and meetings he'd forgotten to eat.

"Sorry, boss. Didn't realise you'd be dropping by." Kite handed one of the bulbs to Alvera and set another down on the table next to Kojan's bed. "I'd offer you mine, but I added extra halsi flakes and I know how you dachryn are when it comes to a bit of spice. Can't have you stuck in the bathroom all night when we're meant to be saving the galaxy."

Rivus let out a half-hearted growl. "Do I need to remind you who you're speaking to, Merala? I'm not one of your space-jockey grunts you can trade insults with."

"A trade implies you give as good as you get. All you ever do is stand and scowl." Kite grinned and then turned to Kojan, the humour fading from his face. "Shouldn't he be awake by now?"

"He's coming around," Alvera said. "I wanted to bring his cybernetics back online slowly. They've sustained a lot of damage over these last few months."

She brushed her hand under her nose as she spoke, and her fingers came away with small spots of red. She stared at them with a blank, distant expression, then hastily wiped them on the bottom of her shirt and turned back to the monitor.

Before Rivus could say anything, Kojan groaned and slowly pushed himself up on his elbows. The metallic casing that curved around one of his eyebrows blinked with a green light as he stretched his neck from side to side.

He let out a breath. "Did you find anything?"

"Only the bug in your retinal implant."

"So she *was* tracking me." Kojan pushed himself straighter, wincing at the effort. "Damn it. Part of me hoped she was bluffing. Do you know what this means? She was in my head for months, watching my every move, listening to every conversation. She was a step ahead of us the entire time, and I let her win, as always."

"It wasn't your fault. You didn't know."

"I should have." Kojan gave a bitter laugh. "No wonder Shaw found us so easily back on Rellion. If I'd figured this out sooner, he'd never have been able to come after us. Eleion might still be alive." He picked up the ceramic bulb from the table, holding it between his hands. "Did you kill her this time?"

Alvera stilled. She looked the same as she had when she'd stood over Ojara's crumpled body. Her tired, pale features held all of the same helplessness, all of the same guilt.

Eventually, she lowered her head. "She was still alive when I left."

Kojan looked up at her. "And are you satisfied with that?"

"I don't know. Are you?"

"I don't know," he echoed.

Alvera put a hand on his shoulder. Kojan didn't shrug it off, but there was a coolness with which he accepted the gesture that made Rivus uneasy. It was too much like how things had been between him and Tarvan at the end. The chill in the air, the stiff voices and deflected glances. Everywhere he looked, he saw their alliance splintering under its own weight. The worst part was knowing there was nothing he could do but watch it break.

He cleared his throat. "Captain Renata, a word? I have something I need to discuss with you."

Alvera checked the monitor a final time before following him through the sliding doors. Once they were out in the corridor, she released a long, heavy breath and braced herself against the wall.

Rivus tightened his jaw plates. "Are you all right?"

"Tired," she said, closing her eyes. "Just tired." She took another deep breath and snapped her eyes open again, pulling her face into a smoothed-out mask. "What was it you needed?"

Rivus hesitated. "This strike team Rhendar is putting together...it will be made up from the heavy hitters. Sioleans and Idran-Var, mostly."

"You don't trust them."

He flinched at her directness. "We could do with someone who knows the enemy. Someone who might know how to shut down the Omega Gate if they make it that far."

Alvera arched an eyebrow. "Does that mean you trust me?"

"It's worked so far, hasn't it? Even if we've disagreed, we've had each other's backs."

"I suppose you're right." She leaned back against the wall and sighed. "I'll do it. If there is a way to shut down the Omega Gate and stop the curators coming through, they'll have safeguards and defences. My cybernetics might be the only things that can break through."

"Speaking of your cybernetics..." Rivus trailed off. "Something is wrong, isn't it? I've seen the blood, how exhausted you are. Is it the same virus Kojan had? The quickening?"

Alvera shook her head. "Not the quickening. If it was, I

might be able to stop it. This is something worse. I left part of myself behind to escape the hive. Part of me exists within the curator consciousness, and I don't know if the rest of me can survive without it."

"If you're not up to this—"

"I have to be." She rubbed a hand across her eyes. "I should have died on that waystation. Maybe the only way I can fix what's wrong with me is by going back there. Maybe that's the only way to fix everything."

Her expression hardened, her features shifting into something tough and immutable, as if her human-soft flesh had turned to plates of bone. Rivus couldn't help but shiver at the look on her face, more familiar than he wanted to admit. Alvera wasn't a legionnaire. She wasn't Tarvan.

But she was the only damn hope they had left.

———

By the time Rivus found himself back on the *Lancer*, the Idran-Var war council was already a distant memory. The hours passed by in a blur, each melding into the next. Everything else seemed unimportant in the face of what they were about to do.

The ship's command centre felt different than it used to. Larger, in a way, like there was something missing that once occupied the space there. It took Rivus a moment to realise that the thing missing was Tarvan.

A jolt of grief hit him like a blade under his plating. With everything else that was happening, the weight of all the lives he was carrying, there hadn't been time to think about what he had lost. He had pushed it to a corner of his mind where it couldn't hurt him, never considering how painfully it might rush back.

Rivus drew a long breath into his lungs and held it there until he felt he might burst. When he finally let it go, some of the pain escaped with it. He took another breath, then another, until all he felt was the numbness left behind when there was no more grief to hold on to.

"Later, old friend," he murmured. "When there's time. Until then...well, there's no glory in battle."

Only blood, the echo in his memory whispered.

It took all of Rivus's strength not to shiver at the warning.

He turned towards the holographic interface in the middle of the room. According to the readouts, they were on final approach to the space tunnel connecting them to Ossa. Faint gold and green lights tracked the progress they'd made through the Rim Belt, glowing circles marking the points they'd jumped from tunnel to tunnel on their way back to civilisation. Being back in Coalition space was a comfort, even knowing what waited for them. He was going home.

The clang of armoured boots broke Rivus from his thoughts, and he looked up to see Zal make her way into the command centre, a wide grin plastered across her face.

Rivus let out a half-hearted sigh. Having an Idran-Var aboard the flagship of the legionnaire fleet brought a sting of resentment he couldn't entirely get rid of, but the irritation was tempered somewhat by the fact that Zal and her squad had saved his life during the invasion of Ossa. Rivus had come to recognise her shrewd mind and capability for making decisions under pressure behind her eccentric manner.

"Any word from your war chief?" he asked.

"Rhendar has the *Tressel's Vengeance* lined up and ready to move on our signal," Zal replied, bringing up a holographic overlay on her wrist terminal. "The rest of the fleets are waiting in position. We'll have ships coming through every tunnel in the system, all ready to converge on the Omega Gate."

"And the strike team?"

Zal's jaw twitched. "Primed for their drop. They know what they have to do."

Rivus understood the expression on her face all too well, even if it presented differently on her soft, human features. He knew the fear she must have felt. Venya was part of the strike team. So was Niole.

Thinking about her only brought a fresh wave of bitterness. What she'd done at the Bastion was just another reminder that the Niole he knew now was not the same as the Niole he remembered. Or maybe she was exactly who she'd always been, and Rivus simply never had the vision to see it.

The sound of the command centre doors whirring open was a welcome distraction. Rivus looked up to see a dark-skinned human enter the room, followed closely by another pale human and a jarkaath. The three of them seemed out of place among the stiff-spined and swift-footed officers bustling around the room, like they'd intruded somewhere they shouldn't have.

He walked over to them. "You don't look like legionnaires. What are you doing in the command centre?"

The human at the front bristled, the coiled curls on top of her head shaking. "I was *asked* to come here."

"Ah, you're one of Captain Renata's crew?"

The human flinched, but she smoothed her expression into a careful mask of composure. "Ridley Jones. I'm one of the *Ranger's* crew, yes. I'm to link up with Kojan while he's making the drop."

"Good. Take that comms station over there." Rivus turned to the other human and the jarkaath. "What about you two?"

They exchanged a glance, and the jarkaath shrugged. "Unless you need something stolen or shot, I'm not sure how much use we'll be."

"I'm only here because Riddles over there said it would be the place we're least likely to die," the other human added. "Hey, I don't suppose there's a bar on this ship, is there? You'd think with the size of it..."

Rivus suppressed an irritated grumble. "I don't have time to be your tour guide. If you're not here to help, at least stay out of the way." He turned back to Ridley. "I'll get you set up. It won't be much longer until we're ready to move, and I want all of our systems checked before then."

Ridley followed him over to the long, blinking bank of comms consoles. "You think this will work?"

The question was so raw and honest that Rivus didn't know how to answer. "Which part?" he asked. "Getting them close enough to make the drop? Breaching the gate? Figuring out a way to shut it down from the inside?"

"Well, when you put it like that..." Ridley sank into one of the chairs and scanned through the holoscreen feed in front of her. "There's so much that can go wrong, isn't there? Makes you wonder if we stand a chance."

"If you didn't think we had a chance, you wouldn't be here," Rivus said. "None of us would. We're still in this fight, and the entire galaxy knows it. If you need proof, all you have to do is look around."

He tapped his wrist terminal, magnifying the viewport feeds to display the armada gathered around them. Coalition battleships, Idran-Var troop transports, legionnaire fighters. Dachryn bombers and jarkaath stealth ships. Pirate-branded cargo runners and merc frigates. Everywhere he looked, there was another glimmer of light. The burn of engines lit up the darkness like distant stars. It reminded Rivus of what the Coalition was. Why it had held strong for so many millennia. They were stronger together. They always had been.

It was time to let the curators see that.

He nodded to Zal. "Let's do it."

She clapped her hands together and let out a hoot. "Opening a line to the *Tressel's Vengeance*."

The sound of static echoed through the command centre, followed by Rhendar's calm, mechanical voice. "All Idran-Var fleets have checked in and are ready to launch on your signal, *Lancer.*"

"Understood," Rivus replied. "Ridley Jones, any word from the *Ranger?*"

"On final approach to their tunnel now."

"All right, everyone. Get to your stations." Rivus lifted his head. "That ship is our best hope. Our focus is ensuring the *Ranger* gets close enough to make the drop. Once the strike team makes it onto the Omega Gate, we give the curators hell. Until then, I want every available ship covering their run."

He sensed their eyes on him. Not just Zal and Ridley and the others in the room, but the rest of them out there. The people listening on the other end of the open comms channel. The people sitting in the cold hulls of their ships, waiting to move. The people trapped on planets under siege, praying for help to arrive.

"We won't get another shot at this," Rivus continued, his throat constricting. "We're fighting for the future of the entire galaxy, and it all depends on what we do here. Take a moment to breathe. Look at the people around you. Then put it away and get yourself ready. We're about to move."

The soft clunk of Zal's footsteps echoed through his ears as she came to join him at the viewport. Idran-Var or not, it was a strange sort of comfort knowing there was someone next to him who knew as well as he did what was about to come. She'd lost people back on Ossa too. She'd seen the monstrosity that was the Omega Gate. She was like him in more ways than Rivus ever wanted to admit.

Zal looked up at him, the green light from her cybernetic eyegraft blinking gently. "If you were Idran-Var, I'd be saying something like *idra ti'von grat* right about now."

"I'm not Idran-Var."

"I know. Doesn't make me want to say it any less though." Zal cocked her head. "How about this instead?"

She took off her armoured glove and held out her hand, her palm open and honest. It wasn't a dachryn gesture—it wasn't even an Idran-Var gesture, as far as he knew. There was something about the offering that was uniquely human. Maybe that was why she did it. Maybe this was her way of bridging the gap between her people and his.

Rivus reached out with his own claws, wrapping them awkwardly around her fingers and giving her hand a firm shake.

Zal's grin widened. "Look at us getting along. Maybe there's hope for the rest of the galaxy after all."

A low chuckle escaped Rivus's throat. "One step at a time, Scout Captain."

"Fight well, Supreme Commander."

There was no mockery in her voice, just a quiet understanding that passed between them. A tentative show of solidarity as they stood in the face of oblivion—him in his white cloak and Zal in her impenetrable armour. A heartbeat of peace amongst the drums of war.

Rivus turned to the navigation tech standing at attention by the holodisplay. The glow from the lights danced over the young jarkaath's scales, painting her with tunnel points and fleet positions. At Rivus's command, she stepped forward and opened the main comms line to the bridge, where the *Lancer's* pilot was waiting for his orders.

"Hit the tunnel," Rivus said. "We're moving on the Omega Gate."

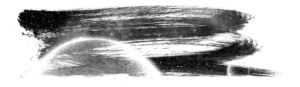

FIFTEEN

Alvera

The tug of acceleration that pulled tight every time the *Ranger* jumped through a space tunnel wasn't something Alvera would ever get used to. Even after the ship had been retrofitted with new inertial dampeners, there was still something about the sensation that left her queasy.

Kojan glanced at her from the pilot's chair. "I told you the dampening fields are more effective mid-ship than up here on the bridge. Shouldn't you be in the hold with the rest of the strike team anyway?"

Alvera shook her head. "Not yet. I want to be here for the approach, make sure everything lines up."

"That's my job," Kojan pointed out.

"I know. And I wouldn't trust anyone else to do it. This isn't a you-thing, flyboy, it's a me-thing. I need to feel a semblance of control again, even if it's just the illusion of it."

Kojan said nothing. His eyes were focused on the nav

display and his hands swiped through holo interfaces faster than she could make sense of. Sitting in that chair, he was one with the *Ranger*, as much a part of it as its engines or hull. It wasn't until now that Alvera realised how much she'd missed, how much time she'd lost.

She pressed the soles of her boots harder against the floor, as if that might stop the shuddering in her legs. "How much longer?"

"Approaching the tunnel exit now. Keep yourself strapped in—we don't know what we'll be coming out to."

The moment the *Ranger* hit normal space again, the acceleration released its hold over Alvera's chest, allowing her ribs to expand and her lungs to swell with deep, gasping breaths. She steadied herself, her head spinning.

"Shit," Kojan said. "You need to see this."

He sent a readout to the feed in front of her chair, and she scanned through the visuals. Thousands of ships. Rail gun fire and plasma cannons streaming across the expanse. Wrecked hulls and engine carcasses littering the void.

"They were ready for us. This place is already a warzone." Kojan shook his head, his face bleak. "We'll never make it to the Omega Gate."

"We have to make it." Alvera opened a comms line to the *Lancer*. "Rivus, are you seeing this?"

His voice sounded more grim than usual, the growl of his vocal cords mingling with the light crackle of static. "Yes," he said. "But it doesn't change anything. You need to get to the Omega Gate. If we have to put ourselves in their crosshairs to cover you, that's what we'll do."

"Understood." Alvera nodded to Kojan. "You heard him. Our only objective is getting to that gate."

"They'll tear us to pieces."

"We have the combined might of the entire galaxy at our

backs. They'll keep the curators off us. As for the rest...all you need to do is what you do best."

The twitch at the corner of Kojan's mouth was so slight she might have imagined it. It wasn't quite a smile, but it was close enough for Alvera to know he was ready for this. He'd been ready ever since the day she'd first shown him the schematics for the *Ranger*. The light in his eyes was dimmer now than it had been back then, the spark of enthusiasm tempered by loss and fear, but his determination hadn't changed. If there was any pilot in the galaxy that could get them to the Omega Gate, it was Kojan Irej.

"Plotting a course," he said, turning back to the nav console. His expression was rigid with concentration, his eyes flitting over the instruments with laser-like focus. "Here we go."

Alvera pressed herself back into her flight chair, bracing herself for the ride. This was the part she hated, the part she couldn't control. Stuck in the belly of a roaring creature made of steel, with only kinetic shields and hull plating between her and the vacuum of space. She couldn't fight what was out there. She could only wait for her own part to come and hope she survived long enough to play it.

"They'll be all over us in seconds," Kojan said. "They know this ship. They know we're the threat."

"What about our backup?"

"The fleets are doing their best to cover us, but there are too many curator ships." Kojan sent another holo readout to her terminal. "You see what's happening out there? For every ship we destroy, another dozen come through the Omega Gate. I don't know what kind of base they've got on the other side of that thing, but they're not running out of reinforcements any time soon."

Alvera closed the readout and pulled up the external feeds, her heart plummeting at the sheer number of curator ships between them and the Omega Gate. They littered the darkness with so many pinpricks of light that they seemed to outnumber the stars. Battleships, cruisers, frigates. It was more than a blockade. It was a self-replenishing armada.

Something rocked the ship violently and she lurched forward, bruising her shoulders on her flight harness. "What was that?"

"Trouble," Kojan said. "That impact blew our shields. A couple more direct hits and we're done for."

"Can you get us out of their target lock?"

"I can try, but it won't last long." Kojan grimaced. "You see their formations, their attack patterns? They're in perfect harmony. They're able to make manoeuvres like they're one ship."

"They might as well be. Shared consciousness, remember? They already know their next move without even thinking it." Alvera frowned, a slow tendril of understanding unfurling in the back of her mind. She was missing something. Something calling to her from the empty parts of her mind that had once been full, once been lived in.

It hit her beneath her ribs, in the place still raw and aching with loss. "No," she breathed. "It's worse than that. They know *our* next move without even thinking it.

"What do you mean?"

"Chase." Her name caught in the back of Alvera's throat. "She was part of the *Ranger*. Traces of her programming still exist here even though she's gone. Not enough to be self-aware, but if the hive managed to absorb them when they took her..." She paused. "That's why we were able to escape the temporal net. The waystations recognise the *Ranger* as a curator ship."

"You're saying they're in our systems?"

"Yes. Chase was part of this ship, and now she's part of their hive. Everything we do is something they've already planned for." Alvera straightened. "Kojan, I need you to kill the *Ranger*."

"What?"

"No questions. Do it now. Comms, engines, navigation—shut it all down."

"But we'll be..." Kojan trailed off, but his hands were already flying across the instruments and switches, powering down systems until there was nothing left but basic life support. He shot her a questioning look, and she nodded once before pressing the helmet release on her exosuit. A moment later, the gentle thrum of the air recyclers ground to a halt.

Alvera brought up her wrist terminal and sent a rushed explanation to the strike team waiting in the hold below. *Everything under control. Suit up and stay put. No comms.*

The quiet was unnerving. It was like the *Ranger* had taken a final breath and died. The bridge was still and lifeless around them. No glow of lights from the console, no clicks or whirrs from the instruments. Alvera's weight had left her body when Kojan shut down the inertial dampeners, and now the only thing that kept her from floating was the safety webbing of her flight harness holding her in place.

She set her exosuit to a short-range, private frequency and motioned for Kojan to do the same. "We don't have much time."

"That's an understatement." His expression was hazy behind the visor of his helmet, but she could still make out the incredulity written across his face. "We're completely exposed. One hit, and they kill us."

"That's what Rivus and the fleets are for," Alvera said, sounding more confident than she felt. "In any case, we don't have a choice. We can't do anything without the curators anticipating it. We need to find a way to take them by surprise."

"I hate the thought of them in the *Ranger's* systems," Kojan said. "It's like they've turned our ship against us."

"Not as long as you're still in that chair." Alvera glanced across at him. "It's not the *Ranger* I'm relying on to get us to that gate. It's you, Kojan."

"How? To keep them out of our systems, we won't be able to

use any comms, any weapons, any navigational assistance. I'd have to fly completely unaided, basic instruments only. It's practically suicide."

"Can you do it?"

Kojan didn't say anything. A faint glow came from the cybernetic implants that curved around his eyebrow and down the side of his jaw. The same cybernetic implants that had nearly killed him, thanks to Ojara. Thanks to *her*. What good was saving his life if she was only going to ask him to throw it away again?

Alvera shook her head. "Kojan, I—"

"I can do it."

If it had been anybody else, she might have asked if they were sure. She might have given them a way out. But one look at the certainty in Kojan's eyes was all Alvera needed. She wouldn't insult him by questioning his confidence, or his abilities. Not Kojan Irej. Not in the *Ranger*.

Kojan turned back to the console. "Life support back online. Inertial dampeners back online. Adjusting for basic navigation only. Ready to fire up the engines and burn for the Omega Gate on your command."

"Do it."

The hull juddered around them as the engines roared back into life. This time, there would be no second chances. This time, the slightest mistake would mean their deaths. Alvera wondered how aware of that Kojan was as he worked the controls, his lips pressed together and perspiration beading around his hairline.

The comms console remained dark and unblinking. Somewhere on the flight deck of the *Lancer*, Rivus would be watching them return from the dead, not knowing what had happened. There was no way of alerting him without alerting the curators. All Alvera could do was trust him to protect them.

"Curator ships on our tail," Kojan said, his voice terse.

"Without our threat detection system, I can't pick them up until they're on top of us. If I bring it back online—"

"No non-essential systems. That's how they're figuring out our every move. Avoid their fire as best you can and keep on course for the gate."

"Anything keeping us from getting shot seems pretty essential to me," Kojan muttered, but he settled back in his chair, his hands tight around the controls. Every few moments his brow twitched, and the *Ranger* lurched beneath them. Alvera wondered how close they were to having a hole blown in the hull every time he pulled them into another evasive manoeuvre. Everything was down to his calculations, his instincts. But not even Kojan could keep this up forever.

"Can't shake this one," he said through gritted teeth. "It's only a matter of time before they line up a clear shot. And without the point defence system..."

"I know."

He clenched his jaw. "Better brace yourself then."

Alvera dug her fingers into the strapping of her harness. The *Ranger* had carried them this far. It only needed to carry them a little further.

"Fighter approaching," Kojan said. "It's heading straight down our throat."

Alvera saw it outside the viewport. A sleek, curved fighter with sharp wings and a pointed nose glinting in the distance. Kojan was right. There was no way out of this now. It had them in its sights. All it had to do was unleash a barrage straight at them and they were done for.

She squeezed her restraints. "Kojan, I wanted to say—"

A flash of cannon fire lit up the viewport. Alvera sucked in a breath, waiting for the inevitable explosion of flame and fuel to take her. The whole ship rattled as she closed her eyes and waited. It was taking longer than she'd expected. It should have been over faster than this.

"Did you see that?" Kojan let out a strangled laugh. "About time that asshole came through for us!"

Alvera snapped open her eyes to see Kojan gesturing at the viewport. A ball of fiery debris burned in the distance, quickly snuffed out by the vacuum of space. Above them, a legionnaire fighter dipped into a series of barrel rolls.

Kojan snorted. "Kitell Merala. Not enough for him to save our asses, he has to get cocky about it too."

Alvera released the breath she'd been holding. Her palms were slick with sweat inside her exosuit, and she tasted bile on her tongue. "I told you to keep all non-essential systems off. How did you read his signature?"

"I didn't. I just know it was him. He's got a certain style." Kojan turned back to the flight controls and pulled up one of the viewport feeds. "We're getting close now. I have a visual on the Omega Gate."

Alvera expanded her fingers over the holographic image to magnify it further. The twisted structure made from the waystations was coiled around a beam of light cutting through the darkness of space. A tunnel that led back to wherever the curators came from. If they shut it down, the curators would have no more reinforcements. It would finally be a fair fight.

"You should get to the airlock," Kojan said. "We won't have much time to line up for the drop."

"Understood." Alvera unfastened the strapping around her shoulders and pushed herself to her feet, grateful the magnetic soles of her grav boots were there to hold her steady. "Once we've launched, don't hang around. Get back on comms and tell Rivus and the rest of the fleets to retreat."

"Retreat?"

"Until we shut down the Omega Gate, there's nothing they can do here except get themselves killed. That tunnel spits out more and more curator ships every minute. If we're to beat them, we need to save our forces."

Kojan shook his head. "I don't like the thought of leaving you there with no way out if things go to hell."

"This is what we signed up for. All of us know the risks. Shutting down that gate is the only thing that matters." Alvera paused at the threshold of the bridge. "You're a good pilot, Kojan. You deserved a better captain. Whatever happens next, I wanted you to know that. Stay safe out there."

A tremor danced along the edge of his jaw. "Same goes for you."

Alvera made her way towards the cargo hold, the magnets of her grav boots clinking with each step. The *Ranger* felt different around her with its empty seats and emergency lighting. There had been a time this ship made her dream of the future that was waiting for them. Now, all she could think about when she walked through its quiet corridors was how much they'd lost.

The rest of the strike team was waiting for her in the hold, their gazes expectant and questioning. The dim lights illuminated them all in a red glow, casting shadows across the walls. A group of Idran-Var. Four pale-skinned sioleans. Ridley's crime lord friend from Jadera. They were all here for the same purpose. They would stop the monstrosity that was the Omega Gate, no matter the cost. No matter the sacrifice.

Pain shot through Alvera's chest, but she pushed it away and readied herself at the airlock door. As soon as Kojan gave the signal, they'd open the door and launch into the abyss. Towards the Omega Gate. Towards whatever was waiting for them there.

Her auditory implant gave a soft chime, and the flashing on her wrist terminal turned from red to green.

"All right," she said, lifting her head. "Time to go."

SIXTEEN

NIOLE

Niole's heartbeat echoed in her ears as the airlock doors in front of her parted. She couldn't move. The thought of throwing herself forward was enough to flood her legs with fear.

Then she took a breath, and jumped.

Her limbs lost all their weight as she hurtled through the vacuum. She was an insignificant fleck of matter, ready to be lost if she missed her landing.

Ahead of her, she made out a faint glint of armour. Alvera Renata was like a bullet unleashed, her legs tucked together and her arms stiff by her sides as she shot towards the Omega Gate. Every few seconds, a puff of gas released from the microthrusters in her suit as she adjusted course.

The Omega Gate loomed in front of them, impossibly close now. The beam erupting from its centre was so bright that

Niole didn't dare look directly at it. More and more curator ships appeared every minute, flooding into the darkness.

"On my mark." Alvera's voice came through the comms system in Niole's helmet, strained. "Last thing any of us wants to do is overshoot the waystation rings and go headfirst into that beam."

Niole focused her eyes on the gate's huge, curved arms rushing to meet them. Her helmet's display amplified her vision until she could see each rivet along the metal, each seam where the plates joined.

"Landing targets marked," Alvera said through her ear. "Making final approach."

A green holodisplay flickered into life across Niole's visor, guiding her towards the zone Alvera had pinpointed. It was close now—all she had to do was keep her thrusters in check and get ready to make contact.

Alvera swung her legs around from behind her and hit the hull with the soles of her boots, the magnets locking into place with a blinking light. Niole followed suit, bracing herself for the impact. A shockwave rippled through her knees as she slammed into the surface of the gate. The pull of her feet against the hull was a comfort she never knew she needed. A reminder there was something anchoring her to safety, holding her back from the void.

Niole turned around to see the rest of the strike team arrive, all of them stiffening as their boots snapped and took hold. She spotted the familiar silhouette of Venya's huge, hulking frame and the diagonal glow from Serric's visor, and allowed herself to release the air from her lungs. The first part was over. They'd made it.

"Those of you who can flare are up next." Alvera glanced between them through her helmet's transparent visor. "I need you to tear us a way through. Once you've breached the outer—"

A burst of red lit up the darkness and something hit Niole's chest as a violent blast of energy threw her backwards. She barely had time to register the click of her boots as the magnets released, sending her tumbling off the surface of the gate.

Before she had time to scream, Serric's hand wrapped around her wrist, as tight as a vice. He hauled her back in, only releasing his grip after her boots had once again secured themselves to the metal underfoot.

Serric spun around. "What the hell was that?"

The tall, red-skinned siolean who'd been introduced as Skaile gave a withering snort and gestured to the hole at her feet. "She asked for a flare, she got a flare."

Niole looked down. The metal had crumpled in on itself in places and disintegrated in others. Skaile had ripped it apart as easily as if it had been made of paper.

Alvera shot Skaile a hard look but said nothing as she lowered herself through the hole and disappeared below. After a moment, the comms line crackled in Niole's ear. "We have a way in. According to my readouts, we've cut into an access tunnel that will give us a route into the main part of the gate. It's a tight fit, but we should be able to make it."

Venya grunted. "Tight for a human? Someone better stay behind me in case I need a push."

One by one they slipped through the opening, edging past the exposed cables that had been left in the wake of Skaile's flare. Niole moved cautiously across uneven floor panels and around fallen joists, the light from her helmet torch illuminating the tunnel. After a while, the shadows gave way to an artificial glow up ahead.

"Interior airlock system," Alvera announced over the comms line. "This will bring us out into one of the main sections. From there, we'll be able to navigate our way around more easily."

A faint hiss echoed around the tunnel as the doors opened.

Niole followed Venya through, stepping into a large corridor with a wide walkway and curved ceiling. Floor-level lighting faded into the distance, giving an eerie glow to the gloom surrounding them. Dust clung to the walls, but there didn't seem to be any structural damage. The place was abandoned, but it hadn't been left to rot. Something, or someone, had kept it alive.

Alvera tapped her wrist terminal and swiped through a number of feeds, the glow bouncing off the polymer of her visor. Then she retracted her helmet. The joints of her suit whirred gently as they folded back in on themselves, revealing her tired, pale face.

"Essential systems are still online," she said, her voice echoing off the walls. "Oxygen levels are stable. My guess is we're not the only ones on this gate. Be prepared to meet resistance."

"That's what we're here for, isn't it?" Skaile removed her own helmet, shaking her long red headtails loose. A nasty gouge ran down one of them, so deep it was a wonder it hadn't severed it.

"We're here to find a way to disable the gate and shut down the tunnel," Alvera said, her voice taking on a hard edge. "If there's an opportunity for us to do that without getting ourselves tangled up in a fight, we'll take it." She narrowed her eyes. "And if you pull any more shit like you did back there, you'll be on your own. If you can't listen to—"

"I didn't come here to listen," Skaile snapped. "I came here to kill the things that took my planet from me. You think I'm going to wait around for an *order* from you, human? That's not how I operate. I see a problem, I remove it. Permanently."

Before Alvera could say anything, Serric stormed forward, his flare shimmering around his armour. "You want to talk about problems?" he said, his voice like ice. "You almost got

Niole killed with your little stunt up there. As far as I'm concerned, the only problem that needs removing is you."

Skaile's grin widened. "You want to try, Idran-Var? Don't make the mistake of assuming that armour of yours will save you."

The corridor crackled with the swirling of their flares, the tension so thick Niole feared it might burst loose. The stirrings of her own flare surged across her skin, begging to rush free. She didn't want to think about what might happen if she released it.

Alvera stepped between them, the lines on her face deepening. "Enough," she said. "We don't have time for this. If you two want to stay here and kill each other, that's up to you. The rest of us will do what we came here to do. If you want to come with us, then fall in line. If not, the least you can do is stay the fuck out of our way."

She motioned to the rest of them with a jerk of her head and made off down the corridor, the click of her boots sharp on the floor. After a moment, Jasvan and the other *ilsar* from the Bastion followed her.

"Serric," Niole said quietly, putting a hand on his arm. "This isn't worth it. Save your anger for the curators."

Serric didn't say anything. The blue-green of his flare still swirled around him as he stared at Skaile, his expression indecipherable under his helmet.

Across the corridor, Skaile tilted her head. "The human captain has more spine than I gave her credit for. There aren't many people in this galaxy who'd put themselves between two sioleans ready to flare. I'm trying to decide whether that makes her brave or stupid."

"I'm not a siolean," Serric said. "I'm Idran-Var. You'd do well to remember that the next time you put one of my people in danger." He stood stiff and unmoving, his flare rippling in the air between them. Then he let out a breath, the sound crackling through his helmet. "Whether the human is brave or stupid, she's right. We came here to stop the curators. That's the only fight worth my time."

Skaile drew her mouth into a tight-lipped smile. "Wise decision. But if you ever change your mind, you'll find me more than willing to accommodate you." She turned away, leaving trails of her flare behind her like a red mist as she followed Alvera and the other *ilsar* down the corridor.

Venya stared after her, then holstered the rifle she'd been pointing at Skaile. "I'm no expert on sioleans, but I couldn't tell if she was threatening you or flirting with you there, Squad Leader."

"Move out, *jal-var*," Serric said curtly.

Venya made a noise from inside her helmet that might have been a cough or a snort of laughter, then motioned for the rest of the squad to join her as she trudged off.

After the echoes of their clanging footsteps faded into nothing, Serric pulled off his helmet. His brow ridge was set in a stony frown, and a familiar twitch of anger danced along his jaw.

"Serric," Niole began. "I—"

"She could have killed you," he said, his voice strangely hollow outside the filters of his helmet. "Before that, it was the warden back at the Bastion. Before that, it was Tarvan. There was a time not so long ago when that wouldn't have mattered to me. But things have changed, and I'm not sure it's for the better."

Niole's stomach knotted. "What do you mean?"

"We both know what happens when we fight, when we resist. Our fellow warriors die. Our friends die. It's something we accept as Idran-Var. Or at least, we're meant to." Serric shook his head. "Niole, I wanted to tear her apart for even coming close to hurting you. If I hadn't managed to grab you before..." He scowled. "I might have brought this whole gate down around me, mission be damned. That's not the mark of an Idran-Var. It's the mark of an *ilsar*."

"It's the mark of someone who cares about his squad. If it had been Venya—"

"It's not the same." Serric's flare surged again, fierce and insistent, and Niole's rose to meet it without hesitation. The air pulsed between them like they were pressed against each other skin to skin instead of separated by armour. Heat spread through her headtails, filling her with an ache for something she'd never known she was missing.

When he let go, her heart was racing. "You don't have to worry about me," she murmured. "I'm capable of taking care of myself."

Serric looked away, his features twisted with an emotion Niole couldn't place. All she wanted to do was reach out and touch him, to feel his flare leap to meet hers.

Serric placed his helmet back over his head, securing the seals in place around his neck. After a moment, he turned back to her, his expression once again hidden behind his mask. "This isn't about what you're capable of, Niole. It's about me doing something I won't be able to walk away from."

The shiver of energy across her skin faded to numbness as he withdrew from her. His flare slipped out of reach, retreating behind a barrier she couldn't see, leaving her fumbling after something that was no longer there. She hadn't expected it to sting so much, to *ache* so much. She'd spent so long pulling away from him, shirking back from the stirring he always managed to provoke in her. Now he was the one running.

He was right. Everything *had* changed.

Serric let out a long sigh. "All we can focus on now is shutting down this gate. If we fail here, nothing else will matter anyway. Whatever this is, we'll figure out a way to deal with it later."

Niole swallowed the hard lump in her throat. "Understood."

If Serric heard the stiffness in her voice, he did nothing to show it. He turned on his heel and marched after Alvera and the others, his boots clicking with each brisk stride.

Niole hurried to keep pace with him. Navigating the stretching corridors and criss-cross tunnels that made up the entrails of the gate was like walking blindly into a trap. It was all too easy to imagine the curators stalking their footsteps, waiting for their chance to strike. It was like the walls themselves were watching them, following their movements from the dust-coated ventilation grates.

Ahead of them, Alvera led the way. The dim blue glow of the floor-level lighting caught the edges of her face, casting her features in a ghostly sheen. There was a weight to her brow that reminded her of Rivus, but Niole pushed that thought away as quickly as it came. She already had too much to worry about without dredging up that wound.

After a while, Alvera came to a halt and pulled up her wrist terminal. "We're at one of the control stations."

Niole's heart leapt. "Can you disable the tunnel from here?"

"I don't know. Each individual waystation had a control station of its own. We might need to initiate shutdown across all four of them." She pointed at the doors. "In any case, let's start with this one."

The control room was nothing remarkable, just a small, windowless chamber buzzing with the noise of the generators lining its walls. In the centre of the room was a console with a holoprojection suspended above it. Niole recognised the curved arms of the waystations, twisted together to form the Omega Gate. A single red light blinked from deep inside one of the sections, so faint she could barely see it.

"That's where we are," she said. "We're lucky we landed close to one of the control stations. Each one of these arms is kilometres long. If we need to get to the rest of them, this isn't going to be over any time soon."

"One thing at a time," Alvera said, positioning herself in front of the console. "First, let's see if my cybernetics still have it in them to give these bastards a fight."

She bowed her head and started working on the console. The strain was clear across her face—the vein pulsing in one of her temples, the red webs spreading in the whites of her eyes, the tremor dancing along the edge of her jaw. A trickle of blood ran from one of her ears, and her skin turned ashen as she hunched over the console.

"I'm in," she managed, her voice thin and rasping. "Just need to..."

A low groan reverberated around the room as the generators powered down. A moment later, the emergency lighting flickered and died, plunging them into darkness.

Niole's head split open with the agony of a million screams. She dropped to her knees, pressing her hands against the sides of her helmet. She couldn't keep it out. It was like something had burrowed its way into her head and was clawing at her skull to break free. It roared in her ears and sent pain shooting through her synapses until she could no longer hold herself upright.

Across the room, the console exploded in a shower of sparks, sending Alvera flying backwards until she hit the floor with a crack. The others were falling too, clutching their heads as they collapsed. The pressure in Niole's head raged and swelled, threatening to burst.

Then it all disappeared.

———

The stiffness in Niole's limbs told her she'd been out for a while. Her head was thick with fog, still buzzing with the echoes of her own screams. It was distant now, like a dream already fading. But the whispers lingered, soft and hushed at the base of her skull.

Muffled voices reached her ears as she rolled over and strained her eyes. Everything was a blur. She could only make out the hazy shapes of the others around her.

Something tightened around her shoulder, and she flinched.

Kill them.

The thought was like a bolt of electricity through her brain, departing as quickly as it came.

"Just me." Serric's voice was strained. "Can you stand?"

Niole allowed him to help her to her feet, trying to ignore the way his hand tightened around her waist as she swayed on her trembling legs. "What happened?"

Serric jerked his head across the room. "I think we'd all like to know the answer to that."

Alvera's face was pale and sickly as she looked back at them, a shadow behind her eyes. The sight of her filled Niole with a weak rage she couldn't understand. Everything felt wrong. Even Serric's steadying hand was an unwelcome weight, and it took all of her control not to jerk away from him.

Alvera looked between them all. "If the curators didn't know we were here already, they do now," she said grimly. "Getting to the rest of the control centres just got a lot harder."

"The rest of them?" Skaile stepped forward, her red skin paling in disbelief. "You're telling me this didn't work?"

"It's as I suspected. There are four waystations powering that beam. Four control centres. I managed to shut this one down, but—"

"But what, exactly?" Skaile's eyes glinted dangerously. "You set something off. Something that messed with our heads. If you think I'm going to let you drag us around these waystations, pressing buttons until you fry all our brains—"

"You'll do what?" The venomous edge to Serric's voice startled Niole, and she quietly reached for her flare. "It's not like any of us can walk away from this now. We don't have a way off this gate."

"Because of *her*." Skaile rounded on Alvera. "You've led us all to our deaths, and for what? A problem you and your outlander friends created in the first place." She curled her fist, and a red glimmer rose from her armour. "I've had enough. I came here for the chance to kill something. If I can't have the curators, I guess I'll make do with you."

The air sizzled, but the burst of energy that lit up the room was blue-green in colour, not red.

Skaile flew back, hitting the wall with a sickening thud. Her face contorted into a snarl as Serric held her with his flare. Her throat bulged as she writhed and fought to free herself, but Serric's grip only grew tighter.

"That's enough," Niole said, reaching for his arm. "We can't afford to—"

Serric spun around and sent a burst of his flare straight at her. Niole barely had time to register the air leaving her lungs as she flew back and landed hard on the floor.

For a moment, there was only confusion. Then it was gone, and she pushed herself back to her feet, rage thickening her throat as she called her flare close to her skin.

She let it loose, sending a crushing wave straight at Serric. The whispers at the back of her skull hissed as he fell to his knees. Not even Idran-Var armour was enough to keep her out. She would force her way through the metal and into his skin, into every blood vessel and synapse and piece of tissue, ready to tear it all apart and—

Gunfire echoed off one of the walls and Niole ducked down, releasing her hold on Serric. When she raised her head, Venya was standing stiff and square-shouldered, her plasma rifle pointed straight at her.

Before Niole could summon another flare, Venya whirled to

one of the sioleans from the Bastion and fired a barrage of plasma bolts into the middle of his head. The siolean fell to the floor, his helmet riddled with scorch marks and sizzling flesh.

Then Niole saw Alvera. The whispers filled her head with a pleasant buzzing that drowned out everything else. She felt the surge of Serric's flare as he and Skaile traded violent blows. She smelled smoke and burning plasma from Venya's wild flurry of shots. None of it mattered. All she cared about was crushing the human captain in the grip of her flare.

Niole stepped forward, but something jolted through her stomach, sending her flying. Her lungs squeezed themselves free of air. Her limbs burned like they were on fire. She gritted her teeth against the pressure on her bones, but she couldn't fight it.

Her eyes fell on Jasvan, standing in the middle of the room with his arms wide. A pulsing white barrier shimmered around his exosuit, expanding further and further until it filled the entire room. Serric was caught in it like she was. So were Skaile and Venya. Another one of the Bastion sioleans was lying on the floor, his body torn and crumpled, his blood splattering the wall behind him.

The only one unaffected was Alvera. She hobbled into the middle of the room and clutched a hand to her forehead like she was trying to hold the pieces of herself together. A pained grimace twisted her lips, and blood dripped from her nose and ears.

Enough. The voice was Alvera's, but not as Niole had ever heard it before. It made the whispers rise up in fury, and for the first time since reaching the control station, the fog in her brain lifted. Something had a hold of her. Something had burrowed its way into the inner workings of her mind and pushed her out.

It's the curators, Alvera said, her voice cutting through the confusion in Niole's head. *They're infecting your cybernetics, trying to absorb you into their hive mind. You need to fight them.*

The whispers rustled furiously at the base of Niole's skull, their outrage leaving claw marks on the inside of her head as Alvera's words pushed them back.

Niole let the remnants of her flare drift free from her burning skin and locked eyes with Jasvan. "You can let me go. I know who I am again. For now, at least."

Jasvan didn't say anything in reply, but the pressure around her chest loosened and faded away. Her lungs were raw and aching, her head pounding. But the pain wasn't the worst part —it was knowing that the whispers were still lingering there, waiting to creep back in.

One by one, the others were freed from the shimmering white bonds of Jasvan's flare. Skaile dropped to the floor, dazed and bloodied, a severed headtail clutched between her red fingers. Serric stood stiff and silent as he surveyed the carnage that had unfolded. Venya looked down at the plasma rifle in her claws, the barrel still steaming. Then she turned her huge, heavy head to the dead sioleans on the ground. "I did that," she said, her voice low and gravelly. "I don't understand why."

"It's the curators," Alvera repeated. Her voice was different now that it was no longer in their heads. Just as sharp, but thinner too, like it had been honed to the point of breaking. "I should have expected this. What need do they have for defences when they can turn our own minds against us?"

"You coped fine," Serric said.

"I've had practise. But every time I try to hold them off, they kill me a little bit more." She wiped the arm of her exosuit across her bloodied nose, then turned to Jasvan. "What I can't understand is how he was able to shut them out when the rest of you couldn't."

"He doesn't have cybernetics," Niole said. "Not even a translator. They ripped everything out of him when they imprisoned him in the Bastion."

Alvera arched an eyebrow. "Lucky for us that they did, otherwise we'd all be dead."

Niole shuddered. "What do we do now? I still feel those... things. I don't know how long any of us can hold them off for."

"You can't. You have to leave."

Skaile gave a weak snort. "That's the first thing anyone's said that I agree with," she said, her voice rasping. "Dying for a lost cause isn't what I signed up for."

"We all knew the risks," Niole said. "The entire galaxy is depending on us. If we give up now—"

"Who said anything about giving up?" Alvera crossed her arms. "All I said was that you need to leave. None of you can help me now. If I'm to shut down those other control centres, I need to do it alone. Once you get back outside, your cybernetics should be safe from the curators' signal. Call the fleet for pickup. Give yourselves a chance to fight again."

Skaile was the first to leave, limping out the door still clutching her severed headtail in one hand, dripping angry splotches of blood in her wake. Venya followed, her footsteps stiff and wooden, her claws shaking around the still-smouldering plasma rifle.

Niole drew a breath as Serric crossed the room and put a hand on her shoulder.

"Are you all right?" he asked gruffly. "I didn't mean to—"

"I know. Neither did I."

Serric gestured towards the door. "Let's go, before it's too late. Jasvan, are you coming?"

"No." The big siolean's expression was impassive across his eerie white skin. He stood still and thick-shouldered, unfazed by the tension as they all turned their gazes towards him.

"No?" Niole repeated.

He shrugged. "I might not have a translator to pick up the

finer details, but I understand enough. I understand this human needs to survive. I understand I'm the only one who isn't affected by this place." He glanced at Serric. "I understand this is the only reason you broke me out of the Bastion."

Serric winced. "That doesn't matter now. Nobody is forcing you to stay."

"Nobody could, even if they wanted to." Jasvan grunted. "This is my choice. I always thought I would die down in that prison. Never asked for a second chance. Never considered what I'd do if I got one. This seems like a good way to use it."

Niole shook her head. "But—"

"We need to go." Serric's voice was low and urgent. "This is his choice, Niole. He can still make a difference here. Our fight will come soon enough."

She nodded, unable to speak.

Serric started towards the doors, pausing to turn his head back one final time. "*Idra ti gratar*, both of you. You fought well."

A grim smile unfurled across Alvera's face. "We're not done fighting yet."

Every step Niole took was weighted in lead. The echo of her boots resounded in her ears. She was running again, like she always did. It didn't matter that it made sense. It didn't matter that it might be the only way to fight another day. All that mattered was the fear returning. The fear of never getting far enough. The fear of getting caught. It hollowed out a space in her chest and spread its ice-cold tendrils there until she could barely move.

She was running. They all were. And if Alvera failed, Niole couldn't see a way for any of them to stop.

SEVENTEEN

KOJAN

K ojan stepped out of the *Ranger* to the ear-splitting pitch of sirens. The *Lancer's* forward hangar was in chaos as he made his way down the access ramp—fighters taking off as quickly as they were docking, flight crew and mechanics rushing around, frantic messages blaring out over the intercom.

He jumped into one of the ship's express tramways headed to the operations centre. The last thing he'd heard before docking with the *Lancer* was Rivus ordering all fleets to pull back. Since then, there had been radio silence. Maybe the Supreme Commander could give him some answers.

The sirens still blared as Kojan jumped off the tram and made his way through the pristine white corridors of the command deck. By the time he reached the ops centre, his heart was hammering. He barely had time to catch his breath before he was face to face with the towering presence of Rivus Itair.

"Good, you're here," Rivus said, grinding his plates. "We got word that another temporal net has been triggered around the perimeter of the Omega Gate."

Panic ripped through Kojan's chest. "The strike team?"

"We don't know. It wasn't the strike team who contacted us. Their comms are still down. Most likely they're deep within the gate now, unable to reach us."

"Then who..." Kojan trailed off as Rivus brought up a vidlink. There, flickering in front of him with a look of wry resignation across his purple skin, was Kitell Merala.

"Who else?" Kite said, but the forced humour in his voice didn't match his eyes. "You know me, always the last to leave the party. My squad made it out in time, but I got caught by the temporal net. Now I'm stranded here waiting for the curators to find me and pick me off."

"The net doesn't affect the curator ships?" Kojan asked, his mouth dry.

"Apparently not," Kite said. "I've killed my engines, trying to play dead, but it's only a matter of time."

"There must be something we can do."

"There's not." Kite's voice was heavy. "I'm dropping comms now, going dark. It's a long shot, but maybe they'll overlook me. If not..." He sighed and saluted Rivus. "It's been an honour serving with you, Supreme Commander."

Rivus grunted. "Now's the time you choose to start using formalities?"

"As good a time as any, I figure." Kite glanced at Kojan. "Guess we'll never get that showdown after all, human. It's a shame—I'd have enjoyed teaching you a thing or two."

Kojan forced a laugh loose from his throat. "The things you'll do to avoid losing, huh?"

The ghost of a smile spread across Kite's features. Then it wavered, and it was gone.

Rivus stared at the empty spot where the projection had

been, his plates shifting as he clenched and unclenched his jaw. Dachryn wore their grief differently to humans, but these past few weeks had given Kojan more than enough practise when it came to interpreting. Each of them had lost something. Each of them had learned to carry that pain in their own way.

"The *Ranger*," he said suddenly, straightening his spine. "It escaped a temporal net once before. I can fly in, grab Kite, and fly back out. It won't be easy, especially if they've still got fighters swarming around, but I can—"

"No," Rivus said, his voice strained. "We can't risk you or your ship rescuing a single fighter. If the *Ranger* is our only way to breach the temporal net, it may also be the only way to get us back to the Omega Gate if the strike team fails. We need to give ourselves a way to destroy that thing."

Kojan blanched. "So we abandon Kite? I thought he was your friend."

"He is. Perhaps the only friend I have left in this galaxy." Rivus's eyes were bright with anguish. "I know what I'm sacrificing. If there was another way, I'd take it. But I can't throw away the galaxy's only lifeline on one person, no matter how much they may mean to me."

"You can't be serious." Kojan looked around the room for support. The Idran-Var captain with the cybernetic eyegraft grimaced and turned to the viewport. Ridley glanced over from her seat at the comms station, her features pained and sympathetic, but she said nothing either. The room was quiet with unspoken grief for a decision nobody wanted to make.

Kojan couldn't bear the burden of that kind of responsibility. He couldn't shoulder the weight of billions of lives like Rivus could, like Alvera could. But a single life...that was something he could carry. That was something he could save.

He tapped his wrist terminal and sent a launch notice to the hangar. "With all due respect, Supreme Commander, I don't fall under your chain of command. If Alvera can't be contacted, then responsibility for the *Ranger* falls to me. And I'm going to get Kite."

Rivus glared at him. "Did you hear nothing I said? We can't risk it."

"Are you going to detain me? Lock down the hangar? Shoot down the one ship that might give us a fighting chance against the curators?" When Rivus didn't answer, Kojan snorted. "I didn't think so. I'm taking the *Ranger*, whether you like it or not. If you have a problem with it, you can deal with me when I get back."

Rivus's bone-plated expression was as stony as ever. Then something in his hard features broke. "I hope you're half as good a pilot as you think you are," he said gruffly. "You'll need to be if you plan on getting back here in one piece."

"More than half. If there's one thing I was put in this galaxy to do, Supreme Commander, it's fly."

"Kite certainly seemed to think so, and I know how difficult he is to impress." Rivus's jaw plates twitched faintly. If Kojan didn't know better, he might have thought it was a smile. "Bring him home. Chain of command or not, that *is* an order."

———

Back in the hangar, a small crowd had gathered around the *Ranger*. Kojan navigated his way around sprawling fuel lines and automated cargo skiffs until he got close enough to recognise Cyren's lean shoulders and mottled scales.

She hissed gently as he approached, her yellow eyes gleaming. "Glad we caught you before you rushed off again. It's good to see you."

"Likewise. How is the manufacturing going back on Kaath?"

"Better than we could have hoped, thanks to you." Her throat thrummed. "Production lines are in full swing, and we're fitting more and more iskaath with trauma regulators each day.

Now all we need is somewhere to put them. Lucky for me, I have an idea."

"What do you mean?"

Cyren gestured to the group behind her. "This is my nest's finest selection of mechanics, medics and techs. Not to mention a couple of logistics officers, and we might even have a chef in there, too." She made a show of craning her long neck around. "All of them good people. All of them looking for good work."

Kojan nodded. "Rivus will be happy to hear it. We could use some—"

Cyren cut him off with a gentle snicker. "We didn't come here for the Supreme Commander, Kojan. We came here for you."

"For me?" Warmth flushed his cheeks. "What are you talking about?"

Cyren motioned towards the *Ranger*. "Eleion told me what that ship meant to you, what it meant to your people. It was a symbol of hope—a promise of a new future out there waiting for you. We iskaath understand that better than anyone. That kind of ship deserves a full crew, not just a pilot. No matter how capable he is." Her eyes twinkled. "I know we won't be able to replace the people you've lost, but—"

Kojan didn't let her finish. He did the only thing he could think to do and threw his arms around her.

Cyren patted his back with her claws. "I'll take that as a yes."

Kojan pulled back, his cheeks burning. "It will be good to have you aboard. You're right—the *Ranger* deserves a full crew. It's been empty for far too long."

Someone behind him cleared their throat. "We getting a fucking move on then? I hear we've got a legionnaire to rescue."

Kojan spun around and met the amused grin of Maxim ras Arbor. He ambled up in his modified power armour, the casing gleaming under the hangar lights.

Sem stood next to him, a sombre expression on his face. "I know what it's like to be trapped in a temporal net," he said quietly. "And I'm still a Coalition soldier. If you're heading out to save Merala, count me in."

Kojan eyed Max. "And you?"

Max shrugged. "Figure if I keep playing the hero, someone might start paying me. It's not like there's credits coming from anywhere else."

A sharp laugh tore from Kojan's throat. The unexpected company filled him with a belonging he'd been missing ever since he lost Eleion. The sight of them all gathered at the foot of the *Ranger's* access ramp, ready to fill the places that had been empty for so long, was enough to bring the prickle of tears to the back of his eyes.

He looked up at the *Ranger*. *A symbol of hope*, Cyren had said.

"All right," he said. "Let's fly."

———

Sometimes it was easy to forget how vast space was, how lonely a single ship could be. They'd left the *Lancer* far behind, the ship unable to follow them across the perimeter of the temporal net. If things went wrong, they were on their own.

The hum of instruments around the bridge faded as Kojan shut down one non-essential system after another. As risky as it was, Alvera's plan had worked last time. He couldn't take any chances when it came to the curators.

He waited for the silence to seep in, but there was a heartbeat to the *Ranger* that hadn't been there before. It resonated in the clanging of boots against the metal floor, the soft hiss of iskaath chatter carried through the vents from the deck below.

He had a crew again. He had a place. None of them were on their own.

The gentle clack of bare claws underfoot tore him from his thoughts. Cyren slid into the co-pilot's seat, stretching her legs like Eleion used to.

Kojan smiled. "She always complained the chair wasn't built with an iskaath tail in mind."

"She wasn't wrong." Cyren snickered and eyed the lifeless instruments. "How do you expect to reach Kite's position if you don't have all your navigational data?"

"It's all in here." Kojan tapped the side of his head. "I downloaded his location into my cybernetics. I may not be able to link up with the *Ranger's* systems, but I can get us there."

The glowing projections of flight vectors and nav points streamed from his retinal implants like a faint overlay on top of the real world. His cybernetics didn't have access to the *Ranger's* real-time data with the systems powered down, but the information was enough for him to point the ship towards Kite's last recorded location. They weren't far out now. All he had to do was reach Kite before the curators did.

"Okay, Cyren, make sure you're buckled up. I'm going to take us—shit!"

Something rocked the back of the ship and the emergency diagnostic feed lit up with a warning light, pointing to an electrical fire two decks below.

"We got their attention," Cyren said.

"Took them long enough. Guess we're not as easy to track when they can't use our own systems to spy on us." Kojan adjusted the controls. "Looks like most of their heavy hitters fell back to the Omega Gate when the temporal net went up. These fighters must be on patrol. I'll do my best to keep us out of their fire."

Cyren hissed. "You call that keeping us out of their fire?"

"As long as our engines are still running, we're winning."

The words left Kojan's mouth with more bravado than he felt. All around them were the drifting wrecks of ships torn apart by the curator fleet. The splintered hull of a huge dreadnought floated overhead. No lights illuminated its empty viewports, no fuel blazed from its dead engines. It just hung there, suspended lifelessly in the temporal net.

Kojan sent the *Ranger* into a steep dive through the dreadnought's hollowed-out wreckage, banking to avoid the struts and floating pieces of hull blocking his way. The curator fighter followed, sending a flurry of cannon fire after them.

The rear of the ship rocked again, and Kojan slammed the controls forward with as much force as he could muster. The engines below him roared. The wreckage was closing in around him. The slightest lapse in concentration could send them spiralling. One errant twitch of his fingers could turn them into a ball of flame.

Kojan jerked on the controls to bring the ship around in a turn so sharp it ripped the air from his lungs. Adrenaline surged through him. Across the bridge, Cyren let out a wheezing gasp. Then they were gone, free from the wreck, shooting forward with only the expanse of space in front of them once more.

Kojan whirled the ship back around. Every breath burned his chest as he waited. Then the viewport lit up with a flash of blue, and the tightness across his ribs loosened. The curator fighter following them was gone, swallowed up in the explosion inside the belly of the dreadnought. It was over, at least for now.

He refocused his retinal implants on the navigation overlay. "We're almost at Kite's position. According to Rivus's data, his ship should be a little way past the debris field."

Kojan pushed on the controls again, easing the *Ranger* forward. The scattered remains of crippled ships thinned out, returning them to the vast openness of space.

Then Kojan saw it: a lone legionnaire fighter in the distance, swallowed by the dark. It looked so small out there, so exposed. If there was any glow coming from the inside of the cockpit, it was too faint for him to see.

Cyren glanced at him, the spindles on her neck quivering. "Is that your friend?"

Kojan nodded, his lips pressed together in a grim line. Kite's fighter still looked intact, but that was far from a guarantee he was alive. The curators might have breached the hull and left him choking in the vacuum, or riddled the cockpit with spray from their rapid-fire cannons. Until they got closer, there was no way of knowing.

"Taking us in," he said, his voice hoarse. "Send a message to your rescue team down in the hold and tell them—shit, no, no, no!"

Another trio of curator fighters appeared through the viewport, flashing past like three gleaming bullets.

Panic seized Kojan's chest. They didn't care about the *Ranger*. They were heading straight ahead, straight for Kite's crippled fighter.

There was no time to do anything else. No choice.

"Bringing weapons systems back online," he said, tapping the sequence into the console.

"I thought we couldn't—"

"I know." Kojan opened a channel to the rest of the ship. "Max, I need you on targeting assist."

The line crackled into life. "Didn't you say we weren't supposed to—"

"*I know.* The situation has changed, all right? Just do it."

Cyren fixed him with a steady look. "This means the curators will be able to access the *Ranger's* systems again?"

"We can handle three fighters."

"And if they signal for backup?"

Kojan didn't answer. All he could think about were those fighters bearing down on Kite's ship. Kite, who had helped him on Kaath even when he didn't agree with him. Kite, who had saved him from Shaw in the factory tunnels. Kite, who'd been trapped out here covering their retreat.

"I owe him," he said quietly. "We all do."

Cyren parted her jaws in a faint smile. "You remind me so much of her sometimes." She unbuckled herself from her harness and pushed herself from the co-pilot's seat, squeezing his shoulder with her claws as she passed.

"Where are you going?" Kojan asked.

"The medbay. I want to make sure we're ready for him when we bring him in."

Something sharp lodged in his throat. "Thank you, Cyren."

The gentle click of her claws on the walkway faded, leaving him with nothing but the hum of instruments for company. Lights from the console switched on in sequence, bringing the bridge back to life.

Kojan wrapped his hands around the controls. "How are those targeting solutions coming along, Max?"

"Locked and loaded. Go get those bastards."

The roar from the engines filled Kojan's ears as he pushed the *Ranger* back to full speed. The curator fighters were too far ahead to catch, but they couldn't outrun a missile.

He adjusted the targeting console for Max's input and the interface turned green as the missiles launched. He couldn't see them through the viewport feeds—they were too small out there, and space was too dark. All he could do was wait.

A flash of blue-white light erupted in the distance, expanding outwards in a sphere. The nav console lit up with warnings of debris shooting outwards from the starburst centre as the fighter disintegrated. Another followed. Two direct hits. That only left—

"Last target still in play," Max said over the intercom. "It managed to shake the missile and is still on approach. I don't know if we have time to—"

Another burst of light bloomed in the viewport, and Kojan's stomach twisted. "What happened? Did we hit it?"

For a moment, there was only silence. Then Max let out a sigh, making the line rush with static. "No, we didn't."

Kojan stared out the viewport. The curator fighter was already out of sight, no doubt retreating to the safety of the Omega Gate. All that was left was the far-off scattering of debris. Fragments of the fighter that had been blown apart. Kite's fighter.

The knot in Kojan's stomach tightened. They couldn't have lost him, not after coming so close. It wasn't right. It wasn't *fair*.

"Bringing up an open channel," he said, his voice scratching. "Kite? This is the *Ranger*. If you're out there, please respond."

The comms interface blinked in front of him. It was hopeless. He owed it to the others—his *crew*—to turn the ship around and get back to the *Lancer*. There was nothing more he could do here.

He cleared his throat. "Kitell Merala, this is Flight Lieutenant Kojan Irej of the *Ranger*. If you're out there, please—"

"—respond. Yeah, yeah, I heard you the first time."

Shock flooded Kojan's body, and he jolted upright in his chair. "Kite? That's really you?"

"How many other Kitell Meralas did you expect to find out here?" His voice was thin and tense, like every word was an effort draining him. "It's me. For now, at least. Not sure how much longer I'll last if you don't move your ass and haul me out of here."

"I don't understand. Where are you? How did you survive?"

"Ejected myself when I saw the fighter coming. If I'd left it a minute later, I'd have been caught in the blast." Kite let out a groan. "Didn't manage to avoid the debris though. A piece of my landing gear ripped through my flysuit, and I'm losing air fast. So I'd appreciate it if you moved along as quickly as you can."

Kojan adjusted the nav console, honing in on the small blip coming from Kite's flysuit. "We have a team of iskaath on standby with tethers and rescue gear. Hold on."

Kite coughed. "It's not like I'm going anywhere. The temporal net knocked out the manoeuvring controls in my flysuit. That's why I couldn't get clear. I've been drifting ever since I launched myself from my fighter."

"Not for much longer. We're coming up on your position now."

It was strange how nervous Kojan felt now that the hard part was over. Evading fighters, carrying out high-risk manoeuvres—those were things he could control. All he had to do was sink into the seams of his pilot's seat and become one with the *Ranger*. Everything else was background noise when he was flying.

Waiting was a different matter altogether. Kojan watched the iskaath jump out of the hold on their long tethers and attach their rescue cables to Kite's damaged flysuit. He drummed a rhythm on the console to distract himself, then wiped his slick palms against his shirt.

The tension in his shoulders only loosened when the doors to the bridge opened and Kite hobbled through, dressed in an oversized human cargo suit and wincing with each step.

Cyren followed him in, the slits of her nostrils flaring. "I told him he'd be better off in the medbay until we had time to assess his injuries, but he insisted on coming here."

"And I told you there was no need to fuss. I've been in worse scrapes than this one." Kite limped forward and braced himself on the back of the co-pilot's seat. "Thanks for the save. I suppose this makes us even now, doesn't it?"

"Who's counting?" Kojan turned his attention to a new light blinking on the interface. "We have an urgent message coming in from the *Lancer*. I guess they noticed our comms system was back up and running."

Kite leaned forward. "Let's see it."

The connection flickered, then Rivus appeared. He let out a heavy sigh when he saw Kite. "Good to see you made it, Merala."

"Still in one piece, boss. The *Ranger* came through."

"No heavy damage to the ship?"

Kojan shook his head. "A couple of scrapes and scratches, but we're in good enough shape to make it back to the *Lancer* for repairs. We should be with you in—"

"There's been a change of plan," Rivus interrupted. "While you were gone, a distress call came through from the strike team. They've requested immediate extraction from the Omega Gate."

Panic flooded Kojan's insides. "They couldn't shut it down?"

"I don't think so. There was a lot of interference, so we didn't get the entire message, but it's clear they're in trouble." Rivus gave him a pointed look. "Any intelligence they might have recovered from the gate could be vital to us winning this war. With the temporal net in the way, you're the only one who can get them out of there."

The fatigue Kojan had been keeping at bay lapped at his muscles. He couldn't remember the last time he'd eaten. Sleep was something he'd forgotten how to do. There was always one more mission, one more fight.

But there had to be. If there wasn't, it meant they had lost.

He shook himself, scattering the haze from his head. "We can do it. The *Ranger* hasn't let us down yet. It won't be easy, but we're operating with a full crew again. The best, in fact. We'll do everything we can to bring the strike team back."

Rivus nodded. "Fly safe, *Ranger*. We'll be waiting for your return."

The connection died. All Kojan could hear was Kite's stilted breathing and Cyren's claws clicking nervously on the floor. He knew what he was asking of them. But that didn't make asking it any easier.

Before he could say anything, Cyren let out a soft hiss. "It's never going to stop, is it? Not until we win."

"Or they do," Kite muttered.

"We won't let that happen. Not as long as we fight to protect our home, our nest." Cyren stared at Kojan, her yellow eyes weary but resolute. "We're with you. We'll have a chance to rest once this is over, one way or another. Until then, we'll do whatever is asked of us. It's what Eleion would have wanted."

Kojan's throat tightened. "This is for her."

"This is for all of us." Cyren bobbed her long neck. "I'll let the others know we're ready to move again. I assume the two of you have things covered in here." She curled her tail, a gentle snicker following her down the hall as she left.

Kite sank into the co-pilot's chair. "I spent months hunting down this ship. Feels strange to be here."

Kojan cocked an eyebrow. "A bit presumptuous of you, isn't it? Taking that seat, I mean."

"Count yourself lucky I'm not kicking you out of yours. I still outrank you, remember."

"Anywhere else, perhaps." Kojan smirked. "But not on this ship. Not on the *Ranger*."

He ran his eyes over the board of instruments and switched the connections off one by one. If they wanted to make it to the Omega Gate undetected, they'd need to go dark again. No weapons, no comms, no help from any of the state-of-the-art systems Chase used to inhabit. Just him, the controls, and the rumbling of the hull. It was the kind of company he could get used to. Even if he did have to share it with Kitell Merala.

Outside the viewport, darkness waited. The Omega Gate was somewhere out in its depths, nothing more than a pinprick in the distance.

Kojan pushed power to the engines and felt a rush of satisfaction as the *Ranger* roared in reply. "Ready?" he asked.

Kite nodded, his eyes bright. "Thought you'd never ask. Come on then, Flight Lieutenant. Let's see what this ship of yours can do."

EIGHTEEN

ALVERA

E very step Alvera took was a fresh kind of hell.

She bent over again, clutching her knees to steady herself. Every muscle felt like it was about to give way. Each breath came sharp and shallow, too feeble to give her lungs the air they needed. But she couldn't stop. No matter how weak she got, no matter how much her body begged her to give up, she had to push on. There was no other choice.

Through the fog in her head, she vaguely became aware of Jasvan's presence next to her. He didn't ask if she was all right or offer a steadying hand; he just waited, as silent as ever.

Alvera pushed herself upright and wiped the moisture from her brow. "I'm fine. No need to stop."

Jasvan didn't answer, of course. Without a translator—without any kind of cybernetic implants—it was impossible for him to understand what she was saying. Their journey into the heart of the Omega Gate had been largely silent, and Alvera couldn't help but find something strangely comforting about that.

She forced her legs into motion again. All she had to do was stay alive a little longer. With Jasvan's help, she'd managed to shut down another control centre. Now, there were only two more left.

The constant pressure from her cybernetics was taking a toll on her body. At the last control centre, she'd vomited blood and passed out before she managed to finish the shutdown sequence. The curators had crept into her head, whispering at the nape of her neck. They wanted her to fail. They wanted this to kill her.

Alvera gave herself a violent shake. It was getting harder and harder to keep the curators out of her mind. They crept in through her implants like poison, infecting her, corrupting her. Chase wasn't there to stop them anymore. She was on her own.

The next control centre was up ahead. All of the waystations had the same snaking system of corridors and junctions, the same layout of access tunnels and maintenance hatches. Alvera was intimately familiar with them now. In a strange, twisted way, it felt like she was home.

That's the curators talking, she reminded herself. *I don't belong to this place.*

The doors to the control centre hissed open in front of her, parting their metal jaws to let her in. Inside, the main console stood tall in the middle of the room, its lights blinking like it was welcoming her.

A chill ran through Alvera's blood. She knew what the connection would do to her cybernetics. It was only a matter of time before it became too much for her body to handle.

"All right," she said. "I'm going for it."

Jasvan didn't give any sign that he'd heard her. He took up position at the doors, his towering frame stiff as he wrapped his hands around his rifle and waited.

"Good talk," Alvera muttered, turning to the console.

She closed her eyes and let her cybernetics take control. The subconscious workings of her mind reached out with invisible tendrils and created links and connections from the software in her head. She'd never fully understood how it worked. There was always a part of her that ceded control over herself, that let her implants fix the problems she couldn't. Before, that part of her had been Chase. Now it came from the absence of her, the empty spaces she'd left behind.

A burst of pain flooded her head as the connections strengthened and took hold. The ache spread from her temples to the base of her skull, throbbing more with each passing second.

Alvera opened her eyes. The holographic interface awoke in a faint glow. Her cybernetics had bridged a connection between her mind and the console. That was the easy part. Now, she had to fight with everything she had to bend it to her will.

A muffled bang echoed through her ears, but she ignored it. She was already in too deep. If she didn't give the curator systems her entire attention, they would push back against her implants and turn her brain to mush. They'd come close twice already.

Focus, she told herself. *Focus on bringing the whole fucking thing down.*

Out of nowhere, a hand grabbed her shoulder. Alvera jerked back, every nerve in her head screaming like it was on fire. It was like her cybernetics had overloaded. She couldn't see anything past the spots clouding her vision, couldn't hear anything but the buzzing in her ears.

The vice-like grip loosened, and Alvera shook it off. She blinked the haze away to see Jasvan towering over her.

"What are you doing?" she demanded, gasping for breath. "You can't disrupt the connection like that. You could have killed me."

Jasvan raised his rifle and pointed it towards the doors. "Enemy," he said.

A cold wave of dread ran through her, rooting her to the spot. She should have known this was coming. It had been too much to hope for that the Omega Gate would remain empty as she worked to deactivate the remaining control centres. Every time she linked up with a piece of the curators' technology, they saw her. They knew what she was trying to do.

Now they had sent their thralls to stop it.

"How many are coming?" Alvera asked. "Where did they— damn it, you have no idea what I'm saying, do you? Hang on, I'll see if I can pull up a translation programme on my wrist terminal."

Before she could move, Jasvan reached out a hand and pushed her back towards the console. "Hurry. I'll hold them off."

"But what if you can't..." It was no use. Jasvan gave her a blank, uncomprehending look and turned back to the door, his rifle steady in his hands.

Alvera whirled around to the console and opened up the connection again, nearly biting through her tongue as the pain returned. It was sharper than ever before. More concentrated, more precise. The curators knew the parts of her brain to target, where to apply the pressure most. She couldn't let it distract her. The only thing that mattered was shutting down the console.

The world outside the confines of her head faded to black. Somewhere across the distance, the ping of gunfire ricocheted off the walls. Smoke filled her nostrils, but she paid it no attention. She was in the curators' systems now. She didn't exist outside of the streams of code and corrupted data her cybernetics had plugged into. She was the flaw they'd never accounted for, the bug that could bring down their whole machine.

Something hot seared the back of her thigh, and she became vaguely aware of a warm trickle running down her leg. Pain, but a dull, far-off kind of pain. A pain that could be pushed away and revisited later, if there *was* a later.

She was nearly there. The systems crumbled in bursts of green and gold on the console's interface. The strain of her lungs and the frantic thump of her heart against her ribs didn't matter anymore. Her body would hold out as long as it had to. She was *winning*.

A crackle of electricity erupted from the console. The shock threw Alvera back, sending her sprawling on the floor. She lay there, dazed and blinking as the room came back into focus. A small stream of sparks leapt from the console's cracked interface as she fought her way back to her feet.

"Just one more," she said. "Jasvan, we need to—"

Another bolt of pain split open Alvera's head, bringing bile to the back of her throat. This time, it wasn't from the exertion of using her cybernetics. It was the curators. They were in her brain, searching for something, digging away at her with claws they didn't possess, scraping and scratching at the tissue until they found what they were looking for.

An image from her memories bloomed in her mind: a base nestled among barren ash plains and drifting snowfields. Volcanoes spewing ice into the perpetual night. Fissures in the ground so deep and volatile it was like the planet had cracked apart at the seams.

Alcruix. They were coming for Alcruix.

Alvera tasted blood on her tongue. She had to warn Rivus and the Idran-Var. She had to reach the last control centre and hope that shutting it down would cut off the curators' reinforcements. She had to stay alive.

Jasvan was half-shrouded by a cloud of thick black smoke, his armour splattered with different colours of blood. He sent a barrage of shots into the corridor, then drew back, grunting as he adjusted the settings on his rifle.

His eyes locked with hers as she stumbled forward. His unnaturally pale face sported blotches of grey, and his mouth twisted in an expression that might have been exhaustion or rage or something else entirely.

"Dropships," he said. "They're latching onto every access point along this arm of the gate. There's too many of them between us and the last control centre. We'll never make it."

Alvera drew her gun from her belt and set her jaw.

Jasvan chuckled. "I don't need a translator to understand that look, human. I know when someone is itching for a fight. But I've been in enough of them myself to learn what battles to pick. This isn't one of them."

Alvera ignored him and started forward, only for one of Jasvan's arms to shoot out and pin her roughly against the wall. "Let me go," she snarled.

He fixed her with an unnerving, empty stare. "Tell me this, Alvera Renata. Is there anyone else in the galaxy capable of doing what you do? Can anyone else shut down these control centres?"

Alvera opened her mouth to reply, then snapped it shut again and shook her head.

"I didn't think so." Jasvan loosened the pressure on her chest. "If you die here, who wins but these curators? Better to live for another chance to destroy them. Only you can do that. You owe it to the rest of the galaxy to survive."

A chill crept in somewhere around Alvera's sternum. The last time she'd taken on that kind of responsibility, it had set her on the path to where she was now. She knew what that kind of weight would do to her. She knew the kind of monster she'd need to become to shoulder it. No matter how hard she tried to escape it, it would always be there, clawing at her heels, dragging her back to face all the things she'd done because she was the only one who could stomach doing them.

Was it not better to die here trying to do better? Was that not enough for the galaxy?

Even as the thoughts crossed her mind, they were already scattering, carried away by the depths of her own realisation. She couldn't escape this. She'd never been able to escape it.

Alvera opened her wrist terminal and tapped a message into the translation programme. A glowing line of strange-shaped glyphs sprang up on the holoprojector, hanging between her and Jasvan.

What are you doing this for? it read.

Jasvan held her questioning gaze with his empty black eyes. "Same reason as you, human. I know what it's like to be born into this galaxy to fulfil only one purpose. My entire existence has been as a weapon." The air shimmered from the pulse of his flare. "This may be the only time in my life where that grim truth can do some good."

Alvera followed him out the doors, flinching at the blinding light of his flare as he sent a white wall of energy down the corridor. He stood in the middle of the floor, a guttural roar ripping from the back of his throat. Past the fading light of his flare, Alvera saw the outlines of the approaching thralls. Armoured boots clunked off the floor. A bullet hit the fluorescent light above her with a ping, shattering the glass.

There were too many of them to hold off. Even for him.

"Go," Jasvan groaned.

Alvera forced her muscles into motion as they screamed against her. This wasn't how she wanted to leave. *All of us go, or none of us go.* The old words were a mockery in her head, an echo of all the promises she'd made and all the ways she'd failed in keeping them.

She only dared to glance back for a moment, but a moment was enough. She saw Jasvan's broad, towering frame, a silhouette against the light of his flare. The curator thralls were on him now, illuminated in flashes as he sent wave after wave of energy towards them. They were unrelenting. Unstoppable. It was only a matter of time before the corridor descended back into darkness and the thralls trampled over his bloodied, broken corpse in pursuit of her.

She had to keep running. Even though her lungs burned and her mouth tasted of blood and bile. Even though her broken body was ready to collapse from under her.

The interior airlock they'd come through was just ahead. Alvera charged through and fumbled with the control panel to seal the doors behind her. Any time she could buy might be the difference between surviving this nightmare and falling back into the curators' clutches.

She pressed forward, navigating her way through the narrow access tunnel until she came across the loose wires and fallen beams scattered around the hole Skaile had ripped in the gate's outer shell. She hauled herself over the edge, clicking her grav boots against the smooth surface and letting out a long, rasping breath.

She was out. She'd achieved that much, at least.

The black of space above her was cast in a glow from the monstrous beam coming from the middle of the Omega Gate. It cleaved through the darkness, a fissure through the fabric of space. More curator ships poured out, arriving from whatever factory of mass production, mass-fucking-destruction, the curators had on the other side. More guns fabricated from their infinite armouries. More bodies bred in their labs—thralls with no consciousness, no memory.

They'd keep coming through. And she might have given up the only chance of stopping them.

Another dropship landed further along the arm of the gate, and Alvera took cover behind one of the nearby generators. Even now, more thralls poured in, coming to kill her. She wondered if Jasvan was still alive. Then the ache in her chest reminded her that it didn't make a difference.

An urgent yellow light pulsed on her wrist terminal. Being back outside the Omega Gate's hull must have reset her comms connection. Alvera swiped through several diagnostic screens and re-established the link, breathing heavily when Rivus appeared in front of her.

"I couldn't get it done," she said, the words sticking in her throat. "They sent in dropships, flooded us with thralls. Jasvan stayed behind so I could get out, for whatever that's worth."

Rivus held his bony face plates stiff and unmoving. Then he shook his head, his composed mask cracking. "Everything has gone to shit here too. The Idran-Var flagship—the one the war chief is in charge of—it broke off and ran. Nobody has been able to reach it, not even Zal."

"You should do the same."

Rivus's jaw plates shifted. "You want us to give up?"

"Not give up—retreat. Before it's too late." Alvera grimaced. "The curators got into my head. They know about Alcruix. They're sending the bulk of their forces to wipe out whatever is left of us. If we're to make a stand against them, it has to be there."

Rivus paused, his green eyes considering. "We could regroup somewhere else. Consolidate all the ships we have left and plan another assault."

"There's no time. They're coming *now*. We have to give them a fight. We have to keep their attention on that planet. It might be our only chance."

"You have a plan?"

"Maybe. I don't know if you can call it a plan. More like a last hope."

"Desperation has a way of making the impossible seem within reach, doesn't it?" Rivus gave a short laugh. "Kojan picked up the rest of the strike team not long ago. I'll tell him to come back for you. The *Ranger* is pretty banged up, but if the bulk of the curator fleet is focused on advancing towards Alcruix, he might be able to carve himself a clear path."

Part of her wanted to refuse. Part of her wanted to tell Rivus to forget about her and concentrate on keeping everyone else alive. She was done fighting. Done struggling. Done forcing herself to survive when all she wanted to do was slip away and let someone else pick up the burden.

She thought of Jasvan holding off the thralls below. Chase's sacrifice back on the waystation. All so Alvera could have a chance at stopping this.

"Understood," she said, her voice cracking. "I'll watch for Kojan."

The line fizzled out, leaving Alvera with nothing but her own laboured breathing for company. All around her, the curator ships were moving. A quartet of huge engines blared with fiery light as a destroyer crawled past, its roar swallowed by the vacuum. A squadron of fighters followed in an arrow-head formation, their wings like silver blades cutting through the black.

Alvera brought up her wrist terminal again. The connection pulsed, waiting for an answer on the other end. Then it flickered into life and she was met with the formidable, steel face of Rhendar.

"You're still alive then?" he asked, his voice even. "I was beginning to have my doubts."

"For the moment," Alvera replied. "What's going on? Rivus said you took the *Tressel's Vengeance* and left the allied fleet."

"You know what's going on, Captain Renata. This is what we agreed to back on Alcruix. We need a contingency."

The metallic edge to his voice was perfectly neutral, but Alvera couldn't help the shudder that ran through her body at his words. It was too soon for this. She thought she'd have more time. She thought she'd have a chance to bloody the bastards before giving up everything to beat them.

"This *contingency* means sacrificing New Pallas," she said, her voice low. "Do you understand that?"

"I do. And so did you when you agreed to this."

His words rang in her ears, leaving her with no escape. He was right. The mission to shut down the beam had failed. *She* had failed. They were out of options.

Her heart wrenched as she thought back to New Pallas. Its filthy, smog-thick atmosphere. Its skyscraper towers built on layers of poverty and grime-covered streets. Its blood-red sunsets and the acid rainstorms. Its people, starving for more than food and medicine. Starving for hope. Waiting for them to return with the promise of a new future.

So many mistakes leading to this point, this critical moment. So many words given and broken. What was one more after everything she'd done?

"Forgive me," she whispered, the words cracking a hole in her chest. There was nothing more she could do for New Pallas. She had to let it slip away through her fingers, leaving it to its fate as she faced her own.

The comms line crackled as Rhendar waited for her reply.

"Do it." Alvera swallowed, her throat burning. "Send the asteroid."

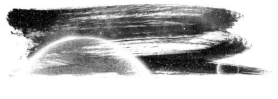

NINETEEN

Rivus

Rivus stood in silence as the *Lancer* burned back towards Alcruix. The engines were pushed to their limits, eating through as much fuel as they could spare, but on a ship this size, even the most desperate pace felt like a crawl. There was no tightness in his gut from the pull of acceleration, no jolt from the abrupt transitions in and out of the space tunnels. The inertial dampeners were powerful enough to hold down a small city, but they also made it feel like time had stopped. Like they weren't moving fast enough to stop what was coming.

The thought sent a shudder through Rivus's plating. Their time was up, in every way imaginable.

He turned his attention back to the room. Silence had fallen over the ops centre, so thick it clung to the walls. The dimmed lights had cast most of the people gathered there in shadow, but Rivus's eyes were drawn to Alvera Renata, her pale face illuminated in ghostly tones from the holoprojector in the middle of the room.

She looked close to death. She slumped in a medical hover-chair, the crook of her arm home to several buried needles pumping her with fluids. A pair of thin breather tubes ran from her nostrils to a nearby oxygen tank, and she stared blankly ahead, her eyes grey-lidded and drooping, the sunken rings around them like permanent face markings.

She'd given all she had, and they'd still not been able to win.

The hologram stuttered, and Rhendar stepped back into view. Rivus couldn't help the way his insides flooded with anger at what the Idran-Var war chief had proposed.

No, not proposed, he thought to himself. It was worse than that. Rhendar had already set his plan in motion. He hadn't waited for a consensus—hell, he hadn't even given them the courtesy of having a damn discussion. A contingency, he'd called it. A desperate, violent gamble that only made sense if all else was lost.

As hopeless as things were, Rivus wasn't ready to admit that yet.

"Sorry for dropping out there," Rhendar said, his voice crackling on the other end of the line. "As you can imagine, we're not in the best place for a strong signal."

Rivus couldn't see much in the way of the background behind Rhendar, but he was more than capable of imagining it. A desolate hunk of rock from the reaches of the Rim Belt, more than two dozen kilometres across. Rugged, rocky ground made of mountains and craters in equal measure. No atmosphere, just space and stars surrounding them.

Another asteroid. Another unthinkable weapon centuries in the making. A colossal bullet of rock and metal with engines the size of tower blocks strapped to its surface. Defensive encampments bored into the rugged terrain, outfitted with enough aerial defence cannons and missiles to take out a small fleet. The Coalition ambassadors had been foolish to believe their old enemy would ever have stopped at Alcruix. What should have been an atrocity never to be repeated had instead shown the Idran-Var the promise of what they'd created. Of course they'd made more of them.

He should have known better. *This* was who the Idran-Var were.

Alvera cleared her throat. When she spoke, it was with a harsh, rasping voice that sounded like crunching glass. "What's the situation out there?"

"We're making solid progress and haven't encountered any curator forces so far. Our aerial defences will be a match for any ships that get too close, and there's not much in the way of weaponry that can stop a rock this big." Rhendar folded his arms. "The biggest threat we face is if the curators drop a few hundred of their shock troops on the asteroid's surface. I have a small garrison here, but it's not enough to stand up to any real assault. If the curators overwhelm us and hijack the engines, they could change course and divert away from the target."

Rivus couldn't help himself anymore. "Away from Ossa, you mean," he said, the words coming out in a snarl. "The planet you're so eager to destroy with this stunt of yours."

"The target is the Omega Gate," Rhendar said, his mechanical voice as calm as ever. "This isn't an act of vengeance, Supreme Commander. I have no desire to bring down any more destruction on your capital than it has seen already. But at this point, collateral damage is inevitable."

"Collateral damage?" A growl rumbled in Rivus's throat. "You're talking about crashing an asteroid into an orbital superstructure. If the fallout from the collision gets dragged into the gravitational pull of the planet, you're talking about hundreds —maybe thousands—of strikes. Some kilometres in diameter.

That kind of impact won't just annihilate any survivors, it will make the planet uninhabitable for millennia to come."

"And if we do nothing?" Alvera's voice was soft as she met his eyes, but there was an underlying brittleness to it, like it might crack and break. "If the curators win, it's not just Ossa that will be annihilated. The lives of everyone in the galaxy are at stake."

"So we sacrifice an entire planet for the desperate hope that we might still be able to save everyone else?"

"We don't have a choice," Alvera said. "There's no other way to take out the Omega Gate. The temporal net renders any kind of technology useless. Our ships would be immobilised before they could get close. But we've observed asteroids and other astronomical objects pass through the net unaffected." She turned back to Rhendar. "All you need to do is lose the engines before you hit the perimeter. Do you need reinforcements to make sure that happens?"

"I'd rather not commit any more lives to this than I need to." A long sigh escaped Rhendar's helmet. "If you have reinforcements, use them to give the curators a fight at Alcruix. Keep them occupied, make them concentrate all their forces there. It might be our best shot at keeping these engines burning."

Out of the corner of his eye, Rivus saw Niole flinch. "You're not coming back?" she asked.

Rhendar tilted his head. "I plan on seeing the job done," he said gently. "Nothing more, nothing less."

"Then let us help you. We can take a shuttle and be with you in—"

"This is not your fight, Niole. These Idran-Var are ready to pay the price I asked of them. All of them have things they wish to atone for, debts they wish to repay. This is their opportunity to regain the strength they lost when they lost their armour. It's not a place you belong."

She faltered. "Claine? Is he with you?"

"Amongst others, yes." Rhendar nodded. "He will never be able to undo what he did when he led Tarvan Varantis to Vesyllion. But he can save more lives than his actions took. Perhaps now, at the end of all things, that is all we can ask for."

Rivus ran his claws down the already-fraying edge of the white cloak around his shoulders. He'd tried to live up to the promise it held, but the mantle of the Supreme Commander had already been bloodied by the time it came to him, and he'd let it happen. He couldn't forget his complicity in Tarvan's actions. Couldn't forgive it, either. Was Rhendar right? Was all that was left for them now the chance to save more than they condemned, even if that meant more lives lost under his watch?

Rivus glanced around the room. Niole stared at the floor, her shoulders hunched, her expression bleak and distant. Alvera's face was so gaunt and pale it was almost translucent. Rivus recognised their haunted expressions all too well. None of them were free from the ghosts they'd left behind.

Maybe this was the price of survival. Maybe there would always be a price as long as there was someone left who was willing to pay it. But it wouldn't be him. Not this time.

"I won't be a part of this." The words felt hollow as they left his throat, carrying with them an echo of betrayal. "I can't do what you're asking of me. I accepted this white cloak to protect the innocents in this galaxy, to protect the Coalition. No matter how much of it is left, I won't abandon it now. I won't abandon Ossa."

The hologram flickered as Rhendar shifted his weight. "You can't stop this," he warned, his voice taking on a harder edge. "This rock will hit the Omega Gate, no matter the cost."

"I don't care about stopping you. I care about saving them," Rivus bit back. "The temporal net doesn't stretch as far as Ossa itself. I'll go back and evacuate as many civilians as the *Lancer* can carry in the time that's left. As for the rest...their blood is on your hands."

He walked out, ignoring the murmuring voices that followed him as he stalked down the corridor and retreated into the quiet of a nearby observation room. It was blissfully empty; all he had for company was the viewport feed projecting the depths of the void outside. Even the stars had faded from view. Maybe here, he could steal a few precious moments to himself.

"Rivus? Can we talk?"

Niole stood in the doorway. Without waiting for an answer, she stepped inside and tapped the access panel, sealing the doors behind her.

A harsh laugh escaped the back of Rivus's throat. "Niole, I mean no offence, but you're the last person in the galaxy I want to talk to right now."

She blanched at his words like he'd struck her, and an involuntary growl escaped his throat at the resulting guilt that bubbled up inside him. After what she'd done, she deserved everything he said and more. But the hurt on her face needled between the gaps in his plating, creeping into the parts of him that should have been hardened to her by now.

"I know how difficult this must be," Niole said gently. "I know how much Ossa means to you. But if we're to have any chance at winning this war, we need to destroy the Omega Gate. Surely you see that."

"I abandoned Ossa once already for the sake of winning this war. I left its people to the curators, left the cities burning as I fled to join this alliance." Rivus ground his teeth. "Some of those people are still holding on. Still fighting back. If we give up on them now, we might as well give up on the entire galaxy."

"It's not as simple as you make it sound."

"Simple?" Rivus echoed. "You think anything about this is simple? I know how much easier it would be if I could turn my back on them and give Rhendar my full support. If I could accept the loss of a few million here to save a few trillion elsewhere. But if that's the kind of Supreme Commander you wanted in charge, then maybe you should have kept Tarvan alive."

The rush of anger behind his own words caught him off guard. Saying Tarvan's name out loud was enough to stir it up again, to bring all the rage and resentment swelling to the surface. But it wasn't Niole he was angry at, not anymore. It was Tarvan. For leaving him with this legacy. For being the kind of ruthless bastard who found it easy to make these decisions. For being the kind of leader Rivus could never be, not when it mattered most.

Niole stepped back, her black eyes shining under the lights. "You're right," she whispered. "You're not Tarvan. If he were here, we'd never have made it this far. The reason we're still in this fight is because of you."

Rivus's chest seized around his lungs. It was too much like the voice of an old friend when all he saw in front of him was a stranger. Too much of a reminder that even now, there was a connection between him and Niole that battlelines and bloodshed hadn't been able to break.

"I won't take the entire Coalition fleet with me to Ossa," he said, his voice cracking on the words. "Only the *Lancer* and a small escort. The rest can stay behind to defend Alcruix. That's the best I can do."

"What about you?" Niole furrowed her brow ridge. "This evacuation... You won't be able to save everyone before the asteroid strikes. How long are you planning to stay on Ossa?"

"As long as it takes."

Niole stared at him, her mouth half open like she wanted to say something. Her skin shone blue as the wisps of a flare danced along her arms. Then she snapped her mouth shut and nodded before heading towards the door.

When she reached the threshold, she paused. All Rivus could see was the hunch of her shoulders under her long headtails. She didn't look at him. She just held herself there with her back to him, like walking away was as impossible as turning back around.

"I know it's not fair of me to ask, but considering what's about to happen..." Niole broke off, her voice trembling. "What happened between us, this rift we opened up...do you think if we make it out of here alive, we might ever have a chance of healing it?"

The question was so honest, so painfully raw, that all Rivus wanted to do was push it away, push *her* away. It ripped open the wounds he'd tried to ignore, brought back the memories he'd tried to forget. Her flare, Tarvan's broken body, a stained white cloak crumpled among the ash.

There was a part of him that wanted to say yes. A part of him that wanted to believe he could forgive her. A part of him that pondered how their lives might have turned out if it hadn't been for that fateful day in the training grounds of Cap Ossa all those years ago.

"You're right," he said tightly. "It's not fair of you to ask."

The words hung between them in the ship's recycled air. Then they were gone, and Niole pushed herself through the doorway without another word.

Rivus stared after her, watching the light from the corridor spill into the observation room. He half hoped her shadow would reappear, giving him another chance to make things right.

But when the doorway darkened again, it was not Niole. Instead, Alvera Renata limped her way into the room, her face twisted in pain as she struggled forward one step at a time. She fought her way to one of the couches near the viewport and sank into the leather, dropping her mobility aids to her feet with a heavy clunk.

"You're making a mistake," she said.

Rivus gave a weary sigh. The human captain had made for

an unlikely ally these last few months. She'd stood by him when nobody else had. She'd saved his life. But there was something about her presence that made him feel like he was in the company of a ghost.

"How can you bear it?" he asked. "All these things you've done, all these lives lost at your hand...how can you keep going?"

"I can't." Alvera stared back at him, her eyes dead. "An asteroid is heading towards the Omega Gate, ready to destroy whatever hope New Pallas has left. And I can't stop it. I *agreed* to it. I'm giving up everything I ever promised, everything I ever fought for, everything I ever killed for, just for the chance it might give the rest of the galaxy a shot at seeing the other side of this."

"And you don't think the cost is too high?"

Alvera tensed. "Don't talk to me about the cost, Rivus. I know it all too well."

Rivus thought about saying something. Maybe there was a way to get through to her, a way to change her mind. Then he shook his head. Alvera had made her decision. They all had.

Instead, he extended his claws towards her, mirroring the gesture Zal had shown him. Alvera looked at him, surprise flashing across her face. Her mouth widened, and she slid her soft human fingers into his grasp.

He closed his claws around her hand. "It was a good fight."

"While it lasted." Alvera's smile faltered. "One way or another, it's coming to an end. I have to admit, I'm looking forward to it being over."

She gave his hand a final shake and limped out of the room. The doors sealed themselves shut behind her with a soft hiss, closing the room off to the garish light pouring in from the corridor outside.

Being alone again should have brought Rivus some measure of relief, but the empty observation room didn't hold the kind of solitude he'd expected. Alvera's parting words lingered with him for company, prodding at the places his plates met until he could no longer ignore them. It was unsettling to think the same woman who'd shouted down the ambassadors and broken through a military blockade to save her people was the same woman resignedly accepting her end now. Alvera Renata had never seemed like the kind of person to go out with a whimper.

Outside the viewport, the endless abyss of space stretched out in front of him. Even with the *Lancer's* regulated environmental controls, it left him cold. There was so much darkness it was hard to remember the places where light endured.

Rivus understood Alvera's exhaustion. He felt it in his own bones, in the ache of his muscles and the stiffness of his plates. Sometimes, in the quiet of his own mind, he too wished for the fight to be over. But that time was not now. As long as Ossa still endured, as long as his people still fought, then so would he.

Even if he had to do it alone.

TWENTY

RIDLEY

The floor of the shuttle bay was cold and hard underneath Ridley's back as she adjusted her position for what felt like the millionth time. Spending the last three hours curled up in a cramped corner of the hangar was taking its toll. The chill from the floor had crept its way into her joints, and her muscles were stiff and aching as she rolled over again, doing her best to block out the animated chatter and rumbling engines.

"Are you awake?" Halressan hissed.

Something prodded Ridley in her side, and she whipped around to see the tip of Halressan's boot hastily withdraw. "What the hell?"

Halressan narrowed her eyes. "I knew you weren't sleeping."

"I was trying to."

"Well you're pretty poor company, aren't you?" Halressan

stretched her legs and let out a groan. "I can't feel my ass. How much longer until we get a ride out of here?"

Ridley fought the urge to roll her eyes. "I told you, we have to wait our turn. The *Lancer* is a huge ship and there are only so many surface transport shuttles to go around. We'll be back on Alcruix soon enough."

"You think that makes me feel any better? Returning to that creepy planet to wait for the curators to come kick our asses isn't exactly my idea of a good time, babe."

"I don't think it's anyone's idea of a good time, *babe*, but it's not like we've got much of a choice, do we?" Ridley pressed her fingers into her temples. "Sorry, I didn't mean to say it like that. It's just..."

"I know." Halressan's voice softened. "You don't have to explain. You're scared. So am I. Even Skaile is scared, though she'd kill you before she ever admitted it."

"That's when you know things are bad."

"It could be worse." Halressan slipped her fingers between Ridley's. Her skin was icy, but that didn't stop the rush of warmth that flooded Ridley's chest at her touch. "No matter how bad shit gets, at least we're in it together."

"You make it sound so romantic."

Halressan drew her mouth into a smirk and leaned forward. "I try my best."

The gentle pressure of Halressan's lips against hers sent an urgent flutter through Ridley's stomach. She'd never get used to this, not if they had all the time in the galaxy. There was something about the fierce taste of Halressan, the scent of her skin, the steely intensity of her eyes, that made Ridley shudder under every kiss. The brush of her lips, the insistence of her tongue, it was enough to make everything else melt away. All she felt was the heat in her cheeks and the need for Halressan pooling in the deepest parts of her. She couldn't think of anything else but that *want*, that feeling of—

"Oh, that's just great. The humans are doing their mouth mushing thing again."

Ridley pulled away sharply, her face hot. Drexious was standing over them with a perturbed expression, holding a bulb of foul-smelling liquid between his claws. Next to him, Fyra bit into a halsi stick and stared determinedly ahead.

"Fuck off, Drex," Halressan said pleasantly.

"All I'm saying is nobody wants to see that. All that soft flesh squishing and sliding together, it's disgusting." He cast a side-long glance at Fyra. "Wait, you sioleans have lips too. Don't tell me you do the same thing?"

Fyra gave a serene shrug. "I can't speak for the sioleans of your time, but my kind were certainly familiar with the concept. Maybe you should try it sometime. It might make you more agreeable."

Drexious bristled. "You know what? I'm going to take my bark tea somewhere else. Maybe find a dachryn or two to hang out with. At least I'm not likely to see any kissing from *them*." He flicked his tail. "But don't forget to call me if we get a spot on a shuttle. I don't fancy being left alone with these military types. If I'm not careful, they might expect me to actually fight at some point."

As he sauntered off, Ridley's vision blurred in front of her. Sleep had spared her from the tears for a little while, but now that she was awake, it was difficult to keep her thoughts from drifting to the unrelenting grief that had wrapped itself around her.

"Hey." Halressan's voice was a murmur at her ear. "We can still get out of here. We might not get far, but we could buy ourselves a bit more time before...you know..."

Ridley wiped the tears from her eyes. "I can't stop thinking about the asteroid. If it destroys the Omega Gate, the tunnel back to Exodus Station will collapse. For us to survive, New Pallas has to die. Even if we win, how am I meant to live in this galaxy knowing what we did to those people we left behind?"

Fyra stopped crunching on her halsi stick. "Your human colony hasn't been evacuated yet?"

"We didn't get the chance." Ridley dug her nails into her palms. "The Coalition ambassadors set up a jamming rig around the waystation to stop us contacting New Pallas. Alvera managed to blow it up, but we don't know if the message she sent ever reached them. We were too late."

"No." Fyra lowered herself to the floor, her halsi stick hanging halfway out of her mouth as she spoke. "There's still time before the asteroid hits. Weeks, maybe. Not enough time to evacuate an entire planet, but enough to save as many as you can."

"It's impossible. There's no way to communicate with them."

"There is." Fyra reached into the folds of her tunic and drew out the small black data cube she'd been holding on to ever since they woke her from cryostasis. The box gleamed against her pale lilac skin, its sides seamless and perfectly smooth. It looked more like a trinket than a piece of ancient technology. "I told you once that this device contains records of our entire civilisation. It was once the most valuable piece of tech in the galaxy. Maybe it still is."

Ridley frowned. "What do you mean?"

"There were...other things stored on this data cube. Classified secrets. Technological discoveries. The dachryn went to war with us over the contents of this box." Fyra wrapped her four fingers around it. "In my time, the dachryn were the final colony to make it through the waystations. Just like you, they triggered the signal to the destroyers. The rest of the galaxy blamed them for what was coming. We wanted to punish them, to have their colony pay the price for what they'd done."

"Sounds familiar," Ridley muttered.

"There is too much about the galaxy that feels familiar," Fyra said. "That is why it's hard for me to watch this. I've seen it all before. All the same defeats, all the same mistakes." She rolled the box over in her palm. "The technology stored in this device was our greatest triumph, and our greatest shame. We developed a way to harness the waystations' signal to allow instantaneous communication to the colonies. But when the dachryn needed it most, we withheld it from them out of fear and vengeance."

Ridley froze. She couldn't move. She couldn't *breathe.*

Fyra held her gaze, her eyes bleak. "I don't want this galaxy to feel familiar. I don't want to make the same mistakes we made in the past." She pressed the glittering data cube into Ridley's hands. "This is all I have left of my people. They charged me with protecting what was left of us in the hopes that a few might survive and rise to fight again. But this isn't my fight—it's yours."

Ridley closed her hands around the data cube. Its sides were smooth and slippery against her skin, the metal cool to the touch. It felt like a heartbeat in her hands, a lifeline to the people she'd lost. "You're saying I can use this to contact New Pallas?"

"I'm not sure how it works. I was a soldier, not a technician." A knowing look spread over Fyra's face. "But from what I understand, you're quite the expert when it comes to decrypting the secrets of my people."

"I'll need some kind of satellite uplink to connect to. When we get to the surface, I'll ask one of the Idran-Var if I can..." Ridley trailed off. "Wait, you're not coming with us?"

Fyra shook her head. "My days of fighting the destroyers are long past."

"Then what will you do?"

"I'll stay on board the *Lancer* when it departs for Ossa and help the evacuation efforts. If we're as close to the end as everyone believes, I'd like my last moments in this galaxy to contribute something more than a lifetime of violence." Fyra's mouth stretched into a sad smile. "Maybe when I see my old friends again, I can meet them with my head held high."

She pushed herself up from the floor and dipped her head in a sombre bow. "If you hadn't woken me from that pod, I'd have slept through another extinction. Maybe it would have been easier that way. But if this helps you to save some of your people—no matter how fleetingly—then I cannot regret it. Not when I'd have given the galaxy for the same chance."

"Thank you," Ridley said, the words sticking in her throat. "Whatever happens, I hope it ends with you finding the peace you've been searching for."

"As do I."

Ridley watched her go, unable to suppress the emotions rushing through her. Too much regret. Too much fear and pain. But underneath it all, something new rose inside her, a kernel of hope pushing its way through all the despair.

She looked down at the data cube, its sides glittering under the hangar lights. It looked too precious, too delicate, for the power it contained. Of all the treasures Ridley had ever uncovered, all the ancient artefacts she'd worked so hard to detail and decipher, this was the most important. Not because it held the key to their past, but to their future.

"Halressan," she said. "Grab your rifle and get ready to threaten some people. No more waiting around. We're getting on a shuttle."

———

The Idran-Var had been surprisingly amenable to Ridley's request for satellite access. She'd expected them to dismiss her out of hand, but all it had taken was the mention of reinforcements for Zal to point her in the direction of an uplink station a few klicks away from Alcruix's main base.

The building was little more than a cramped, dimly-lit room attached to the base of the huge satellite dish. Its air recyclers groaned and stuttered as Ridley worked, drowning out the howling wind and tectonic rumbling from outside. The single window was coated in a layer of grime, but all the view had to offer was ash rain and towers of ice. The most important thing was the data cube hooked into the mainframe in front of her.

"I still don't understand why you couldn't have done this back at the main base," Halressan said, pulling her thermal jacket around her. "They're not exactly lacking comms equipment, are they?"

"Zal said this is the longest-range relay they have. I need to give myself the best possible chance of making this work." Ridley shrugged. "Besides, I prefer working somewhere a bit more remote. Means there are less distractions around."

"Present company excluded?" Halressan ran her hands along Ridley's shoulders. Ridley gave a long, satisfied groan at the way Halressan's fingers worked along her muscles, pressing in all the right places to loosen the tension that had crept in.

"Present company excluded," she agreed. "For now, at least. But if you keep doing that, I'm going to find it difficult to keep concentrating on this data cube."

Halressan held up her hands. "Just trying to help. You've been at this for hours now. Don't you think you should take a break?"

"I don't have time for a break. New Pallas doesn't have time." Ridley turned back to the cube. A single golden light on the side of the device pulsed gently as she started another transfer. Streams of data flashed up on the interface, too fast for her to make sense of. Somewhere, buried under all these layers, was the information she was searching for. All she had to do was delve through the lifespan of a civilisation to find it.

"I still can't believe Fyra gave me this," she said. "All their history, all their languages and culture, it's all in here. This data cube is the only place they exist now. If I had a repository of all that was left of New Pallas, I'm not sure I could have parted with it so easily."

"Nothing in that box will bring them back. No number of records will ever be able to make up for what Fyra lost." Halressan slid onto the bench next to her, shadows dancing across her pale features. "Those weeks I spent with her on that planet...I saw what I would have become without you. Fyra survived, but she has nothing to live for. That's why she gave you the data cube. Holding on to it was more than she could bear."

Ridley squeezed her hand. "I'm glad you came back. I don't know how I would have got through these last few weeks without you. You're the only thing that—"

The holofeed above the mainframe lit up in a glimmering green. Her modified translation programme had found something in the files.

"Is that it?" Halressan asked.

"I think so, but I can't be sure until..." Ridley trailed off. If it didn't work, if she failed... The thought was too much to bear. Each thump of her heart bruised her ribs. Each ragged breath clawed at her lungs. Her whole body felt like it was going to melt into the ash-covered floor. "Halressan, this is something I need to do by myself. *For* myself."

"No distractions, right?" Halressan smirked. "I'll head back to base and wait for you there. Go talk to your people."

Ridley listened to Halressan's footsteps, the click of her boots fading with each step. She waited for the hiss of the outside door and the sharp crunch of ice underfoot. A gust of wind blew in and sent a chill down her back. Then it was gone, and the grumbling chatter of the air recyclers was all she could hear once again.

The green light on the mainframe pulsed, and Ridley sent the programme to her wrist terminal. All she needed to do was upload it to the satellite and wait.

She settled herself into one of the booths on the other side of the room. The chair was old and musty, with more holes than leather. A slender microphone protruded from the console, giving off a faint crackle of static. Her reflection shimmered in the empty holoscreen in front of her. Her cheeks were gaunt, her eyes wide and fearful. But there was a strength to her jaw she didn't recognise, a hardness to her features she'd only ever glimpsed in others. For better or worse, this galaxy had changed her. It had given her a second chance.

Now it was time to give the same to New Pallas.

Ridley opened a link to the satellite. For a moment, there was nothing. Then the holoscreen lit up to display a flashing symbol, the ancient siolean glyph for *establishing connection*.

Every breath of recycled air resounded in her ears like an echo. Time had slowed, holding the room in some kind of stasis. Her legs grew numb. Her eyes became dry and itchy from the effort of keeping them open.

When the microphone crackled, Ridley thought she was imagining it. Then another burst of static rushed through and she jolted in her chair, staring at the place the sound had come from.

The holoscreen changed, revealing a place she'd only ever laid eyes on once and never expected to see again.

Exodus Station's control room.

Ridley's mouth turned so dry she couldn't trust herself to speak. The control room wavered in front of her eyes like it might vanish. All she wanted to do was press a hand against the holoscreen to check that it was real, to make sure she wasn't dreaming.

"...you hear me? I repeat, you are using one of our secure... without authorisation. Identify yourself."

Ridley scrambled to clean up the connection. "Exodus Station, do you read me? This is Ridley Jones of the *Ranger*."

"Who?"

"Ridley Jo— I mean...never mind. I'm part of the *Ranger's* crew. I left through the waystation with Alvera Renata."

"Never heard of you." The holoscreen feed sharpened into focus and Ridley was met with the irritable features of a grey-bearded comms officer in Exodan dress uniform. He peered into the camera, his frown deepening. "We've not had word from the *Ranger* since it left Exodus Station more than a year ago. So I'm asking you again to identify yourself."

"I already told you, my name is Ridley Jones. I'm part of the *Ranger's* crew and I have an urgent message I need to deliver to—"

"If the *Ranger* made it, then why am I not talking to the captain?" The officer folded his arms. "Where is Alvera Renata?"

"Unavailable. But—"

"How convenient."

Fury rose in Ridley's chest. "You don't believe me? Then check the *fucking* manifest or get me someone who isn't going to waste time neither of us has!"

The officer's face contorted and turned red, but before he could say anything else, the feed disappeared, replaced by the bright white light of the blank holoscreen once more. Ridley stared at it in horror. Had she blown it already? Had she riled up the officer so much he'd cut the connection?

Then the screen flickered, and another face came into view. A solemn man with dark brown skin and soft, searching eyes stared back at her. "Ridley Jones, it's good to meet you. I apologise for the behaviour of the comms officer there. This past year has been...difficult, for all of us."

Ridley stared back at him open-mouthed. "You know who I am?"

"Alvera spoke highly of your accomplishments when we worked together to draw up the *Ranger's* crew. I've learned over the years to trust her judgement." He smiled. "My name is Felix Udo. And with Alvera gone, I suppose that makes me commander of Exodus Station."

"Commander, I..." Ridley trailed off, the rest of her words trapped behind the hard lump in her throat. Exodus Station was there in front of her, separated only by the holoscreen. Somewhere past it, out of sight, was New Pallas. *Home.*

It hadn't felt real until now. It had been too easy to put it out of her mind. She'd been trying to survive, like she always had. And somewhere, past the uncharted reaches of dark space, so had they.

"Please, call me Felix." The commander shifted awkwardly in his chair. "I was never one for titles and formalities. Neither was Alvera, come to think of it. Can I ask..." The glint in his eyes faded. "Is she alive?"

"More or less." The last time Ridley had seen her, Alvera's face had been grey and sickly, her eyes dark with shadows and her cheeks sunken and pale. She'd looked like she was running on nothing more than desperation. Ridley wasn't sure how long a person could last like that. "I suppose you could say this past year has been difficult for us too."

Felix's face fell. "Of course. You said you had something urgent to tell us."

Ridley closed her eyes. Everything she'd been through, everything she'd fought for, it had all come down to this. She'd come all this way to deliver a death sentence. Maybe she should have told Alvera, let her handle it like she handled everything else. But for a reason she couldn't understand, Ridley knew it *had* to be her.

"We're out of time," she said, her voice thin and fragile around the words. "This new galaxy we found ourselves in, this place that was meant to be our future, is under attack. We're fighting back, but the odds..." She shook her head. "The situation is desperate. We're desperate."

Felix straightened. "You need military support? We've had an armada standing by for the last year, waiting on word from the *Ranger*."

"It won't be enough. And that's not the worst of it." Ridley took a breath. "In a matter of weeks, the space tunnel linking Exodus Station to the waystation in this galaxy will collapse. No more ships will be able to make the jump across dark space. New Pallas will be cut off for good."

For a moment, she thought the feed had frozen. Felix looked back at her through the holoscreen, deathly still, his mouth half-open. A heavy silence hung over them both, bridging the unfathomable space between them.

"In a matter of *weeks?*" Felix repeated in a whisper. "We can't evacuate an entire planet in a matter of weeks. There's not enough time."

"I know," Ridley said, tears thickening her throat. This wasn't how it was meant to happen. *All of us go, or none of us go.* That was Alvera's promise, the promise they'd all believed in. Now it was in so many pieces it was impossible to pinpoint the exact moment it had broken.

"And the captain?" Felix asked, echoing her thoughts. "I can't believe she'd accept this. I can't believe she'd give up."

"Alvera sacrificed everything to send a message that never reached you in time," Ridley said. "She fought for New Pallas with everything she had. She crossed lines nobody else would, for better or worse. There's only so long a person can carry that kind of weight, even her. I don't think there's anything left in her to give."

Felix chuckled, the sound of it thin and faint. "If there's one thing I know about Alvera Renata, it's that there's always something left in her to give. I just wish I could have been there to see her do the impossible one last time."

"Felix, I—"

He cut her off with a wave of his hand. "We all knew this was a long shot. If it had been anyone else leading the mission, I'd have given up a long time ago. But even if New Pallas is lost, we can still save some of our people. Alvera gave us that. You gave us that."

Ridley's cheeks flushed. "What will you do?"

"We'll load up our evacuation carriers with as many people as we can in the time we have left," Felix said. "It won't be easy. Too many desperate people trying to get off planet and not enough shuttles to carry them. In all likelihood, this will turn into a bloodbath."

"It won't end there," Ridley said. "Those who make it will be arriving to a bloodbath too." She hesitated. "I know this is hardly the time to ask for favours, but there's something you could do to help us. You won't be able to fill all the evac transports before the tunnel collapses. If you sent one ahead, empty, there's a planet that could desperately use it right now."

"Empty? But..." Felix hesitated. "No, you're right. We don't have time to fill the transports we have—each one is the size of a small city. We'll crunch the numbers and send what we can spare ahead of the evacuation, along with the military fleet."

"Thank you, Felix. And I'm sorry."

"Don't be. We'll save as many as we can. We'll survive as best we can." He gave a tight smile. "It's the one thing Alvera never really understood. She always wanted to save everyone. People like you and me, we understand that's not always possible. Sometimes, the only thing you can do is fight to the next day and hope there's still a familiar face or two when you get there."

Ridley frowned. "What do you mean, people like you and me?"

"I might have lost the accent over the years, but when you

grow up in the darkness like we did, you never forget where you came from. Or what you had to do to survive."

Ridley couldn't speak. The commander of Exodus Station, Alvera's right-hand man, wasn't an Exodan. He wasn't even a topsider. Felix Udo was a surfacer.

Like her.

"I didn't know," she said. "I assumed... Is that why you agreed to help me?"

"I agreed to help you because you reminded me of the captain," Felix said. "Or at least, the parts of her I like to remember. The parts of her that still scrambled to save everyone when the fight was lost." He regarded her with a sad smile. "The truth is, I don't know you. I don't know whether you're acting under Alvera's authority, or if she's even alive. But I have a feeling you and her are on the same side, even if she makes it difficult to see that, sometimes."

Ridley wanted to push his words away, to forget he'd ever said them, but they crept in and burrowed their way under her skin. Her anger at Alvera was still there, a hot ember smouldering under everything she'd done to suppress it. Anger at who she was, at who she'd forced herself to become. But Felix was right. They were on the same side. Even at Alvera's worst, they always had been. She couldn't lose sight of that. Not now they were so close to the end.

"Will you..." The words caught in her throat. "Should I tell her you're coming?"

Felix shook his head. "The captain and I already said our piece to each other. We both knew what this might cost us. She's done her part. Now I have to do mine."

Ridley swallowed. "Then I guess this is goodbye."

"For the two of us, at least." Felix bowed his head. "But look out for our ships, Ridley Jones. They'll be out there. They'll be coming. Look out for New Pallas."

"I will."

His smile lingered on the holoscreen, then disappeared. Ridley sank back into her chair, her throat tight from holding back tears. They had lost. No matter how many they managed to evacuate from New Pallas, no matter how many they saved, they had still lost. Maybe this was why Alvera had become so dangerously desperate. Maybe this was what had broken her.

A soft hiss echoed from the doorway, and the gusting wind outside returned with a chill. The whisper of it racing across the back of her neck was enough to break Ridley from her thoughts. She had to get back to the main base. She had to tell Kojan and Alvera about the reinforcements coming to help. She had to tell Rivus about the evac transport on its way.

"Halressan?" she called. "Good timing. I was about to…"

A shadow fell across the doorway and Ridley froze. The shape was too bulky, too stiff in its movements. The footsteps scraping along the floor were nothing like Halressan's easy gait. The strained effort of deep, guttural breaths punctuated the silence, coming closer with each passing second.

For a fleeting moment, she thought she was imagining things. It was her mind playing tricks on her, nothing more. She was back in the *Ranger's* fuel line, the smell of oil burning her nostrils as she held her body still. Waiting for him to find her. Waiting for him to drag her out of her hiding place and press the barrel of his gun against her head like he'd done to all the others. She'd escaped him that day. She'd never seen him since. It wasn't him. It *couldn't* have been him.

Then Shaw stepped out of the shadows, and she screamed.

TWENTY-ONE

NIOLE

P utting on her armour had become a ritual for Niole. She slid each piece into place around her undersuit, shivering every time the joints clicked together. It was like pulling a second skin over herself, one that was made to withstand more than her fragile body of muscle and sinew and bone could ever endure. The shell around her made her feel like she had some kind of guardian protecting her. It made her feel like she could do anything.

Even this.

She scanned the base's departure manifest until her eyes fell over the entry for the small shuttle she'd registered under a false identification code. It was still there. Her deception hadn't been discovered. Not yet, anyway.

A pinch of fear tightened her gut. It wasn't just the worry of being caught—it was what would happen if she got away. Rhendar had told her to stay on Alcruix. Disobeying his order went against every one of Niole's instincts. But the alternative was leaving him on that asteroid. It was accepting she would never see him again. She couldn't let that happen.

A soft chime echoed off the walls, and Niole froze as the access light on the door panel turned amber. It couldn't have been Venya—Niole had already made sure she was on one of her perimeter patrols. Zal was still on the *Lancer*, attempting to convince Rivus to stay and fight with them. That only left—

"Rhendar gave me the master override codes for every door in the base before he left," came a muffled voice from behind the door. "I'd rather not have to use them."

Serric. Of course, it *had* to be Serric.

Niole bristled. "Are you not familiar with the concept of privacy? I'm in the middle of something right now."

"That's exactly what I'm afraid of." Serric's voice took on a harder edge. "Come on, Niole. Open up."

There was nothing else she could do apart from ping him the access code. She waited for the door to open, for her plans to come tumbling down around her. Maybe Serric would understand. Fyra, maybe he'd want to come with her. She couldn't imagine him being too pleased about getting left behind either.

The doors slid open and Serric marched through. He wasn't in his armour—just casual cargo trousers and a loose shirt that let Niole see more of his chest than she was prepared for.

She gulped down the nervous flutter in her throat. "How did you know I was here?"

Serric fixed her with a hard look. "Felt your flare from three floors up. You can't hide from me. You can't hide what you're up to, either."

Niole's headtails flushed with warmth. "I don't know what you mean."

"Really?" He folded his arms. "There are some Idran-Var who live in their armour. Not you, though. When you put your armour on, it's for a reason. And if that reason is what I think it is, you and I are going to have a problem."

Niole forced a laugh. "You got all that from me putting on my armour? Been watching me that closely, have you?"

Serric scowled and let his flare disperse. Niole's skin tingled as it withdrew. Part of her wanted to reach out towards him, but he took a pointed step back from her, a sullen look settling over his features.

"You can't go," he said shortly. "You heard what Rhendar said. Everyone who went to that asteroid is as good as dead. Our fight is here, with the living." He hesitated and ran a hand over his headtails. "If this is about what I said back on the Omega Gate, you have to understand—"

"It's not about that. It's not about you, or us, or anyone else out there." Niole clenched her jaw. "It's about Rhendar. I was lost until I met him. He *found* me, Serric. He saw me when nobody else did. He knew who I was better than I did and did his best to show me even when I didn't want to see it."

"You think I don't know how that feels?" Serric's headtails flushed dark. "He was the closest thing I ever had to family. He gave me a place to belong, an enemy to fight. He helped make me who I am, and he did the same for you. Throwing your life away on his behalf isn't the way to honour that. It's a betrayal of everything he would have wanted."

Niole stepped away from him, his words stinging her cheeks. "You of all people should understand. How many times did you needle me about running from a fight? How many times did you tell me I needed to accept this part of myself? And now, when I'm finally ready to take a stand, you're trying to stop me?" She snorted. "Great timing, Serric."

"I've learned how to pick my battles."

Niole cocked her head. "You sure about that?"

Before he could reply, she pushed past him, bolting towards the door. For a moment, she thought she'd made it. The glow of the panel blinked in front of her, millimetres from her fingertips.

Then Serric's arms wrapped themselves around her waist and pulled her back.

Her feet ripped away from the ground as he threw her to the floor with a heavy clang. Niole barely felt it through her armour, but the force of the impact sent a gasp rattling through her. Something furious boiled up inside her, rising like a wave, and before she knew what she was doing, she'd drawn her flare into her skin and released it in a vengeful burst.

Serric stepped to the side and caught the blast with his own flare, wrapping it around himself in a spiral before letting it soak back into his skin. He didn't send it back at her. He didn't move at all. He just stood there, shoulders square and brow ridge smooth, holding her in the measured calmness of his stare.

Niole pushed herself back to her feet, tasting blood as she ran her tongue across a tender gash on the inside of her cheek. The metallic tang of it only stoked her anger. "Is that it? What's the matter, Serric? I've never known you to back down from a fight."

He still didn't move. "That's not what this is. If it was, you'd be in far less danger."

"What's that supposed to mean?"

"Keep going with this ridiculous display and you'll find out."

Niole sent another blast from her flare towards him, casting the room in a bright blue light. This time, she caught Serric square in the chest, sending him flying into the wall. He staggered back to his feet, his eyes dull and unfocused as he brought his hand to the back of his head and pressed gingerly. His fingers came away flecked with blood, and he lifted his chin to meet her eyes.

"Not a good idea, Niole."

A flare sprung from his skin in a shimmering blue-green haze. It surrounded him, swirling like it was yearning to break free and come for her.

Her own flare rose to meet it, too impatient for her to control. It pulsed against his, and her body flooded with the fierceness of it, the swelling of energy between them filling like a bubble about to burst.

The realisation seized in Niole's chest. Serric was right. This wasn't a fight. It was something else. Something that terrified her and exhilarated her in equal measure. Something she wasn't sure she could stop, or if she even wanted to.

She released her flare, catching Serric off guard and snapping his head back like he'd taken a blow. He stared at her, his eyes expressionless in their appraisal. Then he gave a dark smile.

The next thing Niole was aware of was something hot slamming into her. Serric's flare pushed her back against the wall, holding her there in its grasp. Her armour was no protection against the crushing weight pinning her down. It was a weight she couldn't escape from. A weight she wanted to surrender herself to, even knowing all that it would do, all that it would *mean*.

Serric stepped towards her, closing the distance between them. His body was only a breath away from hers. There was nowhere left to run. No way left to fight it. But Niole didn't want to fight it, not anymore.

The muscles in Serric's throat twitched with the pulse of his heartbeat. Close enough to taste. Close enough to...

She leaned forward and pressed her lips against his neck.

Serric froze. It was like they were caught in time, held in some kind of stasis. All Niole felt was the brush of his skin against her lips and the energy that rushed between them.

Serric jolted back, his face paling even as his headtails deepened in colour.

"Niole..." he warned, his voice little more than a growl. But he didn't say anything else. He just looked at her, his fingers clenched as his flare surged around him.

"Niole," he said again, but this time there was something else in his voice, something low and throaty and full of the same want, the same need, that was boiling up inside her.

The pressure of his flare disappeared. Then he was on top of her, pushing her back with the strength of his own body, wrapping his hands around the delicate part of her scalp where her headtails met the nape of her neck. His lips crashed into hers with a desperate kind of fury, and she was kissing him back, kissing him so violently that her own flare leapt from her skin again.

It was hard to tell which one of them started to remove her armour first. All she could hear was the clunk of metal as each piece fell to the floor. Each smooth piece of casing she took off stripped her of her shell, until there was nothing left separating them but the thin fabric of their clothing as they tumbled onto the cramped sleep couch at the side of the room.

"Have you ever done this before?" Serric said from above her, his breath warm against her face.

"Not with a si—" Niole caught herself. "Not with an Idran-Var."

"Do you want to?"

She answered him with another kiss, and he sank his weight down on top of her, pressing her against the couch. Everything faded away apart from the sensation of the sheets beneath her and the smoothness of his body against hers, every part of him lithe and taut with longing. His eyes fixed onto hers, never letting go even for a moment.

The pulsing of their flares against each other was so intense Niole couldn't tell where hers ended and his began. The need for him rose in her again and again, sending a violent shudder of pleasure through her headtails each time it came. Time melted away from them, the hours passing in flashes of light, in blurs of breathlessness and spells of sleep. Niole sank herself into the scent of him, the brush of his body against hers, the taste of his lips, and pushed away all thoughts of it being over, all thoughts of leaving. For these last precious moments, there was only Serric.

If only that could have been enough.

———

There was no real concept of dawn on Alcruix. No brightening of the sky, no grey bleed of daylight, just the ever-present black cloak of space draped from horizon to horizon. Even when the base was bathed in its weekly cycle of solar light, each hour moved into the next with no change. It was only the artificial morning glow of the room's window that told Niole it was time to go.

She slipped out from under the sheets and pulled on her undershirt as she padded across the room, the floor like ice beneath her bare feet. Pieces of her armour lay scattered, and she gathered them up, careful as she lifted them to make sure they didn't clink too loudly and wake Serric. The sheets had formed an outline over the long curve of his spine, gently rising and falling as his steady, sleeping breaths echoed around the room.

The last few hours had changed the way it felt to click the pieces of her armour into place. Each of her movements held a hesitancy that hadn't been there before. When Niole had made the decision to leave, she'd only thought about getting to Rhendar. She hadn't considered what she might be leaving behind. Now, the thought of walking out the door wrenched at a part of her she hadn't known existed.

Her helmet stared at her from its place on the locker, the

empty visor fixing her with its blank gaze like it could see right through her.

You're still running, it seemed to say. *You're always running.*

Niole ignored it and scanned the room for her last piece of armour. She was missing her vambrace, the one Rhendar had given her. The part that reminded her most of where she belonged, where she had *chosen* to belong.

"Looking for something?"

She spun around, her heart racing. Serric sat upright on the sleep couch, the sheets gathered around his hips as he leaned forward to pluck her vambrace from the floor. He held it between his hands, staring at it with a furrowed brow ridge. His lean arms were made of nothing more than sinew and muscle. Under the dim sleep lights, Niole saw the patchwork of faint white scars that marred the blue-green skin of his chest and shoulders. Reminders of the battles he'd fought, the battles he'd won. If there was to be one more this morning, she wasn't sure there was a way she could come out on top.

"Take it." Serric tossed her the vambrace so quickly she almost fumbled it to the floor.

She clutched it to her chest, the metal warm from his grip. "Just like that?" she asked. "I thought you'd at least try to stop me."

"It's yours, isn't it?" Serric shrugged. "I have no right to keep it from you. Just as I have no right to keep you here. If you're set on joining Rhendar on that asteroid, I won't stand in your way."

Niole slotted the vambrace into the gap between her wrist and elbow, shivering when it snapped into place. It was duller than the rest of her armour. It didn't have the same fresh sheen as the parts around it. But there was a weight to it that held her like an anchor. Its tarnish told a story; it reminded her of what it had cost her to get here.

"What made you change your mind?" she said quietly.

Serric let out a long sigh and dipped his head forward,

letting his headtails spill over his shoulders. "We don't have to do this, Niole. You got what you wanted. Better we leave it at that."

"I'd rather we didn't." She swallowed. "We both know there's a good chance I won't be coming back from that asteroid. If there's anything left to say, I want you to say it."

Serric looked back at her. "I've been fighting my entire life. Fighting to survive, fighting because I had to, because I wanted to...it's what I've always done. I always thought I'd reach a point where I didn't need to anymore, but it never came. Not for me." He fixed her with a measured stare. "You're not going to that asteroid to fight. You're going out there to be with him at the end. You found something out there that's worth more than fighting for. Something that's worth dying for."

"Is that such a bad thing?"

"Maybe not." A wry smile twisted his lips. "If I'm being honest, I envy you. It took me too long to admit it, even to myself, but I care for you, Niole. More than I ever thought myself capable of. And if that was enough for me, I'd put this entire base on lockdown before I let you leave." He shook his head. "But the fight will always be part of me. I don't think I'll ever be able to stop. I don't think I'll ever *want* to. You deserve more than that."

"Serric..." Niole reached out and laced her fingers between his. Her flare stirred inside her again, but it was quieter now, full of yearning. "You don't have to—"

"I do. It's who I am." He pulled away. "But it's not who you are. Be glad of that."

His words sent a stab of pain through her. Her heart hurt— it *ached*—but not for herself, not this time. It hurt for Serric, for the existence she could imagine all too easily. There was a reason his flare had always called to her. Niole would have drowned herself in it a thousand times over if he'd let her. She'd have lost herself in all of the power, all of the pain.

Looking at him was like looking at all she could be, all she was capable of being.

That was what frightened her the most.

"You're right," she said, her throat tightening around the words. "But Fyra, I wish you weren't. I wish there was a way for—"

"*Idra ti gratar,* Niole," he said gently. "You fought well. But it's over now. You can go. Find the old man and tell him goodbye."

"I will." She choked down the rest of her words. Nothing else she could say mattered now. It would only make the pain worse.

Maybe Serric was right. Maybe they should have left things alone.

She grabbed her helmet from the locker and tucked it under her arm as she walked towards the doors. Every clunk of her boots rang with a finality that made her ache. The soft whirr of the doors became whispers in her ears, filling her head with a thousand reasons to stay. The spotlights in the corridor trailed into the distance, promising a path she'd never be able to turn back from.

"*Idra ti vestar*, Serric," she murmured. "You fought better. You always have."

She stepped into the corridor, leaving the doors to close behind her before she could change her mind.

TWENTY-TWO

KOJAN

Getting drunk had never been something that particularly appealed to Kojan, but if there was ever an excuse to knock back a few drinks, it was the end of the damn world.

Not just the world, he reminded himself. *The entire galaxy.*

He pinged his balance of credits to the bar terminal and threw back a shot of liquor that burned his throat on the way down. It wasn't pleasant, but it warmed his stomach and blanketed his head in a comforting fog that kept the darker thoughts at bay for as long as the buzz lasted.

The bartender loaded the rest of the drinks onto the tray and Kojan gathered it up, trying to keep his balance steady as he navigated towards the booth in the corner where the ras Arbor brothers were waiting. He slid the tray onto the table and sank back on the firm leather couch, wondering if the echoing in his ears was from the alcohol or the noise from the bar.

Max picked up his glass of cloudy ale and raised it in a mock salute. "To the Idran-Var and what they think passes for hospitality around here. At least they make their armour better than they make their drinks."

Sem snorted and clinked his glass against Max's. "To the fact we're still alive to complain about shitty drinks."

"To New Pallas," Kojan said, his words louder and more slurred than he intended. "Who won't have much longer to worry about how shitty or not their drinks are."

He joined his glass with a heavy clunk and then thudded it back down onto the table, ignoring the pointed glance Max and Sem exchanged. There was a dull ache growing in the back of his head now, pushing its way through the haze he'd wrapped himself in. Maybe the drinks were a mistake. Keeping the pain at bay had seemed like a good idea at the time, but now that it was creeping back, its hold on him was tighter than ever.

"I hated how far Alvera went to save us," Kojan said, half to himself. "All the lines she ever crossed, all the lives she ever risked, all for that promise she made: all of us go, or none of us go. And now that she's let go of it, I hate her for that too."

Max shrugged. "Either the asteroid destroys the Omega Gate and some of us see the other side of this shitshow, or it doesn't, and we all fucking die. Not much of a choice, is it?"

"That's what we said about abandoning the Rasnian systems," Sem said, a soft hiccup escaping from his throat. "Will there ever come a point when it's too much? How many more people are we willing to sacrifice for this to be over? How many people need to be left standing at the end for it to be worth it?"

"We're not the kind of people who are meant to have the answers to those kinds of questions." Max took a long slug of ale. "Better that way, if you ask me."

"Always the easy way out with you, isn't it? Can't be the one to blame if you were just following orders, right?" Sem rolled his eyes. "Especially if those orders come with a nice sum of credits attached."

Kojan tuned out their arguing and took another drink. The beer was thick and foamy in his mouth, too stale to be enjoyable. Each gulp he forced down his throat felt like a punishment, but he was too far past the stage of caring. Losing himself at the bottom of a glass was the best thing he could do right now. The *only* thing he could do right now. The alternative was to face what was coming, and he wasn't ready for that yet. Nobody was.

He tore his eyes away from his drink and let his gaze wander around the crowded bar. A wide-eyed siolean lounging on one of the nearby benches giggled and sidled closer to the jarkaath next to her. A group of dachryn huddled together to watch two humans having an arm-wrestling contest, their low, rumbling laughs carrying through the air. He spotted Ridley's girlfriend at one of the holographic gambling terminals, a drink in one hand as she swiped through the controls with the other.

It was all so *normal*. It could have been any dive bar on New Pallas. All of them were here for the same reason—trying to blow off a little steam, trying to forget there was a war going on. But past all the music and chatter and drinks, there was a nervous tension in the room that was palpable. It stuck to Kojan's skin, clinging to him as if to remind him the rest was an illusion. There wasn't enough alcohol in the galaxy to help him forget what was at stake here.

He pushed himself to his feet, swaying from the sudden movement. "I'm going to talk to her."

"Her?" Max raised an eyebrow. "You mean Alvera? Are you sure that's a good idea, given your current...condition?"

"For once, my brother and I agree on something," Sem said. "You should go back to your quarters, Kojan. Sleep it off. You'll regret the headache enough in the morning without adding a confrontation with Alvera into the mix."

"She needs someone to talk some sense into her." Kojan waved them off and drained the rest of his glass. "Don't worry. I can handle Alvera Renata."

"Make sure to fill us in tomorrow morning." Max gave a wry smile. "If you make it that far."

Kojan ignored their chuckling and made his way back to the operations sector of the Idran-Var base. His ears were still tinny and muffled from the thump of music, and the glare from the corridor lights made his eyes water. He brought up his wrist terminal and sent Alvera a ping, his stomach lurching when she responded with her location.

Shit, maybe this wasn't such a good idea after all. Maybe Max and Sem were right, and talking would only make things worse. Too much had changed between him and Alvera over the last year. Too much disappointment and resentment on both their parts, still lingering like an old wound.

You deserved a better captain, she'd told him.

Maybe he did. Maybe they all did. But she was all they had, and they needed her now more than ever.

Kojan found her in one of the quiet rooms. She sat cross-legged on a plump cushion in the middle of the floor, eyes closed and breathing steadily. The soft blue lights from above cast her in a gentle glow, reflecting the paleness of the white walls onto her skin. A loose strand of grey hair fell across her face, and she brushed it aside before opening her eyes.

"Hey, Kojan," she said.

He clenched his jaw. "Hey."

Now that he was here, it was hard to remember what he'd wanted to say. Words weren't enough. All he wanted was for her to understand. To fix all the things she'd broken, and all the things she hadn't but that needed fixing anyway. There was nobody else capable of it. It all came down to her. In a way, it always had.

"There has to be another way," Kojan said, his voice cracking. "If that asteroid hits, if the tunnel collapses...everything we fought for will have been for nothing. The whole reason we came here will die with us. New Pallas will be lost forever."

Alvera stared at him bleakly. "You think I don't know that? You think I haven't known that since the start of all this? I tried everything. No matter what it cost me, or what it cost those around me. It still wasn't enough."

"So that's it? You're giving up?"

"What else do you want me to do?" There was a bite of anger in her voice, a heat that fizzled in the air between them. "There's no solution here that sees New Pallas survive. If the Omega Gate isn't destroyed, they'll be arriving to a galaxy-wide grave. The curators will sweep right through them without a fight."

"You *promised* them."

"And look where that got me. Look where it got us all." Alvera uncrossed her legs and pushed herself to her feet, a vein pulsing in her temple as she rose. The lines on her skin seemed deeper from this close, like scars of age and exhaustion. "It's over, Kojan. I've done all that I can."

"Bullshit." Something white-hot bubbled up in his chest. "You can't go as far as you did and decide it's time to stop. It's too late to back down now. I might not have agreed with the things you've done, but you did them anyway. You never cared what I thought, what anyone thought. It was always about you. And now things have gone to hell, you want to hand that off to somebody else?"

Alvera narrowed her eyes. "That's not what I'm doing."

"Of course it is. You've given up. You can't face the fight anymore, so you're waiting to die." Kojan snorted. "You have your own kind of quickening inside you, don't you? But instead of your cybernetics eating away at you, it's everything you ever did in the name of New Pallas. Everything you ever failed to do for them. It's rotting you from the inside out, and you'd rather let it destroy you than find a way to stop it."

Alvera blanched. Something in the hardness of her eyes slackened, like she was looking right through him to something he couldn't see. All the sharp edges of her features had frozen, as if she'd turned to stone in front of him.

Then she shook herself. "Enough," she said, her voice cold. "I need you to leave, Kojan."

"Don't worry, I'm going." He walked towards the door, his blood boiling with every step. He should never have come here. It was another mistake. Another regret on top of so many.

He glanced back at her from the threshold. Alvera had her back to him, her shoulders stiff and hunched. "You did the unthinkable so we didn't have to, and I've always resented you for it," he said quietly. "Maybe that wasn't fair. But you chose this responsibility. You *took* it. That means it's up to you to fix it. And this time, I don't give a damn how you do it. Just get it done."

Kojan stumbled back into the corridor, his head reeling as he headed towards his assigned quarters. The throbbing in his temples spread all the way around his head, creeping into the nape of his neck. He needed to lie down. He needed somewhere he could sink into the embrace of sleep and forget about all of this.

Before he had time to send his code to the access panel, the doors hissed open in front of him and Cyren rushed out of his room, her tail swishing in agitation.

"Kojan!" Her yellow eyes widened. "I've been looking for you everywhere. You didn't respond to my ping."

"I didn't see it." A wave of exhaustion crashed over him. "Cyren, this isn't the best time. I need to—"

"You think I'd have sliced into your quarters if this wasn't important?" she asked, the scales around her nostrils rippling. "One of the Idran-Var passed on some security footage. You need to see this."

"Can't it wait? I'm really—"

"Look." She brought up a holofeed on her wrist terminal and ran through the recording until she reached a still frame showing the exterior of the base. "See there? Do you recognise him?"

At first, Kojan couldn't be sure. His head was still fuzzy from the alcohol, and the image was hazy. The shadowy figure was caught mid-step in a stalking prowl, his head covered with a hood. It could have been anyone.

Then he looked closer and saw the sheen of cybernetics surrounding a dark, gaping hole where an eye should have been.

His whole body turned cold. "Shaw. No, it can't be."

"He's here, Kojan. Somewhere on the base. You're in danger."

"Not just me." Fear leapt in his throat. "He'll be after Ridley too. I need to find her."

"I tried to ping her too. She's not answering."

Kojan thought for a moment. "The bar. Halressan was down there earlier. Maybe she was waiting for her."

Cyren nodded. "Let's go."

He stormed back through the corridors, taking the steps three at a time. The fog around his head had lifted. Shaw was here. Still hunting them even as the galaxy burned. Still set on making them pay. There were only so many times they could slip out of his grasp. Sooner or later, he'd find them. Maybe he already had.

The bar was just as he'd left it, thumping with low, pulsing music and thick with the stench of ale and sweat. No gunfire, no terror. Not yet, anyway. Kojan scanned the benches and booths until his eyes fell across the bright purple of Halressan's leather jacket.

"Over there," he said to Cyren.

Halressan was in one of the smaller booths next to Drexious, a steaming tray of ground meat and sticky vegetable skewers placed between them. The aroma made Kojan's mouth water and stomach churn at the same time. Only two plates. Only two drinks. Ridley wasn't here.

"Where is she?" he said, fighting to catch his breath.

Halressan arched one of her pale blonde eyebrows. "What are you talking about?"

"Ridley. You need to tell me where she is."

"She didn't tell you?" Halressan sent him an appraising look. "Then I'm not going to either. She's in the middle of something important. Doesn't want to be disturbed. The rest is none of your business."

"None of my..." Kojan broke off, grinding his teeth. "Do you have any idea how—"

Cyren wrapped her claws around his arm. "Let me show her the footage."

She tapped her wrist terminal and brought up the recording. Kojan shuddered as the feed flickered into life. Watching it back a second time was worse now that he knew who it was. Every one of Shaw's stalking steps sent a fresh wave of dread through him.

"His name is Artus Shaw," he said. "Did Ridley ever tell you about him?"

Halressan watched the feed, her face turning more and more ashen with each passing second. All the disdain in her expression had drained.

"How long ago was this?" she asked, her lips trembling.

Cyren swiped through the feed. "About an hour."

"Ridley told me about him. She told me what he did to your

crew, what he would have done to her if she hadn't escaped."
Halressan looked sick. "And now you're telling me he's here?"

Kojan leaned down in front of her, forcing her to meet his
eyes. "Where is she?" he asked again.

"Alone." Halressan's words sent a chill through him. She
glanced at Drexious, then back at him, and swallowed. "We
need to go. Right now."

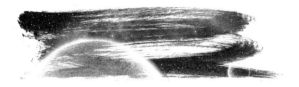

TWENTY-THREE

RIDLEY

Shaw braced himself on either side of the doorway and stretched his mouth into a twisted grin. The red light from his retinal implant pierced the darkness, casting what was left of his face in a bloody glow. The rest of his eye socket was empty, pulling in Ridley's gaze so she couldn't escape.

"The surfacer." His voice was thin and ragged. "The *slete*."

It shouldn't have been able to hurt her, not after all she'd been through. But the word still wormed its way through Ridley's defences, reminding her of her place in the galaxy. Someone who didn't matter. Someone who was *obsolete*.

"What is it about you?" Shaw continued, tilting his head to one side. "What makes you so damn special?"

Ridley's tongue stuck to the roof of her mouth in terror. Her limbs froze in place. *Special?* She might have laughed if she'd been able to. There was nothing special about her. If there was, she might have been able to save New Pallas. She might have been able to save herself. "Why are you here, Shaw? What do you want from me?"

"Answers." He tightened his jaw, exposing the threads of torn muscle and tissue held together by his cracked cybernetic plating. "How did you manage to contact Exodus Station when nobody else could? How did you manage to gain the respect of these Idran-Var? How did you get away without a scratch while I was left to rot?"

"You can't be serious." Rage swelled through Ridley's fear. "Everything that happened to you, you brought upon yourself. You chose to release Ojara. You chose to murder the *Ranger's* crew. You chose to go up against Alvera. Did you really think you could win that fight? That she would let it go?" A snort of laughter escaped her lips. "You deserve every bit of pain that has come your way and more."

Shaw pulled his lips back in a feral sneer. "You want to talk about deserving? None of you sletes should have been on that ship in the first place. We should have left you to rot on New Pallas." He took a long, rasping breath and steadied himself on the door frame. "It might be too late for that now, but at least I can stop your precious evac ships."

Ridley froze. "What are you talking about?"

"I heard what you told them. The space tunnel connecting Exodus Station to this galaxy will collapse when that asteroid hits. So maybe I'll send them another message. Maybe I'll tell them the tunnel has already been destroyed, that any of their ships that come through will be lost in the void or broken up into pieces as they're sucked into a black hole. They won't leave. They'll die on that pitiful excuse for a planet like they were always meant to."

"You can't." Horror clamped up Ridley's throat. "It's not just New Pallas—they'll be evacuating Exodus Station too. Those are your people."

"I have no people." Shaw's ragged features contorted into a

fury that turned her insides cold. "Look at what your captain did to me. My body is beyond repair. My cybernetics are beyond repair. The only reason I haven't put a bullet through what's left of my skull is because I owe her a debt that needs repaid."

"You'll never be able to kill her."

"I don't need to." Shaw's face split into another manic grin. "I'm going to destroy her the way she destroyed me. I will take everything from her and leave her with only her failures for company as she dies." He straightened his spine, his face twisting at the movement. "I'll start with you, Ridley Jones. I'm going to take that data cube from you. Then I'm going to kill you and leave your body here for your precious captain to find."

His frame filled the doorway, blocking Ridley's escape. She was normally so much better than this, so much more prepared. Back on New Pallas, she'd never have dreamed about shutting herself in a room without some kind of contingency. She'd gotten too comfortable, too safe. Too used to having someone at her back. Halressan wasn't here to save her this time. It was just her and this monster.

A cruel smile crept over Shaw's face. "There's no way out for you. I made sure of it this time." He stretched out one of his hands, his cybernetic bone reinforcements peering through the burned-off skin over his knuckles. "Now, give me the data cube, or I'll take it from your cold, dead body."

Ridley tightened her grip around the black box, its smooth surface growing slippery in her hands. If she surrendered it to Shaw now, he'd undo everything she'd fought for.

And if you don't, he'll kill you and take it anyway, she reminded herself.

She had no choice. It came down to what it always did: survival. No matter what the cost, no matter what the consequences.

"Have it your way," Ridley said. "If you want it, it's yours."

Time slowed down. The smile on Shaw's face widened millimetre by millimetre, like a vid stuttering through the individual frames. He stood motionless as she drew her arm back, clutching the data cube like it was a grenade she'd armed. Then she threw it straight at his vicious face.

Ridley didn't wait to see the cube hit its mark. She'd already turned away and crossed the distance to the window in a few desperate strides. There was no slowing down. No time for doubts. The ash-stained glass was in front of her, the only thing left in her way.

She dipped her head and launched herself at the window. The impact rattled through her like a blow, stunning her. Then it was gone, and she was falling, falling to the ground with nothing to stop her. Her ears filled with the sound of splintering glass. The shards rained down, biting at the back of her neck and across her arms and hands. She bit back a cry of pain as blood splattered the grey-dusted ground.

A dull pain twinged in her left knee. The window was higher from the ground than she'd realised. She'd landed awkwardly, twisting her legs and scraping her palms raw and bloody from where she'd braced her fall.

Slivers of glass glinted from her forearms as she pushed herself back to her feet. No time to assess her injuries now. She had to move.

A furious roar tore through the thin atmosphere. Shaw stood in the empty window, his half-formed jaw snarling as he looked at her. He steadied himself and leapt down from the opening, the broken glass crunching under his boots.

"I'll kill you," he said, his voice a low, rasping mutter. "I will leave you in pieces across this mountain. That bitch girlfriend and the lizard scum you tag along with won't ever find what's left of you. I'll make sure of it."

Fear flooded Ridley's chest. Shaw's hatred burned through

in every word. She couldn't bring herself to imagine the things he'd do to her if he caught her, the ways he'd make her suffer. Thinking about it only made the terror worse. If she wanted to escape, if she wanted to survive, she had to push it away.

She pulled her breather mask up around her nose and willed her limbs into action. The terrain underfoot was a mixture of compacted ash and ice-encrusted rock. Every step she took was an invitation to slip and fall. And a fall was sure to mean death, whether at Shaw's hand or on the grim, steep sides of the mountain.

Every breath came sharp and shallow, even with the oxygen aids in her mask. This wasn't what she was cut out for. She wasn't fierce and strong like Halressan. She wasn't quick and nimble like Drexious. She didn't have Alvera's resolve or Kojan's reflexes. Out here against the elements, against the monster pursuing her, Ridley felt shamefully, vulnerably *human*.

Obsolete, the wind whispered to her. *That's what you are. That's all you'll ever be.*

Ridley craned her neck. Shaw had closed the distance between them, but not as much as she'd expected. He was struggling to drag himself across the sliding gravel and volcanic rock. Whatever Alvera had done to him, it showed in the strain of every movement. Maybe neither of them would make it off the mountain alive.

"You can't run forever." Shaw spat a shower of blood over the ash at his feet. "You're weak. You've always been weak. I should have pushed you off the shuttle the first time we met, just like I did to that other slete."

He cracked his fist against his palm. Ridley remembered the sound all too well. Sometimes when she closed her eyes, she still saw the surfacer fall. She still heard his skull shatter as it hit the ground. That was the first time she'd realised what Shaw was capable of. The first time she'd caught a glimpse of the monster behind the mask.

Even after all this time, she still hadn't learned that lesson well enough.

Shaw lunged towards her, letting out a furious snarl from the back of his throat. The movement was so sudden, so desperate, that Ridley didn't have time to react. His shoulder collided with her waist, knocking the air from her lungs. A jolt of pain shot through her elbow as she landed. The crushing pressure of Shaw's weight pressed her into the jagged rock underneath. Then it was gone, and she was tumbling down the side of the mountain, her head spinning as she clattered across the ash-covered ground. Every new bump and thud rattled her brain inside her skull until she couldn't tell which way was up anymore.

When she came to a stop, she could hardly breathe. Her oxygen tubes had been knocked loose from her nostrils, and she fumbled to reconnect them, gasping for air. Every part of her body felt bruised and broken. She didn't know how far she'd fallen or where she'd ended up. A fog settled over her head, clouding everything but the pain.

Ridley lifted her chin and tried to catch her bearings. The wind had picked up, thickening the air with swirling ash and sharp fragments of ice. Its bite nipped at her skin until her cheeks were raw. She focused her eyes on the rugged terrain in front of her, and her stomach lurched as she caught sight of Shaw.

He was hunched over, holding one arm limp at his side. The side of his face that still looked human was covered in a bloody mask, with streaks of red running from a deep gash in his forehead. Bone reinforcements jutted through his skin, making him look like more of a machine than ever.

Then Ridley spotted the gun.

It was lying on the ground between them. Shaw must have lost it during the fall. If she reached it before him, if she closed the distance before he could...

Ridley leapt forward and snatched the gun, scrambling back out of Shaw's reach before he could charge her down again. Her heart thumped furiously as she wrapped her hands around the cold metal and levelled the barrel at Shaw's head. There was a tremor in her arms that had nothing to do with Alcruix's icy atmosphere. Her fingers brushed over the trigger like glass, like they might shatter into pieces.

Shaw stumbled and fell to his knees, bracing himself against the ground with one arm. He looked up at her, his tongue lolling red in his mouth. He wasn't afraid. That terrified her more than anything else. Even now he was still smiling, his torn lips like the foaming jaws of a rabid animal.

He coughed and spat blood onto the ground at her feet. "You won't do it."

Ridley tightened her grip around the gun, trying to ignore how much it was shaking. He was wrong. She could do it—she *had* to do it. It didn't matter that he was hunched over like a wounded animal. It didn't matter that the touch of the gun felt wrong in her hands. It didn't matter that her mouth was dry and her chest had seized up, like her body was shutting down. Shaw was a killer. He'd executed the crew of the *Ranger* without a second thought. This was only payback for those deaths. This was only justice.

"You're a coward." Shaw leered at her. "You always were. That's why you hid rather than face your fate back on the *Ranger*. Even now, you can't bring yourself to pull the trigger. You don't have the stomach for—"

He stopped mid-sentence, his jaw gaping and a circle of red blooming in what was left of his forehead.

Ridley froze. Her hands were shaking, still wrapped around the gun, but the metal was cool in her hands. There was no wrench as the bullet left the chamber, no sting in her palms from the kickback. It was still and quiet, waiting for a brush of the trigger that hadn't come, that would never come.

She turned around. Halressan stood a few metres behind her, her own pistol still smoking in the frosty air.

"She doesn't need the stomach for it," she said softly. "She's got me."

Ridley let the gun fall from her hands. In two steps, she was in front of Halressan, her heart hammering, her hands running over her armour, her lips moving but finding no words.

"Don't," Halressan said tightly. "Don't thank me. Don't apologise. Whatever you're going to do, just...don't."

Ridley kissed her.

It was different this time. No warmth flooded her cheeks, no desire pooled in the pit of her stomach. It wasn't want, or even need, it was *home*. She pressed her lips against Halressan's, losing the taste of her to the low, choking sobs wracking her chest. But Halressan pulled her close and kissed her back with a tenderness Ridley hadn't known she was capable of. All she wanted to do was dissolve into the softness of her, the gentle caress of her touch. She felt the trickle of tears down her cheeks, then the brush of Halressan's fingers as she wiped them away.

"I couldn't let you do it," Halressan said, her voice hoarse. "Not like that, putting him down like a wretched animal."

Ridley shook her head. "I've killed before."

"Not like this. Not somebody who was already beaten, helpless to do anything about it. Not in that kind of cold blood." An angry tremor danced along Halressan's jaw. "That's why he wanted you to do it. He wanted that kind of horror to stay with you forever. I couldn't give him that kind of power over you. Couldn't let him haunt you like that."

Ridley brushed her fingers across Halressan's cheek. Her skin was soft and cold to the touch. "Do they haunt you?"

"Some of them." Halressan leaned forward and pressed a gentle kiss against Ridley's forehead. "Not this one. Never this one."

Ridley closed her eyes and slipped back into Halressan's arms. For a few precious moments, all she could feel was the strength of her embrace holding her together. The wind howled around them, but she was numb to its sting now. A violent quake ran through the ground under her feet, but the rumbles of a broken planet didn't matter anymore. Not if she could stay like this forever.

"Ridley?"

She opened her eyes. Kojan was at Halressan's shoulder, his dusky skin paler than she'd ever seen it, his eyes circled with dark lines. Drexious stood next to him, tail swishing, frost forming patterns across his scales.

Before Ridley could say anything, they stepped forward and looped their arms around her. Another sob tore free as they huddled around her, encircling her, holding her close. Shaw was gone. He'd never hurt her again. Here, surrounded by these people she loved—her friends, her *family*—she was safe.

Even if it was only for a little while.

Ridley disentangled herself from the knot of their arms and wiped the remaining moisture from her eyes. "We need to get back to base."

"Cyren is waiting nearby with the skiff." Kojan ran his eyes over her face and arms. "Some of those cuts look nasty. We'll get you to a medbay so you can get patched up."

"There's something I have to do first." Ridley glanced at Shaw's body sprawled across the rocks. He was smaller in death, somehow. His expression was blank and empty as he stared up at the sky, one eye distant and glassy, the other an empty socket glowing with the red light from his retinal implant.

It seemed fitting, in a grim, twisted way, that his cybernetics should outlive him. All the parts of him he thought made him better than her—made him *more* than her—didn't care that the rest of his body had given up. In death, he was as human as she was.

The red light from his empty eye followed her as she approached, and Ridley couldn't help but shudder as she knelt next to the blood-soaked ground and wrapped her fingers around the black box that had slipped from his lifeless grasp. She had the data cube. She had her line back to New Pallas. Now, all she needed was a welcoming party.

"I need to get to the operations centre," she said. "There's a message I have to send to the Supreme Commander."

———

By the time they reached the base, Ridley's pain had increased tenfold. The deeper gashes on her arms still oozed with blood. Her knee twinged every time she put weight on it. All she wanted to do was lie down and sleep for a week.

But she couldn't. Not when there was so much at stake.

She allowed Halressan to ease her into one of the hover-chairs, wincing as she sat down. Kojan and Drexious were working at one of the consoles while Cyren paced back and forth, her tail swishing with every stride. The room was fraught with nervous energy, making Ridley's stomach churn. Maybe Kojan was right. Maybe she should have gone to the medbay first. She'd be no use to anybody if she passed out from the pain.

"Damn it." Kojan hit one of the holoscreens. "The *Lancer* has already left. Logs show it finished refuelling hours ago and departed for Ossa soon after. Rivus is gone."

"Send him a priority message," Ridley said. "He can divert to the Ulla system before continuing on to Ossa. He'll need those evac ships from New Pallas."

"Trying to establish a connection now." Kojan frowned. "Taking a little longer than expected. The signal is bouncing around off the comms relays in this system. It's like it can't find a way through."

"Keep trying."

An uneasy quiet settled over the room. The tension felt like a cord pulled too taut, ready to snap at any second.

A whirr broke through Ridley's thoughts as the doors slid open and Zal burst into the room, her face pale and hair bedraggled.

"You won't get through," she said hoarsely. "It's too late."

Ridley turned cold. "What do you mean?"

"The curators are already at the edge of the system. Our forward patrol couldn't get a message back to us through the ships' comms systems, so they dispatched one of the scouts to deliver the news in person. I don't know what happened to the rest of them." A dark look fell across Zal's face. "Nothing good, I expect."

"A communications blackout," Kojan said faintly. "They did the same in the Rasnian systems. Shit, I should have realised."

Fear tightened Ridley's throat. "We need to get word to Rivus."

"You think it would make a difference, even if you could?" Zal scoffed. "The Supreme Commander made his decision. He won't let himself abandon Ossa. Stubborn *malré* is running off to get himself killed fighting for a lost cause."

"Isn't that what we're all doing?" Kojan said. "We knew the curators were coming here. We stayed to put up a fight, to keep them occupied so Rhendar and the others on the asteroid have a chance to pull off the unthinkable. If this is the end, I don't blame Rivus for spending these final few moments trying to do right by his people."

Zal let out a long, heavy sigh. "In any case, it's impossible. We're down to short-range communications only. Cross-planet channels and orbiting satellite systems is as good as it gets from here on out. Rivus Itair is beyond our reach now."

"Not exactly."

Ridley snapped her head towards Kojan. He was staring back at her, his jaw set in a determined line.

"The *Ranger*," he said. "I can catch him."

"Even if you make it to one of the space tunnels, there could still be a lot of curator ships between you and the *Lancer*." Ridley shook her head. "Alvera won't want to risk—"

"I'm not asking Alvera," Kojan said, his eyes fierce as he stared back at her. "I'm asking you."

Ridley couldn't answer. Those kinds of decisions had always been made by people with the stomach to live with the consequences, people made of hard fights and harder losses, people who could carry the weight of hundreds of thousands of lives on their shoulders without breaking under it. That had never been her. She'd never *wanted* it to be her.

"Go," Ridley said finally, her words leaving her mouth in someone else's voice. "Find Rivus. Tell him New Pallas is coming to help."

Kojan straightened. "Stay alive until we get back, all right? One way or another, we're getting that New Pallas reunion."

He turned towards the doors, Cyren following closely on his heels. He left a stillness in his wake, a silence that seemed like it might smother her. This might be the last time Ridley ever saw him. She might have just said her first goodbye. It wasn't likely to be the last.

Halressan cleared her throat. "And the rest of us? I assume we have a better plan than sitting on our asses waiting for the curators to come kill us."

Ridley looked at Zal. The Idran-Var scout leader was hunched over the console like she was bent under the weight of what was coming. It was her planet that would serve as the battleground for this fight, her people who would stand here alongside their old enemies in defence of the rest of the galaxy.

It would be too much for anyone else to handle. But the Idran-Var weren't just anyone.

"What are we going to do?" Ridley asked softly.

Zal looked up, the hint of a grim smile dancing at the corners of her lips. "What we always do," she said. "We resist."

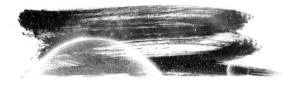

TWENTY-FOUR

ALVERA

Alvera was no stranger to a fight. She'd done her share of killing—some of it justified, some of it a stain she'd never be able to wash out. She'd seen her share of bodies, friends and enemies alike.

But this wasn't a fight. This was war.

The Idran-Var base was on high alert, sirens blaring and corridors heaving with bustling bodies. The armoury had been emptied, the weapons lockers stripped bare. Everyone who knew how to hold a gun had geared up for the coming battle. Those who didn't hunched themselves over holoscreens and consoles, putting their own brand of violence to good use through the base's weapons systems and targeting arrays.

Alvera pulled the chestpiece of her exosuit over her head, wincing at the strain in her shoulders. It was more difficult than it used to be. Her muscles didn't have the same strength anymore. Her lungs took a little more effort to fill each day. She'd spent too many years pushing them to their limit. Now, it was all catching up with her.

She walked into the war room to find it empty apart from Zal and Serric, who were in the middle of a heated discussion.

When Zal saw her, she straightened her spine. "Good. At least *someone* is still here."

Serric shot her an irritated look. "Don't start this again."

"Start what? You were the one who let one of our best warriors pack up and leave."

"Niole made her choice. It wasn't my place to interfere."

"It never stopped you before, did it?" Zal sighed. "We're outnumbered, Serric. We need every fighter we can get."

Alvera crossed her arms. "That's what I'm here for. Where do you need me?"

"Everywhere." Zal ran a hand through her bedraggled hair. "We've got a formidable network of orbital defences that should hold off any heavy bombardment for a while. Targeting cannons built into asteroids, satellite-guided missile systems, proximity charges set along a variety of orbital approaches. But even if we hold the curator dreadnoughts at bay, we won't be able to stop their smaller ships getting through. That will be their plan of attack. They'll overwhelm us with ground troops until there's nothing left to defend."

"They have the numbers," Serric said. "All they need to do is keep throwing bodies at us until we're overrun. That's where we could use your help."

"What did you have in mind?"

"Your cybernetics can hack their systems." Serric gave her a sidelong look. "I know it doesn't come without cost, but if you could disrupt some of their transport shuttles and stop them from landing..."

"I'd need some kind of connection." Alvera frowned. "If I got onto one of their shuttles, I might be able to use its systems to link up to the rest of them. I could send some kind of rogue code into their navigation consoles or burn out their engines."

"It's worth a shot," Zal said, tapping her chin. "But you'll need support to cut a path through to one of their shuttles. I'll contact some of the heavy hitters and see if any of them are up for the job."

Alvera stiffened. "That's not necessary. I won't risk anybody else."

"Save the heroics, human," Serric said dryly. "The curators had us beaten on the Omega Gate because we were in their territory. They won't find it as easy now they're in ours."

Alvera followed his gaze to the window. Beyond the glass, she saw the faint white-blue plume of ice and gas spouting from a skyscraper-tall cryovolcano. The unstable ground rumbled under her feet as the planet's broken surface groaned and shifted. The thin black atmosphere bled into space, littered with fragments of rock and metal that had been pushed into orbit all those centuries ago. Alcruix wasn't a planet that knew peace. Alvera couldn't help but find something reassuring in that.

"All right," she said, releasing a long breath. "Who did you have in mind?"

———

The scream of a missile pierced through her helmet's earpiece, and Alvera scrambled behind an icy outcropping to shield herself from the shower of rocks and shrapnel that exploded from the rugged ground only metres ahead. Even through her helmet's filtration systems, she smelled burning. Everywhere she looked, more curator dropships burst through the canopy of ash, opening their doors to release the next swarm of thralls onto the battlefield.

"Well, isn't this the most pleasant of reunions?"

Skaile huddled beside her, lips drawn back in a familiar sneer. A shimmering red glow rose from her armour as she sent a flare into the midst of the incoming curators. A crackle ripped through the air, splitting a fissure in the terrain as it raced towards the enemy and consumed them in a burst of red.

"Nice work," Alvera said. "Try to keep it aimed at the curators this time instead of turning on us again, will you?"

"Don't worry, they'll pay for their attempts to get into my head," Skaile replied, her eyes gleaming. "Only I get to decide who I kill."

She leapt back to her feet and stormed through the rubble, summoning another surge of energy. Alvera followed her, each step crunching through scraps of battle underfoot—shards of armour, hollowed-out artillery shells, the broken bodies of the fallen. The curators had begun their assault mere hours ago, and already Alcruix wore the scars of their brutality. Smoking craters, burned-out defence outposts, scattered wreckages of fighters and ground transports.

"Looks bad, doesn't it?" Venya appeared at her side, a huge rocket launcher strapped to her shoulder. She towered above Alvera, as broad and hulking as a mountain made of metal.

Alvera nodded. "I'm sorry."

"Don't be. This planet is tougher than you know. There's nothing those bastards can do to it that we've not done already. If it survived the Idran-Var, it can survive this." Venya eyed Skaile as she let loose another flare. "I know some sioleans can be...*unstable*...but she's something else."

"Just be glad she's on our side."

"I'm not sure she's on anybody's side. Unless there's a side for indiscriminate violence and chaos." Venya chortled. "In any case, she cleared a path for us. We should keep moving."

"What about ras Arbor?"

"Right here." Max jumped over a hastily-dug trench, carrying a long-barrelled sniper rifle in his hands. He'd modified his Rasnian exosuit with pieces of Idran-Var plating, and the utility belt around his waist was laden with so many explosives that Alvera worried he'd leave nothing behind but a burning crater if he tripped.

She focused her eyes across the terrain, wincing at the shock her retinal implants gave her as she enhanced her vision on a smoking shuttle in the distance. "I see a downed curator transport. It's been hit, but it looks mostly intact. If we can reach it, I might be able to get into their systems."

"Sounds like we have a target." Venya gave a satisfied grunt. "Let's move. I'm not about to let Skaile have all the fun."

Alvera followed her, weaving from one makeshift barricade to another. She took shelter wherever it was offered, from the shelves of volcanic rock jutting up from the planet's surface to the smoking ruins of abandoned transports. Her helmet echoed with the sounds of war, the blanket of her own breathing muffling the explosions and screams around her. She ignored the bodies littering the ground as the smell of scorched flesh burned her nostrils. Everywhere she looked there was more death, more violence. This was what she'd helped bring upon the galaxy. This was what she had to answer for.

"Watch out—we've got a velliria!"

A huge, insectoid alien descended from above. Its steely wings clicked and clattered as it swept its way along the ground towards them. Even at a distance, Alvera could see the gape of its mandibles, their serrated prongs splayed wide in a mixture of tissue and flesh, saliva dripping from the roof of its mouth.

She fired a barrage of shots from her rifle. Some of them hit flesh with a soft *thunk-thunk-thunk*, but more still bounced harmlessly off the velliria's metal plating. The alien let out an ear-splitting shriek but continued its advance, bearing down on them as a blue-coloured pus began oozing from beneath its metallic carapace.

Dread twisted Alvera's stomach. If the thralls felt pain, it didn't stop them. They didn't know what it meant to pull back in a tactical retreat. They certainly didn't know how to surrender. They were nothing but empty shells, stripped of the consciousness they once had. Bred from leftover genetic material for the sole purpose of killing. When one fell, a thousand more were already waiting to replace it.

This would be their fate if they lost, Alvera realised. One by one, they'd fall. Maybe it would take centuries. It didn't matter. The curators had all the time in the galaxy.

The velliria was close now. The biological signal it emitted was a sharp pain coiling around Alvera's nerves. In a few moments, she'd be paralysed.

"Skaile, I need you to take care of that thing!" she yelled. "The rest of you, keep moving. We're not far from the shuttle."

Another burst of red flashed across the edge of Alvera's vision, and the sound of tearing flesh and shattering metal rang around her ears. She didn't wait to watch the velliria fall. More curator thralls were already swarming around them. Max lined up a shot with his rifle and put a bullet through the beady yellow eye of an approaching azuul. Venya was further ahead, wrestling with one of the sharp-fanged, blue-coated creatures that scurried around on six legs. The smoking battleground had become a blur. Everything faded into the distance apart from the next enemy in front of her, the next target for her gun.

The downed curator ship was ahead, half engulfed in a plume of black smoke pouring from one of its engines. Alvera wrapped her hands around the edge of the access hatch to pull it open, but the door wouldn't budge. She tried again, her forearms aching from the effort.

"It's jammed," she said. "Must have been damaged during the crash."

"Allow me." Venya marched forward and pressed her huge shoulder to the edge of the door. Something inside the mechanism groaned, then the whole door fell away, crashing to the floor of the shuttle like it had been made from a sheet of plastic.

Venya cracked her jaw plates into a grin. "You're welcome."

Alvera pulled herself through the gap. Inside, the shuttle was a mess. Half the consoles were blown out with electrical fires, and there was no lighting apart from the glow of the red emergency beacons dotted along the wall.

"You really think you're going to find something functional in this wreck?" Skaile followed her in, removing her helmet with a grimace. The deep red pigment of her skin had paled with exhaustion, and Alvera couldn't help but let her eyes flit over the ragged stump of the headtail she'd lost on the Omega Gate. Not that losing an appendage was likely to slow Skaile down, if half of Ridley's stories about her were true.

"This part of the shuttle looks pretty burned up, but there might be a viable control system further inside," Alvera said. "I'll go on ahead. The rest of you stay here and bunker down."

She stepped through the wreckage towards one of the adjoining corridors. Some of the floor panels had come apart during the crash, and the emergency lighting had failed entirely, leaving the rest of the corridor in darkness.

Alvera adjusted her retinal implants with a neural command, and her vision brightened. This was what they'd created cybernetics for back on Exodus Station. To be able to see things. To be able to survive in places they weren't meant to. To become stronger, smarter. To become something *more*. They'd been walking the same path as the curators without knowing it.

A faint glow from up ahead cut through the gloom. One of the door access panels was still functioning. Alvera pressed her hand against it, gathering her breath as she waited for her cybernetics to hack the encryption. The panel turned green and the doors slid open with a gentle whirr, opening up into a small server room. Towers of processors stretched from floor to ceiling, still humming with power. Lights flashed across their holographic interfaces, beckoning her closer.

This was something she could work with.

Alvera closed her eyes and opened the connection. Immediately, her head flooded with pain. Every nerve, every synapse, pulled so tight it was ready to snap. A million needles probed her mind, each one more intrusive than the last.

The consciousness of the hive brushed against her mind like a whisper. The curators wanted her back. They wanted to break down her mind and catalogue her memories in their endless archive, so the part of her that was once Alvera Renata no longer existed.

You are but a single mind. The voice came from everywhere and nowhere, filling her head until there was no room for anything else. *A single life. So fleeting, so inconsequential. Yet you persist in this arrogance, in this delusion. There is no power in the individual. Only in our connections, our collective thought, can we achieve true meaning.*

Alvera gritted her teeth. "You only say that because you've forgotten who you used to be. You don't remember what it was like to have a single thought of your own. If you did, you'd know it's not in our nature to go down without a fight."

You are not the first to fight, the hive whispered. *You are not the first to believe you can win. But you live in a galaxy of our design. We are history and memory, past and future. You already belong to us. You* are *us. You cannot escape it.*

"We belong to no one." Blood dribbled from Alvera's nose, and she wiped it away. "Look at the Idran-Var. Look at the people we fight beside. Individuals. Single lives. All of them fighting together. Not because we're part of some collective, part of some shared consciousness. But because we *choose* to. As people. As friends. As enemies. As all of the mistakes we've made along the way."

That is why you will fail, the voice said, echoing against oblivion. *Tell us, Alvera Renata, what happens when the desires of the individual come into conflict with the needs of the collective? What happens when all that you fight for no longer aligns with what you must do to win?*

Darkness engulfed Alvera's vision. Then the shadows lifted, and she was back on solid ground. Back on a street she'd walked down a hundred times, a street made of crumbling grey concrete suspended kilometres above the surface. Back below an orange-red sun fighting to push through the smog that lingered around the pinprick spires of the highest skyscrapers. Back on the planet she'd left behind, amongst the people she'd abandoned.

It was New Pallas, but not the New Pallas Alvera remembered. It was a vision of what she'd always feared, the future she'd been fighting to ensure they never saw. The skies were unnaturally still and empty, devoid of shuttle lanes and skycars. Tower block windows gaped at her, shattered glass spilling from the frames like broken teeth. The pathways and plazas that once bustled with life had become wastelands, home to nothing but rubble from the decaying city around them. There was no noise but the smothering silence of death.

This was what was coming for them. This was what she'd condemned them to.

"You think showing me this will change my mind?" Alvera said, her words ripping from her throat with a snarl. "You think I don't see this every time I close my eyes? I know what will happen to New Pallas when we destroy the Omega Gate. I know the price my people have to pay to see the galaxy free of you."

Her vision shifted once more, sending her hurtling through the reaches of dark space until the stars were lost to her. This place was far beyond the sprawling edges of the galaxy, far beyond anything she could comprehend. The darkness was absolute, unending. It was a void containing no life or light.

That's when she saw them. The waystations. Four huge, curved structures. Not conjoined into the Omega Gate, but separate stations in the familiar shape of sweeping rings. Their ends didn't yet meet. Parts of them were exposed to the surrounding vacuum, showing their inner workings like a carcass gutted. Only now did Alvera see the stream of construction ships around them, the glint of machinery across the distance.

"You're already building replacements," she whispered. "Even if we win, you'll just start this all over again."

The curators' voice whispered back. *Let this be a reminder of the patience we possess that eludes you. Ours is a purpose millions of years in the making. If you destroy our waystations, we will simply replace them. Whether it takes a thousand years or a hundred thousand, it makes no difference to us. Our memory is endless. You are not.*

She'd been so tired. So ready for it to be over. Acceptance had settled deep into her bones, promising her the chance to rest if she could only get through this final part. She knew now she'd never be able to rest, not as long as the curators existed.

Kojan was right. She couldn't stop, not after all she'd done. It was up to her to fix things, no matter what it cost her, no matter what it cost anyone. The blood on her hands was only a reminder of that. All the terrible things Alvera had ever done, she'd done because *that's what she fucking did* to people that got in her way.

It was time for the curators to learn that.

"I thought I was done making promises," Alvera said, choking the words out. "But you had to go and piss me off, didn't you? You have no idea how big a mistake that was, but you will soon. Because I swear, I will be the end of you."

She tore away from the connection, letting out a gasp as the curators' tendrils ripped away from their hold on her mind. A burst of pain shot through her and she fell to the floor, her exosuit hitting off the surface with a clang.

An urgent chirp from her wrist terminal rang through her head, and Alvera focused on the holographic readings it was throwing up. She was going into cardiac arrest. A fog descended around her head, darkening the edge of her vision. She'd soon drift away, lost to—

A swift shock jolted through her chest. She thrashed on the floor, eyes wide open and head reeling. Her nerves tingled with the remnants of the electric current that had shot through her body, and after a moment, she remembered how to breathe.

Her trauma regulators. The cybernetic solution she'd engineered to keep her crew alive. Her way of making amends for the quickening, for the virus she'd created. It wasn't the first time they'd saved her. Where she was going, it was unlikely to be the last, either.

Alvera pushed herself back to her feet, sucking in a shallow breath. She knew what she had to do.

The gold-and-green readout displayed her heart functionality, flashing warning signs at her, but Alvera swiped it away to open a communications link. Every passing second dragged on longer than the last as she waited, hoping it wasn't too late.

Eventually, the connection crackled into life, and Ridley's dark features flickered in front of her. "Captain," she said, the word stiff in her throat. "I thought you were helping fend off the invasion."

"I was. I am. But something happened, and I need your help." Alvera swallowed. "Where are you right now?"

"Holed up in one of the Idran-Var bunkers. We're under heavy fire, but the defences are holding strong. We're expecting reinforcements from the Belt Cabal soon. That should take some of the heat off."

"I'm coming to get you. We'll need to find Kojan too, and the *Ranger*. I'll explain everything when I get there."

A shadow flashed across Ridley's eyes. "That won't be possible."

Alvera's stomach turned cold. "Ridley, please. Whatever I've done, whatever you think of me, I'm asking you to put it aside. I need your help."

"It's not that simple." Ridley's expression softened. "Kojan is gone. He took the *Ranger*."

"He took the ship?" Alvera shook her head, dazed. "But...why?"

"I found a way to get a message to New Pallas. I spoke to someone there—an old friend of yours." Ridley looked away. "They understand what the tunnel collapsing means for them. But as long as they still have time, they're going to send ships. They're coming to help us win this war."

Alvera could hardly breathe. *All of us go, or none of us go.* The promise echoed in her ears, a reminder of everything she'd failed to do, everyone she'd failed to save. But Ridley had done the impossible. She'd done what Alvera couldn't do. Now there was a chance. It had to be enough.

"Ridley, I..." Alvera broke off, her throat thick with emotion. "You've done more than anyone could have asked for. I wouldn't be asking you for more if it wasn't important. But this won't stop at the Omega Gate. Even if we destroy it, the curators will return. They're already building new waystations. It doesn't matter how long it takes. At the end of it—and there will be an end—they'll win."

Ridley stared at her. "Unless?"

"Unless we put a stop to them. Together," Alvera said. "I need you, Ridley. You and Kojan are the only ones who can help me see this through. Please, if not for me, then for the people you saved from New Pallas. Help me give their children and their children's children a galaxy they can call home. Not for a few millennia, but forever."

The other end of the line fell silent. Ridley's face was frozen, so still that Alvera wondered if the connection had cut off.

After what seemed like an eternity, Ridley met Alvera's eyes. "All right," she said. "Tell me what we need to do."

TWENTY-FIVE

RIVUS

L eaving Alcruix was the right decision. There was nothing more Rivus could do on that broken horror of a planet, nothing more he could give that he hadn't given already. If Alcruix was to be the site of the galaxy's last stand against the terror coming for them, he could accept that. He just couldn't accept that it would be his.

But the more distance Rivus put between the *Lancer* and the Rim Belt, the tighter the tugging sensation in his chest became. Like a thread anchored to something he'd left behind, ready to snap. It wasn't pain, not exactly. It wasn't guilt either. Just a strain beneath his plating he couldn't shake.

He tore himself from his thoughts and turned to one of the navigation technicians hovering around the bridge. "How are we doing?"

The young jarkaath snapped to attention. "Everything looks good, Supreme Commander. Still no sign of any curator ships in this sector. The human captain was right when she said they were sending the bulk of their forces to Alcruix."

Rivus ground his jaw plates together. He thought of Alvera Renata's grim, grey-featured tenacity that had always impressed and unsettled him in equal measure. He thought of Zal's easy camaraderie—friendship, perhaps, if such a thing was possible between a legionnaire and an Idran-Var. Too often, his thoughts turned to Niole, bringing with them that bitter concoction of rage and grief and regret for all the things that could have been. Leaving her behind was like reaching for something that wasn't there, like discovering an old scab had fallen off a wound that had never existed.

"You seem troubled."

Rivus spun around to see Fyra watching him, her expression unnerving. On the surface, she looked like any other siolean. Her pale lilac skin was smattered with white markings, and her headtails hung supple and loose around her shoulders. But underneath, she was something different. Something ancient. Something that had survived the impossible.

Rivus forced a laugh. "I'm always troubled. Nothing new about that."

Fyra joined him at the viewport. The external feeds showed nothing but darkness. Only the glint of distant stars told them they were not alone. Their far-off pinpricks of light did little to comfort Rivus. One of them was Ossa. One of them was the planet he'd failed.

"You made a difficult choice back on Alcruix," Fyra said. "For what it's worth, I understand how you feel. I've made my share of difficult choices."

"I keep waiting for it to get easier, but it never does." Rivus hesitated. "Are you really who the sioleans say you are?"

Fyra let out a dry chuckle. "I'm exactly who *I* say I am. What the rest of them say about me is beyond my control."

"Stories about you survived when nothing else did. Your

people held on to them, remembered them when they lost everything else. They call you a goddess."

"I never asked to be worshipped." The humour disappeared from Fyra's voice. "Or remembered, for that matter. All I wanted was to see my people survive. I thought by joining Ridley, by returning to the galaxy I once called home, I'd be able to fill some of that hole inside me. But it's hard to feel like anything more than a stranger when all the faces I knew are gone, when all the people I loved have been forgotten."

"What was it like?" The question left Rivus's jaws before he could stop it. "Sorry, I don't mean to—"

"It was like this," Fyra replied. "Desperation. Division. Everybody doing what they thought was right. And in the end, none of it was."

An uneasy silence fell between them. It settled over Rivus's shoulders, bearing its weight down on him. All his certainty around leaving Alcruix suddenly seemed tenuous, like the thing he'd been clinging to so tightly might evaporate at any moment.

"I chose to come with you because I could not bear to fight again," Fyra said. "Not after having already fought and lost. It's too much for my heart to take."

"You think we'll lose?"

"I know it's not what you want to hear, but the truth is, I've seen this play out before. I know what happens next." She sighed. "I once pledged my life to the service of this galaxy. As I understand, you did too. Helping you evacuate Ossa is the only way I can honour that before I meet my fallen friends in whatever place lies beyond this one."

Her words left Rivus with a chill that seeped through the hairline cracks between his plating, into his core. He'd never been afraid to die. He'd always accepted that each battle might be his last. But swearing his life to the legionnaires didn't mean that he welcomed the prospect of death. It didn't mean he was looking for it. He couldn't imagine what it must have been like for Fyra, so displaced from the time she remembered, so removed from everything she'd once fought for. It seemed like she'd already accepted the death that should have claimed her all those years before.

Someone behind him cleared their throat, and Rivus turned around to find Kite hovering by one of the consoles, shifting his weight between one foot and the other.

"Sorry for interrupting, Supreme Commander," Kite said, glancing between them both. "A word, if you have time?"

"I'll leave you to it," Fyra said smoothly, gathering the folds of her tunic and making for the exit.

Kite stared after her, half-hunched in the awkward bow he'd stumbled into. His headtails were flushed with colour, and he had a dazed look on his face that Rivus couldn't help but chuckle at.

"Never had you down as the religious type," he said.

Kite shook himself upright and sent him a scowl. "I'm not. Or at least, I wasn't. Having one of your people's ancient goddesses turn up to make small talk has a way of changing things though." He eyed Rivus, raising his brow ridge. "Sounded like a cheery conversation."

"She does have a certain way of steering any topic towards hopelessness and despair," Rivus admitted. "Not that I blame her, with everything she's been through."

"I still can't wrap my head around it all," Kite said. "Sure, she was a goddess to us, but it didn't *mean* anything outside the religious sects back on Sio. To most people, she was just a name you'd use as a curse, or a blessing. To find out she's so much more than that, well...it makes you question everything."

Something in the tone of his voice made Rivus pause. "You think we should have stayed on Alcruix, don't you?"

"That wasn't what I—" Kite let out a breath. "Look, boss, I told you I'd go wherever you needed me. I won't pretend I didn't want to stay, but I wasn't there when Ossa fell. I didn't see what happened there like you did. If you say it's our duty as legionnaires to go back and save who we can, I'm with you. I only hope that—"

"Supreme Commander!" One of the navigation techs leapt to their feet, their eyes wide with alarm. "Something appeared on the scanners—an incoming ship on an intercept trajectory."

Rivus stormed towards the nearest holofeed, bringing up the data in a glimmer of green lights. "Ready the defences. I want our targeting systems online and ready to blow that ship apart as soon as it's in range. We're not taking any chances when it comes to the curators."

"It's not the curators."

Rivus whirled around. Kite was staring at the holoscreen, his brow ridge creased as he scanned through the data. "How can you be sure?"

"I recognise that ship's profile. It doesn't match any known curator vessels." Kite brought up his wrist terminal and swiped a holographic overlay onto the feeds. The swirling green lines and edges matched up exactly. "I figured as much. You don't spend months hunting down a rogue ship not to remember its signature when you see it. That's the *Ranger*."

"The *Ranger*?" Rivus shifted his plates. "What's it doing here?"

"I'd say we're about to find out."

A few minutes later, the comms console in the middle of the room shimmered into life and Rivus was met with the flickering features of Kojan Irej. The human looked tired. The warm tones of his skin were blotted with shadows, and there was a sunken appearance to his cheeks. But despite it all, his eyes glittered with something Rivus hadn't seen in a long time, something that made his chest seize.

Hope.

Kojan let out a long breath. "You were burning hard,

Supreme Commander. For a while there, I didn't think I'd catch you."

"I didn't realise we were being chased," Rivus replied. "Though I'm pleased to see it was a friendly face following our trail and not the curator fleet."

"The curators have a bigger target in mind." A dark look flashed across Kojan's face. "They reached Alcruix. The allied fleets are doing their best to hold them off, but I'm not sure how long they'll be able to hold out for."

There it was again. That tug in Rivus's chest, buried under bone plating and muscle and sinew. A part of himself he hadn't known existed until he'd had to leave it behind on that forsaken planet, alongside his old enemies. Alongside his old friends.

You had to leave, he told himself. *It was the right decision.*

He couldn't begin to doubt. Not now, not when Ossa was getting closer by the minute. What happened on Alcruix wasn't his responsibility. Let the Idran-Var look after their own planet. His duty was to look after whatever was left of his.

"Is that why you came all this way?" Rivus asked stiffly. "You want me to turn around and go back to help?"

"As impressive as the *Lancer* is, one ship isn't going to help us now," Kojan said. "We need more. A lot more. That's the reason I'm here."

"What do you mean?"

"Ridley got a message back to New Pallas. They're sending their entire military fleet." Kojan smiled. "We're about to get a shit-ton of reinforcements."

Rivus stilled. "Enough to turn the tide?"

"I don't know. But it gives us more of a chance than we've got right now." Kojan paused. "Ridley also asked them to send one of their evac ships ahead, empty. The *Lancer* may be big, but the New Pallas evacuation transports are like floating cities. They can carry hundreds of thousands of people at a time."

Rivus's throat tightened. "For Ossa?"

"For Ossa," Kojan said. "I know you're keen to get back home, Supreme Commander, but a diversion to the Ulla system is worth the delay."

Rivus couldn't speak. The walls of his throat closed up, grinding together as he tried to breathe. A diversion was the last thing he wanted, but if Kojan was right, if the human colony had a way to carry more people to safety...

"You think they'll come?" he asked quietly.

"Wouldn't be here if I didn't."

There was no promise in the human's words, no guarantee of anything but lost time. That wouldn't have been enough for Tarvan. The weight of his old commander's legacy still hung around Rivus's shoulders like lead woven into his white cloak. It was always heaviest in moments like these, when doubt and fear crept in to cloud his judgement. Sometimes, he wanted nothing more than to cast it off and leave it all behind him. But there were people out there who needed him. That was why he'd taken on the white cloak and all the burdens that came with it. That was why he'd left Alcruix.

"I'm sending you clearance to dock with the *Lancer*," Rivus said, tapping the command into one of the consoles. "Good to have you back on board, Flight Lieutenant. Now let's give your people the welcome they deserve."

———

Rivus had never been to the Ulla system before. The sector was sparse and largely uninhabited, containing only a handful of gas giants and nebulae. The waystation the *Ranger* had arrived through was gone now, turned into one of the twisted arms of the Omega Gate. But the echoes of its presence still lingered in the space it once occupied. Drifting wrecks of the ships that had been caught in the temporal net still floated in the vacuum, mass graves for the crews that ran out of oxygen or supplies before the dead zone lifted.

Kojan stood next to him, shoulders stiff. Human expressions were usually softer than the shifting of dachryn bone plates, but there was a tension in Kojan that made him look like he was made of stone.

"This is it," he said, consulting his wrist terminal. "According to the logs from the *Ranger*, this was where we came through the tunnel, give or take a couple of hundred klicks. If the ships from New Pallas make it through, this is where we'll meet them."

"If?"

Kojan grimaced. "After everything that has happened, everything we've already lost...it's hard to believe that something will go right for once."

Rivus turned back towards the viewport. In the distance, he saw the faint, wisping clouds of a nebula—swirling starburst shapes of pink and gold dusted with the glinting of a thousand stars. Something beautiful amongst all the emptiness around it. A reminder that even out here, in the cold grip of space, there was still light. There was still hope.

He signalled one of the operations technicians on the lower section of the bridge. "Anything?"

The siolean tech shook her head. "Not yet. Monitoring stations don't show any sign of activity. We're the only ones out here."

Rivus growled. Patience was a tall order, especially with the knowledge that every passing minute could be measured in the loss of another life, the obliteration of another city or settlement. It was impossible to keep the doubt at bay. It crept under his plating, burrowing its way into all the parts of him that were soft and vulnerable.

A sigh rumbled in his throat. "I can't afford to linger here much longer. Every moment we delay, more people on Ossa die. We only have a small window to evacuate before that asteroid hits."

"I know." Kojan swallowed. "I thought they'd be here by now. I thought we'd finally... I'm sorry, Rivus. I brought you all this way to chase down a lost hope."

"Supreme Commander?" The siolean operations tech got up from her station. "Sorry to interrupt, but something is happening to our monitoring systems. They're glitching, like something is interfering with their signal."

"Could it be the curators?" Rivus glanced at Kojan. "You said they had advanced signal-jamming technology, didn't you?"

The siolean furrowed her brow ridge. "We haven't picked up anything on our long-range scanners. There's some kind of anomaly messing with our sensors. Like a ripple, but we can't pinpoint where it's coming from."

Kojan turned back to the viewport. "It's the ships from New Pallas. It must be."

Rivus followed his gaze. The darkness outside was as vast and unending as ever. The colourful swirls from the nebula swam in the distance, out of reach. The glittering of the far-off stars remained still and unchanging.

"There's nothing there," he said gently. "I'm sorry, Kojan, but—"

"Look."

Rivus couldn't see anything. The emptiness swallowed everything else, drawing his eyes in until he forced himself to blink it away.

Then he blinked again.

A ship. A single, small ship, half the size of the *Ranger*, was floating in a pocket of space that had been empty only a heartbeat ago. A silhouette against the stars with sleek, curved edges and blinking lights.

"It can't be," Rivus murmured. "Where did it come from? How..."

The rest of his words died in the back of his throat. Another ship appeared. This one was bigger, with roaring engines and formidable railguns set all the way along its hull. It swept past the first ship, emerging from the darkness like it was materialising before Rivus's eyes.

He took a step towards the viewport. The holofeeds wavered in front of him, daring him to believe what he was seeing. Maybe it was an illusion, some kind of glitch in the system.

Another ship appeared in the distance. Then another. Each passing second brought with it a new arrival. Sleek, nimble fighters. Huge battleships and destroyers. Before long, there were more ships than Rivus could count.

Kojan's lips parted in a breathless laugh. "They made it."

The tension in Rivus's plating gave way to a rush of relief that left him lightheaded. More and more ships spilled out into the darkness, spreading out to make room for the next. It was more than he ever could have hoped for. More than he could believe.

Then the evacuation transport arrived. Rivus couldn't help but marvel at the sheer magnitude of it. It had none of the streamlined curves or sharp angles of the ships that had come before it. Its frame was huge and boxy, like someone had stuck engines onto a city block and sent it into space. Time stilled as it crawled forward, agonisingly slow.

The comms terminal lit up with an incoming connection request, and Rivus motioned to the comms officer to patch it through.

The sombre face of a bronze-skinned human woman appeared before them. "This is the evac shuttle *Endurance* reporting for duty," she said. "We have orders from Ridley Jones of the *Ranger* to assist in a rescue mission."

Kojan took over the comms terminal. "It's good to see you, *Endurance*. Glad you could join us."

"We're one of the lucky ones, I guess. Or not, as it might turn out." A faint smile danced on the captain's lips. "Tell me, is the situation here as bad as command made it out to be?"

"Worse, probably," Kojan admitted. "Still, it's good to see a friendly face. It's been a while since, well..." He broke off, his voice catching. "Never mind, there will be time for that later. Stand by while we send you coordinates for Ossa. We'll be moving out to begin the evacuation soon. Someone will brief you on the way."

"Understood. Tell us where we need to go, and we'll be there."

The line fizzled out, leaving Rivus with nothing but the sound of his own breathing echoing in his ears. The whole conversation had passed him by in a distant blur. Seeing the human captain on the feed, hearing her voice over the comms channel...it didn't seem real.

He glanced back at the viewport. Thousands of ships were gathered now, with more arriving every minute. Enough to bolster their forces, enough to make a real difference.

"Supreme Commander?" One of the navigation techs looked up at him. "I've charted a route to Ossa. Ready to move on your order."

Do it, Rivus wanted to say. *Take us home.* This was what he'd wanted. This was what he'd been waiting for. The evac transport from New Pallas was more of a miracle than he'd ever imagined. He'd be able to save not just thousands, but hundreds of thousands. He'd be able to give the survivors on Ossa the lifeline they desperately needed before the Idran-Var's asteroid turned their planet into an uninhabitable pile of rubble.

Why, then, had his throat closed up around itself? Why had

his plates frozen solid, so stiff and unyielding it was like they'd melded together?

Rivus felt a hand on his forearm and flinched. Fyra wrapped her fingers gently around his plating, casting a pale violet light over them both. She looked at him with her deep, black eyes, somehow knowing. Somehow understanding.

"Go back to Alcruix," she said, her voice so soft he had to strain to hear it. "Your friends need you."

Rivus shook his head. "My *people* need me. I am a legionnaire. My duty is to protect those who need it most."

"You have already done that. You've done more than that." Fyra smiled. "I would have been proud to fight alongside you in my own time, Rivus Itair. But my fight is over. Yours isn't. You can still make a difference to the people you helped bring together."

Rivus turned away. He felt Fyra's eyes on him. He felt the eyes of Kojan and Kite from across the room, the eyes of all the officers and technicians gathered on the bridge. All of them looking to him to make the decision. All of them waiting to see what he would do.

Alcruix meant nothing to him. The curators could obliterate that forsaken planet for all he cared. But it wasn't about Alcruix. It was about the people he'd left behind there, the people who'd believed in him when he'd shouldered the white cloak. Fyra was right—he'd brought them together. He'd put aside his own grief and rage and pain to stand with them. To fight with them, until the end. Until they *won* this damn war.

Fyra must have read something in the shift of his plating, for her smile widened when he turned back to her. "I will look after your people on Ossa," she said. "I will make sure they have every chance to escape before the asteroid hits. You have my word."

"Thank you," Rivus managed, the words scratching like gravel in his throat. "For everything."

Fyra held up a hand, waving away his words. "We did all we could when it mattered most. And if we happen to cross paths once all this is over...well, it will be a new galaxy. There will be time for old wounds to heal. Time to start over, for all of us. That's the future you're fighting for."

Something in her expression chased away the rest of the doubt clinging to him. The tug in his chest was as tight as ever, thrumming with each beat of his heart. Rivus knew where it was leading him. He knew what he had to do.

He met Kite's eyes across the room. His old friend sent him a legionnaire's salute. Next to him, Kojan looked as serious as ever, but the hint of a smile danced at the edge of his mouth.

Rivus gave him a brusque nod. "Flight Lieutenant, get me a line to whoever is in charge of those New Pallas ships. I want everyone briefed and ready to move." He cocked his head. "And make sure the *Ranger* is refuelled and equipped with whatever munitions you need. I imagine you'll want to be at the head of that fleet when we return to Alcruix."

Kojan grinned. "Wouldn't want to be anywhere else, Supreme Commander."

"Good. We're going to come up against one hell of a blockade. We'll need every ship at our disposal if we're to drive these bastards back, from our biggest destroyers to our smallest fighters." Rivus glanced at Kite. "I assume your squad is up for a bit of trouble, Merala?"

Kite snorted. "Like you have to ask."

A fierce swell of elation coursed through Rivus. For the first time since wrapping it around his shoulders, the white cloak felt like it belonged to him. It cascaded over his armour, weightless. This was why it had come to him. This was what he was meant to do.

Finally, he understood what it meant to be Supreme Commander.

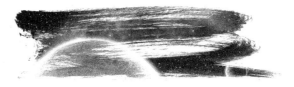

TWENTY-SIX

NIOLE

A warning light flashed across the cockpit walls as the asteroid appeared on the shuttle's scopes. Niole swiped away the alert and keyed in an override command to remain on her current course. The detection system was only doing its job —under any other circumstances, she'd have accepted the correction and moved well clear of the approaching asteroid. But the chunk of rock and metal burning through space wasn't a threat. It was exactly where she needed to be.

She watched it through the viewport, a huge mass of jagged mountains and trenches the size of a city, eclipsing the stars behind it as it raced towards Ossa. Even from a distance, the glow from the massive engines was visible against the darkness of space. The reactors had been built into the rock, designed to boost the asteroid along its path and detach before hitting the temporal net around the perimeter of the Omega Gate. The asteroid's velocity would do the rest.

Niole gritted her teeth against the turbulence as she brought her shuttle around the wake of the engines and looked for a landing zone. Two aerial assault cannons stared up at her from a nearby plateau, their huge barrels following her as she surveyed the area. The barren, rocky terrain was littered with the wrecks of various types of assault craft and troop transports—some Idran-Var, some of a more alien design.

A shiver raced across her skin. Rhendar was right. The curators had come here to stop them. If they managed to gain control of the engines and send the asteroid off course, it would all be over. The Omega Gate would remain intact. The curators would keep coming. No matter how strong they stood, no matter how hard they fought, they couldn't win against those kinds of numbers. The only hope the galaxy had left was cutting off their supply of bodies.

Niole's stomach lurched as a flash illuminated the rugged landscape. She could see the fighting now. A swarm of curators were advancing on an Idran-Var defensive encampment, pinning them back against the steep sides of one of the asteroid's towering ridges.

She tightened her grip on the shuttle's controls and pushed it into a dive. It was no fighter—and Niole was no pilot—but she had enough second-hand knowledge of weapons systems to line up her targets and squeeze the trigger. The rattle from the cannon echoed around her head as she sent a flurry of bullets into the curators below.

Elation surged through her as she whirled the shuttle around and brought it down near one of the makeshift barricades. If nothing else, she'd bought a little time. She'd saved some Idran-Var who might not have made it otherwise. That had to be worth coming here, no matter what happened next.

She unbuckled herself from her flight harness and punched the door controls. Outside, a line of Idran-Var waited for her, their weapons pointed warily as they circled around her shuttle.

Niole stepped forward, raising her hands. "I'm here to help. Can anyone tell me where—"

"Tails? Is that you?"

One of the Idran-Var holstered his gun and reached both hands to his collar to twist off his helmet. A delicate breather mask covered the lower half of his face, but there was no mistaking the smile beneath it. It shone across his skin, crinkling the corners of his eyes.

Niole's heart leapt. "Claine!"

He ran towards her and pulled her into a hug. His pale-yellow hair had grown back in loose curls around his head, and there was a light in his eyes that had been missing the last time she'd seen him. He looked a different man compared to back then, when he'd been confined in a cell, bruised and beaten for the part he'd played in bringing the legionnaires to Vesyllion. Some of the youthful charm had been lost from his soft features, leaving behind something more aware, something more mature.

"What are you doing here?" Claine asked, pulling away. "This mission was meant for those of us who disgraced our armour. We're here to earn it back, so we can die as Idran-Var. You don't need to be here, Niole. You were always one of us, even when you couldn't see it yourself."

"That's exactly why I need to be here. Rhendar saw the parts of myself I was too scared to look at. He showed me who I really was. I couldn't let him..." A painful lump caught in Niole's throat. "I need to see him before this ends."

Claine's face fell. "We received word that the outpost at the other engine had fallen. Rhendar took half our squad and headed out to capture it again before the curators could sabotage our flight path." He grimaced. "That was a day ago now. We've heard nothing since."

Niole's insides turned to ice. "But the asteroid is still on course, isn't it? He must have secured the engine and taken back the outpost."

"At what cost?" Claine looked at her bleakly. "If he was alive —if any of them were alive—we'd have heard by now. Rhendar knew what was at stake. He knew what he was walking into. He'd have done whatever it took to make sure the curators couldn't have that engine."

The pain that tore through Niole's chest wasn't something her armour could protect her from. It wasn't something she could push away with a flare. It held her in its grip, crushing her until she could hardly draw breath. Not Rhendar. She couldn't let herself believe it.

"I need to find him," she said, forcing the words out. "Will you be able to hold out here for a little longer?"

"As long as it takes." Claine smiled sadly. "Rhendar told us to stay here and protect this engine with our lives. I let him down once. I won't make that mistake again."

Niole glanced around the encampment. The rocky ground underfoot was strewn with the bodies of Idran-Var and curator thralls alike. Overturned transports and burned-out shuttle wreckages acted as barricades. The aerial defence towers loomed over them on the ridge above, watching the empty sky. But still, they burned towards Ossa. The curators had not yet broken through to the control room nestled in the base of the massive engine. Claine and the others had done all that Rhendar had asked of them and more.

"What happens when the engines detach?" she asked. "Will you have time to get away before the asteroid hits the temporal net?"

Claine shrugged. "We lost most of our shuttles in the fighting. I don't see how any of us are getting off this rock now. But we all knew this was what might be asked of us."

"I'll come back for you," Niole said. "I'll find Rhendar and bring him here. We can leave in my shuttle before we get caught in the temporal net."

"I don't think—"

"I'll come back," she repeated. She couldn't hold his gaze any longer. Claine was a different person to the young *jal-var* she'd met on Vesyllion all those months ago. The boy was gone now, replaced by someone she hadn't yet got the chance to know. She wanted that chance. She wanted Venya to have that chance. Fyra, if she could only see him now...

She pushed the thoughts from her head as she slid back into the cockpit and fired up the shuttle's engines. There was no time to dwell on what their future might hold, not when it was still so far out of reach. First, she had to get them all out of here. And she wasn't doing that until she found Rhendar.

The shuttle skimmed across the surface of the asteroid, cutting through the non-existent atmosphere with ease. Niole guided it over the jagged ridges and gaping crevices in the rocky surface, never taking her eyes from the glow on the horizon. The second engine cast a purple-orange tint against the surrounding darkness, its distant light showing her the way.

She didn't see what was left of the encampment until she was right on top of it. The whole area was a blackened crater, the barricades and sentry posts blown to pieces. It was too quiet, too still.

Niole landed the shuttle and stepped outside. There was no sign of Rhendar. No sign of any Idran-Var. Just a hollowed-out hole in the ground. Even in the gloom, she could see glints of armour buried under the debris. Some of it was Idran-Var, but there were curator bodies too. Torn-off limbs and chunks of flesh. Corpses limp and broken, scattered carelessly across the rubble.

"What happened here?" Niole murmured to herself. "What did you do, Rhendar?"

She trudged towards the edge of the crater. The engine was

right above her now—she felt its heat as it roared silently into the vacuum, burning furiously in bursts of purple and orange. Rhendar had kept it alive.

At what cost? Claine's words echoed through her. The entire encampment had been obliterated, turned into a smouldering grave for both Idran-Var and curator alike. Finding Rhendar—finding *anyone*—seemed like too much to hope for.

Something glinted near the base of the engine. The entrance leading into the control centre had been reduced to a pile of rocks, but something in it had caught her eye. Something in it had moved.

Niole stumbled across the loose, shifting ground, her heart pressing painfully against her ribs. She saw something amongst the rocks: an outline of metal peeking through the rubble, illuminated by the soft red glow from a visor she knew all too well.

"Rhendar!"

His weight was heavy on her shoulder as she looped her arm under him and dragged him free. If he was able to move, he didn't show it. His arms hung limp at his sides and his legs trawled through the rubble as she half-pulled, half-carried him back to the shuttle. The only thing telling Niole he was alive was the faint crackle of static that rushed through her helmet earpiece every time he drew a breath.

"Hold on," she whispered. "I'm getting you out of here."

She set him down in one of the flight chairs and strapped the webbing of the harness over his armour. The plating was dull with scorch marks and scratches. Had he been caught in the same explosion that had caused the crater? If so, what kind of state was his body in?

Niole jumped as Rhendar shot his hand out and grabbed her by the arm. "I told you not to come here," he said. "This isn't your fight, Niole."

His voice flooded her with a warmth that rushed through

her entire body. "I choose what I fight for now. You taught me that."

"Then I didn't teach you enough." The red glow of Rhendar's visor wavered as he rolled his head to the side. "I can't let you die here with us. There are people out there who need you, more than you know. I need you to carry on for them after I'm gone."

"You're not going anywhere." Niole slid into the pilot's chair, firing up the shuttle's engines with shaking hands. "We'll get you to a med centre. There are still some nearby systems that haven't been overrun by the curators. You have to hold on until—"

"I'm dying," Rhendar said, his voice oddly gentle for the finality in it. "My armour served me as best it could, but I always knew there would come a time I asked too much of it. A time where it could not protect me from what I had to do."

Niole glanced at her wrist terminal, her heart breaking with each scan Rhendar sent over. Multiple breaks and fractures. Internal bleeding. Organ failure. Too much trauma for a body to endure, no matter how strong the shell around it was.

"I took out our entire encampment to stop the curators getting to that engine," Rhendar said quietly. "The Idran-Var I brought here were killed in the blast from the explosion, because that was what I had to do to protect the rest of them. In sacrificing them, I succeeded where Tarvan Varantis failed." He let out a pained grunt. "The Tyrant paid the price for what he did that day on Aurel. It's only fitting that I do the same here."

"You're nothing like Tarvan. You saved us. You saved me." Niole's throat tightened. "There must be something we can do."

"Set us down," he said. "Somewhere along the ridge. If the curators return, someone needs to stay behind to hold them off. All I need is a vantage point and my rifle. That's enough to see me through until the end."

"Not a chance," she shot back. "I'm getting you back to

Claine and the others. We still have time to get out of here before the engines detach. If we—"

"Niole." His voice was so thin, so weak, but it held an authority that had never faltered, not since the day she'd met him. "You've already disobeyed my orders once. Don't make the mistake of doing it again."

The words hung in the air between them. Niole couldn't refuse him. She'd never been able to refuse him. From the moment he'd offered her an armoured hand back on Pasaran Minor, he'd given her a home she'd never known she was missing. He'd given her a place to belong. She'd have done anything he asked of her.

Even this.

"Setting us down," she said, anguish welling in her chest. "Fyra, forgive me."

Niole brought the shuttle to the summit of the sprawling ridge overlooking the engine base. From here, she could see the full reach of the huge crater that marred the rocky surface below. She didn't know how many bodies were buried under the rubble there. She didn't want to know. All she knew was the grief for what Rhendar had done, for what he still had to do.

"We're getting close." Rhendar dragged himself over to a small, rocky outcropping and propped himself against it. But he wasn't looking out over the crater—he was looking in the other direction, towards the path the asteroid was following. Towards Ossa.

Niole saw it in the distance now: a faintly-shining sphere amongst the darkness, its jewel tones shrouded in the orange glow from the fires that still burned there. Impossibly far away, yet too close to escape. The planet she'd once called home. The planet she'd run from, then fought to save. It seemed oddly fitting that this, of all places, should be where the end came.

"There was a time I would have given anything to see that planet burn like it's burning now," Rhendar said, his voice thick with exhaustion. "Strange that when I look at it, all I feel is sorrow."

"We tried."

"I know. That doesn't mean a dying man isn't allowed to have his regrets." He shifted against the rock. "There are so many things we could have done differently, could have done better. It took too long for me to see it. And now that I'm here... the end has a way of giving perspective."

Niole lowered herself to the ground next to him and slid her hand into his. On the horizon, Ossa loomed larger and larger with each passing moment. The scale of it terrified her. But this was where she was meant to be. At Rhendar's side.

The red glow from his visor flickered faintly against the black sky. "I'm proud of you," he said quietly. "Finding you on that backwater farmstead gave me a piece of my life I never knew was missing."

He lifted his hands and brought them to the sides of his helmet. The seams released with a hiss, and a faint puff of air dispersed into the vacuum.

Niole grabbed his arm. "What are you doing? If you remove that helmet in front of me, it will mean you are no longer Idran-Var."

"I no longer need to be Idran-Var," Rhendar said, his voice half-distorted through the modulator. "If I am to die, I would rather die as your friend. As your family. Maybe that means more to an old man than the weight of all the things he's done in the name of his armour."

Niole kept her hand wrapped around his vambrace. It was difficult to know whether the trembling through her arm was coming from his body or her own. She'd never known pain like this. Never known belonging like this. Seeing his face had never mattered to her, not until now. Not until it mattered to *him*.

One by one, she released her fingers from around his wrist. Rhendar tilted his head, giving her one last Idran-Var smile before lifting the helmet and placing it on the ground between them both.

"There it is," he said softly. "It's over."

She'd always known he was human, but she'd never imagined what he might look like under the strength of his armour. Gone were the stern lines spanning his visor. Now, all Niole saw was the softness of him. Golden-brown skin, faintly creasing at the corners of his dark, sparkling eyes. Lines of green ink chasing their way up his temple, markings so faint and faded they looked like they were from another life. A smile so honest it was like it held all the warmth in the galaxy.

Niole swallowed. "I don't want to leave you here alone. You deserve more than that."

"I got to see you with my own eyes," Rhendar said. "I got to see you become the person I always knew you could be. That's all I need."

His helmet lay on the ground between them, its glassy veneer reflecting the shadows. The visor looked strange without the red glow coming from behind its slits, like it already knew there was a part of itself destined to fade out and disappear.

Rhendar lifted it from the ground. "I want you to take this. You could do great things as one of the *varsath*."

Niole stiffened. "You know I can't do that. Serric should have it. He was always meant to have it."

"The galaxy isn't the same as it used to be, and even if we win this fight, it won't be the end," Rhendar said gently. "If the Idran-Var want to survive, we have to change. Clinging onto these old wounds, these scars festering with hatred and anger... it will only destroy us. When I look at Serric, I see the death of our people. And maybe that's for the best. Maybe the Idran-Var need to die for this galaxy to heal."

"You can't mean that."

"I've seen what pain can do to the best of us. I've seen how it lingers through the centuries. We Idran-Var make a point of inheriting that pain. We use it as a reason to keep fighting." Rhendar shook his head. "It doesn't have to be that way. In you, I see a future for our people. A future free from the violence we've always necessitated as part of our existence. It's easy to storm headfirst into a fight. Turning away from one, now that's something not many people can do." He smiled. "Even I've never managed it, until now."

Niole's stomach twisted. She couldn't do this. She couldn't accept what he was offering her. The weight of it was too much.

"Don't ask this of me, Rhendar," she whispered. "It will tear us apart."

"The Idran-Var? Or you and Serric?" He gave her a knowing look.

Niole flushed. "It might as well be the same thing. Serric belongs in that armour. He's been fighting for it his whole life. There's nobody that knows what it means to be Idran-Var more than him."

"There's more than one way to be Idran-Var," Rhendar said. "You understand that in a way I didn't. In a way someone like Serric will never understand. Resisting is violent, sometimes inevitably so. But it can be quiet, too. It can happen across a theatre of war or in the battlefields of your own head." He wrapped his hand around hers. "Never be afraid to remind yourself of that, as you reminded me."

Niole looked down as he set the helmet in her lap. It stared back at her, the visor blank and empty. Rhendar's face. The only face of his she'd ever known. All those times he'd watched her with an expression immutable and made of steel. All those times he'd tilted his head in his customary smile. That was all she'd be able to see whenever she looked at it. She'd see him every time she saw her own reflection. Rhendar, staring back at her. Part of her for as long as she chose to carry him with her.

The golden glow encircling Ossa was becoming brighter by

the minute. Niole watched it grow closer, one hand in Rhendar's, the other clutching his helmet. Soon, she'd have to go. Soon, she'd have to leave him. But until then, all she wanted to do was remain at his side, taking in the view.

Perspective, Rhendar had said. That was what he'd given her.

The faint whirr from his breather mask brushed against her ears, then fell silent. She waited for the next one, but the only sound that came was the soft hum of a comms line with nothing at the other end. His shoulder rested against hers, the leaden weight of his body pressing into her like an embrace.

When Niole looked at him, his eyes had closed, but the ghost of his smile still lingered on his lips.

"*Idra ti gratar*, my friend," she whispered. "I'll never forget what you did for me."

Ossa was a bright ball of light now, growing so large she could almost reach out and touch it. In a matter of minutes, the huge clamps keeping the engines in place would release, allowing the asteroid to hurtle through the temporal net. It was time to go.

Niole pushed herself to her feet and took one last look at Rhendar. He seemed peaceful in death, like all the burdens and echoes of violence he'd carried with him through the years had drifted away, leaving him as nothing but a man. Not Idran-Var, but her friend. The closest thing to family she'd ever known. A man freed from the shackles of all the fighting that had ever been asked of him. A man who finally knew peace.

By the time Niole made it back to the encampment, the clamps had already begun to detach around the engines, moving with a slow, mechanical groan. She held the shuttle hovering above the rocky surface while Claine and the other Idran-Var clambered on.

When the last of them made it on board, Claine turned to her. "Did you find him?"

"Yes," she said, glancing at the helmet from its place on the console next to her. "You were right. He knew exactly what he was walking into. He always did."

Claine's face fell. "I'm sorry. I know what he meant to you. He was a good man. A good leader."

Niole nodded. "He showed me who I was. Even at the end, he was still showing me who I was."

Claine studied her, his pale brows knitting together. "What happens now? Where do we go from here?"

Rhendar's helmet stared at her under the dim lights of the cockpit, the glow from the instruments bouncing off the metal in ripples of colour. It was like he was still watching her. Like he still had his eyes on her. Wherever she went, she'd take him with her.

We're more than the sum of flesh and matter inside these metal shells, he'd told her once, offering her his hand. *You can be too.*

"Alcruix," Niole said, her heart fluttering. "We've got a galaxy to save."

TWENTY-SEVEN

Rivus

R ivus had always been quietly overwhelmed by the sheer
vastness of space. The ever-stretching darkness had a
magnitude to it he couldn't help but feel in awe of. Now, with
the broken, shattered carcass of Alcruix on the feeds once
more, space seemed impossibly crowded. Hundreds of thousands of ships surrounded the planet, engaged in battle. As far
as interplanetary warfare was concerned, this was up close and
personal.

He watched them on the scopes—legionnaire fighters
harrying battleships ten times their size, Belt Cabal cargo
runners tearing through the enemy with modified railguns
strapped to their hulls, an Idran-Var destroyer blasting an
approaching troop transport to dust. The entire galaxy had
come together to hold off the curators.

Rivus opened a line to the *Ranger*. "How are things out
there, Flight Lieutenant?"

"We're in formation and ready to hit them where it hurts," Kojan replied.

"Glad to hear it." Rivus gave an appreciative grunt. "I'm taking a team of legionnaires planetside to bolster the ground defences. Merala and his squad will escort us down, then rejoin you. Take any opening to push back their fleet. The people we left behind on Alcruix need all we can give them."

"We'll keep them busy. You get down there and give them hell from us." Kojan paused. "Good luck, Rivus. I hope I'll see you again on the other side of this."

"Likewise. Fly safe out there."

The shuttle touched down on one of the ice-encrusted landing pads and opened its doors to Alcruix's fierce, swirling winds. The ash-thick atmosphere echoed with gunfire and explosions. Smoke shrouded the dark sky, reflecting the sounds of missile fire like thunder. Far-off yelling and anguished screams called from across the distance, muffled by the fighting.

Rivus glanced at his legionnaires, their green cloaks hanging loose around their shoulders. Scuff marks and scratches marred their white power armour, but there was no expression among their faces that betrayed anything other than quiet determination.

One of them, a young jarkaath with silver-dusted scales, met his gaze with her keen yellow eyes. "Orders, Supreme Commander?"

Rivus shifted his plates. "Our job is to protect the people of this galaxy. Some of them might look like our old enemies, but in this fight, we stand together. Idran-Var, Coalition, legionnaire...none of that matters, not in the face of these things we're up against. We'll fight them as one, until there's nothing left of us to fight." He let a rumble loose from the back of his throat. "Now, move out!"

The Idran-Var operations base looked different to how

they'd left it. Most of the landing pads had been reduced to rubble, and everywhere Rivus looked he saw burning transports and smoking defence turrets. The trenches outside the main entrance were bursting with bodies of both Idran-Var and curators alike, their limbs limp and unmoving.

Part of him was surprised the Idran-Var hadn't abandoned the camp entirely. The infrastructure was too spread out to bunker down and outlast an extended assault. There were other outposts on the planet in more defensible locations, where their makeshift fortifications would be more effective. But this was where the Forge was. This was where the Idran-Var mined the precious metal they used in their armour. Abandoning it would have been as good as admitting defeat. And if there was one thing Rivus knew about the Idran-Var, it was that they didn't give up without a fight.

"Let's get down there," he shouted over the raging wind. "If there's anyone coordinating a groundside resistance, that's where they'll be."

He stepped into the carriage of the landing pad's elevator, his stomach lurching as the contraption shot towards the ground. The beams screeched when the platform shuddered to a halt at the bottom of the giant stilts, and Rivus pushed open the door with as much force as he could muster, spilling out onto the ash-covered terrain with his plasma rifle tight in his hands.

In front of him, a wave of curator thralls pressed their way across the battleground. When one of them fell to a well-placed flurry of gunfire or a blast from a hidden landmine, the rest continued on like nothing had happened. No backwards glances, no concern for their injured or dead. They were nothing more than empty husks. Too disposable to have any kind of significance. Too replaceable.

Rivus turned to the legionnaires. "Circle around. We'll hit

their flank and cut off their approach to the base. It might help relieve some of the pressure on this entrance."

He set off across the uneven ground. The clunking of his boots filled his ears as he quickened his step, navigating his way over the bloody trenches towards the oncoming swarm of thralls. For once, the white cloak around his shoulders felt weightless. Before he'd been Supreme Commander, he'd been a fighter. A warrior. A protector. This was something he knew how to do.

A nearby azuul reared up its leathery white skull and let out an ear-splitting howl, flecks of saliva spraying from between its needle-like teeth. Rivus levelled his rifle at it and fired a round of plasma bolts. The shots hit their mark, sizzling the creature's exposed flesh around its jowls and sending it into a frenzy. It thrashed its thick arms, catching one of the smaller, blue-furred thralls on the side of the neck and sending it to the ground with a splintering snap.

One of his legionnaires followed up with a flare, sending a burst of yellow-tinged energy straight at the azuul. She was no *ilsar*, but the blast was still powerful enough to knock the hulking alien to the ground while another one of the squad sent an incendiary round into the back of its skull. The creature convulsed, its limbs flailing wildly. Then it stilled, another life-less corpse among the hundreds of others scattering the area.

No glory in battle. Only blood. The old mantra rang through Rivus's ears, an echo of a different time. So much had changed since the days at the academy, where he'd sparred with his friends underneath the blossoms of the orchard, pretending at something he hadn't been able to comprehend. Now he was on the homeworld of his old enemy, and his former friends were nothing more than ghosts reminding him of his failures and the failures of the Supreme Commander before him. But he had changed too. He wasn't the same dachryn he used to be. He wasn't Tarvan.

He was better than that.

Rivus holstered his rifle and drew his varstaff from his belt, the electric current humming into life as he extended both ends. One of the blue mammalian-like thralls snapped its head towards him, its fangs slick and wet. Rivus stepped cleanly out of the way as it leapt for his throat and brought the varstaff down across its back with a crack. The creature's fur and flesh singed, and the varstaff crackled violently as he whirled it back around, ready to follow up with another attack.

Before he could land his next blow, the thrall fell to the ground, a smoking wound between its four beady eyes. An Idran-Var hunkered down in one of the trenches gave him a nod from behind their helmet, and Rivus returned the gesture.

We stand together, he'd told his squad. Legionnaire and Idran-Var, fighting together. Dying together. He still couldn't believe it. The gentle hum of electricity coursing through his varstaff was a reminder of a life so far out of reach he'd forgotten how he'd ever lived it. Here he was, holding the only weapon in the galaxy capable of searing through Idran-Var armour. And now he was using it to defend them.

After a while, the relentless swarm of curator thralls eased off like a tide slipping back from shore. All around them were fallen bodies and scattered weapons piling high around the perimeter of the base.

One of the Idran-Var motioned to Rivus. "There will be more of them. Best take some time to regroup and replenish any ammo or incendiaries you need. We'll be back out here soon enough."

Rivus secured his varstaff to his belt as the huge reinforced doors of the bunker slid open with a metallic groan. The bite of wind disappeared once he stepped inside, and he took his helmet off with a deep sigh. Part of him wanted to wince at the relief that rushed over his plates. Returning here shouldn't have felt easy. It shouldn't have felt like coming back to somewhere he belonged. He wasn't Idran-Var, he was—

He stopped in his tracks, his thoughts scattering as he found his path blocked by a familiar face.

Zal.

The small human woman stood in a plain cargo suit, her hands on her hips as she fixed him with a glare. "You're back."

Rivus nodded. "Things changed. I realised I needed to—"

The rest of his words died at the back of his throat as Zal drew back her fist and threw it at him, right between the eyes. The impact barely registered in his brain, but he heard the sickening crack of bone and Zal's enraged scream as she whipped her hand back, nursing bloodied knuckles.

Rivus blinked. "Did you just try to *punch* a dachryn with your bare fist?"

"Stupid...boneheaded...bastard," Zal grunted, tears streaming from her right eye. "You're lucky I hadn't picked up my gear yet, otherwise it might have been a bullet through that thick skull of yours instead."

"You're angry at me for coming back?"

"I'm angry because you left in the first place, you idiot." Zal slumped against the wall. Her skin was pale and tired, with blue-green circles around her eyes. "We could have used you and your legionnaires. We're getting crushed out there."

"I'm here now."

Zal let out a hoarse laugh. "For all the good it will do. We've already lost so many. The *varsath* insist on fighting on the front lines, so our leadership has been decimated. Serric only comes back to eat, sleep and shit—I've barely been able to get a word out of him since the invasion began. Rhendar intends on staying on that asteroid until it hits its target, and Niole somehow got it into her head that she needed to be there with him."

"Niole?" Rivus froze. "She's gone?"

"You hadn't heard?" Zal shook her head. "I'm sorry."

There was a time not so long ago when the news might have filled Rivus with relief. A galaxy without Niole in it would be a simpler galaxy, a galaxy more in balance. A galaxy where her loss might make the grief and pain of losing Tarvan somewhat even. Instead, all that swept over him was a cold, unflinching numbness. The thought of her out on that asteroid, hurtling through the gullet of space towards the Omega Gate, towards her end...it didn't fill him with satisfaction. All it did was wrench at the part of him he fought so hard to keep buried, the part that always yearned to imagine what could have been.

What happened between us, this rift we opened up...do you think if we make it out of here alive, we might ever have a chance of healing it?

There would be no answer to her question now. Just another regret on top of the rest of them.

"Rivus?" Zal's voice shook him from his thoughts. "All grievances aside, if you're here to fight with us, I welcome the help. But first, you should speak to Alvera."

"She's still alive?" Rivus said. "She didn't look well the last time I saw her."

"She looks even worse now. But she's tough. I don't think she'll let herself die until she's done whatever it is she needs to do. She seemed pretty desperate to get a message to Kojan, but with the curators jamming all communications in and out of the system..."

"He's with me. Alongside a whole armada from New Pallas."

Zal's eye widened. "The human colony?"

"We got our reinforcements. Now we need to make them count," Rivus said. "I'll talk to Alvera. It's been a while since I've had the chance to deliver any good news. Might as well take the small victories when we can get them."

"Let me know if there's anything you need. The Idran-Var are ready to do our part, as always." Zal gave a wry grin. "I'm sorry about the punch. But if I hadn't hit you for leaving, I might have kissed you for coming back, and that wouldn't have done either of us any good."

Rivus choked. "No, that's probably for the best." He hesitated, grinding his jaw plates. "For what it's worth, you can count on me to do my part too. I'm ready to fight to the end, wherever that takes us."

"Careful, Supreme Commander. You're starting to sound like one of us." Zal smiled. "Go find the captain. And when you come back, we'll show the curators how big a mistake they made when they forced the Idran-Var and the legionnaires onto the same side."

―――――

It didn't take Rivus long to find Alvera. News about his return had spread around the base faster than he could walk, and he met her halfway down a corridor near one of the medical centres, her cheeks flushed and her eyes wide.

"Kojan," she said breathlessly, not sparing a single word to acknowledge the fact Rivus was back. "He's with you?"

"In a manner of speaking," Rivus said. "The *Ranger* is out there at the head of the New Pallas fleet. Kojan is right where he should be, right where he's needed. What's so important that you need to call him back?"

Alvera faltered. A disbelieving expression flashed across her face at the mention of New Pallas, taking away all the years and battle-worn lines and leaving her looking like an awed child. For a single, terrible moment, Rivus thought she was going to cry. Then it was gone and the mask returned, as hard-edged and unyielding as ever.

"I need the *Ranger*," she said stiffly. "No other ship will do."

Something in her words made his plates twitch. "You're planning on going back there, aren't you? To the Omega Gate."

"I don't have a choice. There's something I need to do."

A growl ripped loose from deep in Rivus's chest. "You do realise there's an asteroid heading right for it, don't you? Even if you make it there in time, you'll never get off before it hits."

"I'm aware of that."

"Then why do this? Your ships from New Pallas are here, and more are coming. It's not all of them, but you could never have saved all of them. Neither of us could, no matter how much we wanted to believe it." He softened the edge of his voice. "Throwing your life away on that gate isn't going to change things."

"I don't intend to throw my life away," Alvera said quietly. "But you're wrong. It could change everything. If we win today, it will buy us a few millennia at most. The galaxy will forget we ever faced this kind of horror. But sooner or later, the curators will come back. I've seen it. Destroying the Omega Gate will only slow them down. I need to get to them from the inside. I need to destroy the hive itself, and I can't do it alone. I need the *Ranger*. I need my crew."

The words left her mouth with a weight wrapped around them, leaden with regret in every syllable. Their echo circled the pit of Rivus's stomach, leaving him cold.

"This is the end, isn't it?" he said, his voice little more than a murmur.

Alvera nodded. "For the galaxy's sake, I hope so."

"Then I won't stand in your way." Rivus grimaced. "But there is one problem. What makes you think Kojan will agree to this? I know you two have history. Something tells me he won't come running back just because you ask."

"I don't blame him. If I ever had his trust, I lost it a long time ago." A wistful smile pulled at the corner of Alvera's mouth. "Lucky for me, I know someone who might be able to get him to listen."

———

"No way."

The connection stuttered with interference from the space battle raging overhead, but there was no mistaking the defiance in Kojan's voice. The holofeed wavered in and out of focus as he folded his arms, his features sullen and stiff. Rivus felt the tension in the crackle of static that followed every word.

Next to him, Ridley rubbed her hand across her forehead. "At least hear her out. You have to understand—"

"The only thing I understand is that I've got thousands of ships from New Pallas fighting for a galaxy they didn't know existed until a few days ago. Dying for people they've never met." Anger flashed across Kojan's eyes. "And you're asking me to abandon them for some desperate plan we don't know will work?"

"Yes." Alvera's voice was quiet, but it carried the same hard edge it always had. She stepped closer to the comms terminal with a steadfast expression. "You told me I had to fix this. You said you didn't give a damn how I got it done, as long as I did it. I'm telling you, this is what needs to be done."

"This wasn't exactly what I had in mind." Kojan glanced at Ridley. "You're on board with this? You believe she can shut down their network from inside the Omega Gate?"

Ridley's expression was neutral as she looked down at the floor, quiet and unblinking. Then she snapped her gaze back up again. "I believe we only have one shot at giving this galaxy any hope for the future. We came here for our people. The next time the curators come around, we won't have an Alvera Renata." She nodded at her old captain, her expression relenting. "For better or worse."

Something shifted in the room at her words. A look passed between the two humans—if not forgiveness, then perhaps understanding. It stirred an emotion in Rivus he couldn't place, filled with longing and regret.

Even Kojan's prickliness seemed to deflate. The stiffness in his shoulders loosened, the heat in his eyes replaced by dim exhaustion.

"I'll need to refuel and restock our missile supply," he said. "But it won't be easy. The *Ranger* is like a homing beacon to the curators. The moment I touch down on Alcruix, they'll send every thrall they've got straight at the ship."

Rivus grunted. "Let me worry about that. I have my legionnaires, and I know an Idran-Var or two spoiling for a fight. We'll hold the hangar long enough to give you the time you need."

"Will it be enough?" Ridley asked.

The room wavered before Rivus's eyes. The three humans melted away, and all he saw in the reflection of the empty holoscreen was his own face staring back at him. Except it wasn't his own face—it was Tarvan's. Grey markings and keen blue eyes, eyes that had always been so sharp they'd pierced to the very heart of him.

You've gone too far this time, old friend, said Tarvan's ghost. *Standing side by side with the enemy. Forgetting what they've done, who they are. What kind of Supreme Commander are you? What kind of legionnaire?*

Rivus brushed the words aside. Tarvan was gone. He was all that was left. The decisions he'd made. The alliances he'd forged across grief and battlelines and vengeance. The people he'd fought for. The people he was still fighting for, no matter what kind of armour they wore.

We are all Idran-Var now, Rhendar had said.

Rivus finally understood what he meant.

"You ask if it will be enough?" He turned back to Ridley, tensing his plates. "It will have to be. *We'll* have to be. We didn't unite the whole galaxy just to fall apart when it matters most. If I can't promise you anything else, I promise you this: not a single curator thrall will make it into that hangar as long as I'm alive." Rivus glanced at Alvera. "See that everything is in place to receive the *Ranger*. I'll gather as many fighters as we can spare and meet you there soon."

Alvera drew her lips into a tight smile. "Sounds awfully like a last stand, doesn't it?"

"Only if we lose, Captain Renata." Rivus marched towards the doors, his white cloak billowing in his wake. "And I don't plan to."

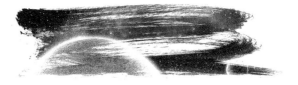

TWENTY-EIGHT

RIDLEY

The cocktail of nerve-stasis drugs coursing through Ridley's veins was more than potent enough to numb her to cyber surgery, but that didn't make it any easier to bear the scraping sound of the scalpel as it prised the implants loose from the bed of tissue in which they'd been seated.

Ridley drew another shaking breath, fighting the paralysis that had taken hold of her limbs. All she wanted to do was throw off the medic's invasive touch, but her body betrayed her, bound by the choice she'd made to submit to this.

"We're almost there, Ridley." Alvera's voice was muffled and distant. "They just need to stitch you back up and flush the nerve-stasis from your system. A quick course of stims and you'll be back to yourself in no time."

Ridley might have laughed if she'd been able to. Back to herself? Trying to imagine what that looked like was like trying to return to a state of being that didn't exist. The person she'd been on New Pallas—the skinny surfacer with no cybernetics who'd scrapped for everything to survive—was gone. She'd changed so much she barely recognised who she used to be. Not because of the bloodied implants lying on a sterilised tray at her bedside, but because of who she'd become out here.

A dull tingling sensation spread through her fingertips and toes. The paralysis was wearing off. Her limbs grew hot and heavy, and after a few minutes, Ridley felt strong enough to sit up. She couldn't see anything past the bandages wrapped around her head and over her eyes to help with the headache.

"Take it easy." Alvera's voice sounded different without the auditory implant sending signals to her brain. Like it had stretched thin, missing some of the timbre that had been there before.

"I'm fine." The words left Ridley's throat dry. "At least, I think I'm fine. It's hard to tell."

"Does it feel different?" Alvera asked. "Without the cybernetics, I mean?"

"A little numb, I suppose. Like there's a fog in places I used to be able to see clearly." Ridley shrugged. "What does it matter? It's not like I can change my mind now. It's done."

"If you're not up to this—"

"I never needed them before. If I survived back then, I can survive now." Ridley stretched her neck, wincing as a jolt of pain shot into the base of her skull. "Look, Captain... Alvera. I know you have plenty of regrets. Plenty of things you feel guilty about. This doesn't have to be one of them. I chose to do this. I know what's at stake, and I know this is the only way to get you where you need to be. I want to do my part. Let's leave it at that."

"Understood." Alvera cleared her throat. "I'm going to check on the *Ranger* and update Kojan. In the meantime, you have a visitor."

The soft tap of Alvera's footsteps faded across the floor,

replaced by a heavy, metallic clunking coming closer and closer. Ridley reached up to the bandages secured around the back of her head, then froze when a pair of armoured hands wrapped themselves gently around hers, drawing them away.

"It's best you leave those on, sweetheart," Halressan said. "You still need time to recover."

Ridley could smell her now. Steel and sweat and the fresh bite of Alcruix's atmosphere, mingled with something sharp and rusty. "Is that blood?"

"Not mine." Halressan let out a long breath. "It's hell out there, Riddles. I thought I knew what a good scrap was, but this...it's something else. No matter how many we kill, they keep coming."

Ridley squeezed her hands. "You don't have to go back out there. You've already done more than enough."

"The funny thing is, I thought I would be scared." A faint laugh tumbled from Halressan's throat. "But everyone out there is ready to fight until the end. The Supreme Commander and that turquoise siolean with the bad attitude? You'd never believe it, but they move like they've had each other's backs their whole lives. There are Coalition veterans working alongside mercenaries and pirates from the Rim Belt. Shit, I even saw Skaile ripping apart one of those huge aliens that was about to shoot Drex. They're all fighting for a chance at their future." Her voice cracked. "Turns out, so am I."

A painful ache crawled up Ridley's chest. "Let me look at you," she whispered. "Please."

Halressan's gauntlets slipped out of Ridley's hands and began working away at the knots holding the bandages in place. The brush of metal against her skin sent a shiver down Ridley's back, and when the soft fabric fell away from her face, she found her cheeks wet with tears.

"There you are," she said.

The brightness from the overhead lights was painful, but

not as painful as seeing Halressan in front of her and knowing it might be the last time. Her features swam into focus, blurred edges sharpening and taking shape. The pale marble-smoothness of her skin. The hard edge of her jaw. The flinty look in her grey eyes. All Ridley wanted was to dive into her and never come back up.

Halressan took off her armoured gloves and stroked a tear from Ridley's cheek. "You went through with it."

Ridley forced a laugh, but it tore from her throat like a sob. "You always said I was enough without my cybernetics. You said I had to see it for myself."

"Not like this." Halressan's voice cracked. "Not if it means I have to lose you."

Ridley leaned forward and pressed her mouth against Halressan's. The kiss was wet and soft, leaving the taste of salt on her lips. "I don't want to lose you either," she said. "But I have to do this. I'm the only one who can."

"You *don't* have to do this," Halressan said, her voice rough and fraying at the edges. "You don't have to go out there and get yourself killed so people will think you're special. You already know you are. *I* already know you are. So stay with me. If you're going to die, die beside me. Die letting me protect you until our last breaths."

All Ridley wanted was to say yes. She wanted it so badly it tore at her heart and left her bruised and aching. She couldn't imagine leaving this galaxy any other way than with Halressan's arms wrapped around her. Nothing else mattered when she was this close. Close enough to feel Halressan's breath on her cheek. Close enough to smell the faint perfume of her skin. Close enough to see the sheen across her grey eyes as they filled with tears.

"I love you," Halressan whispered, and Ridley was broken.

She pulled Halressan close and kissed her again, kissed her through the tears and the long, wracking sobs coming from both of them. The taste of her was bittersweet. Each time their lips brushed, Ridley wanted more. Even if it was agony. Even if it might destroy her.

"I love you too," she said, her words catching in her throat. "That will never change, no matter what happens."

Halressan pulled back. Her skin had turned red and blotchy, and her eyes were bloodshot. There was a tremble in her throat and a ghostly pallor to her cheeks that made her seem on the cusp of passing out. She looked more shattered than Ridley had ever seen her, but no less beautiful for it.

"How long do we have before the *Ranger* finishes refuelling?" Halressan asked, her voice thin.

"About an hour."

"Then we have an hour. We have that much, at least." Halressan traced Ridley's lips with her finger. "If these are the last moments we spend together, I want to spend every one of them with you."

A rush of warmth spread through Ridley's body and pooled in the pit of her stomach, making her insides flutter. Her cheeks burned as she met Halressan's gaze. "They set up a private recovery room next door. With a bed. If you wanted, we could—"

The rest of her words were lost to a gasp of half-shock, half-delight, as Halressan scooped her up in her arms and carried her across the floor. The recovery room was cramped and dimly lit, with only a footlocker and a small cot inside, but the only thing Ridley cared about was the firm grip of Halressan's arms around her as she gently laid her down against the sheets. Ridley sank into the softness of them, panting as Halressan straightened and gave her a coy smile.

"You have no idea how long I've been wanting to do this," Halressan said, her voice low and husky. "Ridley, you are—"

"Are you going to keep talking, or are you going to take that damn armour off already?"

Halressan slid off one of her vambraces. It dropped to the floor with a clatter, the sound of it sending a violent shudder of anticipation through Ridley's legs. She swore and fumbled with the ties at the back of her neck, almost ripping the medical gown in her urgency to get it off.

By the time she'd cast it to the floor, Halressan was completely, *beautifully*, naked in front of her. The soft light from the muted bedside lamp danced off her pale skin, illuminating all the dips and curves and freckled markings Ridley had never seen before. She swallowed, painfully aware of the shape of Halressan's body, of the wiry muscles and the slope of her breasts and the ridges of her hipbones.

Ridley bit her lip and forced her eyes back to Halressan's, sucking in a breath as she saw the same want, the same need, reflected in her grey gaze. Ridley's entire body raced with a heat burning her from the inside out. She'd never wanted *anything* as badly as she wanted this.

"Come here," Ridley said. "*Please.*"

Halressan's cheeks flushed pink and her lips parted as she slid one knee, then the other, onto the bed. The way Halressan slid over her, the way she leaned in until there was only a breath between their lips, was so coiled and purposeful that Ridley was ready to melt underneath her.

Halressan glanced down at her, a smile tugging at the corner of her mouth. "Is this better?" she murmured.

Instead of answering, Ridley slid her hands into the softness of Halressan's long blonde hair and pulled her into a kiss. The taste of Halressan's lips against hers, soft steel and endless longing, sent a rush between her thighs that made her whole body shiver. She sank further into the sheets, a moan escaping her throat as Halressan pressed down on her more fiercely with each deepening kiss.

Ridley moved her hands from the tangle of Halressan's hair, trailing her fingers down the nape of her neck and feeling a rush of exhilaration when she drew a small gasp from Halressan's lips. She ran her touch over every part of her she could reach, taking it all in. The roundness of her shoulders, the smooth arc of her spine, all of the places that fit the sweep of Ridley's hands so perfectly it was like they'd been made for her. The drum of her heart against her ribs had become a pulse throbbing through Ridley's whole body, under her skin, between her legs.

Halressan nipped at her lower lip, leaving it gently stinging from the graze of her teeth. "Stay there," she whispered.

Easier said than done, Ridley thought. She buried her hands in the sheets and squeezed so tightly her fingers ached as Halressan shifted her weight and inched slowly down her body, trailing deft kisses in her wake. Each brush of her lips was agonisingly inadequate, just the lightest touch against her collarbone, the underside of her breasts, the edge of her hip. It left Ridley's body quivering with the delicacy of it, desperate for more, for...

Oh.

There it was. This was what she'd been waiting for, longer than she'd ever known. The missing piece of her body, of her soul. It was never the cybernetics. It was this feeling of surrender, of giving herself to someone so entirely and getting all of them in return.

Ridley arched her back, yielding herself to Halressan, knowing that no matter what happened next, at least for this moment, she was completely hers. She closed her eyes and let go of everything but the racing of her heart and the warmth surging between her legs. The galaxy didn't matter. The insistent caress of Halressan's mouth against her skin eclipsed everything else. This feeling—*wanting*, and being wanted—was all Ridley had ever needed. For the first time in her life, she'd slid into a place where she completely, utterly belonged.

———

An hour wasn't long enough. Ridley could have spent eternity in those few precious moments stolen before the storm. She could have lost herself in them, lost everything else but the beat of Halressan's heart against hers as they lay together in that tiny, cramped cot, legs entangled and foreheads damp with sweat.

Ridley took her clothes out of the footlocker, pulling a padded vest over her head as she flicked her eyes back to the bed. Halressan was lying face down, her frost-blonde hair spilling across her shoulder blades as she mumbled something into her pillow. Ridley was tempted to wake her, but something raw and aching inside her stilled her hand. They had already said their goodbyes in the best way she could have asked for. Anything else would only be filled with pain and regret. That wasn't how she wanted to remember their parting. That wasn't what she wanted Halressan to remember.

She clipped the thin strap of her wrist terminal back together and slipped out the door, sliding it shut behind her. The harsh glare from the med centre lights assaulted her still-tender corneas, but she blinked the tears away and pushed the pain to the back of her mind. If her body hadn't recovered fully, she'd need to make do. There wasn't enough time left for anything else.

The *Ranger* was waiting in the hangar when she arrived, sleek and shining under the lights as the maintenance crew worked to unhook the huge fuel lines snaking across the floor. Ridley's heart wrenched at the sight of it. The *Ranger* had carried so much hope for them once. Maybe it could give them a little more before the end.

"Good, you made it."

Ridley turned to see Alvera coming out of the hangar's control centre. She was already geared up in her exosuit, and her hair was pulled back in a tight bun, accentuating the sharp angles of her face more severely than usual. There was a time Ridley might have snapped to attention upon seeing her so in control, so pristine. That awe had long since faded and died, but so too had the resentment she'd been holding on to. All she saw when she looked at Alvera now, sallow-skinned and bleak-eyed, was the last lifeline leading back to New Pallas.

"I wasn't sure you were going to show up," Alvera said. "Not that I would have blamed you. I didn't realise about your..." She glanced in the direction of the med centre and cleared her throat. "Well, if I'd known, I'd have tried to find someone else. Another way."

"There is no other way. We both know that." Ridley let out a breath. "Maybe I never understood that before, but I do now."

Alvera clenched her jaw. "You were right to judge me for the things I did. I kept telling myself I didn't have a choice, as if that would make things better. As if that would take some of the guilt away. But the truth is, I always had a choice. So do you."

Ridley hesitated. The captain was offering her a way out. A way to extricate herself from this desperate mission. A way to return to Halressan so they could meet their bitter, glorious end together.

"I made my choice," Ridley said, her voice hollow and distant to her own ears. "This is what I have to do."

"I understand." Alvera smiled sadly, then turned back to the *Ranger*. "We're ready to go. Just waiting on a few final touches."

Footsteps echoed from inside the *Ranger*, and a few seconds later, Kojan made his way down the access ramp with a purple-skinned siolean Ridley recognised as Kitell Merala. The two of them were in heated conversation, barely paying attention to anything but the holopad they were passing back and forth between them.

"Don't tell me how to set up the flight trim on my own ship,

Merala. I don't know what kind of junk you're flying these days, but believe me when I say the *Ranger* handles differently."

"I'm trying to save you from being blown to atoms when it turns out you can't pull out of a manoeuvre in time. If you'd let me make a few adjustments..."

"Nice to see you're stuck in the same argument as when I left an hour ago," Alvera remarked. "But I'm afraid we're out of time. If we're to reach the Omega Gate before the asteroid hits, we need to leave now."

"We're ready to launch," Kojan said. "Kite agreed to escort us as far as the temporal net to back us up against any curators that might give chase. After that, we're on our own." He put his arm on Ridley's shoulder. "It will be good to have you back on board. Feels like a lifetime ago we last did this."

Ridley patted his hand. "It's good to be back."

"All right. Head on board and find your stations. I'll be—" Alvera turned to the hangar doors with a frown on her face. "For fuck... What is it now?"

A dozen soldiers stumbled through the doors, their battle suits stained with blood and grime. Ridley's heart leapt frantically as she picked out all the faces she recognised. Rivus, one of his bone plates split right down the middle, his white cloak tattered and stained with ash. Zal, Venya, and the surly-looking siolean she remembered as Serric, all huddled together in their gleaming Idran-Var armour. Maxim ras Arbor and his brother Sem, bruised and bloodied. Drexious standing tall in full combat gear, supporting the weight of a limping Skaile.

Rivus shot Alvera a dark look. "The curators have breached the perimeter. We've brought everyone back to defend the hangar itself, but it's only a matter of time before they break through. You need to go."

Skaile hobbled across the hangar floor, her lips twisted into her usual sneer. "Well, my dear outlander, I suppose this is it. Try not to die, will you? It occurs to me that if we somehow manage to win this, you might be a useful person to have around when I'm building my new empire out of the ashes of these broken worlds."

Ridley couldn't help but chuckle. "I knew you were starting to like me."

"Breathe a word to anyone else, and I'll tear you apart." Skaile flicked her eyes towards Drexious. "This war of yours has put me in the deeply uncomfortable position of owing my life to that pathetic excuse for a jarkaath. Remind him that if he ever tries to collect on that debt, I will end him. Painfully."

Skaile limped away as Drexious sauntered over, his jaws split in a sharp-toothed grin. "Let me guess, she was telling you how much she likes me now, right?"

"Something like that."

"It's my natural charm." He pulled her into a hug, his arms stiff and awkward. "You definitely made things interesting for a while. Not counting the times you almost got us all killed, of course."

Ridley forced a smile. "Always time for one more when I get back."

"I'll hold you to that." Drexious let out a soft hiss. "Stay safe, Ridley. Or if you can't do that, at least stay alive. The galaxy would be a more boring place without you in it."

As Ridley opened her mouth to reply, an explosion rattled the hangar. Somewhere behind the reinforced doors, gunfire erupted, followed by yells and screams. There was no more time for goodbyes. The curators were here.

Rivus drew his varstaff and exchanged a look with Serric, whose armour was rippling with reflections from the blue-green surge of his flare. "Go now," he said sharply. "We'll hold them off."

Ridley tore herself away and followed Alvera up the *Ranger's* access ramp. This was it. There was no taking back the decision she'd made. No turning around now, not even if—

"Wait!"

Halressan sprinted across the hangar floor, her cheeks flushed with colour and her blonde hair flying wildly in all directions as she stumbled up the foot of the ramp. She crashed into Ridley in a tangle of steel limbs, wrapping her arms around her and pressing her lips against hers in a final, furious kiss.

"Come back to me," she said, panting heavily.

Ridley choked back a sob. "I'll try."

There was no time to say anything else. The ramp was already retracting into the *Ranger's* hull with a mechanical groan. Halressan stepped off the end, her grey eyes bright and shining as she pressed her lips into a trembling smile. Ridley watched her the whole way, right until the doors slid shut in front of Halressan's beautiful, stricken face and left her with nothing but the darkness of the hold.

The metallic clunk of the locks sliding into place carried with it a finality that made Ridley shudder. The rumble of the engines through the hull seeped all the way into her bones. Suddenly, the hold didn't feel like part of the *Ranger* anymore. It felt like a tomb.

"Head up to the flight deck and get strapped in," Alvera said. "Kojan will be launching soon."

Ridley nodded, but her feet wouldn't move. A trickle of fear found its way into her limbs, turning her muscles to ice. It was too much. To know that this was the end, to know she had a part to play in whatever was coming... It was meant for someone else. Someone like Alvera, or Rivus, or...

No. It was meant for me.

The thought was fierce and unbidden, rising up from a place inside her she hadn't known was there. It pushed out the doubt. It rang through her head in Halressan's voice, in Skaile's voice, in Ridley's own voice, singing with the truth of it. Even without the cybernetics, even when she'd scrapped for survival every day of her life on the wretched, decaying surface of New Pallas, even when they'd called her a *slete* and told her she didn't matter, she'd never hated who she was. All she'd hated was the fear that who she was would never be good enough.

Now, she knew better.

"Ridley?" Alvera stared at her through the darkness, her face obscured by shadows. "Are you ready?"

She was the only one who could do this. Not because of any cybernetics, but because of the person she'd made herself into without them.

Ridley met Alvera's questioning gaze. "I'm ready."

TWENTY-NINE

ALVERA

The journey back to the Omega Gate passed in the distant haze of a decision made. A decision Alvera would never turn back from, even if she could. She wrapped herself in a thick fog of pain and memories, losing herself to the steady thrum of the *Ranger's* engines like she was the only one on board. A ghost among the living, already haunting the empty spaces she was about to leave behind.

This had been her ship, once. She'd stood on the bridge next to Kojan in the same exosuit she wore now and spoken words they'd all needed to hear. Words they'd all needed to believe in.

All of us go, or none of us go.

The promise still pulled at Alvera even now, but it didn't possess the same hold over her it once had. She'd left that part of herself behind. It was out there somewhere, far across the reach of dark space, waiting for the rest of her to follow. There was no going back now. No point in wondering how long her withering body might last before it gave out completely. The blood in her lungs and black spots in her vision were far from the worst enemies she'd fought off. If death was coming, it would find its match in Alvera Renata.

"Airlocks are aligned. You're good to go." Kojan's voice broke through her thoughts. A piece of her old life, reminding her of what she had to do. A light to guide her through the approaching darkness. Alvera wanted to hold on to the memory of his dry tone, the way he hesitated over his words. She wanted to hold on to everything.

Instead, she could only say, "Thank you."

"Don't thank me yet," Kojan replied. "I still don't like this. The last time we came to the Omega Gate, we couldn't get this close. Now, they let us fly right up and dock with one of their airlocks? It's like they don't even care."

Alvera shook her head, the motion sending a stab of pain through the back of her eyes. "The opposite, in fact. They wanted me to come back here. They know this station will be the end of me."

It was the first time she'd admitted it out loud. The words lingered long after she closed her mouth, echoing in the awkward silence between them. Alvera didn't care. She'd known the truth long enough. It was past time the rest of them learned to accept it too.

She turned to Ridley. "Let's go."

Ridley shot one last glance at Kojan and nodded, her mouth set in a thin, determined line. The scuffed legionnaire flysuit Kite had acquired for her was too big for her body, turning her narrow shoulders and small frame into something clunky and unwieldy.

"Once you get me where I need to go, get the hell out," Alvera told her as the airlock doors shut behind them. "The

Ranger can't wait forever. Sooner or later, that asteroid is going to hit. You all need to be far, far away by the time that happens."

"We'll do our best." Ridley took a breath. "Listen, Alvera...it hardly feels like the right time to say this, but I wanted to tell you before we go in there that despite everything that's happened, I'm glad you chose me. I'm glad I got to help fight for New Pallas. No matter what else I may regret, I'll never regret that."

Alvera wasn't sure whether the tightness in her chest was from the swell of sentiment or the dying ache of her slowly-collapsing lungs. "Me neither," she managed. "Choosing you is one of the few decisions I won't regret after I'm gone. One of the few decisions I can be proud of. New Pallas doesn't need me anymore, Ridley Jones. It's got you."

The corridor stretched out in front of them, the gaping jaws of a throat Alvera was all too familiar with. Every time she walked into the darkness, she knew she might not come back out again. This would be no different.

"Here," she said, pressing her gun into Ridley's hand. "It's better off with you than it is with me. The curators will get in my head. They'll try to make me stop you. If it comes down to it, save yourself."

Ridley looked down at the gun, then back at Alvera, horror-struck. "I can't kill you."

"If it gets that far, you wouldn't be killing me. You'd be killing one of their thralls." Alvera pinched the bridge of her nose. "Without your cybernetics, the curators can't get to you. That's why I brought you here. No matter what it takes, no matter how much I lose myself, you need to make sure I end up in one of their control centres. I'll take care of the rest."

"How are you going to stop them?"

The fading beat of blood through Alvera's veins seemed to hurry at the question. Her own body was a stranger to her now, and the parts of her that weren't numb ached with a gnawing pain that hadn't given her a moment's respite in weeks.

"The curators might be the memory of the galaxy, but those memories can't exist without some kind of system to catalogue them," Alvera explained, each word an effort. "Even Chase couldn't survive without her hardware. Wherever they are, whatever pocket of dark space they're hiding in, they have a server. They have a brain. A big fucking cybernetic brain." She leaned against the wall, straining for breath. "And as it happens, I brought just the thing to kill it."

Ridley stared at her, mouth half-open, her dark skin taking on an ashen pallor. "Alvera, what did you do?"

Alvera offered a tight smile. "What I had to do. Like always."

She could feel the quickening's needle-point teeth eating away at her from the inside. The virus ran through every piece of her cybernetics, corrupting the code in her implants, telling them to turn against the body they'd protected for so long. It spilled poison into her blood. It chewed at her organs and tissue, devouring the parts of her she didn't need anymore, the parts of her that were human. Every passing second brought with it a new agony, but it was an agony that was keeping her alive.

Kojan had given her the idea. His drunken accusation back on Alcruix had burrowed its way to her heart, awakening an idea that terrified and exhilarated her in equal measure. The more Alvera had thought about it, the more plausible it had seemed. It was strangely fitting, in a way—the quickening was her engineering, her virus. It was only right that it should be her end. At least this way, she could make it the curators' end too.

"I need to link my mind to the hive one last time," Alvera said, meeting Ridley's desolate gaze. "I'll give them exactly what they want. I'll let them absorb me into their consciousness."

Ridley swallowed. "And the quickening?"

"It will corrupt their programming, wiping out every memory they've ever collected. Those memories *are* their consciousness. Without them, they don't exist." Alvera balled her fists. "This is the only way to stop them coming back. The only way to destroy them for good."

"If what you're saying is right, if this works..." Ridley's eyes gleamed. "Alvera, we could call off the asteroid. We could defeat the curators and still keep the waystations. New Pallas would have time to evacuate everyone."

"No." The word left Alvera's throat harsh and cold, echoing off the station's grim walls. "It's too late for that. If we call off the asteroid now, we won't get another shot if things go wrong."

"But—"

Alvera doubled over, fighting the spasm that shot across her chest. After she regained what little breath her lungs could hold, she straightened her spine, grimacing at the effort. "Look at me. I don't know if I can do this. I don't know if my body will survive long enough to get the job done. I won't ask the galaxy to gamble its life on my ego, not when I've done so much damage already. If this doesn't work, at least the asteroid will buy you some time. Maybe centuries, maybe millennia. Maybe enough time to find something that *will* work. I wish there was a way to save New Pallas, but this is the way it has to be."

Ridley pressed her mouth shut. A thousand emotions flickered across her eyes, darkening them like a shadow. Her shoulders stiffened in the metallic casing of her borrowed flysuit. She looked like someone who'd stared into the void and lost themself in the nothingness of it.

"I understand," Ridley said quietly. "I wish I didn't, but I understand." She lifted her chin, her eyes bright and resolute. "Tell me where we need to go."

Alvera gave a grim smile. "To the heart of this place, so I can put a bullet through it."

———

At some point during the excruciating trudge through the snaking network of tunnels, Alvera's legs stopped working. It was like all the tendons and ligaments holding her wasting muscles in place had frayed and snapped, leaving her limbs too feeble to support her weight. Ridley did her best to drag her along, but even using her as an anchor couldn't stop the stutter in Alvera's steps.

It's taking too long. You'll never make it.

If the voice in her head was her own, Alvera was long past recognising it. Her thoughts had become muted and distant, drowned out by the whispering at the base of her skull. The curators had taken root in her mind again, eating away at her as ravenously as the quickening. They pressed their twisted, ugly presence against the synapses in her brain, searching for a way in.

You can't keep your mind from them. It's already theirs.

Alvera licked her lips, tasting blood on her tongue. It was hard to tell if it had come from her nose or her constant cough —her body's betrayal was unceasing and infinite. Her headache had spread to her temples and now pulsed painfully behind her eyes. She was losing herself, if she hadn't lost already.

The station's abject gloom only grew more lifeless through the lens of her failing implants. What little colour there had been in the dreary corridors and soulless tunnels leached out and died, leaving her with nothing but grey shapes bleeding into each other. The room around her might have been familiar if she'd only been able to see it. She felt like a stranger returning to a home she couldn't remember.

"This is it." Ridley consulted her wrist terminal. "Going by the schematics you sent me, this is where we need to be."

Alvera stumbled forward, catching herself on something smooth that hummed with electricity. The final console. The last remaining link to the place the curators were hiding, far across the chasm of dark space. She'd made it.

"This is where *I* need to be," Alvera corrected, tiredness seeping into every syllable. "You need to get out of here before that asteroid hits. We've already wasted too much time."

"I can still help you," Ridley said. "I can—"

"No." The word tore from Alvera's throat. "Dying here with me won't make you a hero. You have to live to make that happen. Do everything you can for New Pallas. Help the galaxy rebuild. Go out there and live the life you deserve, the life you've *always* deserved. That's what I need from you, Ridley— not this. Now go."

Ridley gave a final, reluctant nod before wrenching herself away and disappearing back into the belly of the gate. Her footsteps echoed in Alvera's ears until the muffled sound faded, leaving her with nothing but her own ragged breaths for company. She was on her own now. There was nobody left to get hurt.

Nobody apart from her.

Alvera sprawled her weight over the console. Faint holographic lines danced across her vision in colours she could no longer see. A light on the interface blinked, its monochromatic glow dull and dim.

"One last time," she whispered, and surrendered herself to the signal.

Diving back into the curators' consciousness was like returning to a nightmare. Their presence rushed in like a flood, seeping into the cracks in her brain until the sides of her skull buckled and swelled with the pressure. The hive crashed over her, pulling her to depths she hadn't known existed. Their minds tore hungrily at the filaments of her brain and sucked on the memories like parasites. This was what they'd always wanted: to absorb her into their infinite memory. To make her one of them, to make her forget everything about the individual that was once Alvera Renata.

Back so soon?

The familiarity of the voice was enough to make Alvera sob. There was no presence to it this time, not even a wisp of memory, but as diluted as it was, Chase's voice still endured. It reached to her from inside her own heart like it had always been there.

The muscles at the edge of Alvera's mouth still functioned enough to quirk her lips into a smile. "You know me—I couldn't stay away."

I always said I was the smart one. Chase gave an exaggerated sigh. *So now that you're here, what do you plan to do?*

"Win, of course."

Of course. I don't know why I asked.

Alvera pushed her smile further, but it wasn't enough to stop the grief wrenching at her. Was it really Chase, or just the parts of her she'd brought with her? Did it even make a difference anymore? Either way, they would be together again, a fragment of memory amongst trillions of others. A fractured soul reunited for a moment before she killed the hive and ended everything.

Not yet, Chase reminded her. *There's something else you need to do first.*

The curators reared up around her, tugging her mind towards them, but she held them off. Chase was right. Before she gave herself to them, she had one last mission to complete.

Alvera sank into the depths of the hive. She was one mind fighting to comprehend eternity. The scale of the curators' memories was too immense to fit within the boned-in limits of her finite brain.

But she had to try.

She searched for the threads of millennia gone by. She grasped at them, following them to the places they led to, the places she had to go. All the lost colonies the curators hid across dark space. All the planet-sized graves of the civilisations left behind. It was already too late for most of them, but there was still hope for one, if she could only find it.

Too many variables. Too many possibilities. Tens of thousands of isolated rocks. Any one of them could have been New Pallas. If she'd only had more *time*...but time was the one thing she didn't have. The asteroid was coming. There was no escaping it now, even if she wanted to.

Alvera enclosed the memories in her mind, compressing them into data, hoping that none slipped through her grip as she moulded them into what she needed them to be. The heartbeat of the Omega Gate echoed around her. She sensed the thrumming of the generators keeping it alive, the vibrations through its floors as a pair of steel boots clattered their way towards the airlock. She sensed the faint signal of Ridley's wrist terminal, almost out of range.

Alvera threw herself at the connection. Something blinked and flickered in her mind. Then she was back in the hive, and the data was gone.

If her lungs had still been functioning, she might have gasped for breath. Had she managed to complete the transfer before it was too late? Maybe her failing cybernetics were too damaged to cope with this final ask of them, corrupting the process before she could finish it. Maybe Ridley was already back on the *Ranger*, too far out of reach for the connection to go through.

It doesn't matter, Chase said, soft as a whisper. *Either way, there's nothing more we can do for them now.*

"There's still one thing we can do. We can end this."

In the sanctuary of her mind, Alvera saw Chase smile back, then disappear.

It was a beautiful thing, to stop fighting. To give up and accept what was coming. Alvera had been waiting for this kind of peace for years, and now that it was here, all she wanted to do was bask in how *easy* it was. The hive pried away the last defences around her mind, taking the precious parts of herself she'd guarded so fiercely, and it didn't even *matter*. This was what she came here for. This was what she wanted.

"Your experiment is over," she said.

Part of her was vaguely aware when the shell of her body shut down and died, but if there was any pain, she was too far gone for it to reach her. Those weary bones and ruptured organs didn't belong to her anymore; she had no need for them. She was one of *them* now, floating in their fathomless sea of memories, unable to do anything but drown.

She watched with eyes that no longer existed as the virus she'd brought with her emptied into the water, staining it black with its infecting, oozing tendrils. There was still enough of her left to revel in the curators' disbelief, in their panic, as the quickening spread through them like poison. Memories dissolved around her, shutting down parts of the curators' immeasurable mind. She was smaller than a mote of dust. Smaller than an atom. In a few moments, she would no longer exist. None of them would.

The hive reared its ugly head, but there was no power in the cacophony of its collective voice now, just the pitiable kind of defiance that only came with the end of all things. *You will not take us with you*, it said.

Alvera smiled. "All of us go, or none of us go."

The promise died on her lips, one final time.

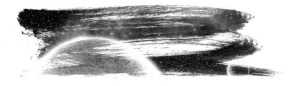

THIRTY

KOJAN

"We have to go."

The gentle grasp of Cyren's claws around his shoulder made Kojan stiffen. He knew the gesture was only meant to comfort him, but something about the pity in her touch made him want to pull away.

He brought up the communications interface on the flight console. "I'll try Ridley again. Maybe—"

"You've been trying for the last thirty minutes," Cyren said. "The Omega Gate jams all outside connections. There's no way of knowing if they're still alive to answer."

"We can't leave them here," Kojan retorted. "I need to do something. I need to go after them."

"Then we'd lose you too." Cyren fixed him with a solemn stare. "The curators would get into your cybernetics and destroy you before you reached them. You *know* this, Kojan. I understand how much it hurts to make this decision, but we can't stay any longer. The asteroid is almost upon us. If we don't leave now, we don't just lose them—we lose the *Ranger*."

Kojan flinched. She was right. The *Ranger* wasn't his anymore. That had changed the moment he'd taken Cyren and the iskaath crew on board. There was life in the corridors now. Engineers working to maintain the ship's beating heart. Technicians keeping its vital systems running. Deckhands and stewards filling the once-abandoned spaces with bustle and purpose. Kojan had welcomed each of them on board. He'd offered them a place here, and they trusted him to keep them alive.

He'd given Ridley and Alvera as long as he could. But he had a responsibility to more than them now.

There can be no right choice with what we're about to do, Alvera had told him. *Remember that, when these decisions come to you instead of me. Try to forgive each other, if you can.*

"I'm sorry," Kojan murmured, and powered up the engines.

The *Ranger* roared into life with a furious snarl, like it was raising its sleek, metallic voice in protest. The vibrations shuddered through the hull and travelled into Kojan's bones, making his hands shake around the controls. He let out a breath as the docking clamps disengaged with a heavy clunk, releasing the ship back into space.

Kojan sent them forward, watching as the Omega Gate became smaller and smaller in the viewport feeds. The huge, blinding beam emanating from its centre cut through the darkness of space, visible even when the rest of the gate had fallen into shadow. If Alvera and Ridley had failed, the only thing that could stop the curators now was the huge chunk of metal and rock hurtling through the vacuum.

"Adjusting our course," Kojan said, swiping through the navigation controls. "We don't want to be anywhere near the path of that asteroid when—" He broke off. "Did you hear that?"

"Hear what?" Cyren shot him a sideways glance.

Kojan listened for it again. The sound was so faint, so fleeting, that he'd hardly dared to believe it. A burst of static amongst the steady hum of instruments around him. It might have been interference. It might have been his own desperate mind giving him hope.

Then it happened again, and the doubts disappeared. Someone was trying to reach them over the comms line.

Kojan swallowed, a flutter rising in his stomach. "I left the line open to Ridley's flysuit. I just thought... I just *hoped*..."

The line filled with a muffled, unrelenting buzz. For a moment, there was nothing but garbled noise. Then came the faint, impossible trace of a voice.

"Is...still out there? I'm...away from..."

Kojan stilled. The words were barely audible over the distortion muddling the line. "Ridley?" His voice cracked on her name. "If you hear me, keep talking. We're trying to clean up the connection."

"Kojan, is that you?" Her voice was sharper now, breaking through the interference. "Please tell me that's you."

She was alive. Ridley was *alive*.

"It's me," Kojan said, fighting to keep his voice steady. "What's your situation? Are you still on the Omega Gate?"

A hoarse laugh crackled though the speakers. "Not exactly. By the time I got back to the docking hatch, the *Ranger* was already gone. I tried to send you a message, but the curators must have been jamming the signal from within the gate. So I jumped."

Kojan froze. "You jumped? You mean you're just floating out there?"

"It was that or hang around to get hit by an asteroid," Ridley said. "I'm trying to put some distance between myself and the Omega Gate, but these manoeuvring thrusters take a bit of getting used to. I keep sending myself around in circles."

"Manoeuvring thrusters?" Cyren shot Kojan a quizzical look. "Didn't Kite's flysuit stop working the last time we were in the temporal net? If it's working now, it must mean..."

"Alvera did it." Ridley's voice came through the speaker, breathless. "Or at least, she did *something*. Enough to knock out the temporal net. We can't count her out. She's still fighting them."

It was more than Kojan dared to believe. The beam tearing a hole through to the curators' dark sanctuary on the other side of the galaxy was still there, shining like a blade. But if the temporal net was down, Alvera had done something to hurt them. How much more could she do?

Ridley's signal appeared on the nav console. She was still within reach. If he turned back now, he could still get to her.

He glanced at Cyren, who responded with an impatient hiss. "Well, what are you waiting for?"

Kojan grinned. "Hold on, Ridley. We're coming."

He pulled the *Ranger* around in a turn so tight it scrambled his insides. The engines roared in agreement as he pushed them to full power, and a painful fluttering spread across his chest at the force of the acceleration. But a little discomfort didn't matter now. The only thing that mattered was getting to Ridley.

The signal from her flysuit held steady, leading them to her like a beacon. Every blink of golden light on the nav console was proof that she'd made it. Proof that she was alive. Kojan watched the iskaath leap out on their rescue cables to bring her into the safety of the *Ranger's* cargo hold, but it wasn't until she was in front of him, her coils tousled and her eyes shining with adrenaline and unspent tears, that he finally released the air from his lungs.

"You made it," he said.

Ridley's smile strained the corners of her mouth. "I always do." She faltered. "Alvera should have been here too. She told me to go, and I left her. I know there was no other choice. I know she had to stay behind. I just wish there had been another way."

"Sometimes there is no other way. Alvera knew that better than anyone." Kojan squeezed her hand. "She's given us a chance. Now we have to get out of here and make it count."

"What about the asteroid?"

Cyren shot them a grim look. "It's close. Too close."

"We'll see about that." Kojan cracked his neck and returned the thrusters to full power. The *Ranger's* hull strained and groaned under the acceleration. Its engines screamed, their capacity pushed to the limit. Every internal component was working overtime, fighting to keep the mechanical systems and instruments alive.

But that wasn't a problem. Kojan trusted the *Ranger* with his life, with all their lives.

"Do you see that?" Ridley bolted upright on the crew couch. "Kojan, do you *see* that?"

The asteroid was so close it swallowed the entire viewport. Kojan's instruments told him it was set to miss them by a little over a hundred klicks, but it was difficult to believe the holographic readings when he could see the huge rock right there, hurtling towards them. It drew them towards it, into its path, ready to crush them into scorched atoms.

"Hold on," Kojan said. "When that thing hits the Omega Gate, a lot of debris will be coming our way. This could be a rough ride."

The second the words left his lips, everything went dark. The asteroid blotted out the viewports with the enormity of its shadow. It snuffed out the light of the Omega Gate's beam, the burning fires ravaging Ossa's surface, the blue-yellow glow from the system's star. It was so close that Kojan could see the ridges and crevasses on its barren, rocky surface.

By the time Kojan released his next breath, the enormous

rock had passed them, hurtling towards the Omega Gate. There was no stopping it now. It was more than a weapon; it was a force of nature. Unstoppable and unrelenting, blazing a path through space.

Time slowed. It was as though the temporal net had sprung up around them again, freezing them in a fleeting fraction of a moment.

Then the asteroid hit.

The feeds stuttered as a brilliant, blinding flash frazzled the external sensors and turned the viewport screens white. Kojan couldn't see the impact. He couldn't see anything but the glare outside. He sucked in a breath, his hands tight around the rattling controls as the *Ranger* groaned around him. His instruments blinked wildly. Warning sirens screamed out from the console.

They were still too close.

He pushed the engines into overdrive, gritting his teeth as the acceleration pinched the muscles in his neck. "The radiation shields," he said, turning to Cyren. "What are we looking at?"

"Sixty percent and falling fast," she replied. "One of the techs is trying to—"

"It won't make a difference. Tell them all to get back to their harnesses and buckle in. The only way we get out of this now is by outrunning that blast."

A proximity alert screeched urgently from the console, and Kojan pulled the *Ranger* into a sharp manoeuvre as something shot past, missing the wing by a matter of metres. Before he had time to readjust, another one came, forcing him to send the ship into a gut-tearing spiral to avoid getting holed.

He heard the splatter of bile on the floor as Ridley retched. "What was that?" she spluttered, wiping her mouth. "Is something shooting at us?"

"It's the asteroid breaking up from the impact with the

Omega Gate," Kojan said tersely. "The explosion sent debris flying in every direction. Hold on while I get us clear."

The *Ranger* shuddered with each wild turn, its engines roaring with the effort he was asking of them.

"Cyren? Give me an update on the radiation shields."

"Holding at thirty-five percent," she said, her yellow eyes unblinking. "Did we make it?"

Kojan eased off on the thrusters as much as he dared. It wouldn't do them any good if he pushed too hard and blew an engine, but as long as there were still chunks of asteroid hurtling through the vacuum, he couldn't afford to let them idle. "We're clear of the immediate fallout, but my instruments are still all over the place. I can't pick up any readings from the Omega Gate. I don't know if it managed to withstand the asteroid, or crashed into Ossa, or—"

"Kojan, it's gone." Ridley's voice came from behind him, soft and trembling. "Look."

Kojan brought up one of the viewport feeds, enlarging it as far as the scopes allowed. The beam was gone. There was no white light tearing through the fabric of space. No curator ships spilling out in their tens of thousands. The Omega Gate's twisted structure, the monstrosity that had formed itself out of the waystations, was nowhere to be seen. All that remained were scraps of lifeless metal drifting across the void.

Cyren let out a pained hiss. "Look at Ossa."

Dread gripped Kojan as he focused on the planet. Every second, a new patch of fiery orange bloomed on its surface, spitting flame and rock into orbit. Huge chunks from the asteroid roared through the atmosphere and shattered against the planet's crust. Shards of metal kilometres wide raced after them, nightmarish blades flung from space towards the defenceless surface below. He watched strike after strike pummel the old Coalition capital until he could bear it no more.

Ossa. New Pallas. Those planets, those *people*, were only the beginning of what this fight had cost them. Their losses would only multiply across the galaxy as more and more reports came in. Planets razed to the ground. Entire systems slaughtered. The thought of it brought bile to the back of Kojan's throat. If this was what victory looked like, it was dark and hollow.

"Rivus sent one of the *Exodus*-class evac ships from New Pallas to help evacuate as many people as possible before the asteroid hit." Ridley looked sick. "Fyra volunteered to lead them. Do you think they made it in time?"

"I don't know. Maybe I can get some readings. Give me a minute to—" Kojan paused, distracted by a light blinking on the comms system. "Incoming connection request. The signature is pointing to a sector halfway between here and Alcruix."

"That can't be right." Ridley frowned. "The curators jammed all long-range communications. How can there be…"

The holoprojector flickered, and the pale, exhausted features of Kitell Merala appeared in front of them. "Shit, it's really you. I sent a ping out in hope, but I never thought I'd get an answer. How the hell are you still alive?"

"I could say the same to you," Kojan replied, disbelief flooding his voice. "What's going on, Kite? How were you able to get a signal out?"

"I was hoping you could give me the answer to that." Kite furrowed his brow ridge. "I don't know what you did out there, but something happened. I left a long-range line open, just in case, and the next thing I knew I started receiving connection requests. A few at first, then dozens. Now I have a queue of a hundred systems waiting on the other end of the line."

"Have you had a report out of Alcruix?"

"I've had reports out of *everywhere*." Kite gave an incredulous laugh. "I don't know how to make sense out of half of them. I'm a fighter pilot, not some smart-ass comms tech. All I know is the situation is a mess. The fighting is still going hard, and I've lost count of the number of systems requesting urgent aid. If we don't get reinforcements to some of them soon, we'll lose them."

"The thralls are still fighting?" Kojan's heart fell. "Then it didn't work. Alvera thought she could infect the curators with the quickening to shut down the hive. But they're still out there. Even if we defeat the thralls, the curators will come back for us. And when they do..." He swallowed the lump in his throat like it was made of glass. "We didn't win. We only delayed the inevitable."

"She must have done *something*," Kite said. "The long-range comms jammer is down. And..." He broke off, his brow ridge sinking deeper. "Wait, I'm getting a real-time transmission through. It's Rivus. Hold on while I patch him through."

The holoprojector wavered again, and Rivus's stony face came into view alongside Kite's. "I saw the communications blackout had been disrupted. I hoped for the best, but I have to admit, I didn't expect this much of a reunion." He glanced between them. "The captain. Did she make it onto the Omega Gate?"

"Yes." Ridley's voice was a quiet murmur. "But she didn't make it back."

Rivus closed his eyes. "I always feared it was too much. There was a moment during the fighting I thought she'd managed to..." He shook his huge, crested head. "Battle makes desperate fools out of the best of us."

"What do you mean?" Ridley leaned forward. "What happened?"

Rivus heaved his shoulders into a shrug. "Something changed. The thralls...they aren't as coordinated as they were before. They're still taking shots at us, but their attacks aren't as aggressive or single-minded as they used to be. They seem desperate. It's like—"

"They're trying to survive," Ridley finished. She sat upright in her chair, stiff-spined and wide eyed. "Alvera didn't fail. She did it. She destroyed the hive."

"That's impossible," Kojan said. "The quickening would have killed the thralls too."

"The thralls were never part of the hive," Ridley countered, her brows knitting together as she rushed the words out. "They were programmed by the curators, but they weren't part of their shared consciousness. The quickening wouldn't have infected them directly—it would have only corrupted the curators' programming."

Rivus looked at her sharply. "What are you saying?"

"I'm saying that without the curators' influence in their heads, the thralls are nothing but the base nature of the species they once came from. They're running on the only primal instinct their bodies have left." Ridley blinked, tears spilling down her face. "Survival."

The word sent a shiver down Kojan's spine. He couldn't imagine feeling any kind of sympathy for the creatures intent on wiping out their existence. But all the same, a kernel of understanding took root inside his chest. The thralls weren't the curators. They never had been. And if all the curators had left behind were mindless bodies just trying to survive, then maybe—

"Could this give us a way to win?" Rivus asked, his bone plates twitching. "Can we defeat them?"

"Do we need to?" Ridley held his gaze, her jaw tense. "You heard what I said. The curators don't have any influence over the thralls' minds anymore. They don't *want* to fight us."

"Then what do you suggest we do?"

"Pull back. Give them a chance to retreat. A chance to *live*." Ridley let out a long breath. "Believe me, they'll take it."

Rivus's plates hardened. "You think we can risk that? If you're wrong..."

"If I'm right, this war is already over. We don't have to lose anyone else." Ridley looked at Rivus bleakly, her eyes dull. "We've lost so much already. We've fought and killed to survive. Why not try a different way for once?"

The silence that followed her question was deafening. What Ridley was asking of Rivus was impossible. To walk away from a fight they finally had a chance of winning. To show the thralls the kind of mercy that would never have been extended to them.

Alvera would have fought until the bitter end—Kojan was as certain of that as he was of anything. But Alvera was gone. She'd taken herself out of the equation. She'd done what she needed to and trusted the rest of them to do their part after she'd gone. Trusted them to do a better job than she had.

Rivus's plates shifted as he stared back at them. For all the hardness of his alien features, there was something underneath that Kojan recognised. Fear. Doubt. The struggle of making the right choice, of making a decision he could live with.

After a moment, Rivus spoke. "I once told my old Supreme Commander not to lose sight of the real enemy. He didn't listen. If he had, things might have been different." A growl rumbled from his throat. "I won't make the same mistakes he did. If the curators are gone, then our fight is not with these wretched creatures they left behind. I won't lose anyone else to a war we don't need to win."

Kojan pursed his lips. "Will the Idran-Var agree to that?"

"The Idran-Var know better than anyone what battles are worth fighting," Rivus said. "They'll understand what needs to be done. We'll withdraw. We'll give the thralls a chance to scatter. If they keep fighting, we'll have no choice but to defend ourselves. But if they leave..."

"We'll be free," Ridley finished softly. "And so will they."

Rivus turned back to her. "Sometimes it's easy to forget what it is we're really fighting for. Thank you for reminding me."

The connection flickered and died. Kojan heard the thump of his heart, the light hiss of Cyren's breathing, the creak of leather as Ridley shifted in her chair. It all seemed so tenuous, so out of place, like this was only the sharp intake of breath before the plunge. Any moment now, the curator fleets would return. The Omega Gate would appear once more as a shadow across Ossa's sun, a horror reassembled from its broken parts. But seconds rolled into minutes, and still the reach of space around them remained quiet. It was empty.

It was *over*.

Cyren turned her yellow eyes to him, her gaze soft and uncertain. "What do we do now?" she asked. "Where do we go?"

"Back to Alcruix," Ridley said. "No matter what happens with the thralls, there are people there who need us." She looked down, frowning at something on her wrist terminal.

Kojan raised an eyebrow. "More trouble?"

"No. At least, I don't think so. It's..." Ridley hesitated. "It's a message from Alvera. The time stamp places it as being sent shortly before the asteroid hit, but it didn't come through until now."

Kojan's stomach tightened. "What does it say?"

"I don't know." Ridley peered over the glowing data. "The message doesn't appear to be corrupted, but the information is garbled. She didn't leave a voice note or any kind of explanation, just chunks of data all jumbled up with no order or purpose to them. It doesn't make sense."

"Not yet, maybe. But it will."

Ridley shot him a questioning look. "What do you mean?"

"You've never come across a puzzle you haven't been able to crack." Kojan smiled. "If Alvera sent it to you, it's because she knew you'd be able to figure it out."

Ridley looked down at her wrist terminal again. In all the time Kojan had known her, she'd never backed down from a challenge. He'd bet the *Ranger* itself against her backing down from this one.

After a moment, Ridley closed the holographic interface. "Maybe you're right," she allowed. "But it's a puzzle that can wait for another day. Right now, I've got a very important vid call I need to make."

She unclipped herself from her harness and squeezed his shoulder before disappearing down the corridor. Kojan listened to the faint tap of her boots against the floor until the click faded from his ears, swallowed by the other sounds coming from the *Ranger*. It was like Ridley had melted into the ship itself. She was part of it now, just like he was. Just like Cyren and the iskaath who'd left behind the home they knew to find their place in the galaxy.

The people might have changed, but the nest remains.

The memory of Eleion's words was a warm embrace. The *Ranger* echoed with loss, the reminder resounding through empty spaces once occupied by those no longer with them. But it had a new crew now. The people who had made this ship their home, like he had. Not connected by anything as tenuous as blood or birth, but by the space they'd chosen to share with each other. The one thing Ojara, for all her influence and power, had never been able to give him. A family.

And now, finally, it was his.

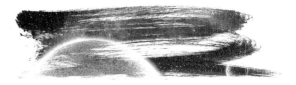

THIRTY-ONE

NIOLE

Alcruix had changed.

It wasn't just the stillness of it, though that was unsettling enough. Every time Niole walked past one of the bloodied trenches or burned-out wreckages left behind from the battle, she couldn't help but imagine how the planet must have looked only a few short weeks ago. Bodies piled high on the ice-encrusted ground, shrouded by the stream of ash pouring from the sky. Bullets and plasma bolts flying across the rugged terrain, filling the thin atmosphere with the scream of gunfire. Smoke and scorched flesh clogging up the filters of her helmet.

Now, the bodies were gone. So were the curator thralls that had descended on the planet in their tens of thousands, their corrupted minds programmed with nothing but violence. Whatever the humans had done on the Omega Gate, it had worked. The moment Rivus and Serric ordered their forces to pull back, the thralls had scattered. All they'd left behind was a quietness, like their withdrawal had caused a vacuum that sucked the resolve from everyone who'd been fighting. It didn't feel like victory. It just felt...empty.

Niole shivered. She'd stepped onto a world she thought she knew only to find something missing, something she'd never get back. Rhendar's absence echoed through every corridor, every room. His loss stalked her every step.

He should have been here. The thought was like a blade between her ribs. *He saved us. He saved me.*

She watched the recordings again and again, until the sight of the asteroid crashing into the Omega Gate was burned into her eyes. She could play every frame of it in her head. The ruptured stillness as the mass of rock and metal made impact. The sunburst flare that erupted from the gate's twisted heart, lighting up the darkness of space. The spherical explosion of asteroid matter and debris blasting outward.

What the recordings didn't show were the people they left behind. The civilians on Ossa who hadn't made it to the evac ships in time. The human captain who'd returned to the Omega Gate to bring down the hive. The broken bodies of the Idran-Var who'd fallen in defence of a plan that had only ever been a desperate contingency.

And Rhendar. Finally—for the first time in his life, perhaps —at peace.

Niole glanced at his helmet in its place on the locker next to her bed. Its blank visor stared at her, painfully empty without the red glow coming from inside. She still hadn't summoned the strength to pull it over her headtails. The moment she accepted it was hers was the moment she admitted he was no longer coming back for it.

A hiss from the door cut through her thoughts. "Are you ready? Zal is waiting for us in the—" Serric broke off as he cast his eyes over the helmet. "It doesn't matter. I can handle this alone if you need to—"

"No, it's fine." Niole pushed herself to her feet. "I should probably be there."

Serric paused. "Yes," he said. "You probably should."

Niole flinched at the tension that thickened in the air between them. The silences they'd shared over the last few weeks were heavy with all the things neither of them had been able to bring themselves to say.

She followed him into the corridor, falling into step half a stride behind him. She saw the twitch that danced along his temple, the hard line he'd set his brow ridge into. The turquoise of his skin was pale from exhaustion, and his cheeks had turned gaunt in the time she'd been away. Not for the first time, a pang of guilt pulled tight in Niole's stomach. She'd left him here. She'd chosen dying with Rhendar over fighting with Serric. That decision had left a fracture between them that was almost tangible. She felt it in every clench of Serric's jaw, every averted gaze.

"Good, you both made it." Zal glanced up from her holoterminal, her face weary. "I know we've had more pressing matters to attend to over these past few weeks, but this can't wait any longer. We need to discuss what to do about the thralls."

"They're going to be a problem," Serric said, pacing back and forth. "We've got scattered hordes of mindless creatures roaming the galaxy with no real understanding of who or what they are. It's only a matter of time before there's trouble."

"Perhaps." Zal's cybernetic eyegraft blinked as a thin smile stretched across her face. "But there's also an opportunity to learn from them. These thralls are the only living evidence of civilisations long eradicated. If we could study them, we might be able to find a way to communicate with them. Can you imagine the possibilities?"

Niole's stomach twisted. "Study them? Like in a lab?"

"Not like that." Zal shook her head vigorously. "I already have enough corpses to keep me busy with autopsies for months. No, what I mean is that we send out probes and trackers to monitor their movements. We observe them. We see if there might be any hope of—"

"You want to leave them to run around the galaxy completely unchecked?" Serric shot her a hard look. "What happens to anyone who stumbles across them and pisses them off? This isn't one of your research projects, Zal. These thralls, these *things*, aren't a juna or vinehound you can slap a tracker on and observe in the wild. We've lost too many of our people for you to believe that."

Zal glared at him. "I'm well aware of what they're capable of. I'm also aware of the fact that they are the last of their kind. Every single one of those creatures belongs to a civilisation the curators wiped out. Do we not owe it to them to give them a chance? Is that not what we'd have wanted for our own people if we'd been the ones removed from existence?"

"They're lost." Serric shrugged. "It would be a kindness to put them out of their misery."

"We were all lost once," Niole said quietly. "That's what made us Idran-Var."

She blanched as they both turned towards her, Zal with a half-smile tugging thoughtfully at the side of her mouth, Serric with a measured look that only pulled harder at the knot of discomfort lodged in her gut. This was what she'd been afraid of. She'd never asked to be the one people looked to. She'd never wanted it. All it made her want to do was shrivel into her own skin and disappear. Better that than suffocate under the weight of their expectations.

Zal cleared her throat. "In any case, we have no war chief anymore. It will be up to each *varsath* to make these kinds of decisions for their own people." She glanced at them both. "With that in mind, I hope you two figure out whatever this is between you soon. Our people are looking for someone to lead them. They deserve better than to be kept waiting."

She gathered up a handful of datapads and left the room. The heavyset doors slid closed behind her with a low mechanical whirr, reverberating through Niole's ears until she could barely hear herself breathe. Being left alone with Serric made the room smaller, like the walls were closing in around her. Like the filtered air was slowly draining as the tension grew thicker and thicker.

"I don't want it," she whispered. "It should have been you."

Serric stiffened. "You have no right to say that. Rhendar gave you that helmet. You accepted it. You should be wearing it now. The fact that you're not is an insult to his memory."

"I accepted his helmet as a reminder of our friendship," Niole bit back, curling her hands into fists. "But that doesn't mean I can accept what he offered with it. He might have given it to me, but he also gave me a choice. He reminded me of another way."

"You don't have to run from this."

"I'm not." She shook her head. "I'm Idran-Var. But I'm *more* than just Idran-Var, and I can't lead our people knowing that." She reached out a tentative hand and brushed his face. "It has to be you."

Serric lifted his dark eyes to meet hers, his expression as unyielding as ever as he searched her gaze. Looking for some kind of assurance, maybe. Looking for some kind of sign that he could take what she was offering him.

"Niole," he said, his voice low. "You don't understand what—"

She pressed her lips against his, fierce and insistent. He froze, then leaned into the kiss, exploring her mouth with his own as he pulled her against him. Warmth raced through her, sending a rush from the pit of her stomach to the ends of her headtails. His flare surged again, and her own rose to meet it. Volatile. Violent. Never at peace. Maybe this was how it would always be between them. Maybe she didn't care.

Serric broke away first. The shimmer of his flare danced across his skin, scattering reflections across the black glint of his eyes. "I could have done it, if you'd given me the chance," he said, his voice strained. "I could have followed you."

Could you? The question went unvoiced, but Niole could tell by the flicker of unease across Serric's face that he'd heard it all the same. It lingered in the air between them, waiting for an answer that would never come, if only because they both knew the unbearable truth of what it was.

Niole forced her mouth into a smile. "This is my choice, Serric. It's what I need to do. And you...you'll do what you need to do. For the Idran-Var."

He nodded slowly. "A new fight. A new beginning, for all of us."

With Serric, it's always a fight. He doesn't know how to do anything else. Rhendar's old warning echoed in her ears like an omen. Maybe he was right. Maybe Serric's way would mean the end of the Idran-Var. But that wasn't something Niole could control. All she could do was take the last gift Rhendar had given her and follow it to its end.

Perspective.

She knew what she had to do.

———

"You're leaving?" Venya gave an outraged grunt which quickly descended into a deep groan of pain. The medical cot creaked under her weight as she writhed, her orange eyes narrowing in agony.

Niole winced. "You need more meds?"

"Pain meds are for children and humans." Venya stopped

thrashing and sent her a glare. "I can deal with a little pain. What I can't deal with is you telling me you're leaving."

"There's something I need to take care of," Niole said. "Besides, it will give you time to recover before we get back in that sparring ring. I owe you a few rounds."

"You'll be waiting a while," Venya said, a guttural laugh tearing from her throat. "I don't think I'll be setting foot in a sparring ring anytime soon."

Niole's stomach turned cold. "It's that bad?"

Venya gestured to Claine. "Show her."

Claine peeled back the thin medical blanket draped over Venya's torso, revealing the full bulk of her bone-plated body underneath. The entire right side of her red-coloured exoskeleton was splintered and crushed, pieces of bone flaking onto the bedsheets underneath. Her leg lay unnaturally stiff, like the carcass of a limb that no longer belonged to her. Niole didn't need a med tech's expertise to know what it meant.

Venya met her eyes with a mirthless smile. "Looks like my fighting days are behind me."

"You don't know that." Claine huffed and folded his arms. "The human colonists have cybernetic technology far beyond anything we've been able to develop. They'll be able to fix this."

Niole placed a hand gently on Venya's crest. "And if they can't, there's more than one way to be Idran-Var. Rhendar told me that, before..." She swallowed. "He always had a way of seeing past the surface. If I learned anything from him, it's that we're more than our armour. More than our bodies. You are Idran-Var, Venya. That's all that matters."

Venya let out a dry chuckle. "Keep dropping wisdom like that and you'll be joining Serric as one of the *varsath*."

Niole kept her expression steady. As far as the rest of the Idran-Var knew, Rhendar had chosen Serric to replace him. Only Zal had guessed at the reason for the tension between them over the last few weeks, and she had been pragmatic enough to leave it be. This was how it had to be, for the sake of the Idran-Var. For the sake of their future.

"About that…" Claine cast her a sidelong look. "If Serric is one of the *varsath*, that means nobody is allowed to see his face now, right? How is that going to work when you two…well, you know? Does he leave the helmet on, or—"

Venya swung at him with her good arm, drawing a yelp from Claine as she cuffed him across the shoulder. "You idiot. If Serric catches you saying anything like that, he'll reinstate your execution. You know he'd love the excuse."

Claine paled. "He wouldn't." He glanced at Niole. "Would he?"

Niole laughed. The sound surprised her at first, bubbling up in her throat like something that hadn't been released in too long. She couldn't remember the last time she'd laughed, the last time she'd had *reason* to laugh. But something about Claine's panicked expression and Venya's cackling amusement drew it out of her in waves, filling her with something light and wonderful.

"My friends," she said, reaching out her other hand to wrap her four fingers around Claine's five. Her heart swelled at the three of them joined together, interlinked across all the things that made them different, connected by the things they shared. "No matter how I got here, I'm glad this is where I ended up. I'm glad this is where we all ended up." She stood up and smiled. "Try not to get into too much trouble when I'm gone, will you?"

"No promises." Venya widened her cracked jaw plates into a grin. "Come back soon, Niole. *Varsath* or not, our people need you."

"I know."

But there were other people who needed her too.

———

Ossa was nothing like the planet Niole once knew. There was no trace of the lush greenery or bursts of colour she'd taken so much joy in as a cadet. The blue-yellow sun had been snuffed out behind an opaque cloud of dust and ash, smothering the planet in a shroud of pulverised rock. Daylight didn't exist anymore, only the perpetual gloom of a sky that would no longer brighten. Not in her lifetime, at any rate.

She made her way through the unrecognisable wasteland that had once been the training grounds, scanning for the faintest remnant of something she remembered. Blocks of sandstone crumbled beneath her boots. Not a single tree from the orchard remained. It was like death itself had swept over the old capital of the Coalition, leaving nothing behind but the spat-out bones of everything it had consumed.

Up ahead, Niole saw a familiar silhouette against the hazy, dirt-thick air. Rivus stood with his back to her, his white cloak hanging limp around his shoulders, so still he looked like part of the terrain itself. The only thing left that hadn't yet fallen to ruin and decay.

Niole stepped carefully across the rubble, joining him as he looked out over the desolation. "Seeing it like this, it doesn't feel like we won," she murmured.

"We didn't win. We survived."

"Not everyone."

"No." Rivus clenched his jaw plates, his breather mask sliding over the angles of his face. "It would have been worse if we hadn't had the evac transport from New Pallas. We saved hundreds of thousands that would have died otherwise. But that's little comfort to the hundreds of thousands more we left behind."

"No word on survivors?"

Rivus gave a harsh laugh. "The planet suffered dozens of orbital strikes. Some from the asteroid, some from the debris from the Omega Gate. I saw the feeds. The shockwaves levelled entire cities. The atmosphere burned. And now"—he gestured to the blackened sky above—"anything that did survive won't last long. The temperature has already plummeted in the few weeks since impact, and it will fall further. Ossa is lost."

His words turned Niole cold. It was one thing to read the reports and watch the newsfeeds, but another thing entirely to stand on the planet she'd once called home and see the devastation with her own eyes. Rivus was right. They hadn't won, they'd only survived. And their survival had come at the cost of Ossa.

"I am sorry, Rivus," she said, her heart breaking on the words. "If there had been another way…"

"There wasn't. I know that now." He shook his huge, crested head. "I was so angry, so desperate to believe we had a choice, but we didn't." He shifted his plates, his eyes still fixed on the barren landscape stretching out in front of them. "I'm sorry too. Rhendar sacrificed himself to save this galaxy. Not just for his people, but for all of us. He gave more than most legionnaires ever could. I won't forget that."

"Neither will I."

They stood in silence, nothing between them but the stillness of the air, thick with vapourised rock. There was a time not so long ago that the quiet would have been unbearable, laden with everything that had happened between them. Now, it felt different. Maybe it was coming back here and seeing the things they'd lost. Maybe that was what it had taken for them to understand each other.

Perspective, Rhendar had said.

"This is the place you attacked me that day," Rivus said, his voice low. "The place where everything changed."

Something sharp lodged itself in Niole's throat. "I remember."

"For the longest time, I thought I was angry at you for what you did. But it wasn't about that." Rivus let out a rumbling sigh.

"It was about what happened after. You ran. You left me with the scars of what you did. All the pain, all the hurt of not being able to understand, and you just left."

"I was afraid. I didn't know who I was or what I was capable of." Niole looked down at the vambrace Rhendar had given her, letting the blue shimmer of her flare escape through the metal. "I do now."

"Maybe that was something we both needed to learn," Rivus said. "I resented you for moving on while I was left behind, but you didn't move on at all, did you? Neither of us did. Not until now." He fixed her with the intensity of his green eyes. "You asked if I thought there might be a chance to heal the rift between us. If you're willing, I'd like to try."

He reached into the strapping of his armour and pulled out a bundle of green fabric. Niole's breath caught in her throat as he unfurled it, revealing the intricate stitching forming the insignia of the legionnaires. There, close enough for her to reach out and claim it, was the cloak she'd once wanted for so long. It hung in Rivus's grasp, fluttering gently in a non-existent breeze. Hers, if she wanted it. Hers, if she could find it within herself to accept it.

"I can't," Niole said quietly. "I'm Idran-Var."

"Was it not Rhendar who said we were all Idran-Var now?" Rivus said. "The Coalition no longer exists, but that doesn't mean there's no longer any need for the legionnaires. We protect the people of the galaxy who need protecting." The rough edges of his voice caught on the words. "Tarvan lost sight of that somewhere along the way. This is my chance to do better. Maybe it can be yours, too."

Niole teetered there on the threshold, caught between it all. Everything she had ever run from, everything she had tried to belong to. All the things she was and all the things she could have been. All the warring parts that somehow coexisted within her. Idran-Var. Legionnaire. She hadn't been able to give herself fully to either because of the hold the other had over her. But what if she didn't need to be one or the other? What if she could be both?

She wrapped her hand around the green cloak and shivered as Rivus released it into her grasp. The soft spill of fabric against the hard casing of her armour should have felt wrong, but instead, it was like a missing piece falling into place. "Could you give me a moment?" she asked. "There's something I need to do."

Rivus nodded. "I should get back to the *Lancer*. There's a lot of work to be done. Whatever you decide, you know where to find me. Goodbye, Niole."

"Goodbye, Rivus."

She waited until the heavy crunch of his footsteps disappeared, then let out a long, shaking breath. Her hands trembled as she pulled the folds of the cloak apart and set it around her shoulders, tying it in place with a roughly-made knot. The fabric was weightless against the shell of her armour, but that didn't stop the way her spine straightened under its mantle, the way her body flooded with all the rush of a flare when she looked down and saw it flapping against her chestpiece.

There was just one thing missing.

Rhendar's helmet clinked gently against her armour from where it hung on her belt. Niole reached down and unlocked the clasp, her fingers numb as she brought the helm up to look at its faceless visage. It was like holding Rhendar between her hands, staring into the only eyes of his she'd ever known until the end. The helmet stared back at her as if it was waiting to see what she would do next.

There's more than one way to be Idran-Var, Rhendar had told her.

Maybe this was it.

Niole pulled the helmet over her head. Her vision turned black until the holographic display inside the visor lined up with her eyes and showed her the world again. Something crackled in her ear as the comms line linked up to the rest of her armour. Piece by piece, system by system, the helmet accepted her. It became hers.

For a fleeting moment, Niole's mind filled with the vision of how she must have looked. Dark, glassy armour, caked in a layer of grime and dust. A green cloak draped around her shoulders, the folds of it falling down her back. And a helmet, staring out across the bleak landscape with thoughts of a brighter future behind the thin slits of a visor glowing red. Everything she was, finally together as it should be.

Idran-Var.

Legionnaire.

Her.

THIRTY-TWO

RIDLEY

Tyvoth's three distant suns didn't hold the same heat as Jadera's single, ferocious star, but that didn't mean the planet was any less hostile. The terrain surrounding the makeshift landing pad where Ridley's shuttle had touched down a few days before was arid and mountainous, bleak grey against the faint, orange-tinged atmosphere. The moment Ridley had stepped outside, her nostrils had burned with the stench of sulphur. The planet was a backwater rock tucked away in one of the Rim Belt systems, too unwelcoming for anyone in their right mind to ever have settled there.

Which made it perfect, of course, for the Outlaw Queen.

"Well, what do you think?" Skaile shot her a fearsome grin. The rich velvet-red of her skin had only deepened since arriving on Tyvoth, and the faint glow of her flare rose around her in a carmine haze. Despite the severed headtail and nasty gouge on her brow ridge, she looked more striking than ever.

The touch of the planet's radiation seemed to have renewed her vigour, returning the wicked glint in her eye that never meant anything but trouble.

"It's...something," Ridley managed. "I assume there's still some work to be done? A *lot* of work?"

Skaile's grin turned into a scowl. "Wipe that look off your face, outlander, or I'll remove it permanently. It might not look like much now, but by the time you're back from this pointless scouting mission of yours, it will be the flourishing beginnings of my new empire."

Next to her, Fyra let out a pointed cough. "*Your* new empire?"

"What?" Skaile glared at her. "You think because you're providing some bodies that you get a stake? Be grateful I let you and your ship full of outcasts land here in the first place. If you want a cut of the profits, you'll work for it. Just like everybody else."

Ridley followed Skaile's gaze across the horizon, where the huge, blocky hull of the *Exodus*-class evacuation transport lay nestled among the rocks, the size of a small city. By all accounts, it should never have been able to make a controlled landing in atmo. It would certainly never be spaceworthy again. Instead, it was the beginning of something new. The heart of a fledgling city that would spring up around it, no doubt filled with the same black markets and dens of debauchery that Jadera was once known for.

Skaile caught her expression and let out a short chuckle. "Having second thoughts, outlander? Do you want me to convince you to stay? I admit, you're a significant improvement on the cowering piece of dead weight you seemed to be when we first met. You might actually turn out to be useful after all this."

"A compliment? From you?" Ridley grinned. "Careful, Skaile. Next thing you know you'll be inviting Drex over to sip bark tea and talk about the galactic restoration programme."

Skaile snorted. "All I'm saying is that if you ever find some sense in that small human skull of yours and change your mind, you know where to find me. We both know you'll eventually need the credits."

"I appreciate it. Truly."

"See that you do." Skaile drew her lips into one last sneer and turned on her heel, making her way back towards the huge, fallen evac vessel with purpose behind every step.

As Ridley watched her go, something tugged at her. Part of her seemed to know she'd end up back here again, one way or the other. It was difficult to tell whether the thought excited her or filled her with dread.

Fyra sighed, the sound brittle against the thin atmosphere. "Everything has changed. Yet somehow, I feel like I've seen this play out before."

Ridley glanced at her. Tyvoth's radiation had brightened her purple skin into a yellow-green colour, and there was a new calmness across her smooth features. The planet suited Fyra as much as it suited Skaile, however unlikely they were as partners, or whatever manner of arrangement it was they'd brokered between them. Ridley wasn't sure she wanted to know the details.

"Are you sure you know what you're getting yourself into?" she asked. "Do they, for that matter?"

Fyra shrugged. "They don't have much of a choice. Ossa is gone—they have no home to return to. They could leave and join the millions of other refugees looking for some kind of sanctuary out there in the galaxy, but that's no guarantee of a better life than the one they might be able to build here. Skaile offered them a chance to be part of something. It might not be the life they knew back on Ossa, but they'll adapt." A serene look fell across her face. "As I have."

"There are ways of adapting that don't involve helping build a new criminal empire," Ridley said with a wry smile. "But I take your point. Sometimes all you can do is whatever gets you from one day through to the next."

"A lesson we've all learned, myself included." Fyra nodded at one of the landing pads in the distance. "Over there. I believe that's your ride."

Ridley focused her eyes across the grim grey line of the horizon. A familiar silhouette of a ship cut through the hazy orange atmosphere, its thrusters firing as it slowly descended onto the landing pad. The sheen of its hull glinted with the reflections of the three suns, signalling to her that it was time to go.

Ridley shouldered her pack and offered her hand to Fyra. "I appreciate everything you did for us. Whatever we find out there, we wouldn't have been able to do it without you."

Fyra wrapped her fingers around Ridley's outstretched hand. "I wanted to thank you, too. I resented you at first. But if you'd never woken me from that tomb I'd sentenced myself to, I'd never have seen this victory. If I am the last of my people, at least I can go on knowing they did not die in vain. One of them lived to see this day. One of them lived to know peace. I hope your people will know it too."

Ridley looked back at the *Ranger*. It was time for another mission. Time for another new beginning, another chance to claim the future Alvera had promised them.

She smiled. "That's the plan."

———

The first time Ridley had stepped on board the *Ranger*, she'd felt a prickle of unease across her skin. She'd never been able to shake the feeling that someone's eyes were on her, that an Exodan was silently watching her, judging her for where she'd come from, who she was. She'd never believed she belonged here. Never trusted that she was good enough.

Now, the corridors bustled with more than Exodans, more than *humans*. The iskaath crew dipped their heads as Ridley passed them on her way up to the flight deck, the gleam of their eyes offering nothing but respect—maybe even admiration. It wasn't something she was used to. It wasn't something she'd ever get used to.

Ridley nodded back, slipping past their long, lithe tails in the narrow squeeze of the corridor. One of the iskaath had bare jaws, but the other still wore their breather mask and toxin supply pouch. Not all of Cyren's people had taken the opportunity to be outfitted with Alvera's modified cybernetics. Not all of them were meant to.

Ridley understood that better than anyone.

Her fingers drifted to the two incisions on the back of her neck. One was so faint she could barely feel the raised ridges of it anymore. The other was still tender and healing. Both of them were reminders of what she'd given up to be here. Both of them were reminders of who she was now.

Everyone was already gathered on the bridge when she arrived. Kojan sat in the pilot's chair tinkering with the instruments, his brow creased as he and Cyren murmured in quiet conversation. Drexious was sprawled on the spare crew couch, acknowledging her with a lazy swish of his tail. Next to him, Halressan pushed herself to her feet, crossing the floor to stand at Ridley's side.

"Big day," she murmured, brushing her fingers against Ridley's in a way that sent a shiver racing down her spine. "You nervous?"

"Always."

Halressan smirked. "You've got this, babe. Everyone on this ship would follow you into hell and back. Half of us already have." She pressed her lips gently against Ridley's cheek. "I wouldn't want to be anywhere else in the galaxy."

Ridley's face flushed with warmth, but before she could reply, the comms system chimed.

"Good timing." Kojan tapped the console. "I have a link to the legionnaire scouting patrol and our basecamp back on Ras Prime."

The holoprojector flickered into life, revealing the shimmering, translucent features of Kitell Merala and Max ras Arbor.

"Do we have an update?" Kojan asked.

"The rip site is ready and waiting for you," Kite replied. "We've triple checked along all projected vectors, and the path is clear. If you're still sure about this, that is." He raised his brow ridge. "That ship of yours has been through a lot already, and now with these retrofits adding extremely complex tunnel-punching technology into the mix... Are you sure the *Ranger* can handle it?"

Kojan rolled his eyes. "I know you're not stupid enough to question my ship, Merala. There's nothing the *Ranger* can't handle."

"Right." Kite grunted. "It's just that you still owe me a rematch from our skirmish at Hellon Junction, and if you think you can get out of it by getting yourself sucked into a black hole somewhere—"

"I haven't forgotten." Kojan grinned. "Winner gets the beers in?"

"As long as it's not that disgusting excuse for ale your Rasnian friends are so fond of. That shit will make you sick for days."

On the other line, Max chuckled. "It's not our fault your weak siolean stomach can't handle a proper drink. Maybe you'll think twice the next time you go pint for pint with the ras Arbor brothers."

Ridley bit back a laugh as Kojan sighed and switched channels. "All good on your end, Max?"

"Grateful for the distraction. I'm stuck in the middle of too many bureaucrats trying to figure out the best way to hold an election in the middle of a shitstorm." He groaned. "And I thought I was done with politics."

"Any news about…" Kojan trailed off, his jaw clenching.

Max seemed to understand. "Still nothing concrete, but Rellion got hit pretty hard after we left. She's likely among the millions of dead who haven't been identified yet."

"I know Ojara better than to believe those odds." Kojan snorted. "If there's no confirmation, I wouldn't write anything off. And if she's still alive out there, she'll be back."

Ridley touched his shoulder. "We've earned a lot of goodwill with the legionnaires. We could contact Rivus and ask him to put some feelers out."

"No." Kojan shook his head. "All my life, I let Ojara control me. I won't give her that kind of power over me any longer, regardless of whether she's alive or dead. Either way, it's over." He cracked his neck. "Besides, there are a lot of Rasnians looking forward to meeting their brothers and sisters from New Pallas. It's time to bring our people home."

"Copy that," Max said, nodding sharply.

Kite gave a legionnaire's salute. "Safe flying. See you when you get back."

The connection fizzled into silence. For a moment, it was peaceful—just the rumble of the engines through the hull and the hushed, expectant breaths of everyone gathered on the bridge. The quiet before the storm.

Kojan turned to her. "I guess this is it. Have you picked a set of coordinates yet?"

Ridley's thoughts drifted to the data packet Alvera had sent her from her final resting place on the Omega Gate. She'd spent the last few months poring over it, staring at the feeds until her eyes burned, drawing on every scrap of knowledge to decipher the jumbled code. At first, nothing made sense. Then Ridley realised the truth staring her in the face all this time: it was just another language—and she was a translator.

After that, all she needed to do was get to work. Patterns emerged, swirling into sense before her eyes. She unscrambled references to celestial objects, coordinates located in places far beyond the reach of any star charts they possessed. She began to grasp what Alvera had been pointing to, what she'd been trying to tell them. Their old captain was leading them home. Back to New Pallas.

Or at least, she'd tried to. But the deciphered data didn't just point to one planet—it pointed to dozens of them. For all Alvera had done, all she had sacrificed, she hadn't been able to narrow it down. Maybe she'd run out of time. Maybe there were limits even she couldn't breach.

Ridley let out a sigh. Her mouth was dry, her palms slick with sweat. How had Alvera done this? How had she managed to make these kinds of decisions? The weight of expectation spread across her shoulders, bleeding into her spine, crushing the breath in her lungs. It was an impossible choice. Any one planet would take years to reach. They'd have to punch multiple tunnels across millions of light-years, pushing their technology to the limits. Every false lead meant more time for New Pallas to suffer alone.

How could she choose? If someone else were here, if Alvera were here—

New Pallas doesn't need me anymore, Ridley Jones. It's got you.

The memory rang through Ridley's head as clearly as if Alvera had been standing next to her. It pushed out the cold touch of fear and doubt that had nestled itself in her sternum. They *would* find a way home. They *would* save New Pallas. Alvera had always believed that. She had to believe it too.

"Ridley?" Kojan cleared his throat. "We're all with you,

whatever you decide. All you need to do is tell us where to go...Captain."

Ridley let her eyes drift down the list of possible matches projected on her wrist terminal, waiting for some kind of sign. Nothing came. All she could do was make the right decision, or keep trying until she did.

She turned to the viewport, to the promise of the unknown, and smiled.

"Let's go home."

AFTERWORD

Thank you for reading! The Waystations Trilogy has been more than three years in the making, and if you're here with me at the end, three books and 350,000 words later, I just want to say thank you for coming along for the ride.

If you enjoyed Those Who Resist (or indeed any of the books in the series!), please help other people discover the Waystations Trilogy by leaving a review on Amazon or Goodreads. Word of mouth is so important for independent authors and helps more books like this get written!

Want to see what's in store next? Sign up for my author newsletter for exclusive updates, sneak peeks and release news!

bit.ly/scrimscribes

ALSO BY N. C. SCRIMGEOUR:

THE WAYSTATIONS TRILOGY

THOSE LEFT BEHIND

THOSE ONCE FORGOTTEN

THOSE WHO RESIST

THE EXODUS BETRAYAL

Go back to where it all began and discover Alvera's origin story in
this standalone cyberpunk thriller

SEA OF SOULS

Looking for your next fantasy read? Check out N. C. Scrimgeour's
newest series, the Sea of Souls Saga, for a Scottish-inspired dark
fantasy filled with magic, folklore and adventure.

KEEP IN TOUCH

You can keep up to date with future releases by visiting ncscrimgeour.com and signing up for my newsletter, or by following me on social media.

facebook.com/scrimscribes
twitter.com/scrimscribes
instagram.com/scrimscribes
tiktok.com/@scrimscribes

BONUS CONTENT

ALVERA RENATA

RIDLEY JONES

KOJAN IREJ

CHARACTERS AND FACTIONS

Crew of the Ranger

ALVERA RENATA: Human female, mid-50s. Cyber engineer, captain of the *Ranger* and leader of the mission to find a new home for the people of the human colony known as New Pallas. Shares her head with an artificial intelligence known as Chase.

ARTUS SHAW: Human male, mid-20s. Former officer on Exodus station, with experience in special operations and in-field medical treatment. Extensively modified with advanced Exodan cybernetic technology.

CHASE: Artificial intelligence installed within the neural implants of Alvera Renata. Highly advanced technological software that appears to be self-aware with a personality of its own.

KOJAN IREJ: Human male, mid-30s. Pilot of the *Ranger*, son of former Exodus Station council leader Ojara Irej. Medical records show extensive genetic engineering and cybernetic implants—possible explanation for remarkable reflexes and piloting skills.

OJARA IREJ: Human female, early-70s. Former councillor on Exodus Station before her imprisonment for running invasive cybernetic experiments on unwilling participants for New Pallas. Succeeded in her position by Alvera Renata. Mother to Kojan Irej.

RIDLEY JONES: Human female, mid-20s. Originally a New Pallas surfacer before securing a scholarship to Hyperion University for translation and archaeology. Fluent in over a dozen New Pallasian languages and dialects.

Coalition of Allied Planets

KITELL 'KITE' MERALA: Siolean male, late-30s. Legionnaire fighter pilot and leader of Pincer Squad. It should be noted that while Merala's skills are impressive, he suffers from a lack of propriety and professionalism, particularly in front of his superiors.

RIVUS ITAIR: Dachryn male, late-30s. General of the Coalition Legionnaire Corps and second in command to Tarvan Varantis. Formidable warrior with considerable size and strength advantages. Facial plates of exoskeleton damaged from training ground incident sixteen years prior involving [*REDACTED – CLASSIFIED*].

TARVAN VARANTIS: Dachryn male, early-40s. Supreme Commander of the Coalition Legionnaire Corps. Recognised for his unparalleled capacity to get results, no matter what the cost. Note: Any references to the Supreme Commander as

'Tarvan the Tyrant' are unofficial edits and should be flagged to the first available archivist.

Rasnian Systems

GOVERNOR COBUS: Human male, early-60s. Leader of the Rasnian Systems, generally based out of Ras Prime or Rellion. Confirmed political leanings towards secessionism and Rasnian independence from the rest of the Coalition—intelligence recommends keeping activities under close observation.

MAXIM RAS ARBOR: Human male, late-40s. Former mercenary who transitioned into private security, then the Rasnian military police. Formidable combat skills but questionable loyalty.

SEM RAS ARBOR: Human male, late-30s. Left the Rasnian military to join the Coalition fleet. Service history on [REDACTED – CLASSIFIED], one of the ships to have been affected by the [REDACTED – CLASSIFIED]. Combat trained with experience in piloting small and medium-sized military craft.

Idran-Var

CLAINE: Human male, early-20s. Father left the Idran-Var and returned to Coalition space. Contact has been observed between the two. Continue to observe to exploit potential opportunities this may present.

NIOLE: Siolean female, early-30s. Former cadet in the Coalition Legionnaire Corps before desertion. Responsible for deaths of several legionnaire retrieval squads. Known to suffer from the affliction of the *ilsar*—approach with caution.

RHENDAR: Unconfirmed gender, age and species—intelligence suggests human male, mid-40s to mid-50s. Holds the position of *varsath* [translator's note: shield of the people] and therefore does not remove his helmet in public. High-value Coalition target—termination pre-approved.

SERRIC: Siolean male, mid-30s. Son of two prominent Coalition senators who he killed as a child. Highly volatile with unprecedented levels of radiation accounted for in his flare readings, even for an *ilsar*. Recommended for solitary confinement in the Bastion if captured.

VENYA: Dachryn female, early-20s. Considerable brute strength and formidable plating, especially for a dachryn of her age.

ZAL: Human female, late-30s. A highly-skilled scout and scientist. Possibly responsible for bioweapon assault on Herta IV.

Kaath

ELEION: Iskaath female [translator's note: *egg-bearer* would be more accurate here], early-30s. Official job description noted with transport registry is cargo runner, but intelligence suspects smuggling.

CYREN: Iskaath female [translator's note: Really? Again?], late-50s. Adept medic and mother [translator's note: *EGG. REARER.*] to Eleion. No record of any political leanings or offworld travel.

Rim Belt

DREXIOUS: Jarkaath male [translator's note: Why do I even bother?], early-20s. Known thief and smuggler. Rumours of connection within jarkaath intelligence are unverified and unlikely to be accurate.

FYRA: Siolean female, [age: ???]. No records within Coalition databases. Shares a name with ancient siolean goddess. Possible cult leader who used the Rim Belt black market to wipe her identity. To be investigated further.

HALRESSAN: Human female, late-20s. Former Idran-Var turned bounty hunter. Rumoured to be in possession of stolen Idran-Var armour. Retrieve if possible.

SKAILE: Siolean female, mid-30s. Also known as the Outlaw Queen. Runs a crime syndicate out of Jadera Port and exerts considerable influence over the mercenary and pirate gangs in the Rim Belt. Possible *ilsar*—do not approach without Coalition ambassadorial approval.

CURRENT GALACTIC
CIVILISATIONS

Sioleans

Bipedal, smooth-skinned species characterised by their ability to flare. Their skin changes colour depending on the strength of a planet's radiation. They have the ability to absorb this radiation and release it in violent bursts of energy known as flares.

Recognisable for their crown-like brow ridge and numerous head tendrils which split as they grow older—some elders have been observed to have hundreds of intricate headtails which they often wear in braids. Their appearance also includes black, colourless eyes and no discernible nose, just nostril slits.

Many sioleans isolate themselves and don't gather in large groups of their own kind. In high concentrations they are more likely to develop the *ilsar* gene which heightens their ability to absorb radiation but also leaves them in a dangerous intoxicated state, unable to resist violence.

Jarkaath/Iskaath

Reptilian, scaled species who move both bipedally and quadrupedally. They have long, powerful limbs and quill-like spindles along their spine and tail, which often indicate their emotional state. Historically predators with sharp, serrated teeth, long jaws and opposable claws, they are formidable combatants even unarmed.

A schism exists within the species: the jarkaath were the first colonists to arrive in the galaxy, doing so before their iskaath counterparts had even developed space travel. As a result, the jarkaath have adapted to breathe in different environments, whereas the iskaath still rely on breather masks with air filtration and toxin supply if they travel offworld.

This has resulted in a clear distinction between the two subspecies, with prejudice rife among the jarkaath and a reluctance to engage in galactic politics on the part of the iskaath.

Dachryn

Crested, horned bipeds who are famed for their impressive size and strength. Their bone-plated exoskeleton makes them excellent warriors. Their face plates come in many different colours and patterns, from black and white to crimson red.

Famous for both their prowess on the battlefield and their cunning military strategy, the dachryn are somewhat hampered in their galactic influence by their lack of numbers. As a species, they are slow to breed, and much of their colony was lost through war before their arrival through the waystations.

Human

Soft-fleshed and comprising mainly of water, humans are nevertheless tougher than they first appear. They also boast the highest population of a single species within the galaxy, even before the arrival of their colony.

The human colonists from New Pallas also bring with them an impressive understanding of advanced cybernetic enhancements, which allowed them to survive the trip through the waystations even through their inertial dampening technology on their ship was sorely rudimental. These implants improve many of their base capabilities, from neural enhancers and trauma regulators to retinal adjustors and bone reinforcement.

Idran-Var

A collective of exiles and outlaws who reject the Coalition and live on the fringes of the galaxy beyond the Rim Belt. They forsake any connection to the species they biologically belong to and instead consider themselves Idran-Var, a name which translates roughly to 'those who resist.'

They are known for their near-impenetrable armour which is made of a metal alloy found nowhere else in the galaxy but the hidden forge they mine it from. This metal can repel most ammunition, including regular bullets and plasma rounds, but is vulnerable to a high-voltage electrical current. As such, a legionnaire's varstaff is one of the few weapons capable of penetrating an Idran-Var's armour.

Sworn enemies of the Coalition and the legionnaires, the Idran-Var are perhaps most famous for a brutal attack carried out on Alcruix almost a millenium ago, where they hurled an asteroid into a planet and rendered it uninhabitable.

PLANETS AND SYSTEMS

ALCRUIX: A planet scarred by the Idran-Var's asteroid attack almost a millennium ago. The surface is volatile and unstable, with a thin atmosphere and debris floating in orbit. What's left of the planet is dark, volcanic, and icy—suitably unwelcoming to any visitors.

AUREL: One of many similar dwarf planets on the border of the Rim Belt, with a thin atmosphere and barren surface. Its sky is tinged a dark red, held in a state of perpetual twilight, and its surface is bleak and rocky.

JADERA: An inhospitable planet in the Rim Belt with a strong sun and unforgiving desert. There are few settlements here apart from Jadera Port—a bustling hive of criminal activity watched over by the Outlaw Queen, also known as Skaile.

KAATH: The iskaath homeworld consists mainly of swampland and thick forests, though vast areas have been cleared for their production factories. The yellow-tinged atmosphere is deadly to other species but carries the vital toxins the iskaath need to survive.

KRYCHUS: A small, unremarkable planet that would likely be of little note were it not the dachryn homeworld. Its varied topography is interspersed with large, uniform cities and military outposts.

NEW PALLAS: The human colony, located in an unknown region across the chasm of dark space. Overpopulated to the point of decay, almost every part of it has been built over, leaving the people of the planet struggling for clean air, food and resources.

RAS PRIME: Human homeworld, characterised by its alpine climate and lush environment. Access to the planet's surface is restricted to authorised ships to ensure its atmosphere is not harmed—most visitors need to dock at one of the sizeable orbital stations and transit to the surface by solar shuttle.

RELLION: A large moon orbiting Ras Prime, sometimes referred to as its sister planet. While Rellion's thinner atmosphere is still adequate for humans to breathe, conservation is less of a concern. As a result, much more of the moon is built up than Ras Prime, featuring impressive skyscrapers and skycar lanes.

SIO: Still considered the siolean homeworld though large parts of it are abandoned due to the semi-nomadic nature of the siolean species. High in radiation, the atmosphere boasts a near-permanent aurora.

TYVOTH: This arid, mountainous planet can be found in the Rim Belt. It has three suns and a sulphur-heavy atmosphere.

Previously considered uninhabitable, but recent reports show signs of construction activity on the surface.

NEPTHE: A frozen, rocky planet once used as an outpost for scientific research. Now abandoned, only a few empty facilities remain among the dangerous winds and freezing blizzards.

NOVA STATION: One of many pirate stations in the Rim Belt, the dangerous border territory between Coalition and Idran-Var space. The station is home to the notorious Belt Cabal and offers everything from luxurious eateries to dive bars and a sprawling black market.

OSSA: Capital world of the Coalition, famous for its temperate climate, clear blue skies and sandstone buildings. Home of the legionnaire headquarters and training grounds.

PASARAN MINOR: A border planet mainly used by farmers, with twin suns and flat, fertile ground. Because of its proximity to the Rim Belt, it is often plagued by bandit attacks.

PXEN: Located in the heart of siolean space, Pxen is an oceanic planet and home to the Bastion, an underwater prison which holds captured *ilsar*.

VESYLLION: The Idran-Var's chosen homeworld is hostile and ravenous, covered mainly by thick, sprawling jungles and plagued by ferocious storms. Both the flora and fauna are dangerous to anyone who is unprepared.

Printed in Great Britain
by Amazon